Home:
Surviving the Zombie Apocalypse

SHAWN CHESSER

CONTENTS

ACKNOWLEDGEMENTS

For you, Dad. Gone home way too soon.

Maureen, Raven, and Caden ... I couldn't have done this without your support. Thanks to our military, LE and first responders for your service. To the people in the U.K. and elsewhere around the world who have been in touch, thanks for reading my yarns! Lieutenant Colonel Michael Offe, thanks for your service as well as your friendship. Beta readers, you rock, and you know who you are. Thanks, George Romero, for introducing me to zombies. To my friends and fellows at S@N and Monday Steps On Steele, thanks as well. Lastly, thanks to Bill W. and Dr. Bob ... you helped make this possible. I am going to sign up for another 24.

Special thanks to John O'Brien, Mark Tufo, Joe McKinney, Craig DiLouie, Heath Stallcup, Eric A. Shelman, David P. Forsyth, and Nicholas Sansbury Smith. I truly appreciate your continued friendship and always invaluable advice. Thanks to Jason Swarr and Straight 8 Custom Photography for another awesome cover. Once again, extra special thanks to Monique Happy for her work editing "HOME." Mombie, as always, you came through like a champ! Working with you for close to a decade has been nothing but a pleasure. I truly appreciate having a confidante I can trust. If I have accidentally left anyone out ... I am truly sorry.

***

Edited by Monique Happy Editorial Services
mohappy@att.net

Prologue

Sunday - December 26, 2011

Yoder, Colorado

A series of loud thumps sounded in the Ford Bronco's cabin and Daymon Bush found himself fighting the steering wheel just to keep the vintage rig tracking straight on the snow-covered two-lane. As the long travel suspension continued absorbing impacts with zombie corpses camouflaged by fresh snow dumped on eastern Colorado the previous night, Duncan Winters, riding shotgun and gripping the grab bar by his head, fixed the younger man with a hard stare.

"Slow yer roll, Slim," said the fifty-eight-year-old Vietnam veteran in his gravelly Texas drawl. "Feels like I'm riding a broken helicopter through triple-canopy."

"You would know, Old Man," Daymon quipped, his shoulder-length dreadlocks bouncing as the SUV shimmied and bucked. "Lord knows you've ridden your fair share of them into the ground. Three Hueys and a National Guard Black Hawk, if memory serves."

Duncan stared out the window at the vast expanse of white surrounding a distant smattering of weather-beaten structures. Speaking softly, he said, "Six birds, not four. Two were by *controlled* autorotation. And to my credit, on both occasions, I still stuck the landing."

Twelve-year-old Raven Grayson poked her head into the void between the front seats. She said, "We're just glad you're still with us, Duncan." Looking sidelong at Daymon, she added, "Aren't we, *D?*"

"I'm just busting his—" Checking himself, Daymon changed the subject, saying, "What makes you two think this town isn't already stripped clean?"

"Because the foraging parties mostly focused on Pueblo and the communities surrounding Springs," Raven stated. "At least that's what my mom said. She and Wilson went on one trip south of Schriever back when we were staying there."

Duncan faced Raven. Peering into her brown eyes, he said, "I was jawin' with your dad one night around the fire in Utah. He let on that he paid Yoder a visit before you all set off for my brother's compound. Came here looking for a bicycle, for you, but also used it as a sort of training mission. Wanted to know if he could keep you and your mom safe outside the wire."

Staring out the right-side rear window, Raven said, "And we all know how that worked out."

"Cade did his best with what he had," shot Daymon. "Don't you guys ever forget that."

"Easy, big fella," Duncan said, placing a hand on his friend's shoulder. "Concentrate on getting us all there in one piece."

It was clear to Duncan that his friend was still beating himself up over his fiancée's death at the hands of Adrian's people. In a way, Daymon leaving Heidi all alone in their rural home while he went out to forage was akin to what Cade had been doing to his family all along. Though Raven's comment wasn't directed at the younger man, Duncan figured it stung all the same.

"Once I've crashed as many vehicles as you have choppers," Daymon said, "then I'll start heeding your advice. Until then, *zip it!*"

Duncan grimaced and sat back in his seat.

A moment later they passed a roadside sign announcing the town of Yoder and listing its population at a tick over two hundred. Thanks to numerous bullet holes punched through the sign's thin metal skin, the information was barely discernable. If the sign suffered another round of target practice, the unincorporated blink-and-you-miss-it town would become another nameless stop on a desolate highway full of them.

The Bronco's transmission whined as Daymon downshifted. The noise of snow compacting under the tires rose to the level of the engine's rumble as their speed dropped from thirty miles per hour to a slow crawl. Rolling into the west end of town, heat from the noontime sun drawing wisps of steam from the snow blanketing the ground and cars and buildings, it became clear Yoder had suffered the same fate as nearly all the other small towns dotting the map.

On the right was a burned-out mom and pop grocery store. In the lot fronting the place, armored by a foot-thick layer of snow, sat a pair of abandoned vehicles. Arranged in a ragged circle around the small import cars were a dozen or so empty shopping carts. And like creatures lying in wait, many more snow-covered carts dotted the lot's periphery.

On the north side of the main drag, facing the looted grocery store, was a long, low building. Though the front elevation wasn't like the modern-day strip mall—all window glass surrounded by faux stone—the clapboard-sided structure was definitely their turn of the century ancestor.

Flanked on the left by a two-chair barber shop and on the right by a second-hand store was a combo sporting goods/hardware store. Plywood sheets covered the door and windows. Wearing a thick layer of snow, a dozen tangled corpses in various death poses choked the covered entry leading up to the boarded-over front door.

Daymon slowed and parked in the middle of the street, equidistant from the drift of dead bodies and frost-heaved sidewalk bordering the grocery store parking lot.

"Good a place as any," Duncan said, dragging the Saiga-12 semi-auto shotgun from its spot between his knees. Checking the box magazine and confirming it was loaded to capacity with shells, all ten alternating between buckshot and slug, he elbowed open his door and stepped to the road.

Daymon cracked his window a few inches. Once Duncan had looped around to his side, Daymon said, "I have dibs on the rotters in front of the store."

Raven had already collected her Colt Commando carbine from the floorboard. Fitted with a minimalist telescoping stock, stubby SOCOM 556 suppressor, and EOTech optics setup, the Short-Barreled Rifle built for her by an armorer at Schriever weighed considerably less and measured a few inches shorter than her old battle rifle. Halfway out the passenger-side door, she leaned back into the truck and shot Daymon a *You've got to be kidding me* look. Closing the door at her back, she said, "You know the twice-dead don't count."

Calling after her, Daymon said, "They got ears, don't they?"

Shaking his head, Duncan said, "That's cheating, mi amigo."

Raven rounded the front of the Bronco. Matching Daymon's gaze, she said, "I spent *weeks* waiting for Central Planning to approve my paperwork so I could go outside the walls with you two."

Daymon shut down the motor and exited the Bronco. Looking to Raven, he said, "So bureaucracy is a *zombie*, too. Something else to fear? Make your point."

"We all came to Springs together is her *point*," explained Duncan. "Cade's stellar reputation among the population notwithstanding, anything *you* do that's not one hundred percent aboveboard is a direct reflection on *all* of us."

Bending over to examine one of the twice-dead corpses, Daymon muttered, "Point is moot anyway. Someone already beat us here."

"Look," Duncan said, "I've got it on good authority there's a herd a couple hundred strong stalled out down the road just outside of town. There'll be more than enough right ears to go around."

"I get what you're both saying," agreed Daymon. "I don't want to screw it up, either. This is all I got. No way I'm doing any kind of job where I'm required to work inside a building surrounded by a bunch of strangers." Dragging his parka zipper to a spot just below his lengthening beard, he asked, "You going to divulge who this person of *authority* is?"

Duncan smiled wide. "Let's just say I have my sources on the inside."

"Nash?"

Duncan said nothing.

"Shrill?"

Still Duncan said nothing.

Tiring of the banter, Raven turned her attention to the building where her dad had found her that bike all those months ago. Noting that most of the zombies on the sidewalk had been face-shot from near point-blank range, she picked her way through the jumble of frozen extremities, taking care to not step on fractured bones or get too close to the gaping mouths.

Broken glass popped underneath Raven's boots as she entered the alcove and stepped up to the front door. Placing one gloved hand on the handle, she said, "You don't have to work *inside*, Daymon. Why don't you join the New Springs Fire Department?"

Stepping over the sneering corpses, Daymon replied, "I fought forest fires before all this. Out of doors. And I grew up with most of the guys and gals on my team. Learned to ski with them. Drank at the Silver Dollar with them. Went bow hunting with some of them. We were a real close-knit team."

Raven banged a fist on the door. Three hard raps. Cocking her head to listen for anything stirring inside, she said, "Your team were people you trusted. People like *us*."

Scanning the road in both directions, Duncan said, "Bird of the Apocalypse is wise beyond her years."

Raven winced upon hearing the name she had first heard uttered a few weeks ago. Leading Alexander Dregan's youngest son, Peter, to safety had endeared her to him greatly. So much so that the comic-book-loving teen had bestowed her with the nickname. *Hell*, she thought, *Bird of the Apocalypse is a far cry better than Raven Mystique*— an actual superhero in the Marvel universe the youngest Dregan could have saddled her with.

Hearing nothing moving inside the darkened store, Raven tried the handle.

Unlocked.

She swung the rifle around, letting it hang from its sling against her back.

Drawing her suppressed Glock 19 with her right hand, she nudged the door with her left elbow.

The door moved less than six inches, then stopped.

Craning her head, Raven spotted something on the floor just inside the door. Looked to her like a statue carved from wood. Even in the interior gloom she could see it was painted in garish colors.

Putting her shoulder against the door, she pushed with all her strength.

Still it didn't budge.

Holstering the Glock, she said, "A little help here."

With Duncan keeping watch, Daymon and Raven got the door to move halfway through its swing.

Bathed in a thick pillar of light spilling in through the door was a drug store Indian. It had suffered some damage falling to the floor and wore a thick coating of dust. Pebble-sized kernels of broken glass littered the store's wood floor.

Daymon said, "They have one of these statues in the bar where Heidi used to work."

Regarding Daymon sidelong, Raven said, "Kind of a shitty thing to have to look at if you're a Native American who wants to eat there."

Leaning over Raven's shoulder to see inside, Daymon whispered, "Try eating at a Sambo's if you've got my skin tone."

"Sambo's?"

After waving Duncan over, Daymon said, "Sambo's was a restaurant chain whose mascot was a little brown boy with big lips."

Incredulous, Raven said, "And you ate there?"

Daymon shook his head. "They went out of business when I was a baby. My moms told me all about them, though."

Arriving in the alcove, Duncan said, "What's up?"

"We're going in," informed Daymon. "You want to stay here and watch the road? Or do you want me to?"

Patting the Saiga, Duncan said, "I got your six." A brief pause. "You got mine?"

With a slight eye roll, Daymon said, "If I see your *Precious*, I'll grab it for you."

Chapter 1

Suppressor leading the way, Raven squeezed through the door, stepped over the fallen statue, and moved aside to wait for Daymon.

Thanks to many months of exposure to changing climate, the air inside Abe's Value Hardware was ripe with the unmistakable odor of mildew and death. Though the merchandise had been picked over, a lot was left behind. Some was molding in place. It was clear rodents had taken over. Droppings and shredded packaging littered the aisles.

Clutter and cobwebs notwithstanding, the place was a treasure trove of Americana. There were antique tricycles and American Flyer wagons parked on wall-mounted shelves right of the centrally located cashier's stand. Porcelain oil signs and taxidermy game sat on shelves above the door. One sign in particular drew Raven's attention. It featured a thirty-something woman wearing a red polka dot bandanna wrapped tightly around her head. Denim sleeves rolled up, the woman flexed one well-muscled arm. The sign was a throwback to the World War II war effort. The script above the woman's head said it all: *We Can Do It!* She even wore an expression that conveyed all at once an iron will, intestinal fortitude, and moxie—all traits Glenda Gladson constantly reminded Raven she had inherited from her mom, Brook. The retired nurse even went so far to insist that, if cultivated, those traits would one day see Raven walking in her father's footsteps.

Bird of the Apocalypse.

Stepping over the debris field inside the front door, Daymon asked, "What, specifically, are you looking for?"

The sound of his voice in the still environs caused Raven to start. Recovering, she said, "Nothing in particular." No sooner had she said it than her eye was drawn to a stack of plastic toboggans balanced atop a high shelf beside the door.

"Well," he said, "I need to find gas additives for Heidi. That old wispy haired helicopter mechanic isn't as generous with his stockpiles of automotive lubricants with me as he is Duncan."

Straining to reach a rope tied to one of the red plastic sleds, Raven said, "Sergeant Whipper?"

"Yeah, that *dick*."

"My dad beat his butt good. That's why he's so nice to me and Duncan."

"That explains it," said Daymon as a six-inch hula girl on the floor caught his eye. Bending and snatching up the dash ornament, he went on, saying, "Maybe we should stop by Schriever on the way back so I can beat his ass. Perhaps an attitude adjustment would convince him to be a little nicer to *me* in the future."

Raven said, "Only if you want to spend the night in jail."

Shivering at the prospect, Daymon stuffed the hula girl in a pocket.

Raven let her gaze roam the barren shelves. The place had been stripped of most everything useful. No stools or ladders. No brooms or rakes to snag the dangling rope with. Though she'd hit a growth spurt since fall, there was no way she was getting the sleds down without resorting to doing the one thing she had grown to hate the most since losing her dad: ask for help.

Through gritted teeth, she said, "A little assistance here?"

"How many do you want?"

"Four."

"How about we take all six? You can use the extras for barter." Without waiting for an answer, Daymon reached over Raven's head and easily plucked the toboggans from the shelf.

Dust motes swirled and danced in the air as he placed the liberated snow toys by the door.

"Thanks," said Raven. "How tall are you, anyway?"

"Counting my boots and dreads … six-two … ish. Maybe six-three."

"I've got a ways to go," she conceded glumly.

"You're going to be taller than Brook," said Daymon matter-of-factly. "You're already nearly as tall as she was—"

"When my dad killed her. Thought I would never hear myself say those words."

Daymon had no response to that. There really was none he could think of. In fact he was pissed at himself for bringing Raven's late mother up in the first place. So he tried a little distraction: "Help me find the automotive aisle." Patting his pockets, he asked, "You have a flashlight handy?"

Dumb question, thought Raven as she toggled on the tactical light riding the picatinny rail underneath her carbine's barrel.

White cone of light sweeping back and forth, Raven led them down each aisle. Back and forth they went, stepping over toppled paint cans and tubes of caulking and rolls of masking tape.

The automotive aisle was near the rear of the store. Save for a tube of instant radiator weld, a vanilla-scented air freshener tree, and a rock chip repair kit that had been unwanted or got overlooked, the shelves held only a thin layer of dust and a minefield of rat turds.

Daymon pocketed the random items, then reached to the top shelf and pulled down what looked to be a pillow shrink-wrapped in plastic.

Raven said, "What's that?"

"It's an imitation-wool seat cover."

"For Heidi?"

Shaking his head, he said, "It's for Duncan."

"Looks like you're going to have to enlist Duncan to sweet talk Whipper out of whatever you came here for."

Daymon thought, *Master of the obvious.* Out loud he said, "I guess asking Old Man for help is better than busted knuckles and a night in jail."

Barely, thought Raven. Painting the back wall with the light from her rifle, she raised a hand and froze. After holding that pose for a couple of beats and again hearing the faint shuffling noise that had precipitated the pause—shoe soles drawing across wood planking was her best guess—she looked over her shoulder at Daymon and pointed to her ear. *I hear something.*

Daymon had heard it too. Nodding, he set the seat cover on the floor, gripped the neon green handle of the machete he'd named

Kindness, and drew the razor-sharp blade from the scabbard on his hip.

Heel and toeing it to keep the floorboards underfoot from creaking, Raven crept down the center of the store, now and again pausing to peer left and right down gloomy aisles.

After searching what she guessed was two-thirds of the store, Raven's light washed over the moldering corpse of someone she guessed had once been associated with the store.

Perhaps a worker?

Maybe the owner, Abe?

Sitting on the floor, back to a post and legs splayed out, the corpse had been here for a long time. Hair and bone and dried brains clung to the post above the dead man's canted head. Of course, a tiny hole ringed by a raised nub of cartilage was all that remained of the corpse's right ear.

"Keep moving," Daymon whispered. "We couldn't have collected it anyway."

Nodding, Raven stepped over the dead man's legs and pushed deeper into the store.

Three aisles removed from the morbid scene depicting someone's last willful act, they found themselves face to face with the source of the shuffling noises.

Chapter 2

Raven had spotted the pair of fresh turns as she rounded an endcap display piled high with stacked paint cans. She immediately went to one knee, made a fist and held it up for Daymon to see.

Halt.

She watched for a moment as the dead things trundled single file down the lawn care aisle toward her.

It was clear by their actions—arms outstretched, gnarled fingers kneading the air—that the monsters knew they were in the presence of fresh meat.

Thankfully, due to the air inside Abe's being somewhere in the high thirties, every movement the corpses made was painfully slow. And though their jaws were making the usual chewing motions, not a sound was issuing from their open maws.

"They're real slow and not making any noise," Raven noted quietly. "Means they're real close to locking up."

"Good for us," Daymon said. "Bad for them."

As Raven studied the one nearest to her, it completed a plodding step and its dead eyes slowly ranged downward and locked with hers.

The man had been in his mid-forties before first death. He was clean-shaven and had no visible tattoos. The two smallest fingers on one hand were just nubs of bone protruding from a crude bandage. Blood from the injury had soaked the man's jacket sleeve then dried, leaving it almost black and, from the looks of it, stiff as a board. On the corpse's feet were like-new lug-soled Vasque hiking boots.

Though she would have been scared if put in this position before that awful day her dad had been captured and tortured by the Chinese, now, she didn't feel a thing. She was numb to *them*. Over the days and weeks since, she'd become callous to the former humans she used to grieve for.

Craning, Raven saw that the second shuffler was dressed the same as the first. It looked to have been Wilson's age before becoming infected, dying, and coming back hungering for the flesh of the living.

Was he the older one's adult son?

That's all the thought Raven gave the pair. Though the cold had vastly reduced their already compromised speed and dexterity, they were still ambulatory and carrying the Omega virus.

As Raven positioned herself to take on the older of the two corpses, she saw that both still had their right ears.

Easy money.

"Dibs on the dad," said Daymon.

Too late. Already advancing on the first wavering corpse, Raven slipped her rifle around to her back, removed the matte-black Gerber MK II combat dagger from its sheath on her hip, and ducked under the thing's reaching arms. Grabbing a handful of North Face parka, she pulled the living corpse's upper torso downward toward her knife hand and expertly guided the serrated blade into its right eye.

A quick thrust and twist of her wrist was all it took to pierce cranial bone and scramble the brain cradled within.

Daymon was voicing his displeasure at being one-upped when Raven stepped aside and guided the stilled corpse to the floor between them.

There was a solid thud. The dead weight hitting the wooden floorboards sent a vibration shooting through Raven's boots.

"The ear is all yours," she said, going into a combat crouch and advancing on the younger specimen, whose eyes were already devouring her. The hunger conveyed by those lifeless black orbs brought on a hard shiver as Raven dispatched it in the same manner as she had the other.

Once the second kill had crashed to the floor and settled in a semi-fetal position, she stepped back to allow Daymon room to work on the first.

12

A short chopping motion with Kindness liberated the waxen-looking lump of flesh and cartilage from the corpse's head.

Even after having seen Daymon do this hundreds of times, the ubiquitous *thunk-squish* noise always caused Raven's stomach to lurch.

Wrinkling her nose, she said, "I'll do this one."

"You sure?"

"Positive." Without pause, she kneeled next to the twenty-something and grabbed a fistful of curly hair. Though she was wearing leather gloves, they were fingerless, which caused her to feel the gritty accumulation of twigs and bugs in the corpse's greasy, matted locks.

Technique honed from performing the task hundreds of times over the last few weeks, she grasped the fleshy lobe with her off hand. Then, cutting away from herself, she sawed upward until the *prize* was hers.

"Just like it's done in the handbook," said Daymon. He took a roll of plastic sacks from a pocket and handed her one. Originally a staple used by dog owners to police up their pooch's sidewalk bombs, the colorful scented items were perfect for this job and could hold dozens of ears of all sizes and shapes.

Looking up at Daymon, Raven asked, "Should we check their pockets? See where they came from?"

He nodded. "Just check your emotions at the door."

I did that weeks ago. Pausing, she asked, "Do you think they died somewhere out there and turned and then found their way in here after hearing me bang on the door? Or did they get wounded out there and then come in here looking for shelter?"

"These two were doing the same thing we are. Only I'm willing to bet they got greedy and were breaking the law and culling after dark. Chances are they were already in here when you pounded on the door. They were way too mobile to have just recently come in from outside." Lips moving, he looked to the ceiling. "We've been inside less than ten minutes. No way." He shook his head. "No way they came in after us."

Raven emptied the corpse's pockets and spread the items out on the floor. There were energy bars, a pair of empty small-caliber handguns, two wallets, and two fixed-blade knives of questionable quality. And sure enough, each were carrying Ziploc sandwich bags. The younger man's was nearly opaque with some kind of bodily fluid and contained more than twenty severed ears. While the older man had been less prolific, his soiled baggie still contained a respectable baker's dozen.

Rifling through the older man's wallet told Raven he was originally from Connecticut and had been a member of the teacher's union there. For some silly reason, he was carrying around a thick stack of crisp hundred-dollar bills.

Daymon asked, "Where they from?"

She emptied the younger man's wallet. After plucking the license and a folded square of familiar-looking yellow paper off the floor, she said, "They're both from the same address in New Haven, Connecticut." Screwing up her face, she added, "He's forty-six and this one is twenty-two. Different last names, though. Means they're not related."

Pointing out the matching silver rings they each wore on their left hand, he said, "That's because they were a married couple."

"Ewwww," she exclaimed. "North Face is twice as old as the other guy."

"No different than the mid-life crisis Corvette dudes and forty-something cougars who used to prowl Jackson Hole in search of young meat. Look at Hollywood before the world went to hell. Common practice was to trade in the old models for the new as soon as the previous started to show some wear and tear. And I'm not talking Lambos and Ferraris."

Raven had been holding the folded paper in one hand and listening intently. As Daymon's story progressed to car talk, her head slowly took on a slight tilt. Once he paused to take a breath, she said, "Cougars?"

"Recent divorcees or widows with newly done faces. Plastic surgery Botox queens looking for boy toys."

"How do you know North Face was a *cougar?*"

Daymon shook his head. Smiling, he said, "Dudes can't be cougars."

"Why not?"

"Above my pay grade." Indicating the paper in her hand, he said, "Is that what I think it is?"

She unfolded it and gave it a cursory glance.

Daymon said, "Let me have a look."

She handed it over.

After examining the creased page, he shook his head and whistled. "These fools were way out of their lane. Wonder how they got their hands on an all-temperature, all-zone cull license."

She said, "I thought you have to be current or former military to have one."

"Or prove you have proper training," he added. "Face value … these two don't fit the bill."

"Think they got this on the black market?"

Duncan said, "Dollars to donuts, that's exactly where these greenhorns got it." Somehow, he had made his way through the door, over the fallen Indian chief, walked to the back of the store, and rounded the last aisle's endcap—all without making a sound.

Daymon started. "You sneaky bastard," he shot. "How'd you pull off the ninja approach?"

Chuckling, Duncan said, "What I lack in dexterity and flexibility, I make up for with cunning and patience." He nodded at the paper in Daymon's hand. "That's a Golden Ticket, isn't it?"

Daymon closed his eyes and tilted his head back.

Noting the younger man's free hand was at rest on the butt of his Sig Sauer pistol, and that Raven had instinctively drawn her pistol, Duncan raised his hands and apologized for sneaking up on them.

Daymon fixed the older man with a hard stare. "Damn near scared the kinks out of my dreads."

"Not my intention," Duncan drawled. "I thought for sure my creaky old knees had given me away well before I arrived on scene."

"Well they didn't," Raven said, holstering the Glock. Then, parroting something she had once heard her dad say to Wilson, she went on, "That's a good way to get yourself two to the head."

Cackling, Duncan said, "Out of the mouths of babes."

Daymon rose and kick-stretched his legs. "We keeping their ears?"

Making a face, Raven plucked her ear from the bag and placed it on the younger man's corpse. Holding up the soiled baggies bulging with ears, she said, "These are fair game. But I feel that trading Theodore and Liam's ears for credit is inviting bad luck and trouble." She paused. "Knock yourself out if you want to keep yours."

Placing a hand on Daymon's shoulder, Duncan said, "She's right, you know. Capitalizing off of their bad luck *is* bad juju."

Fishing the ear from his baggie and tossing it on the floor between the corpses, Daymon said, "I'm not a ghoul. Someone in Springs might be missing these two."

Nodding, Raven said, "You did the right thing, Daymon."

Arms crossed, Daymon said nothing.

Patting the seat cover he'd scooped off the floor on the way down the center aisle, Duncan said, "Thanks for this, D." Tucking it under one arm, he added, "Now let's get down the road and see if it's worth its weight in right ears."

Raven wanted to know what Old Man meant by the cryptic statement but decided to let it play out.

Chapter 3

Chief Warrant Officer 4 Ari Silver, crack aviator and longtime member of the storied 160th Special Operations Aviation Regiment, worked the stick and pedals with expert precision as the Ghost Hawk helicopter he was piloting rocketed west at a hundred knots, its smooth underbelly nearly skimming the glassy surface of Utah's Great Salt Lake. Save for the lake's aquamarine water and laser-straight run of Interstate 80 stretching away north by west, there was nothing to see but miles and miles of flat, white salt plains.

Now and again Ari would look out the starboard window at the lake's surface and spot the matte-black stealth helo's reflection keeping pace.

Minutes after leaving the Great Salt Lake behind and bumping up over a line of low, ochre-colored hills, Ari had the Gen 3 helo tracking a due west heading. Keeping perfect pace just off the Ghost Hawk's nose, the helo's angular shadow stretched and compressed as it flitted over the occasional depression in the mostly flat landscape.

"Thank you for flying Night Stalker Airways," quipped the wannabe comedian, who was in his mid-thirties and acted like a teenager most of the time. "Next stop, *Bendover* Nevada."

In this case the veteran of many combat tours in Godforsaken hotspots all over the world wasn't kidding. Precisely ten seconds after making the announcement over the shipwide comms, Ari hauled back hard on the stick, causing the bland landscape filling the cockpit glass to instantly give way to cobalt blue sky.

Not one complaint came from the special ops "customers" riding in back. To the contrary, one of the shooters showed his satisfaction by belting out "Yee haw!" and fist bumping the team members near him.

Seated opposite Ari, gloved hands flitting over the large touchscreen making up the majority of the Ghost Hawk's cutting-edge glass cockpit, thirty-six-year-old Chief Warrant Officer 3 Haynes took the abrupt maneuver in stride.

No matter the airframe, Ari liked to hotrod his bird; therefore nothing much fazed the well-muscled African American aviator.

"Two minutes," said Ari.

In response, Haynes said, "FLIR coming online."

"Standard optical," Ari replied. "Fifty percent zoom."

"Copy that," Haynes said. "Standard optical. Fifty percent zoom."

With the helicopter beginning to bleed airspeed and go nose down, all while banking to starboard, Haynes gazed out Ari's window and got a real good look at Wendover Airport directly below them.

Not a single plane remained on the two-strip facility's gray tarmac. Pointing to how hectic the last day was before the President officially grounded all commercial and private flights, a burned-out carcass of what looked to have been a multi-million-dollar Gulf Stream business jet sat forlornly in the center of the wider of the two runways. Though they hadn't escaped damage from the intense heat and smoke, the engine nacelles and a substantial piece of the tail remained mostly intact.

At the end of a long debris field that began amid the wreckage of the Gulfstream were the remains of a twin-prop commuter plane. Having left a good deal of its red paint on the runway and bits and pieces of wing on the infield, the Piper Seneca now rested upside down, its fuselage crushed to half its original height. Strangely, the deployed landing gear looked undamaged and the rubber tires remained inflated.

Seeing the lack of a control tower rising over the public-use field, Haynes said, "That there is the result of too many cooks and not enough chefs."

"Must have been a shit show," Ari said.

As Ari stopped their rapid descent at a hundred feet above ground level and tightened the turn radius, Haynes felt the building Gs push his two hundred and fifty pounds into his seat and was instantly treated to a bird's eye view of West Wendover. It was nothing like he remembered it; the neon lights had all been extinguished. Missing was the hustle and bustle of gamblers arriving from nearby Salt Lake City or race teams going to and from the world-famous Bonneville Speedway. It looked as if the latter crowd had trailered their race cars and fled before the outbreak raised its ugly head in the combined city of fifteen hundred.

Thinking out loud, Haynes said, "You know the Enola Gay's pilots and crew trained for their mission somewhere near here."

"Damn," said Ari, finishing the sweeping turn and leveling the bird out, "we are overflying hallowed ground in aviation history."

Straight off the helo's nose and coming up fast were two massive casinos. Viewed from above, they looked like glass and cement islands surrounded by vast seas of trash-strewn parking lot. The small number of vehicles left behind were no different than all the rest that sat abandoned across America. They all featured grimy window glass, some no doubt with rotten surprises lurking behind them. The vehicles loaded down with people's worldly possessions—static fixtures on nearly every backroad and freeway across the land—sat low to the ground on deflated tires.

Haynes wondered if some of the vehicles belonged to gamblers who had decided to remain on premises and *ride it out*. Which, he decided after a moment's contemplation, was probably no different than *letting it ride*. Didn't matter. With the end of the world drawing tight as a hangman's noose around the neck of the condemned, he was fairly certain both had been losing propositions.

Huge signs fronting the casinos, each perched on fifty-foot poles, had clearly been used for target practice. Slender shards of plastic were all that remained in their metal frames. Brass shell casings littering the street twinkled under the sun. And much like the multitude of dreams shattered within the gambling establishments, colorful drifts of jagged shards of plastic covered the ground all around the blown-out signs.

A handful of twice-dead corpses rotted away in spitting distance from the shattered main doors of a car-choked Flying J gas station. Dozens of ambulatory specimens in search of prey trudged the casino property and sidewalks and city streets.

Tumbleweeds driven across the Great Salt Lake Basin by prevailing winds had collected in alcoves and doorways. One small car had enough of them trapped against its windward flank that the side windows were mostly obscured.

Bringing the helicopter to a dead hover directly over Wendover Boulevard and equidistant to the destroyed casino signs, Ari said, "Haynes, what's the outside air temp?"

"Hovering around fifty-three degrees."

"Shit," said Ari. "We're not going to be able to land the team."

Knowing exactly what that meant, Haynes worked the controls to the FLIR pod. "Searching for a cluster."

The moving image that appeared on the cockpit display between the front seats was also being piped to the troop compartment monitor affixed to the bulkhead directly behind Haynes' helmeted head.

"Zoom fifty more," said Ari.

As Haynes repeated the request back to Ari, he manipulated the controls until everyone looking at a monitor was literally staring the front echelon of a miles-long zombie horde right in the rotting face. Affected greatly by the low temperature, the movements of the dozen or so Zs out ahead of the pack were slow and stilted.

Ari crowed, "Right where Nash said they'd be."

Haynes said, "As per usual, the lady's intel is rock solid. Do you want to drop in over the pacesetters?"

Shaking his head, Ari said, "I don't want to risk having them turn around and start the horde moving back toward Salt Lake. I like them heading the direction they are."

Head moving as if on a swivel, Haynes said, "Copy that."

"I'm bringing us up one hundred," Ari stated. "Find a good-sized cluster between the pacers and main body. I want five to ten minutes loiter time on station."

"Copy that." Sensing the helicopter begin a slow vertical climb, Haynes worked the FLIR camera until the front third of the horde was bracketed on the display. "Here." He tapped a gloved finger mid-screen. "About a mile out there is a cluster of thirty or forty. It's separated from the leaders by a quarter mile or so."

Ari asked, "And the main body?"

Sounding hopeful, Haynes said, "Looks like they're lagging far enough behind to give the *short straw* the time he'll need."

"I concur," Ari said. He looked over his shoulder. "Captain?"

Voice colored with a Hispanic accent, Lopez replied, "Good to go," and flashed a thumbs up.

A second male voice came over the comms. "Short straw is rigged. Readying the devices."

"Copy that," replied Ari. "Be advised, we are backtracking and coming in from their six. Lock and load, gentlemen … one minute to insertion.

Chapter 4

The herd Duncan had insisted they would find east of Yoder was stalled out on the road half a mile outside of town. There had to be at least fifty or sixty of them spread out across the two-lane, and that was counting just the ones that had remained upright after entering the temporary state of stasis following the sudden plunge in temperature a week prior. Another twenty or thirty undead were sprawled out on the ground all around the main body. Snow had mostly covered the fallen corpses. Here and there a gnarled hand or bent knee pierced last night's fresh accumulation.

"There's the *herd* my source spoke of," Duncan noted. "Not quite as big as he led me to believe."

"Beggars can't be choosers," Raven said. "At least you *have* a source. And, damn, that's a lot of ears we're looking at."

Duncan shot a sidelong glare at Raven but held his tongue. The girl was just trying to find her own voice. Besides, in his opinion, a little cursing now and again wasn't indicative of one's true character.

Downshifting and steering over to the approaching lane, Daymon said, "My cut's going to be more than enough to justify the gas Heidi burned to get us out and back."

"I'll kick in for gas," Duncan said. "My entire haul is going into Glenda's account anyway."

Nosing the Bronco onto the shoulder and partway into the roadside ditch, Daymon said, "She still watching you like a hawk?"

Duncan nodded. "And rightfully so," he said, voice betraying a hint of defeat. "I truly need to earn her trust back … *again.*"

"She catch you gambling?"

Duncan regarded the man to his left, his only answer the subtlest of nods.

"If I see you anywhere near the gambling hall," Raven said, "I'm informing on you."

Craning toward Raven, Duncan shook his head. A pained look on his face, he said, "You women. Always sticking together."

The hula girl Daymon had stuck to the narrow metal dash vibrated wildly as the Bronco's left-side tires churned through something semi-solid just underneath the snow. After the last of the herd scrolled by Duncan's window, Daymon tromped the pedal and steered hard right.

The horizon disappeared momentarily, and the old SUV shuddered a second time when the front wheels rolled over the uneven transition between shoulder and asphalt. Then the rig fishtailed as he muscled it back around and got it to tracking down the center of the long, straight run of road.

Daymon put a finger on the hula girl's head to still her wild gyrations. Looking to Duncan, he asked, "How many days have you strung together so far?"

Drawing a deep breath, Duncan said, "Counting today? Fifty-six without so much as a sip."

Slowing the Bronco, gaze locked on the looming post office, Daymon said, "That's a good streak. Congratulations."

If Raven was impressed, she didn't let on. Instead of congratulating Old Man, she parroted Glenda, saying rather icily, "The plug's in the jug. And it better stay there." Then, turning in her seat to see out the back window, she asked, "Where the hell are we going, Daymon? The herd's back there."

"They ain't going nowhere," promised Duncan. Then, regarding Daymon, he asked, "What's on your mind, young man?"

"Those guys back in the store—" began Daymon.

"Ted and Liam," interrupted Raven. "They *all* have names."

"Whatever," said Daymon. "Those dudes didn't walk here all the way from Springs."

Having shifted back around in her seat, Raven said, "You're looking for their vehicle."

Daymon said, "Bingo," and steered onto the L-shaped parking lot that wrapped around the squat brick structure containing Yoder's only post office. Planted in a strip of snow near the front doors was a rusty flagpole scaling large sheets of cracking paint. Hanging limply, the fabric tattered, torn, and faded, Old Glory looked as haggard and weather-beaten as the herd of dead things they'd just passed.

Again the Bronco lurched and gravel popped as the tires found potholes in the unimproved lot.

Pulling around back of the post office, they came upon a lone black SUV parked dead center on a sea of white.

"No footprints I can see," noted Duncan.

Daymon cut a half circle on the lot and parked the Bronco. Shutting down the engine, he said, "It's been here for some time. Judging by the layer of the snow it's wearing, I'd guess it's been sitting here for a day or two. I'm going to check it out. Back in a sec." Without consulting the others, he stepped from the rig and closed the door at his back.

Raven watched the gangly man loop around to the rear of the Bronco. She raised her collar against the chill when he lifted the rear window to take out his gas siphoning kit.

Yard-long length of garden hose and pair of red five-gallon gas cans clutched in one hand, Sig pistol in the other, Daymon stomped through the snow, the Cadillac Escalade visible just off his right shoulder.

Raven noticed that the Escalade had taken a beating at the hands of the dead. Dents and inches-long vertical scratches marred the once-shiny paint on the flank facing the Bronco.

The layer of snow running from the front edge of the hood, up the windshield, and all the way to the back hatch caused Raven to picture a disassembled Oreo cookie in her head.

Oh God, she thought, her salivary glands firing to life. An Oreo cookie sounded sooo good right about now. Add a cup of *real* milk—not the powdered crap they served everywhere in Springs—and she'd just about trade her entire haul of ears for one of each if offered to her right now.

Standing beside the SUV, the sun warm on his neck, Daymon swiped the rime of snow from the passenger window. Looking inside, he learned that the glass moonroof had been left open. Snow had infiltrated the rig, small drifts forming on the front seats and dash.

The black, leather-wrapped lid to the center console was also white with snow.

Finding the passenger-side doors locked, he went around and gained access through the partially open driver's door.

Inside the Bronco, Duncan said, "It's gonna be weird ringing in the New Year inside the walls with all *this* still going on out here."

Raven thought, *Try acknowledging it without both of your parents.*

Voice devoid of emotion, she said, "I'm done observing holidays."

"Why's that?" Immediately regretting the question, he said, "Just take it one day at a time, kid. That's what I'm doing. You gotta remember to keep on livin'."

Seeing Daymon set his gas cans near the Cadillac's rear bumper, she said, "I think you misunderstood me. I've lost so many people in my life that I've decided to treat every single day on this side of the grass as if it was Christmas, New Year's, Fourth of July, *and* my birthday all rolled into one."

While Duncan understood where she was coming from, for someone her age, he wasn't quite sure her new take on the apocalypse was entirely healthy. In his book, holidays and birthdays were milestones to be recognized separately and celebrated to the fullest. It wasn't as if the world had stopped spinning that awful day she was left alone in the house east of Woodruff, Utah. The last day she had heard her dad's voice over the radio. In fact, she had remarked to him just the other day that those barked orders that had saved her life that day would stay with her forever.

Daymon's return from the Escalade shook Duncan from his thoughts.

A gust buffeted the Bronco as Daymon again lifted the rear window. A knife-edged blast carrying snow with it infiltrated the cab as he stowed the gas cans and hose.

Duncan reached over and unlocked Daymon's door. Hinging up in his seat, he said, "Temp is dropping."

Having just received a dose of snow down the collar, Raven said nothing. She was busy helping it down her shirt and grinding her back against the seat to hasten its melting.

As Daymon slipped behind the wheel, Duncan began the inquisition.

"Was that the unlucky couples' rig?"

Daymon flicked the hula girl, starting her bobbing. He watched her dance a tick before touching the pad of a finger to her head, increasing the pressure until she was stilled.

"Well?" Raven pressed.

Staring out across the hood, Daymon said, "It's theirs. Their names are on the registration."

"Makes sense," Duncan said. "The plates are Connecticut. How much gas did they leave you?"

Daymon made a circle with his thumb and pointer finger. Holding the hand up, he said, "Big fat zero. The keys were in the ignition. Lights were left switched on. Which would explain why the battery is dead."

Raven asked, "Why'd they stop *here*?"

"Driver's front tire is flat. Long piece of bone stuck in it. The jack is deployed, and the spare is out on the ground by the jack. Leads me to think they were ambushed trying to change the tire."

Daymon's words rocketed Raven back in time. She was at the wheel of the Ford F-650 on SR-39 in Utah. Eyes glued to the advancing zombie herd reflected in the big side mirror, she was anxiously waiting for her dad to finish adding liquid patch to the truck's deflating tire before the ravenous dead could get to him.

Noting the sudden rise in the girl's breathing and the faraway look in her eyes—thousand-yard stare was what he had come to call the effect that afflicted even the hardiest of survivors—Duncan said, "You can take this next one off, Raven. Me and the kid can lop and bag. We'll share the haul evenly."

Snapping out of the trip down memory lane, Raven hissed, "I'll pull my own weight. Can we go now, or do you need to go *inside* and check your P.O. box for mail?"

Chapter 5

Precisely one minute after pushing south from downtown Wendover, circling back over the airport, and conducting a high-speed sprint east, Ari was holding the Ghost Hawk in a rock-steady hover, a dozen feet above the chosen cluster of walking corpses.

Though muffled due to the exhaust being routed through dozens of feet of ceramic-coated piping inside the stealth helo's airframe, the turbine whine was still substantial when the starboard-side door slid back in its tracks.

Rotor wash heavy with the stench of death and burned kerosene buffeted Staff Sergeant James "Skip" Skipper, longtime crew chief for Jedi One, as he leaned out over the milling mass of undead. Safety tether stretched to its limit, he armed and let fall from his gloved hand a tiny orange noise-making device. The high-tech Screamer was set for one-time use, meaning that once it hit the ground—or any solid object—it would begin emitting through its single tiny speaker a hyper-realistic recording of a dying woman's screams.

With enough juice onboard to run continuously for nearly ten minutes, Skipper knew he had to draw back from the door so his tagger could deploy.

Navy SEAL Petty Officer First Class William "Griff" Griffin, in his mid-thirties, watched as the crew chief hauled himself back inside the helo. Then, after checking his safety harness for the tenth time since Ari's call of "One minute out" came through his headset, the wiry, well-muscled son of a New England lobsterman flashed the crew chief a thumbs up and recited a short prayer only he could hear.

Strapped to one leg was a combat dagger. On the other, secured in a drop-thigh holster, was a Sig Sauer P226. Two spare magazines for the Sig, each carrying fifteen rounds of 9mm, rode in a

Kydex carrier secured to his belt, not that the extra ammo would do much good for Griff against the overwhelming odds represented by the throng of Zs he was about to get up close and personal with.

Now standing before the open doorway, Griff clamped one hand around the cable attached to his harness. In his other hand he clutched a sack containing the items he'd need to complete the mission. To ensure the sack wasn't lost as he was being lowered from the helo, he'd secured its drawstring to his harness with a carabiner.

Having drawn the short straw during the flight out, Griff had quietly accepted his lot, stowed his carbine under his seat, and sloppily jotted down a last will and testament.

Speaking into the boom mike snaking from his headset, the highly decorated former member of SEAL Team 6 addressed Ari. "If you dip me into the horde, I'm coming back as a ghost and I *will* skull fuck you every night in your sleep until the day you die. Are we clear?"

"Crystal," said Ari, his tone all business.

Addressing the mountain of a man up front in the left seat, Griffin said, "Keep your hands on the stick, Mister Haynes. Ari's known to succumb at any given time to the urge to fondle himself."

Smile breaking underneath his smoked visor, Haynes said, "God speed, frogman."

Griffin handed the folded-up will to the stocky, Hispanic captain leading the cobbled-together Delta team. Tugging at his unruly red beard, he said, "Low Rider … you are my executor. If I buy it today, you get my entire collection of X-Men comics. All my other crap, dole it out as you see fit."

Javier "Low Rider" Lopez, thirty-something veteran of combat ops conducted on nearly every continent, nodded and stuffed the paper underneath his plate carrier.

Pointing to the pair of operators sitting side by side, backs to the rear bulkhead, he said, "I'll let Cross and Axe fight over your dildo collection."

Chief Special Warfare Operator Adam Cross, a blond-haired, blue eyed Navy SEAL, responded first. "The Brit can have 'em." Cross laughed at his own joke and patted the SAS shooter on the chest.

Staring down at the shuffling masses, Nigel "Axe" Axelrod said, "Thanks all the same, Cross. You can have every one of Griff's rubber boyfriends."

Ari's voice came over the shared comms. "Ready to deploy?"

"Good to go," Skip replied. The helmeted crew chief, features hidden behind a smoked visor and attached skeleton face mask, turned to Griff and patted the man on the back.

There was a faint whirring noise as Skip drew up the slack in the cable.

Performing the sign of the cross over his chest, Griff leaped into space.

The cable held tight then began to spool out real slow. Griff's every instinct was to draw his legs up, wrap his ankles around the cable above his head, and order the masked crew chief to reel him in.

But he had a job to do.

The straw gods had spoken. And he was chosen ... or, as Ari was wont to say, "The corn holed one."

Griff reached under his plate carrier and came out with the specialized tool he'd be using to tag Zs.

Collapsed, the tool was a foot in length and U-shaped. A single handle coming off the bottom of the U housed an internal spring and featured an external catch. He slipped the handle's nylon strap over his right wrist. Next, he undid locking nuts on the ends of the U, pulled the pair of metal tong-looking arms to full extension, then retightened the locking nuts. Finished, the tool resembled an oversized tuning fork.

Griff waved the yard-long item back and forth in front of him. Seeing it remain rigid against the down blast from the rotor disc, he deemed it good to go. Next, he removed a tracking collar from his bag. The collar was three inches wide, made from some kind of reinforced fabric, and was the same safety-orange as the tiny Screamer wailing below him.

Confirming the small solar collection panel faced outward and that the flexible antenna was unfurled and snugged tightly into the transponder housing, he slipped the collar over the forked end of his tool. While holding the collar in place, he squeezed the handle continuously to start the tines ratcheting apart. Once the band was stretched to twice its normal size, he locked the tool open by thumbing its external catch into place.

Looking groundward, Griff saw that, as designed, the knot of dead they'd chosen was stopped in place and actively searching for the source of the shrill screams, for the fresh, warm meat they knew always accompanied the peals of the dying.

Head down and not eyeballing him was exactly how Griffin wanted the pusbags to remain while he worked. However, a number of them were still staring hungrily in his direction.

He selected a nearby female with a relatively small head and sturdy neck. To let Skip know the number of yards of slack he would need spooled out and the direction he wanted Ari to move the Ghost Hawk, Griff held up two fingers and gestured to his fore.

There was a brief pause, then, as requested, the Ghost Hawk crept forward. As a result, Griff went skimming over the heads of the throng. When he was directly above the Z in the floral print dress, he made a fist. *Stop.* A beat later the helo's forward movement ceased, leaving him but a meat pendulum, swaying subtly, back and forth, mere inches above a multitude of grabby hands.

"Perfect," Griff shouted into the comms. *Famous last words* was what he thought as, either started by the subtle vibrations coursing through the cable, or enacted by a rogue wind gust, he began to spin counterclockwise.

Quickly learning that movements at the end of the cable were nearly impossible for him to arrest once started, and feeling light-headed as a result of the constant change in scenery, he stretched his legs to full extension, keyed in on the tallest Z within reach, and delivered a swift kick to the side of its bowed head.

Three things came of Griff's desperate action.

First, equal and opposite reactions coming into play, the spinning stopped. Flooded with relief, he saw his surroundings snap back into focus.

The relief was short-lived. Because the zombie Griff had kicked in the head was not only very tall, it also possessed a pretty good wingspan.

Working on getting the collar positioned over the female Z's lolling head, Griff felt a crushing pressure envelope his right ankle.

Torn between finishing the delicate operation and getting eyes on what he instinctively knew had happened, he chose the former.

Griff bit his lip against the pain and strained against the harness to get an extra couple of inches extension. Just as he felt his body being pulled off axis—his helmeted head and gravity speeding up the process—the collar cleared the Z's pistoning jaw and he thumbed the catch release.

Unable to celebrate a job well done, Griff drew the Sig, thumbed the hammer back, and rolled his shoulders and head clockwise.

First thing Griff saw was the four long gray fingers encircling the top of his boot. They were opening and closing and slowly inching their way toward his bloused pant leg. He walked his eyes along the spindly arm and got a good look at the snarling creature's narrow face.

Saying, "Not today, McHale," Griff parked the Sig's sights on the bridge of the thing's nose and pressed the trigger two times.

The pair of *pops* from the lethal double tap were mostly drowned out by the cacophony of mechanical components keeping the hovering helo aloft. Altered by the rotor wash, the resulting pink mist bloomed wide on a flat plane, then was distributed to all points of the compass.

Free to go about his business, Griff repeated the process of loading another collar onto the tool. With Mister Murphy on hiatus, Griff was able to locate and tag two recently turned male Zs before the Screamer's battery shit the bed. The timer on his watch read nine minutes and eleven seconds and he was in the process of loading a fourth collar onto the tool when he saw that the horde had drawn dangerously close to the group of pacesetters.

Stabbing a thumb skyward and drawing his knees to his chest, Griff hollered, "Bring me in. Now!"

As the turbine whine picked up and Griff felt the first gentle tug of the winch motor, he dared to look groundward.

The sight of hundreds of dead stares locking on him, and only him, sent a shiver up his spine. Never again did he want to draw the short straw and find himself dangling over a sea of hungry Zs like this.

31

The cold waves and intermittent spasms continued to assail Griff's body even after he was safely inside the helo. Only when Jedi One's door was closed and they were underway did the tremors began to subside. Not until he had buckled in and could no longer see or smell the mega-horde did his breathing return to normal and he was able to fully relax.

"*Pinche demonios*," Lopez muttered. "Shit never gets old, eh, mi amigo?"

Helmeted head resting on the bulkhead, Griff stated, "I've never felt so close to death. Pun *not* intended."

Clapping the winded operator on the shoulder, Lopez said, "Good work, Griff. You just exempted yourself from the next draw."

Smiling at the unexpected good fortune, Griff closed his eyes and settled in for the long ride back to base.

Chapter 6

Daymon drove away from the post office expecting Duncan to let fly some smartass comment in reply to Raven's sharp retort to his suggestion that she exclude herself from the grisly task ahead. When Old Man remained silent, Daymon recognized it as a cue and did the same.

After a short drive west, Daymon brought the Bronco to a full stop a dozen feet shy of the rear of the herd.

Lips pursed into a thin white line, Raven sat unmoving, her gaze directed toward the vast plain to their right. In the front passenger seat, Duncan unsheathed his fixed-blade Bowie-style knife and began to run it across a whet stone.

Once again, Daymon killed the engine and stilled the hula girl with a finger.

During the trip from the post office to the herd, but a stone's throw east of Yoder, the only noise in the cab had been the steady growl coming from the Bronco's V8.

Breaking the silence, Duncan had said, "You know we're going to have to give every one of these things a once-over with the Geiger counter."

As Raven scrutinized the dead things, in her head she heard her dad say: *Work smarter, not harder.*

She said, "Once we're finished culling, why don't we just lay the ears out on Heidi's hood and *then* pass the Geiger counter over them? Then we can just throw away any that cause the thing to spike."

"Bird has a point," Duncan said.

Daymon flashed a half smile. Looking to Duncan, he said, "The girl thinks like her dad."

Nodding in agreement, Duncan said, "Marching orders?"

Daymon shrugged. "Production line? Or we could do the free for all thing and divvy them up on the hood afterward?"

Looking back to Raven, Duncan said, "Anyone have a preference?"

Again, the whole *Work smarter, not harder* thing informed Raven's decision.

She said, "I vote for production line. Free for all wastes too much time." She patted the sheathed Gerber. "And I'll be doing the stabbing."

"I've got a new edge here," Duncan said. "I'll slice."

Shaking his head, dreads whipping his shoulders, Daymon said, "Negative. No disrespect, but that'll take forever. Why don't you guard our six." Dragging a second machete from under the driver's seat, he shouldered open his door and stepped to the road.

Mouthing, "That'll take forever," Duncan sheathed his knife. Still muttering something about young people and discrimination against the aged, he opened the door and stepped out. Perching the white Stetson on his balding head, Duncan hinged the front seat forward and offered a gloved hand to Raven.

Waving away the chivalrous gesture, she squeezed her small frame through the narrow gap.

A chip off the old blocks, thought Duncan.

Eyes narrowing, Raven said, "You going to take the back seat to Daymon like that?"

Duncan retrieved the Saiga from the footwell and closed the door behind them. Dropping the shotgun's muzzle to the road, he regarded Raven. "He does have a point. I have lost half a step. Plus, I kind of enjoy watching him work, what with the two different color neon handles. He gets *Kindness* and *Mercy* going, damn near looks like an airport worker guiding a 747 to the terminal."

Slinging her rifle, Raven said, "Aren't their batons both the same color? When we arrived in Myrtle Beach to see Grandma and Grandpa, the woman guiding us toward the thingy that connects the airplane to the airport was swinging around bright orange ones."

"Semantics," said Duncan. "It's the motion. His long arms windmilling ..."

"I get it," Raven said. "Whatever floats your boat."

Calling out from the rear of the herd, Daymon said, "Well, Old Man, what's it going to be?"

"Hold yer pants," Duncan bellowed. "I'm moving as fast as I can."

As Duncan and Raven edged around the rear of the herd, she stopped now and again to lean over the already fallen specimens and provide them a second death courtesy of her recently inherited Gerber combat dagger.

Brandishing both machetes, Daymon urged Duncan to stand back, then waded into the herd, his blades blurring into twin lethal arcs of Day-Glo orange and green as he expertly split skulls and cleaved ears.

In a dozen minutes the entire herd was down and Raven had successfully freed another fifty-nine earthbound souls with a proficiency refined over the dozen or so beyond-the-wall excursions already under her belt.

Daymon cleaned his blades on a fallen Z's shirt and put them away. Regarding Duncan, he called, "A little help collecting the fruits of our labor?"

With a wag of his head, Duncan said, "You cut them, you police them up."

"It's like looking for needles in a haystack," Daymon moaned.

"When you slice 'em slowly," chided Duncan, "they don't go a flyin' all over the place."

From the middle of the herd where she was hunched over and plucking ears off the snow, Raven called, "Keep your head on a swivel, Duncan. We got this."

"Yeah," quipped Daymon. "*Stay frosty*, Old Man."

"No problem there," Duncan shot. "It's about twenty-five damn degrees. When's it supposed to warm up?"

Head down, eyes roaming the ground, Raven said, "Midweek, they say."

"And how do you know that, Bird of the Apocalypse?" Duncan asked.

"If you'd ever leave the Antlers," Raven said, "you'd know the Town Crier has added a weather report to his list of announcements."

Bird has a point, thought Duncan. After living underground for a couple of months, during which he was topside nearly every waking moment, the luxury of having a room with a view *and* a roof was likely to never get old. *Nesting* was what Glenda called his new behavior. In his mind, for obvious reasons, *hibernating* was the better descriptor.

"I get out," he said. "Every time Max has to go potty and comes scratching at our door, Glenda delegates the job to me."

Finished collecting ears, Raven began picking her way back through the fallen bodies. Curled fingers caught in her boot laces, stalling her forward progress. Kicking away the gnarled hand, she said, "Sounds like the control my mom had over my dad. They were a good team. He used to say she was using Jedi mind tricks on him."

Offering her a gloved hand, he said, "That wasn't *control*, young lady. That was true love."

This time Raven accepted Duncan's offering and leaped off one foot, easily clearing a partially clothed twenty-something. With arms outstretched and a one-eyed stare directed skyward, it looked as if the twice-dead thing had been trying to snatch Raven out of the air.

Walking back to the Bronco via the roadside ditch, Daymon held up a pair of bulging doggie poo bags. "That's all of them, I think."

"What were you picking up after," Duncan joked, "a Great Dane?"

"Nope," Daymon answered. "A dozen ankle-biting Chihuahuas."

Cackling at the visual of the lanky man being led along by a pack of little yappers, Duncan looked to Raven. "Could you see D as a dog walker? Maybe someplace like Manhattan? You know that was a thing"—he turned a slow circle—"before all of this happened. Hell," he added, stifling another laugh, "I may have just found *my* second calling. Think there's enough dogs in Springs to make it worth my while?"

Scrabbling back onto the road, Daymon said, "You could bribe the Crier with a couple of these ears. Have him slip an ad for Dapper Duncan's Dog-Walking Service between the weather and herd reports."

Shaking his head, Duncan said, "We better go before I get to mulling over the crazy idea. Cause if I do, it'll likely take root, and next thing you know, I'll be the one being led along by a pack of yappers."

Raven smiled for the first time in a long while. Twinkle in her eye, she said, "Glenda could finally retire."

Wearing a shit-eating grin, Daymon said, "Well there goes your idea of being a *kept* man."

Pointing to the others, one at a time, beginning with Raven, Duncan said, "You hush your mouth, Miss Grayson. And you, Mister Got-a-spider-perched-on-your-head, you better shut your pie hole, too."

Dumping the severed ears out on the Bronco's hood, Daymon said, "Or what?"

"You give Glenda any bad ideas and I'll nominate you for burial detail."

Raven emptied her bag onto the hood. Regarding Daymon, she said, "Better not cross the Old Man. You can smell those burial detail people from a mile away."

Daymon pantomimed zipping his lips. He went around back of the Bronco and came back with the Geiger counter already powered on and emitting a continuous soft clicking noise. It was a hand-held item readily available before the fall. And though it was a bit bigger than a pack of cigarettes, it looked small in Daymon's hand as he gave it a couple of slow passes over the shriveled ears.

Peering down at the liquid crystal display, Raven declared the ears good to go and began to push individual ears into three separate piles.

Causing them all to throw visible shivers, a big silver hoop earring pierced through one of the ears created a nail-on-chalkboard squeal as its metal post left a long scratch in the Bronco's paint.

"Shit," blurted Daymon. Shaking his head, he ran a finger along the gouge. "It's a deep one."

Duncan said, "Not the first, certainly not the last."

As Raven counted and bagged the ears, she asked, "With all of the vehicles to choose from, why the hell did you pick this relic?"

"Closest thing to Lu Lu I could find. Why? What's wrong with her?"

"Where to begin?" Duncan said. "It's cramped and the heater sucks. It wallows when you run over a sheet of paper. Shall I go on?"

"You two can walk home if you want."

Ignoring the threat, Raven said, "Twenty each for me and Daymon. Nineteen for you, Duncan."

"Why am *I* getting shorted?"

Addressing Duncan, Daymon said, "Just be happy you're not walking back." Regarding them both, he added, "And make sure those bags are double knotted. I don't want Heidi smelling like a burial detail taxicab."

Chapter 7

Eighteen miles west of Yoder, Colorado

Raven shifted in her seat and leaned against the wadded-up seat cover, crushing the plush item down to half its normal size. "This thing is cushy," she said. "Who's it for? Come on, Duncan ... you can tell us."

Shaking his head, Duncan said, "If I tell you—"

"He'll have to kill you," interrupted Daymon. "Old Man is probably going to put it on that ugly burnt-orange Scandinavian recliner of his. I bet it's to keep his hemorrhoids at bay as he watches M.A.S.H. reruns while Glenda's slaving away at work."

Outside Raven's window, bearing only the tire tracks left there earlier by the Bronco's eastbound passage, the laser-straight run of Highway 94 scrolled by like bad news on a heart monitor. Eyes narrowed, she asked, "What exactly is a hemorrhoid? And what is *Smash*?"

Grimacing, Duncan looked to Daymon. "It's your can of worms that just got opened, my friend. Means you get to tell the young lady *all* about 'em."

Daymon's first instinct was to tell her to *Google it*. Instead, he gave her a sanitized definition, likening a hemorrhoid to a pimple, that of which had yet to arrive on her face.

Head tilted, gaze locked on Duncan, she said, "On your butt?"

Duncan didn't respond to the question. Instead, he launched into a bland description of M.A.S.H that had Raven waving him off after a few seconds.

Daymon rolled his window partway down and pointed across the high plain. Cutting Duncan off midsentence, voice full of sarcasm, he said, "Look ... it's our old *home*."

To their left, a mile or so distant, was Schriever Air Force Base. The rambling affair, complete with barracks and a handful of two- and three-story buildings, was garrison to the Air Force's 50th Space Wing: the agency tasked with controlling the United States' small fleet of military satellites.

A dead giveaway to Schriever's main purpose was a Death-Star-looking sphere that no doubt housed all kinds of sensitive communications gear. Further breaking up the horizon were the multitude of antennas and oversized satellite dishes atop the buildings crowding in on the thirty-foot-tall sphere.

Only half joking, Duncan said, "With all those dishes, I bet they already got DIRECTV back up and running."

"Why," Raven quipped, "to torture us with crappy reruns?"

Daymon bumped fists with the tween.

"Here's our welcoming party," Duncan drawled.

Roughly a hundred yards beyond the opposite lane, the recently erected twelve-foot-tall run of concertina-wire-topped perimeter fence was but a gray blur. On the other side of the first layer of defense for the vulnerable base, its twin whip-antennas rising above the coiled razor wire, was a lone Humvee. Protruding from the desert-tan vehicle's roof-mounted cupola, waving a gloved hand above the Browning heavy machine gun, was the same soldier from the Army's storied 4th Infantry Division who'd watched them heading outbound a couple hours prior.

Duncan said, "Well, you going to respond to the sergeant, or just let him continue waving at us like a pageant girl?"

Daymon stuck his arm out the window and flashed a thumbs up. "I'm only doing this for you, Old Man. You know damn well he's bored as hell out here and about to hit us on the—"

On cue, the long-range radio in Duncan's lap emitted a short burst of squelch. A tick later the mobile sentry whose call sign for the day was Boulevard Three-Two began peppering them with questions.

"Boulevard Three-Two hailing the neon-green civilian victor, how copy?"

Raising the radio to his mouth, a half smile parting his lips, Duncan thumbed the talk key. "Boulevard Three-Two, this is Old

Man Actual. Solid copy." Releasing the talk key, he elbowed Daymon and chuckled.

"That's mean," Raven said. "He's just doing his job."

"But he's always so formal," Daymon replied. "Victor? C'mon already. He could have just as easily said *vehicle*."

"How's the hunting out there?" asked the sergeant.

Duncan said, "Well worth the gas it took to get us there."

"Good to hear, brother. When you get back to Springs, hoist a cold one for me. Three-Two out."

Knowing full well *that* wasn't happening, at least if he wanted to live another day, Duncan keyed to talk and said, "Copy that. We'll be thinking of you, Sergeant Bolan. Stay frosty out here." Dropping the radio to his lap, he looked to Daymon. "What's the count up to?"

A look of confusion ghosted across the dreadlocked man's face.

Sighing, Duncan said, "How many cans of spray paint do you have on this wannabe Lu Lu of yours?"

"Try *cases*," Daymon answered. "I just broke open the second one yesterday. So about fifteen cans." He displayed his right hand for all to see. The nailbeds and tips of his fingers were stained green. "I still need to add another coat of paint and one or two of clear."

Mesmerized by the fence scrolling by, Raven said, "Zombie blood and guts are going to show up on it real nice."

Duncan stared dreamily at the roof. He said, "When I got back to the world, my account flush with cash I *earned* in Nam, I wanted to buy myself a Dodge Challenger. Had to be Sublime Green, kind of like your old girl, Lu Lu. I wanted the black hood and accents. Maybe the vertical stickers running down the side."

Upshifting, Daymon said, "Hemi?"

Duncan fixed a *no duh* gaze on his friend. "Hell yeah," he shot. "With the Shaker-style hood, too."

"Why didn't you buy it?" Raven asked.

"Because I drank and gambled my money away. Lasted about one summer. Not the first time I pulled a stunt like that." He fixed her with a no-nonsense stare. Let it linger for a few seconds, then added, "Never, ever pick up that first drink. And if you gamble … set yourself a spending limit."

Raven didn't know what to say to that, so she sat back and stared out the window.

Daymon had heard the stories detailing his friend's many attempts at self-destruction. With nothing to add, he merely shrugged and kept his eyes on the road.

***

A couple of minutes after the first interrogative radio call, they passed a sign announcing the main road into Schriever.

South Enoch Road was a two-lane affair bisecting 94, right to left.

On the left, completely sealing off access to Schriever's distant northwest entrance, was a heavily fortified gate. Erected sometime after Cade and his family left Schriever for the Eden compound in Utah, the new entrance consisted of a heavy iron gate shored up by dozens of HESCO barriers—rock-filled mesh boxes used to construct blast walls.

Similar to the approach to some bases in the Sandbox, jersey barriers lined both sides of the lone drive leading to the gate. And to further thwart a vehicle intent on accessing the base uninvited, additional jersey barriers were arranged perpendicular to the sides of the cement chute. Placed at intervals meant to make incoming vehicles slow to a crawl and zigzag back and forth in order to navigate, the two-thousand-pound cement barriers were also effective at stopping even the largest of vehicles from ramming through.

Flanking the closed gate, with dual guard towers looming over them, was a pair of multi-wheeled Stryker armored vehicles. Sweeping slowly right to left, both roof-mounted remote weapon stations, outfitted with .50 caliber M2 Browning heavy machine guns, acquired the Bronco and commenced tracking its steady approach.

With less than a hundred yards to go to the crossroads, the radio on Duncan's lap emitted a burst of static. Before he could snatch it up, a soldier in one of the Strykers identifying as Boulevard Three-Three was wishing them safe travels.

Waving at the desert-tan, eight-wheeled armored vehicles, Daymon set his jaw and shifted Heidi into her top gear.

Shortly after leaving the crossroads behind, the dense gray clouds that had been hanging over Schriever gave way to wispy horsetails of white that seemed to stretch all the way to the snow-covered flanks of the distant Rocky Mountains.

With another sixteen miles or so to go through what Duncan liked to call "Indian country"—the unpatrolled no-man's land between Schriever and Springs—everyone in the Bronco sat tall in their seats, weapons came out, and all eyes probed the darkened strip malls and abandoned subdivisions scrolling by outside their windows.

As they passed by a six-car pileup, the rusty vehicles still tangled together and languishing in the elements, Daymon looked to Duncan. "When's the last time you heard of a brigand attack going down out here?"

"Day after we got here," Duncan said, covering his nose with his sleeve. "A couple out on a firewood run got ambushed somewhere inside the Yellow Zone. Their rig was found stashed at the wrecking yard we passed on the way out. Both corpses were stuffed into a pair of fifty-five-gallon drums." He went quiet for a moment, unsure if he should say what he was thinking, lest it reopen his friends' old wounds.

"Why hide the bodies?" Daymon said. "Can't throw a rock inside the YZ without hitting one."

In a low voice, Duncan said, "Because they'd been stripped of their flesh."

Having lost his Heidi in a similar fashion, Daymon swallowed hard and focused on the road.

Chapter 8

Two miles west of Schriever, with another two to go before reaching the newly reopened and heavily guarded Colorado Springs Municipal Airport, the pong of decaying flesh riding the crisp afternoon air became nearly unbearable as it infiltrated the Bronco's drafty cab.

Moments later they came upon the latest in a long row of dozens of massive communal graves. Carved into the hard, high plain soil, the rectangular scar in the earth looked to be about the size of a football field. Though the pit's edges were still dark—which led Duncan to believe it was, at most, a couple of days old—it was already filled to brimming with thousands of stiffened twice-dead zombie corpses.

Like whitecaps on an angry ocean, tufts of snow frozen on high spots in the drift of death sparkled like diamonds in the emerging sun. And as if the dead were struggling to stay above water, here and there arms and legs broke the illusory surface.

Duncan found that if he looked real hard, he could make out shriveled heads complete with windblown wisps of hair and mouths frozen in silent Os. As the Bronco clipped on by, the accusatory gazes seemed to follow.

Taking his eyes off the road for a tick, Daymon scrutinized the surreal scene. Recalling the time he had been running outside Schriever's perimeter wire and had inadvertently careened into an open pit teeming with sun-baked corpses, he threw a shiver and felt his heart race. He had thrust his arms out to break his fall but had only succeeded in breaking through taut, pallid skin and putrefying organs. Though the event was old history, as he relived it, he heard in his head the wet *pop* that came when his arm plunged elbow-deep into the dead Z's chest cavity.

At the time he had cursed like a merchant marine and reflexively yanked his arm free of the sucking cavity.

Now, he cringed and strangled the steering wheel as in his mind's eye he saw his hand emerge along with long, greasy ropes of ruptured, feces-covered lower intestine.

The only thing close to surmounting the onslaught of putrid air following his unintended hand plant was the sulphur-like stink of gasses rushing from the bloated corpses that had continued to settle under the weight of his prostrate body.

The eruption of wet farts was quickly followed by tremors of movement and raspy moans as the string of expletives roused an unseen number of *unfortunate* living dead that had become entombed along with their *lucky* twice-dead brethren.

Though he had contemplated retelling the story as a cautionary tale, mostly for Raven's benefit, he shoved the morbid memory away and did a short drum solo on the steering wheel, finishing with a little tap to the side of Hula Girl's head.

Referring to the herd they'd just culled back in Yoder, he said, "That's where our kills will eventually end up."

"By all rights," Duncan replied. "Hell, after what we've been through, that's where *we* should be."

Raven shook her head. "Not going to happen. We're being looked over. I'm sure of it."

Thankful for the diversion, Daymon relaxed his grip on the wheel. "By whom?" he asked.

"Who," Duncan corrected. "Whom would imply there's a whole gang of folks watching our six."

Raven said, "God."

"After all He has let happen to good people down here," Daymon said, "I'm having a real hard time believing He has our best interests at heart."

As if saying *Suit yourself*, Raven shrugged and resumed staring out her window.

Duncan also went silent as he caught sight of humongous mounds of snow-dusted earth that would soon cover the pit and conceal Omega's handiwork from the prying eyes of future generations. Out of sight, out of mind wasn't as easy as it sounded, because there were at least twenty or thirty pits, all containing tens of thousands of bodies. The evidence of the misery Omega had inflicted on man stretched away to the south, as far as the eye could see.

Rising a few feet above the mini white mountains was a pair of *dead sleds*—mega dump trucks weighing three-hundred-tons—each capable of hauling nearly their weight in corpses.

Dwarfed by the haulers and nearby piles of excavated dirt was a vast motor pool consisting of desert-tan D-10 dozers, Day-Glo yellow excavators, safety-orange CDOT road graders, and a trio of oversized steam rollers. Like faithful soldiers awaiting marching orders, dozens of mobile, solar-powered light standards were left arranged in neat lines on the pit's periphery. Whether the heavy equipment was idled by Mother Nature, a lack of warm bodies willing to operate them, or a combination thereof, Duncan hadn't a clue.

Looking to Daymon, he said, "Bet they're going to need someone who knows how to move dirt around. Didn't you do a lot of that in your previous life? Cutting fire lanes and such?"

Flashing the older man a sour look, Daymon said, "Let's keep that little tidbit of info between you and me."

Duncan chuckled and slapped his thigh. "I've got something on you, now, young man."

Soon the view out the left-side windows turned to wide-open snow-covered plain broken up by scrub brush, scattered homesteads, and the occasional white-flocked tumbleweed.

A handful of minutes later, with the stink of death nearly scoured from the cab, the sprawl of buildings and lone control tower making up Colorado Springs Airport materialized off the Bronco's left front fender.

Partially blocking the stunted skyline of the nation's new capital, the airport's sprawling cement footprint was a beehive of activity, most of it taking place north of the runway on tarmac belonging to Peterson Air Force Base.

Massive hangars, some with their floor-to-ceiling rolling doors yawning open, lined the north side of the shared space. A half-dozen black helicopters, their rotor blades tied down, contrasted greatly against the snow-blanketed apron they sat upon.

To ensure ongoing air operations, liberated fuel arrived almost daily aboard aerial tankers tasked with finding and tapping distant underground tank farms.

Convoys of semi-trucks, some of them towing double and triple tanks, were returning weekly from airports far and wide, their full loads of JP8 quickly filling Peterson's vast network of underground storage tanks.

Coming up on treed acreage that had to be a golf course, the four-lane jogged left and became Platte Avenue. Simultaneously, as Peterson Air Force Base slid to the right and filled up the windshield, a pair of A-10 Thunderbolt II jets lifted, one at a time, into the brightest blue sky Duncan had seen in a long while.

The aircraft formed up wingtip to wingtip, passed over the Bronco, then banked hard to the northwest, their twin engines howling like a winter squall.

"A ground pounder's best friend," Duncan said. "Wish we had those birds in Nam. Would've cooled down a lot of hot LZs."

"Having a couple of those on station might have saved you a couple of hard landings," Daymon noted. "Hell, you probably wouldn't have the problem you do now with sitting for long durations."

Exasperation showing in his tone, Duncan said, "The damn seat cover is *not* for me. And my *roids* aren't *that* bad."

Running interference for Old Man, Raven said, "My dad told me those things saved him and Mike Desantos one time."

"Probably more than once," Daymon said. "Your dad was a bad guy magnet. I can't imagine what it was like being around him in a whole country full of bad guys. Must have had to stay *extra* frosty when in Wyatt's orbit."

Raven buried her face in her hands. Stayed in that position for a moment. When she rose up, she wiped her eyes on a sleeve and peered out the windshield. In the middle distance, maybe half a mile away, was the beginning of Colorado Springs' Red Zone—a blocks-wide swath of burned and bulldozed ground that encircled the city just outside its drastically reduced perimeter. It got its name from the no-go zones marked clearly in red on all official maps of the new capital.

In the residential area they were passing through—still technically the Yellow Zone—garbage cans and recycling bins put out in front of some of the homes awaited sanitation trucks that were never coming.

Dead traffic lights swayed lazily over intersections blocked on both sides with inert vehicles shored up from behind by cement jersey barriers.

They passed by a long line of abandoned cars, pickups, and SUVs snaking around the block from a boarded-up Shell station. Someone had spray-painted NO GAS across the sign offering all grades of the finite commodity for an obscenely inflated price.

"Thirty bucks a gallon," scoffed Duncan. "Opportunists sure came out of the woodwork during the outbreak."

"They still are," observed Raven soberly. Lord knows she'd seen her share of them in the months since the Omega virus irrevocably changed her life. And in the weeks since she'd been calling Springs home, she'd come across many more.

Like the blank staring eyes of the infected, grimy windows on homes and businesses long abandoned reflected the green blur of the passing Bronco back at Raven. As they covered the last few blocks to the intersection where zones transitioned from Yellow to Red, she tried hard to picture her home in Portland but only came up with a gray two-story box. The porch roof, she recalled, was buttressed by square columns; the handrails running all around it were supported by metal balusters. The windows, she knew, had white frames bracketed by black shutters her dad had said were put there just for looks.

She also knew without a doubt the front door was black. Because one hot summer day when she was nine or ten, she had helped her dad paint it to match the useless shutters.

Stowing his Saiga on the floor, Duncan said, "Kind of reminds me of the pictures of the No-Man's-Land between Checkpoint Charlie and the Berlin wall. Big difference, though, was that the wall and mined ground and barbwire was there to keep people from *fleeing* communism, not to protect the population from walking dead things and breathers with bad intentions."

Duncan's brief history lesson had snapped Raven back to the present. She looked between the front seats and saw they were now approaching the underpass that marked the start of a half-mile run of Platte Avenue that traversed a wide plain of cleared ground said to be strewn with motion sensors and trip-flares.

Praying the wait wouldn't be a long one, Raven said, "We're here" and started searching for their *welcome* party.

Chapter 9

At first sight of the *Welcome* sign posted just outside the mouth of the El Paso Street underpass, Daymon braked and brought the Ford to a complete stop, leaving its front bumper hovering over the squiggly safety-orange line spray-painted across both westbound lanes.

The sign was far from welcoming. While it did announce Colorado Springs as the new capital of the United States, the rest of the information on it, written in several different languages, was of the instructional variety that concluded with an order for anyone approaching on foot or by vehicle to wait for permission to enter before proceeding forward.

The checkpoint location had been chosen for a number of reasons, the most glaring being the lack of anything standing between it and the perimeter wall fronting the Red Zone.

Constructed from light-gray cement panels sourced from freeways far and wide, the east wall stretched for miles north and south. Finished just weeks ago, the wall was already tagged with graffiti, some of it crude as cave drawings, some of it colorful works of art that had clearly been given much thought before the first line was sprayed.

Referring to the jagged letters making up the nearly indecipherable names and phrases marring many of the panels, Duncan said, "Damn taggers are like cockroaches."

Raven said, "They hit my school in back just after it let out for the summer."

Daymon shut the truck down. "I never saw any of that in Jackson. Chief Jenkins would have shit a brick. Then he would have run down whoever did it and made them spend a day freezing their asses off while they picked up antlers from the elk refuge."

"Ahhh," Duncan said, "the good ol' days. I sure miss them."

Dead ahead, across the razed ground, looking like a postage stamp from this distance, was one of the eastern wall's two entries.

Appearing to hover above the wall on either side of the gate was a pair of guard towers. An enclosed walkway with horizontal firing ports connected the towers. Black fabric stretched across the walkway no doubt shielded from view at least one sniper training his or her rifle on them.

Poking skyward in the middle distance—the tallest among them maybe thirty stories—were the buildings making up the downtown core. Thanks to the recent weather, they stood out starkly against the foothills rambling away westward behind them.

Raven asked, "How do they know we're here?"

Duncan said, "I'm sure there's someone glassing us right now."

Sensing distant eyes on him, Daymon let his gaze travel their surroundings.

Northwest of the Bronco, a trio of huge, snow-dusted burn piles rose up from the parking lot of what appeared to be some kind of sports complex. The rounded tops of the mounds of charred, nearly unrecognizable corpses were almost level with the blackened crowns of the half-dozen mature trees growing in the median directly across the street from them.

Due to Daymon's experience fighting wildfires, the genesis of this massive burn was crystal clear to him. Having flashed off at the burn piles, likely as a result of too much fuel and lax attention, wind-driven flames had jumped the street, flared in the boughs of the nearby trees, and then went on to consume tinder-dry bushes and lawns and structures for blocks and blocks in either direction.

With no water pressure to speak of, the soldiers and volunteers working to sanitize the new capital for arriving survivors could only watch as a half-mile wide swath of eastern Springs burned out of control, only going out once it reached the ground being cleared in preparation for the eastern wall and ran out of fuel.

Shaking his head, Daymon craned and scrutinized the landscape southwest of the intersection. Stretching off for several blocks on a diagonal tangent was what he guessed used to be a city park of significant importance. The snowy expanse of sparsely treed ground rolled away to a nearby lake. Hugging the snow-dappled banks and untouched by wildfire was a row of wooden boat houses. Abutting the boat houses was a long dock home to multiple racks filled with colorful kayaks and stand-up paddle boards.

Near the park's entrance was an abstract stone monument. It sat on what looked to be a marble pedestal erected in the center of a circular plaza. All of the trees ringing the plaza had suffered the same fate as the ones in the median.

Kitty-corner from the plaza was another burn pile. Here and there blackened appendages pierced the snow.

It was a surreal sight to see the park nearly untouched in the midst of all the destruction.

"How did this burn start?" Raven asked.

Daymon gave voice to his theory.

"So how did it jump the city?"

Daymon shook his head. "Two different fires. Shortly after this eastside burn, the mayor called for a volunteer force to be established. Foraging crews went to communities south of Springs looking to loot abandoned stations of their vehicles and firefighting gear. I hear they had to go all the way to Pueblo for engines and spare hose."

Duncan looked away from the burn piles long enough to say, "So how *did* the other fire start?"

"A lightning strike," Daymon said. "And just days after they got this one tamped down."

Raven said, "I'm guessing the mayor's plan was still in motion."

"Yep," Daymon confirmed. "There were multiple strikes up and down the foothills. When all was said and done, wind-whipped flames scorched everything south to north between Interstate 25 and Garden of the Gods."

"Nothing much to burn there," Duncan said, his gaze back to roaming the sky.

Daymon said, "Just red rock spires and juniper."

Raven said, "How'd they save the Air Force Academy?"

"Act of God," Duncan said. "Everyone knows He likes us aviators. How do you think I survived all those *hard landings*?"

"Crashes," needled Daymon.

Duncan waved dismissively. Still scanning the sky, he said, "Damn thing should be here by now."

As the trio waited for permission to enter the Red Zone and begin their controlled approach to the eastern gate, they each struggled to find something to do to pass the time.

Duncan watched a feral dog poking its head into an overturned garbage can. It was no bigger than a Corgi, with the stunted legs to match. Strangely, its white coat bore a multitude of small black spots. Probably the result of a *wham-bang* encounter between a Dalmatian and Corgi. *What a sight that improbable interlude would have been*, he thought with a grin as it scurried from the can and loped toward the windowless shell of a burned-out SUV. Since the tires had been reduced to pools of rubber, leaving the SUV sitting on warped steel wheels, only a six-inch-gap at best remained between the vehicle's running boards and buckled patch of asphalt it sat upon.

Thanks to the dog's low-to-the-ground stance, it crawled under the wreck with maybe an inch or so to spare. Then, totally ignoring the occupants of the bright green intruder, the Corgmation—as Duncan had instantly labeled the mutt—emerged from cover, nosed the ground from the curb to the nearest burn pile, then entered a shadowy crevice and was lost from view.

Raven had been drumming Duncan's seatback and watching the dog, too. Craning to see out the windshield, she said, "What do you think is keeping them?"

Having been staring south down the side street where the bare foundations of razed structures stretched off into the distance, Daymon perked up and looked at his watch.

Regarding Raven, he said, "Lunch?"

Duncan pushed his aviator glasses up on his nose then hunched down in his seat and looked out over the flat hood. Slowly, he scanned the snow-covered expanse of open ground spread out before them. He saw nubs of logged trees and tufts of rolled concertina but couldn't make out much more than that beyond the midway point to the gate.

Straightening up in his seat, Duncan said, "With all the snow, if the damn thing is out there, it should be standing out like a sore thumb."

"Sayeth the guy who weareth the bifocals," Daymon quipped. He cracked his neck and back, then, one at a time, worked on his knuckles. Though he knew they were all bad habits, he'd been doing it several times a day since Heidi's death.

Raven said, "Shhh … I hear it."

A tick later an ominous shadow fell on the hood. As they craned to spot the incoming drone, the soft buzzing morphed to a shrill whine and the insect-looking craft materialized just outside Daymon's open window.

Chapter 10

Pulling a trick out of the Red Baron's playbook, whoever was piloting the source of the buzzing had masked its approach by bringing it in on a gently sloping approach that had it coming straight out of the low-hanging sun.

A couple of seconds after the motor noise enveloped the Bronco, the craft—a four-prop drone about the size of a manhole cover—appeared off the left front fender. The blades were black blurs inside horizontally positioned circular shrouds. Protruding from under the craft's desert-tan main body was a polished black dome.

As if mounting a feeble attack on the Ford, the drone's blurry, insect-like shadow danced back and forth across the hood. This went on for a few seconds while the unseen operator made minute course corrections to steady the craft in front of the windshield.

Having finally attained a semblance of a hover, the drone spun slowly on axis, no doubt to allow the camera in the dome to get a good fix on the truck's occupants.

Speaking in a near whisper, Duncan said, "I've heard about these models, just haven't seen one up close."

Daymon cranked his window open. In a booming voice, he said, "What's up?"

A couple of seconds went by. Finally, as crisp and clear as if the person speaking was just outside the door, a masculine voice asked them to state their business.

Daymon held up the official document that allowed them access to the eastern frontier.

As the drone slipped around to his window, he said, "We were doing a cull east of Yoder."

A few more seconds passed.

Leaning in close to Daymon, Duncan whispered, "I have a feeling there's a bit of an audio delay going on here. You know, like they had on newscasts and such so they could censor the truth. Keep the sheeple from hearing and seeing what they weren't supposed to."

Raven shook her head. "You think everything is a conspiracy, Uncle Duncan. My mom told me tape delay was used so kids didn't have to hear curse words or see bad things like car wrecks or shootings as they were happening on live television."

"Is that what Glenda told you? I'm a conspiracy nut?"

Raven was spared from answering when, again, the voice emanated from the hovering drone. It said, "You can lower the document." Then: "How many in your vehicle?"

"Three," Daymon answered.

The drone moved in closer and rotated on axis, slowly, from left to right, stopping only when it was squared up to Raven.

"Are any of you hurt?"

"Just my feelings," Daymon said. "Any way I can look my interrogator in the eyes?"

There was no response to his question. Instead, the drone panned back and forth, finally stopping where it had started, with what looked to be the front of the craft facing Raven.

Duncan held a hand out to Daymon. "Hundred bucks says it's giving us the once-over with a thermal scanner."

"You're not supposed to be placing bets," Raven hissed. After scanning all points of the compass, she addressed Daymon, saying, "Ask the man what he wants so we can be on our way."

Daymon turned back to face the drone but found that it had flown off and was nearly finished conducting a counterclockwise window-level recon of the Bronco.

Finishing the orbit, the drone hovered off the driver's side mirror and the voice asked if they had been anywhere near the Castle Rock craters or the badlands due east of them where prevailing winds had deposited fallout after the detonation of two low-yield nuclear warheads.

Daymon said, "Nope and nope. And we didn't harvest from any glowers, either. Checked 'em all first with the Geiger."

The voice said, "Follow. Do not deviate."

Watching the drone scoot off to the west, Duncan said, "Pushy fella, ain't he?"

Again stating the obvious, Raven said, "He's just doing his job."

The drone led them down Platte Avenue at damn near thirty miles per hour. Along the way they passed the bulldozed remains of a couple of fast food establishments, a chain hardware store, and a 7-Eleven. Intense heat had warped the convenience store's once colorful sign, leaving it faded and marred with brown, pimply bubbles.

As they reached the gate, without warning the drone lifted away from the Bronco and then dropped out of sight behind the wall.

To their immediate right, planted in the ground on the corner of Platte and North Nevada, was a sign that read *Palmer High School*. What looked to have once been a two- or three-story affair was now a ten-foot-tall pile of rubble. Canted at crazy angles, fractured cement sheets shot through with twisted rebar and sprouting fire-ravaged heating and ventilation equipment kept anyone from approaching the gate from the north.

South of the gate was the fortified single-wide trailer. From previous trips outside the wire, Duncan knew this was where the I's were dotted and T's got crossed. The drab tan building housed medical equipment and was staffed by a doctor and nurse.

Behind the trailer was a pair of futuristic-looking Mine Resistant Armored All-Terrain Vehicles. The M-ATVs were painted in a woodland camo pattern—a mix of blacks, browns, and shades of green—and bristled with guns.

A second trailer behind the first housed a squad of soldiers from the 4th ID. They were armed to the gills and had enough ammo to keep any attackers at bay until a quick reaction force could be summoned from inside the walls.

"More hurry up and wait," Daymon groused.

Duncan said nothing. He was staring at the windowless door and willing someone to emerge through it.

Meanwhile, in the backseat, Raven's attention was drawn to the colorful graffiti on the sections of wall south of the soldiers' billet.

Indicating something that had caught her eye, Raven said, "Are those house-looking thingies some kind of Japanese writing?"

Squinting, Duncan said, "All I can make out is the big writing. Don't ask me what those tangled letters spell out. It's all Greek to me."

Craning to see beyond the first trailer, Daymon said, "Looks to me like Kanji. Chinese figures that have certain meanings. I've seen them on the walls in tattoo shops. Those other things … I have no clue."

Pointing at a big swathe of color, Raven asked, "What's that?"

Daymon said, "The big tag right there is just regular graffiti. It reads … *We are all dead inside.*"

Duncan shot his friend a befuddled look. "How do you get *that* out of"—he pointed across the hood—"*that?*"

Daymon shrugged. He put both hands up so Duncan could see them and began to trace a facsimile of the interconnected letters on his palm for his friend to follow. He got through the first two words and was moving on to *all* when he felt in his chest an all too familiar sensation. It was as if he were standing next to a speaker bank at a Damian Marley concert. Except he heard no lyrics or instruments. Instead he just felt the harmonic thrum that could only belong to one thing: the Ghost Hawk helicopter that used to take his friend on his secretive missions.

Wishing the vintage Bronco had a glass roof, Duncan ran his window down. Removing the white Stetson, he stuck his head out the window and looked skyward.

"There it is," Raven said, pointing at the blue sky above the trailers.

Duncan hunched down in his seat and walked his gaze the length of Raven's arm. Picking up the angular outline of the helo Cade called Jedi One, he said, "Ari's coming out of the sun, too." He sighed and watched the coal-black stealth helicopter pass right to left. "What I wouldn't give to fly one of those black whirly birds."

The third-generation Jedi ride was flying *clean* with its landing gear and weapons stowed internally. The heading it was maintaining looked to be a straight shot to Peterson Air Force Base.

Just as the low-flying Ghost Hawk bumped up to treetop level and disappeared from sight, two MultiCam-clad soldiers stepped from the first M-ATV and the door to the medical trailer hinged open to reveal a person in a white Level B hazmat suit. Wearing gloves and a black facemask hooked to the self-contained breathing apparatus worn on its back, nothing about the form exiting the med trailer seemed welcoming.

"This always feels like jail in-processing," Duncan whispered.

"Prepare to lift 'em and cough?" Daymon replied.

"I heard that," Raven said, a measure of disgust in her tone. "Remember, guys, they're just doing their jobs."

The soldiers stalked over to the Bronco while the person in the suit closed the trailer door and watched their approach from atop the short stack of stairs. Though the face behind the mask was hard to make out, the gesture the suited form made was not.

Elbowing open his door, Duncan said, "Well, kids … our wait is over."

Chapter 11

"No sudden movements," Duncan joked as he formed up outside the Bronco between Raven and Daymon. Looking left and right, he added, "Isn't this cute. We're arranged shortest to tallest."

While one soldier inspected the Bronco's interior and went through their belongings, the other produced a tactical light and a dinner-plate-sized mirror. The soldier thumbed on the light then extended the telescoping handle attached to the mirror. Using the mirror and light in conjunction, he walked around the rig, inspecting its undercarriage, wheel wells, and all of the dark recesses around the V8 engine.

Finished with the cab and backseat area, the first soldier slammed the driver's side door and moved around to the rear of the SUV.

"Easy on the paint," Daymon called. "She's a classic."

The soldier said nothing. Just continued to wave a hand-held Geiger counter over the gear in back. Finished, the soldier regarded the woman in the hazmat suit. "It's clean, ma'am. Rad levels are nominal."

The other soldier pocketed his flashlight, then collapsed the handle and tucked the mirror under one arm. Looking to the woman, he assured her that the Bronco wasn't harboring any biologic residue.

"I could have told you all of that," Daymon said. "We ran our counter over the dead before we culled them."

A lie. However, running the counter over their severed ears after the fact seemed adequate to him. Shoved the *lie* over into the *little white* column.

Voice a bit muffled, the woman said, "No, you didn't. You culled and collected. Then you checked the bounty for rads. That'd probably be my approach."

The first soldier looked a question at the woman.

Nodding, the woman said, "Start with the girl."

Raven was swept for radiation first. Coming up clean, she was led into the trailer by the woman.

Looking his friend in the eye, Duncan said, "Here comes the 'ol'"—he pantomimed squeezing his nipples, then pretended to fondle the family jewels—"*honk, honk, doodle, doodle.* Are you ready for it?"

"Is there a serious bone in your body?"

With a twinkle in his eye, Duncan said, "I think we're about to find out," and bust out in his trademark cackle.

The soldier with the Geiger counter started with Duncan, then moved on to Daymon. Once both men were found to be carrying only nominal levels of radiation, two suited men emerged from the trailer and ushered them inside.

***

After having each received a thorough once-over by a medical professional of their own gender, Duncan and Raven emerged from the trailer.

Duncan was holding his seat forward so Raven could clamber into the Bronco when the trailer door opened and Daymon leaped from the top stair. Though it initially looked as if he had made a successful jailbreak and was making his run to freedom, once his boots hit the churned ground in front of the bottom stair he walked slowly to the Bronco, a definite pep in his step.

Addressing the younger man as he took his place behind the steering wheel, Duncan said, "Why so happy?" He stabbed his pointer finger skyward. "The pretty lady give you a free *oil check* in there?"

As the outer gate began to slide away in front of the Bronco, a purple Mountain Metro city bus was slowly revealed. The late model Gillig was parked parallel to the gate with an older man already in the driver's seat and cranking the engine over. A tick later there was puff of gray exhaust and the diesel growled to life.

Because the bus was weighted down with rubble taken from the Red Zone, it sat real low to the ground and took a lot of gunning the engine from the driver to get moving.

Turning the key in the ignition, Daymon said, "I think the lady doctor is interested in me."

While they waited for the bus to catch up with the outer gate, Duncan looked a question at Daymon.

Out of her seatbelt, arms draped over the seatbacks, Raven did the same.

Gaze shifting between the two, Daymon threw his arms in the air. "Heidi's murder fucked me in the head big time. In fact, it brought back old memories of the cruelty she said she endured as Robert Christian's *concubine*. Still"—he grinned feebly—"a guy has to get back in the saddle. Go on living his life."

Still staring at Daymon, his head slowly panning back and forth, Duncan sighed loudly.

Gaze locked on the trailer door, Daymon bit his lip and returned both hands to the wheel.

Once there was room for the Bronco to slip by the slow-rolling bus, a soldier manning the gate on the inside stepped into the narrow gap and motioned them forward.

As Daymon got the Bronco moving in first gear, Duncan twisted in his seat to face him. Wearing a wan smile, he said, "I think that performance is worthy of an Oscar. About the doc, I think you're full of it."

Before Daymon could mount a defense, Raven said, "What's the doc's name?"

Daymon flicked his eyes to the side mirror and watched the gate close behind them. He ignored the accusatory line of questioning long enough to watch the bus roll back into position.

Working the stick to find the next gear, Daymon looked to Duncan. "*I'm* full of shit? That's rich coming from a guy for whom the truth is Kryptonite. You're so full of bullshit your eyes are brown." He regarded Raven in the rearview, voice softening he went on, "Her name is Sonja. Like the comic book character: Red Sonja. She told me she was a kid doctor and stuck working at a hospital in Salt Lake when it fell."

"Pediatrician," Raven said. "How old is she?"

"My age."

Sounding skeptical, Duncan said, "So, early thirties? I was thinking mid-twenties. Then again, her face was mostly concealed by the mask."

Daymon nodded. "I'm just guessing, though. You think I'm stupid enough to actually ask a woman her age?"

"One time I was so drunk," Duncan mused, "that I asked a woman her age, weight, shoe size *and* if she would like to drink Pina coladas and make love to me in the dunes on a cape."

Daymon said, "Yeah, I heard that song before." He regarded Raven in the mirror. "See, I told you. He's making up stories based on song lyrics. You have any experiences Prince may have memorialized in song?"

Raven said, "Ewwww." Not liking where the conversation was going, she eyed Acacia Park sliding by on the left.

Taking up nearly an entire city block, every tree on it taller than twenty feet touched in some way by the conflagration, the park was now being used as an assembly point for the gate's quick reaction force. Parked side by side, their grilles facing Platte, was a number of military vehicles: M-ATVs, MRAPS, eight-wheeled Strykers, and Humvees in many different configurations. An assemblage of mobile homes and RVs took up the rest of the flat ground behind the makeshift motor pool.

Though not her first time entering the city via the East Gate, the sight of darkened signs over fast food restaurants still got her stomach to rumbling. As they passed a Carl's Jr, she was taken back to her old life. To the Mike's Drive-In back in Portland, Oregon. A special place where memories of eating burgers and fries and slurping milkshakes with her mom and dad had been forged. She recalled how her dad would always comment on the framed prints on the walls, trying to guess the makes and models of the classic cars and hotrods featured in the American-Graffiti-inspired artwork.

Still tuning out the spirited banter taking place between the *adults* in the front seat, she locked her gaze on the distant thirteen-story building she now called home.

Stopping dead center on the snowy two-lane where westbound Platte crossed Cascade Avenue, Daymon shushed Duncan and craned around in his seat.

"Where do you want to go?" he asked Raven. "The Antlers or Penrose?"

Voice devoid of all emotion, she said, "Home."

A little red-faced after going at it with Daymon, Duncan said, "Sure you don't want to go to Penrose? I'm sure Glenda would love some company."

Looking north down Cascade, Raven said, "After all the culling today, a little peace and quiet would do me good."

As Daymon made the turn to the south, Duncan said, "Surely ain't going to find any of that at home. Either Wilson and Sasha will be at each other's throats, or Peter and Sasha will have their tongues *down* each other's throats."

Raven smiled vacantly. "Please drop me off at the park."

Duncan said, "It's pretty cold outside, Raven."

"In case you need a reminder, Duncan, you aren't my parent and you aren't my legal guardian."

That shut Duncan up.

Handing Daymon a scuffed and faded card bearing the Visa logo, she said, "Have them load my cut from the cull on this."

"You got it," said Daymon, pocketing the card. "See who's treating you like the ass kicker you are. Me. That's who." He slid Heidi to the curb on Pikes Peak Avenue and set the brake. Elbowing open his door, he stepped to the road and tilted his seat forward.

As Raven wormed her way out of the backseat, her gaze was drawn to her favorite bench in the park. It was constructed of some kind of dark wood polished smooth from accommodating lots of butts. Facing north by west, it afforded her an unobstructed view of the Garden of the Gods to the west and the Rocky Mountains rising up northwest of the walled-in city.

Endearing her to the particular bench more than any view could was that it sat underneath a deciduous ash tree, one of her mom's favorites.

Daymon stooped over and hugged Raven. Staying in big brother mode, he said, "Holler if you need anything."

Raven slung her carbine and turned toward the park.

"Mind your safety on that thing," Duncan called.

Ignoring Duncan's nagging, Raven made tracks through the snow toward *her* bench. The bench with the small bronze plaque announcing it as a donation to the city made in the loving memory of Charles and Beatrice Goodwin.

The Bronco rocked on its springs when Daymon climbed behind the wheel. Slamming the door, he said, "Apple didn't fall far from the tree."

"Nail on the head," Duncan said. "But I'm afraid that apple is starting to get a little big for her britches."

Daymon was nodding in agreement as he wrenched the wheel over and started the Bronco in a wide U-turn that would see them heading back the way they'd come.

Getting the rig back to tracking north on Cascade, he said, "That's something she's going to have to learn the hard way. No sense coddling her."

Instead of admitting his friend was right, Duncan drummed his fingers on the Stetson on his lap. Finally, looking to Daymon, he said, "You telling the truth about the redhead?"

Daymon said nothing.

Seeing a sly smirk alter his friend's usually stony countenance, Duncan chuckled. "Sonja, my butt."

Chapter 12

At the end of a long, hard cry, Raven remained seated on the bench, fingers on one hand worrying the pair of wedding rings on the chain around her neck, fingers on the other tracing the bestowment plaque's raised letters. She stayed like that, eyes closed, as the events of the last couple of months flicked through her mind like jittery images on an old movie reel.

After spending an indeterminate amount of time thinking about the past, her eyes snapped open, real sudden, as if she'd just arrived at some kind of monumental decision.

Wiping the remnants of grief from her cheeks, she rose and retraced her steps back to where she'd been let out of the Bronco.

Standing on Pikes Place, with the cream-colored hotel looming over her, she had never felt smaller.

Looking up, she saw the wood and stainless railing fronting the balcony to her corner room. Panning her gaze right, she saw similar balconies behind the same run of railing. Though she knew her friends were likely behind the drawn blackout drapes, the long run of unoccupied balconies made the place seem abandoned.

Not quite ready to do the *people* thing, Raven trudged east a block and followed the sidewalk as it jogged right to eventually parallel Cascade Avenue.

She had to walk through a series of interconnected wood pergolas to get to the path leading to the luxury hotel. The path led to the half-circle drive that culminated at a carport, its high ceiling supported by stacked-stone columns.

Beyond the carport was a set of marble stairs leading to a wide landing flanked by planters full of dead flowers. The front doors to the Antlers were twin glass sliders. Rendered inoperable due to the lobby breakers being thrown, a pair of pull doors on either side of the powered panels allowed access to the darkened lobby.

Since the sun was still hovering somewhere behind the Garden of the Gods, the side doors were not locked. In another hour or so, once night fell, the doors would be locked, and the all-volunteer building watch would begin patrolling the premises.

The precursor to the volunteer patrols, a sign that read *Quiet In The Halls! Respect Your Fellow Tenants* remained taped to the inside of the glass sliders.

All alone and about to enter the gloomy lobby, Raven paused long enough to drag the Glock 19 from the drop-thigh holster strapped to her right leg. A quick press check assured her a round was in the pipe.

As Raven pushed through the swinging glass door, in her head, she heard her dad urging her to *Stay frosty*.

The hotel lobby was decorated with touches of the Old West: forked antler light sconces topped with leather shades hung on the wall behind the mahogany front desk. Oil paintings of frontier scenes adorned the lobby walls. A bronze statue of a cowboy breaking a wild bronco sat on a high shelf near the elevators.

Opposite the front desk, Shaker-style furniture with colorful cushions featuring a Navajo print huddled in front of a river-stone fireplace seeing frequent use now that winter was in full swing.

Reminiscent of the warm colors of the southwest desert, the floors from the entry to the bank of elevators were finished with a mix of sandstone, travertine, and marble tiles. Some kind of polished metal inlay was interwoven through all of it.

The walls were white all around. Running the length of the lobby were a half-dozen two-by-two columns paneled in wood a shade darker than the oak front desk. To Raven the wood looked like walnut, the same dark wood used for the floors in their house back in Portland.

Eschewing the elevator, which was known to pause between floors on occasion, Raven made her way to the stairs.

The door to the stairs was propped open, the interior awash in the dull yellow glow of emergency lighting.

The second Raven entered the stairwell, she detected the stench of death mingling with pine, vanilla, strawberry, and new-car-smell.

After giving the shadows under the stairs and behind the door a little scrutiny, she pressed the Glock to her thigh and approached the first of twenty-six identical runs of stairs. Gripping the rail and putting her Danner on the first of three hundred and ninety carpeted steps—steps she knew all too well—she paused and peered up between the rails.

It was the first step … the getting going, that was always the hardest. Every time she stood here looking up at the distant, dim golden spill infiltrating the distant rectangular skylight, a story her dad had recounted to her and Peter the day he was taken came rushing back. Though she knew this wasn't Canada's version of the CDC, and getting to and from her room was *never* comparable in danger or difficulty to her dad donning night vision gear and leading frightened scientists down a pitch-black stairway all the while being groped by dozens of living dead, she was fully aware that Murphy—of Murphy's Law fame—was always trying to insert himself into the equation.

Once her eyes had adjusted to the change in lighting, she spied the colorful clutter of hundreds of air freshener trees tenants had been tying to the handrails since the practice had been adopted a day or two after the hotel was liberated from the dead.

Unlike the Z-choked stairs her dad had emerged from unscathed, here she saw no flitting shadows. No gnarled hands gripping the rails. Heard no wet footfalls or hollow, rasping moans echoing in the enclosed space.

She was alone. However, there was evidence on the carpeted treads and papered walls that at one time living dead had been trapped in here. To make matters worse, after the Zs had all been culled, the stairwell was used as a temporary depository for their corpses.

On a run of three discolored steps eye-level to her was a yellow-green stain of long-dried bodily fluids that still reeked to high heaven. Near the first landing, high up on a wall, were a number of hand-shaped red splotches that no amount of scrubbing could remove.

Throwing a shiver, she started up the stairs.

Leading with the Glock's business end, and giving each blind turn a quick turkey peek, she made it to the thirteenth floor in just under seven minutes.

Heartbeat returning to normal, she stood before the door to her room. A plaque on the door read *Suite 272*.

She slipped the keycard in the reader. Seeing the light go from red to green, she worked the brass handle and entered her room.

Once inside, with the door secured, Raven dropped her pack on the floor and poked her head into the bathroom. Seeing everything was as she'd left it, she stepped into the short hall and let her gaze roam the rest of the room.

All alone.

Just how she liked it.

She propped her SBR in a corner, then placed her pistol and Gerber on the dresser next to the television. Next, she shrugged off her coat and hat, tossing both on the overstuffed leather pub chair angled into the corner between the west-facing sliding door and a narrow window overlooking north Springs.

The blackout curtain on the slider was ajar just enough that a sliver of failing light from the westering sun could be seen peeking around one edge.

For a split-second she was inside the farmhouse east of Woodruff, staring at the papered-over picture windows. There were slivers of light there, too. Only when she had peered out, she didn't see her park and bench and the perimeter wall beyond; instead, her dad had been out there, rifle trained down the narrow gravel drive and trading fire with men on motorcycles. Brass shell casings arced away from the stuttering M4. As the soldiers fell, more were arriving, and with them came the sense of foreboding that had been with her ever since that awful day.

As the growing feeling of dread threatened to take her to dark places she didn't want to revisit, a loud bang in the room next door spared her the pain of doing so.

Ignoring the smartly made king bed beckoning to her, she skirted the centrally located coffee table, made her way to the shared interior door, and pressed an ear to its cool surface.

Listening hard, she detected a low murmur of voices, hollow thuds of footsteps, and snippets of laughter.

Having decided to just show her face before retiring to the solitude of her room, she unlocked her interior door, pulled it open, and knocked hard on the door to the Founders Suite.

Chapter 13

No sooner had Raven dropped her hand to her side and stepped back from the walnut-paneled door, did all conversation cease and someone's approach was announced by a bustle of heavy footfalls.

There was no *Who is it?* or *Raven?*—instead, without warning, the door sucked open and she was staring Tran in the face. The slight Asian American was smiling wide and there was a certain twinkle in his liquid brown eyes. On his head, covering his new high-and-tight haircut, was a red hat decorated with Ferrari's prancing horse logo.

Parking his hands on his hips, he asked, "Why are you back so soon?"

Raven noticed he was wearing what had come to be his new uniform: '80s-era BDU pants in a woodland camo pattern, the cuffs of which were tucked into black combat boots and smartly bloused. Worn over a black thermal underwear top was a black North Face vest. He wore the vest unzipped, which allowed easy access to the Beretta riding in a paddle holster at about four o'clock on his right hip.

"I'm pretty beat," she said, staring at the man's unlined and clean-shaven face. There was no consensus among the younger crowd concerning his true age. Because Tran had once mentioned coming to America as a teenager after the Vietnam war, Wilson insisted he had to be closer to fifty in age than sixty—which was exactly the opposite of how Duncan described his own age when the topic was broached.

When asked, much to everyone's chagrin, Tran would coyly say: "Older than Daymon, but younger than Old Man."

Tran tipped his hat to Raven. "Come in," he insisted. "Everyone is just waiting for dinner." The smile was back as he told her he had a pot of rabbit stew warming on the stove downstairs in the kitchen.

Raven shook her head. Craning to see past the door jamb, she said, "Thanks, Tran … but I'm not hungry. Just checking in. That's all."

Turned out Duncan was mostly wrong about what he thought Raven would find upon coming home. He was spot-on about the peace and quiet component—*that* was nowhere to be found and would only become more elusive after dinner when the board games came out. Conversely, his prediction that either Wilson and Sasha would be at each other's throats, or Peter and Sasha would be French kissing, was all wrong.

Sitting on the loveseat across the room, twenty-one-year-old Wilson and nineteen-year-old Taryn were the ones making kissy face.

Across from the recently married couple, Sasha lounged sideways in a pub chair identical to the one in Raven's room. She had one pants leg rolled up to the knee and the leg propped on a plush pillow.

On bent knee and rubbing on the redheaded teen's slow-to-heal ankle some kind of salve no doubt touted to have *therapeutic and restorative* qualities, blond-haired, blue-eyed Peter Dregan stopped what he was doing long enough to flash a smile at Raven.

Tamping down a flare of jealousy, Raven reciprocated and quickly broke eye contact with the recently orphaned thirteen-year-old.

"Come in," repeated Tran.

"Looks like everyone is *busy*," Raven said. She looked left and right, then made a face. "Where's Max?"

Upon hearing his name, the brindle Australian shepherd rose up from a second pub chair, yawned, and jumped to the floor. Stub tail twitching a mile-a-minute, Max threaded his way between the furniture spread about the finely appointed room. Arriving at the threshold between rooms, he sat by Tran's feet and looked up at Raven.

"Sasha walked him around noon." Tran looked at his watch. "Peter took him to the park to do his business … oh, about an hour

72

ago." He reached into a pocket and brought out two baggies. "Kibble for Max. Venison jerky for you."

Taking both baggies, Raven pointed to her room, then made a fist.

Following the commands, Max padded past her and sat on the carpet, his gaze locked firmly on the two baggies.

"Yes," Raven said, tossing him a couple of treats. "Good boy."

"You trained him well," Tran said.

Nope, she thought, *the family I used for target practice at Schriever trained him well.*

She said, "That was all his old family's doing. We just had to learn what they taught him and the commands he understands. My mom did most of the work."

Wilson called out from across the room, "You playing Monopoly tonight?"

Raven stood on her toes to peer around Tran and wagged her head. "I'm beat," she lied.

Tran said, "Well, he's a good boy," and scratched Max behind the ears. He regarded Raven again. "Want me to bring you a bowl of stew when it's ready?"

She shook her head. "I've got some stuff to snack on."

Tran tilted his head to one side. "You're not going up to Penrose today?"

Raven said nothing. Just hit him with the thousand-yard stare.

"All right," Tran said, his sing-song voice taking a serious tone. "If you need *anything,* you know where you can find me."

It was precisely the response Raven was expecting. She was used to the man looking out for her. After all, it was one of her dad's last requests. And Tran was taking it seriously. In fact, all of the adults had rallied around her and become a sort of extended parental unit.

As Tran was closing the door to the Founders Suite, Sasha began shouting expletives at Wilson.

With zero regret about her decision to isolate instead of listen to *that* for the next couple of hours, Raven backed into her room, shut the door, and threw the lock.

Sighing, she peeled off her gloves and shrugged out of her plate carrier and tossed them on the pub chair with her coat and hat. After doling out some more kibble for Max, she took a strip of jerky for herself and began taking off the rest of her gear.

She removed the empty drop-thigh rig and belt it rode on, stuffed the Glock back in the holster, scooped up the Gerber, then slipped it and the gun belt underneath one of the pillows on the bed. The SBR—round chambered, safety on—went against the wall between the bed and knotty-pine nightstand nearest to the window. Unlacing her Danners, she put them at the foot of the bed, toes facing the door to the unused room.

Every piece of kit got put in the same place.

Every time.

No deviation.

Duncan had come up with a theory as to why, when arriving at Springs together, they found the top floors of The Antlers uninhabited. He figured people were afraid of getting trapped in the building should a horde breach the wall. The one thing the thousands of survivors inside the walls shared was the collective horror they'd endured to get to Springs. No doubt the majority of them spent time hiding from the dead. Maybe on the upper floor of their home or trapped in the stifling heat of their attic.

Lord knows she'd seen her share of furniture choked stairways during her travels outside the wire. Hell, she remembered seeing on more than one occasion entire runs of stairs removed completely, some kind of easily deployable ladder taking their place.

Raven wasn't too worried, though. Before spending one night on the thirteenth floor, she had located all of the stairwells. By day two she had attached to the deck railing two hundred feet of Petzl 10mm climbing rope Daymon had helped her acquire. Stuffed into the slider handle was a pair of thick leather gloves she'd found in the groundskeeper's closet downstairs.

The gloves and rope were her insurance plan should the worst-case scenario came to fruition.

No way she was getting trapped up here.

Staring at her reflection on the television's blank screen, she undressed down to her thermal top and bottoms. She folded the sweater and black BDUs, then placed them on the floor next to her boots.

Max had been watching her the entire time, head cocked to one side, taking it all in.

Getting down to the dog's level, Raven said, "You're lucky … all you have is your fur." She gave him a kiss on the head then planted her palms on the rug.

With little effort and barely breaking a sweat, she performed fifty near-perfect push-ups, fifty so-so sit-ups, and fifty textbook crunches. All of this she did with Max looking on with canine indifference.

After rising from the floor, she went to the closet and took two articles of clothing from their hangers. She slipped the green sweatshirt over her head. It was threadbare, stained with something that no amount of washing would remove, and still a half size too big for her. None of that mattered. That it still carried Brooklyn Grayson's scent was all that did. The second item was so big that she was nearly lost in it the one time she had tried it on. The nearly new Crye Precision top bore MultiCam pattern on the neck and sleeves and still had her dad's scent all over it.

Wadding the top into a ball, she climbed onto the bed and invited Max to join her.

As she lazily stroked his coat, her face buried in fabric that reminded her of better times, the idea of dragging the sat-phone from her pack and placing a call to Penrose came to her.

Almost instantaneously coming to the conclusion that she would just hear a variation of the same old story, she instead switched off the lamp, crawled under the covers, and closed her eyes.

Chapter 14

For Raven, for once in a long, long while, her dreams were good. So good that she subconsciously cursed the electronic trill trying to drag her from a deep REM sleep.

"No," she cried, half in, half out of consciousness. "Mom, Dad … don't go."

She came to with the sensation of hot breath tickling her cheek. Then there was a blurry snout entering her field of view. Before she could mount a defense, Max was planting a sloppy, good morning dog kiss right on her mouth.

The trilling continued even as she was wiping the dog spit on a sleeve and shoving Max back over to his side of the king bed.

Sitting up, Raven saw that the sliver of light around the window had changed from a pus-like gray to a shade of purple closer to lavender than that of Barney, the goofy dinosaur on the television show she used to watch as a kid.

A quick glance at her watch told her it was close to five in the morning. A simple computation in her head told her she'd been asleep for nearly twelve hours.

Her first thought once the cobwebs of a good night's sleep began to drift away was that she needed to get to her backpack to answer the noisy phone. Her second priority, she quickly decided, was that Max had better be taken outside to do his business before he went on the floor.

As Raven's stockinged feet hit the carpeted floor, the phone went silent. She hustled over to her pack and jammed her arm in.

Her fingertips brushed the Iridium handset's smooth case at the same moment the trilling started anew.

Stabbing a finger on the green Talk key, she answered the call with a curt, "What?" Her eyes suddenly narrowed and she listened for fifteen long seconds.

Ending the call without the normal pleasantries, she made like a dervish: throwing on her clothes and gear. Gunning up, she strapped the Gerber to her belt and stepped into her boots. Finished lacing the Danners, she approached the slider and pulled the curtain aside. Downstairs in the park, her bench was still awash in shadow. Though nothing new had fallen overnight, the coverage from several days' worth of snowfall remained.

Beyond the perimeter walls, Garden of the Gods' majestic rock spires were glowing red and orange after having just been hit by the first direct light of morning.

Hoping to rouse someone whose nature leaned more toward malleable than prying, she opened her interior door and banged a fist on the Founders Suite door.

A minute later the door opened.

At once Raven learned her harried knocks had summoned a person who fell into the malleable category.

Surprise in her voice, she said, "Peter?" Before the teen could break sleep's hold and posit a greeting, she was placing Max's leash in his hand and ordering him to get dressed so he could take the dog outside.

Voice barely a whisper, Peter said, "It's happening again ... isn't it?"

Granite set to her jaw, Raven simply nodded.

Peter pinched the bridge of his nose and looked down at the carpet. "Anything for you," he said. "I still owe you for saving my butt."

"Thank you," Raven said. "Pretty soon we'll be even."

Peter rubbed his eyes and yawned. Without another word, he turned and led Max away.

Raven closed both doors and pulled the slider curtains shut. Leaving the SBR, her plate carrier, and the MOLLE rig behind, she stepped into the hall and closed the door behind her.

While waiting for the elevator, she slipped the phone into a pocket, took the time to press check the Glock, then stuffed the extra magazines for it into a cargo pocket.

For once the elevator was reliable, depositing her at the lobby without stalling or stopping between floors.

A twenty-something tenant Raven recognized was pulling guard duty at the lobby desk. She put down the Dean Koontz novel she'd been reading, stood up from the rolling chair, and met Raven in front of the desk.

"Going to school early today?"

Not in the mood for chit-chat, Raven said, "It's Christmas break," and picked up her pace.

Sitting just outside the locked doors and taking up a good portion of the loading area was a purple GMC dually pickup. Wisps of exhaust floated over the pavers, ghosting around the big tires and wending their way underneath the jacked-up 4x4.

Inside the warmth of the idling GMC, with a Hank Williams Jr. standby playing softly over the high-end sound system, Duncan was draped over the wheel and staring in the direction of the dimly lit lobby.

Seeing a pair of silhouettes flit across the lobby, one of them small of stature and walking with purpose, Duncan rolled the volume down and popped the passenger door lock. Then, going against all noise discipline protocols in place, and not giving two shits about waking anyone, he laid on the horn.

As the guard called Eve worked her keys in the lock, she said, "Who is this asshole?"

Raven said, "My crazy uncle."

"Duncan?"

Raven nodded.

"That's not like him," Eve said.

The honking stopped abruptly only to be replaced by the rising rumble of the pickup's high-revving V8.

Eve shoved the slider aside and made a sweeping gesture. "Stay safe out there."

Raven simply nodded and pulled her collar up against the below-freezing temperature. As she hustled to her awaiting ride, her eyes were drawn to the row of buildings two blocks to the east. Backlit by the rising sun, the structures looked to have been honed from black obsidian.

The door hinged open in front of Raven, the handle at chin-level. As it continued a slow sweep by her face, she trapped it with one hand. Taking hold of the strategically placed grab bars, she stepped up onto the deployed powered running boards and monkeyed her way into the cab.

Duncan had the GMC rolling before Raven was buckled in. As he steered onto Cascade heading north, he hit her with a serious look. "Things are going to be different this time." There was a brief pause, during which Duncan looked away. With the truck eating up the blocks toward Penrose, he added, "I promise."

Though twelve-plus years of conditioning dictated Raven smile when presented with good news, all she could muster was a slight head bob.

Chapter 15

Colorado Springs Northern District

Trusting the combination of the GMC's four-wheel drive and its meaty all-weather tires to handle the packed snow covering Jackson Street, Duncan slewed right off of the plowed boulevard without a thought to applying the brakes. Powering through the turn, he stayed on Jackson until reaching the nearest parking lot, where he slipped his rig between a pair of Chevy Tahoes belonging to the Penrose security force. From the looks of the foot of snow atop the rigs, their last patrol had taken place long ago.

Raven had unbuckled her seatbelt and was out the door before Duncan had brought his monster of a pickup to a complete halt. She had sprinted across the road and made the sidewalk before Duncan had shut down the V8.

Someone had taken the time to shovel the sidewalks and driveway leading up to the nearest entrance. With the liberal application of rock salt crunching underfoot, Raven bounded up the stairs and came to a halt in front of a pair of lightly tinted glass doors. Unlike the sliding door at the main entry to the hotel, this one was operational and parted the moment she triggered its motion sensor.

On the door was a plate-sized sticker featuring a pretty good rendition of a Beretta pistol. It sat inside a red circle cut through with a diagonal slash. *No firearms.*

Gun free zones like this had been a norm in the old world. The zombie apocalypse had quickly flipped that on its head.

It was no secret that hospitals had been the first flashpoints of the infection. The universal practice of allowing only on-duty law enforcement personnel to bear arms inside, some would argue, was what allowed the Omega virus to spread so quickly during those first frenetic hours of the outbreak.

Why someone hadn't scraped the sticker off the door here was a mystery Raven didn't care to dwell on.

Sitting on a wheeled office chair just inside the entry was an African American security guard. He was somewhere in his sixties and took his job very seriously. His black shoes were always polished to a high luster. Raven couldn't remember ever seeing a wrinkle on his spotless uniform.

As Raven rushed by, the man tipped his hat. "Hiya, Miss Bird. Mind you walk in the halls, now."

Slowing her gait just enough to show Eddie the respect a Marine who'd served two tours in Vietnam commanded, she passed by the West Tower elevators and made a beeline for the stairwell. Moving as if on autopilot, she clomped up the stairs to the tenth floor, shouldered open the door, and turned to her right.

Unlike the air inside the hotel, the air here was heavy with the antiseptic nose of some kind of cleaner utilizing a common chemical whose name Raven couldn't recall. At the end of the long hall, bathed in the flat white light from overhead fluorescents was the person whom she'd recently spoken with over the phone.

Gaze never leaving Glenda Gladson, Raven commenced a slow trudge down the hall in her direction. As she drew within arm's reach of the woman, the fifty-seven-year-old widow smiled wide and went in for one of her trademark hugs.

Pick your battles.

Still on the fence about what was more annoying, Duncan's cackle or this woman's newfound propensity to be touchy-feely with her, Raven reciprocated.

When they parted, Raven saw there was a sparkle in Glenda's green eyes. She also noticed the door to 10A. Usually closed, it was now standing halfway open.

"This is bullshit, isn't it?"

"Language, Raven." Glenda drew a deep breath. Hands on hips, she said, "It is not … bullpucky."

"What's different then? And why isn't the team here?"

Suddenly the soft rush of air and steady beep of medical equipment was drowned out by the unmistakable sound of rotor blades thrashing the air somewhere nearby.

Since a heavy curtain was drawn over the west-facing window inside 10A, Raven instinctively looked at the drop-down ceiling.

Glenda said, "There's a helipad above the emergency entrance. First time I've heard anything landing down there. And it sure doesn't sound like any Life Flight helicopter I've ever heard."

Raven had been around enough helicopters in the last few months to know it was probably a Black Hawk. As the sound began to dissipate, she dropped her gaze and fixed Glenda with a hard stare.

"What's different? Where's Ramona and Cole and the rest of the team?" repeated Raven, even as she was craning toward the door and peering inside.

In Raven's line of sight was the miniature Christmas tree she'd left here a few days earlier. It was sitting atop a rolling cart and still infusing the room with the heady smell of pine. She'd even taken the time to trim it with lights, ornaments, and some used tinsel she'd scrounged from a supply room back at the hotel. Squares of white paper bearing scribbled words of encouragement were tucked in the branches alongside the ornaments. And thanks to some certain visitors to 10A, the tree was topped with a green beret instead of the usual star or angel.

Hovering a foot off a wall-mounted shelf was a pair of partially deflated Mylar balloons. Though it was hard to make out what the sad-looking misshapen blobs used to be, Raven knew that one was the number three, and the other the number six.

Reminders of Raven's first parentless Thanksgiving—a ceramic pumpkin and plush stuffed turkey—sat on the windowsill, across the room.

Silent as a wraith, a ridiculously tall man in a lab coat emerged from behind the privacy curtain. A nametag on his coat read *R. Cole M.D.* Looking like a kid's toy, a stethoscope was draped over the doctor's giraffe-like neck.

Looking up at the doctor, Raven said, "What's different this time, Doctor Cole? And where's the rest of your team?"

"I think Nurse Gladson should be the one to bring you up to speed."

Voice wavering, Glenda said, "I'm a retired RN, Doctor Cole. I'm just volunteering here."

Making a notation on a ream of papers clipped to the clipboard in his hand, the doctor said, without looking up, "You'll do just fine, Nurse Gladson."

Through gritted teeth, Raven said, "One of you needs to tell me what happened?"—she waved a hand spasmodically before her own face—"Why does he still have to wear all of *that*?"

Glenda sighed. "I was reading to him and saw his eyes doing that rapid eye movement thing behind the lids. Thinking it was the same old, I continued reading—"

"What … happened?" Raven pressed.

Glenda made a face like she was about to cry. "He opened his eyes and looked at me."

Raven's eyes widened as she said, "Did he recognize you?"

A tear traced a path down Glenda's cheek. Dabbing at it with a sleeve, she said, "He must have."

Eyes narrowing, Raven asked, "How can you be so sure?"

Flashing Raven a wavering half-smile, Glenda said, "Because he tried to ask me something."

Skepticism evident in her tone, Raven said, "With that *thing* still jammed down his throat?"

Glenda nodded. "It has to stay in him for now."

Dr. Cole looked up from what he was doing. Meeting Raven's questioning stare, he said, "He's still intubated because he *can't* breathe on his own. And he's still sedated. We will have to slowly wean him off his meds."

Incredulous, Raven said, "It's already been"—she looked at the ceiling, her lips moving as she tabulated the days—"forty-seven days. How much longer will he have to be like this?"

The doctor placed the clipboard in a holder attached to the foot of the bed. Steepling his fingers, he paused for a beat. Finally, tone of his voice showing more compassion than hope, he said, "He suffered a serious head injury. It will be some time before he's back to normal. That is *if* he ever gets back to normal."

"If he's no longer in a coma, why keep the curtains closed?" Recalling the time she spent in a car trunk with Peter, hiding from the Chinese soldiers, she added, "It feels like the inside of a coffin in here."

"He's had his eyes closed for several weeks, sweetie." Glenda looked past the doctor. "His retinas couldn't handle the direct sunlight."

Raven took a tentative step over the threshold. Gripping Glenda's arm, she said, "What did he say?"

"I couldn't make it out entirely," Glenda said. "I told him how his team had rescued him and that they killed all the people responsible for his condition. I told him a helicopter brought him here in bad shape. Then I joked with him about how he'd slept through his birthday, Thanksgiving, and Christmas."

Raven made a face. "Sure he understood all that?"

"I'm certain he did," insisted Glenda. "Because when I finished talking, he tried to speak again. And it came out sounding the same as before. Which got me to thinking about what I had left out of the story."

Hearing a commotion in the hall, the doctor stepped out to take a look.

Raven crossed her arms over her chest. "What was he *trying* to say?"

Again tears pooled around Glenda's eyes. Lip quivering, she said, "Stupid Glenda had a brain fart and forgot to let him know you and Peter were safe and sound. I should have told him that straight away. I was just so damn glad he was awake for real this time." She swallowed hard and dabbed at her eyes. "As soon as I said your name, Raven, and assured him you were here and unharmed, he closed his eyes and his whole body seemed to melt into the bed. I could tell he was smiling on account of how the tube had risen up and the tape holding it in place had gone tight on his cheeks."

Dr. Cole returned, saying, "Better move inside, ladies. We have a herd of men with guns coming this way." He followed them inside and closed the door.

Finally convinced this wasn't another futile false alarm visit, Raven made her way to her dad's bedside. She grabbed his hand and squeezed softly. No change. Still warm, yet no reciprocity.

Where her dad's fingernails used to be, misshapen slabs of translucent material were growing. Though they looked like scabs texture-wise, she'd been told they were indeed fingernails growing in. She'd been told that if they did succeed in gaining a foothold and growing back all the way, they would look *nothing* like they had before the Chinese torturers yanked them out with pliers.

She let her gaze roam his face. Though it was still slack underneath all that facial hair, his eyes were no longer clamped shut. All in all, he seemed to be at peace. After a final furtive glance at the leather band around his right wrist, she let his hand go and looked a question at the doctor.

"Like I said… your dad still has drugs running through his system." He glanced at the door. "And it's likely he's going to sleep for some time before he's ready to have a room full of visitors."

Raven asked, "When are you going to take off the handcuffs?"

"They're called four-point restraints," said the doctor. "They're soft against his skin." He shook his head. "And they're not tight at all. But because he's likely to be combative and tear away the tubes and IV lines when he becomes fully aware, they have to stay on—both for his safety… *and* ours."

Raven said nothing.

A jangling screech from what could only be chair legs being dragged across the hallway floor outside the door drew Glenda's attention. "Who's out there?" she asked.

"Your boyfriend, who is waiting patiently," he answered. "And a bunch of soldiers, who are not."

Raven looked to the corkboard on the wall above the head of the hospital bed. It bore all manner of unit and morale patches, including the Bastion Pale Riders patch that featured the Grim Reaper wearing night vision and armed with a suppressed rifle. Several American flags and a couple of Navy SEAL Budweiser pins—the Special Warfare insignia featuring an eagle clutching a trident and flintlock pistol—had found their way into the mix.

Regarding the doctor, she asked, "Can they all come in? My dad would approve."

"Seeing as how most of them came all the way from Peterson, and that their ride is currently parked on our landing pad, it wouldn't be very neighborly of me to turn them away."

"I'll fetch them," Glenda said as she pulled the privacy curtain aside and strode toward the door.

The doctor placed a hand on Glenda's wrist. "I've got to finish my rounds," he said. "I'll talk to the heathens on my way out."

Halting midstride, Glenda dismissed the doctor with a wave of her hand.

"They're not *heathens*," shot Raven. "They're guys just like my dad. Guys who keep *sheep* like you safe."

Once the doctor had left the room and the door was closed, Raven turned to Glenda. "Why were you crying?" she asked.

Glenda made a face, then said, "Since I lost my two boys to this insane world, I've come to think of your dad as one of my own. As a matter of fact, I've come to think of you *all* as family."

"Would that make me your granddaughter?"

Glenda nodded and dabbed at the tears with her sleeve.

"I've been wondering about all the hugging." Raven moved in close, wrapped her arms around Glenda's midsection, and pressed her cheek to the woman's bosom. "It's all right with me," she said. "I lost my grandmother and grandfather the day this all started." Drawing back and looking Glenda in the face, she added, "I'm real grateful for all you've done for us."

Looking to the unmoving form on the hospital bed, Glenda said, "And I'm grateful for all your dad has done for us."

Chapter 16

Penrose Hospital

Upon receiving the early morning call from Duncan, Ari Silver immediately ceased his pre-mission inspection of the Ghost Hawk he'd be piloting east, on another tagging mission, and paid a visit to First Sergeant Whipper—the cantankerous lifer in charge of maintaining the growing fleet of aviation assets now housed at Peterson. Short of bending a knee and begging, Ari spent five minutes lobbying Whipper to let him "borrow" anything air worthy enough to make the short hop to the new capital.

After making a trio of promises—two that would be easy to fulfill, one not so much—Ari succeeded in convincing the first sergeant to let him take a Kansas Air National Guard UH-60 Black Hawk, fresh off a total tear down and rebuild, out for a supposed "shakedown flight."

The reluctant sounding "yes" had barely crossed Whipper's lips and Ari was burning up the airwaves with his sat-phone, alerting his crew and every member of the Pale Riders team of the new development.

A total of thirty minutes had elapsed between the time Duncan had made his call to Ari, and the hotshot aviator was bringing his borrowed bird in low and fast and settling her gently atop Penrose Hospital's emergency facilities building.

Now, with the group of kitted-out Pale Riders lounging on folding chairs in the crowded tenth floor hallway, Duncan was watching Ari free the faux sheepskin cover from the copious amounts of plastic used to compress it into a neat little cube.

Duncan was standing with his back to the door to 10A and watching Ari unfurl his new acquisition. "What do you think, flyboy? Does it fill the bill?"

Standing back to the wall and bracketed by Haynes and Skipper, Ari smiled and nuzzled the plush seat cover. "This is just what I was hoping for. My ass thanks you, kind sir."

With a tip of his Stetson, Duncan said, "My pops liked to say 'there are two I's in integrity. *I* will ... and *I* did.'"

Folding the seat cover under one arm, Ari said, "Follow through is damn important. Especially in this day and age. Your pops was a smart man, Duncan." He paused to stroke the wool again. Lifting his gaze, he asked, "Did I come through for you all with some solid intel? Or were their ears harvested already?"

"All parties are happy," Duncan drawled. "Even my dreadlocked amigo."

Suddenly the door to 10A opened and out stepped Dr. Cole. Adjusting the precariously perched stethoscope, he said, "Who's in charge of this motley crew?"

Everyone save Duncan looked to Lopez.

Griffin pointed and said, "Captain Lopez outranks us all."

The doctor leaned forward, pushed his glasses up on his nose, and gazed down at Lopez. "Captain Lopez," he said, "I'm afraid you're going to have to send the army here into the room in groups of two. Divide and conquer, so to speak." He went on to tell everyone present the same thing he'd just told Raven as it related to her father's road to recovery. Finished, beginning with Duncan and ending with Lopez, he looked the assemblage over. Gaze lingering on the captain, he reiterated the strict room occupancy rules.

In a grumbly voice, Lopez said, "Understood, Doc." He regarded Skipper. "Get your straws out. We're drawing to see who goes in first."

The crew chief took a clutch of tiny coffee stirrer straws from one of his flight suit's many zippered pockets. "Anyone else get a heavy metal earworm when the doc said motley crew?" Before anyone could answer, he launched into an awful rendition of *Girls, girls, girls*.

With Skipper continuing to butcher the song, Haynes said, "Affirmative. And that song just took me back to my favorite strip club near Fort Campbell." He closed his eyes and smiled. "Trixie … been missin' you, babe."

By the time Skipper had counted out seven straws and was busy cutting them into seven different lengths, everyone in the hall had started a chant to get him to stop the singing.

Quieting the chant with a wave of a hand, Ari said, "You only need to cut four. Us Night Stalkers will go in last."

Skipper shrugged. "I'm used to loitering on station until the ground pounders are finished." Choosing four different-sized stirrers, he discarded the rest. He closed his gloved hand around the straws, tapped the exposed ends with his palm so that they were even, and offered first pick to the Pale Riders' current commander.

Plucking a straw out with two fingers, Lopez held it aloft for all to see.

Unsure of that particular straw's order in the lineup, Skipper proceeded to dole out the rest, starting with Cross, moving on to Axelrod, and ending with Griff.

Brandishing his straw like a mini fencing foil, Lopez said, "Show me what you got, *gentleladies*."

Once again Griff got the shortest straw. Axelrod was next in line from the bottom.

"Looks like me and you have honors, Chief Cross."

Lamenting the fact that he had crapped out again, Griff took a seat in a chair to wait for his turn inside.

"Looks like we got ourselves a classic example of age before beauty," quipped Ari as he pulled up a chair of his own and sat down next to the crestfallen Navy SEAL.

"That would mean I'm dead last," deadpanned Duncan as he stepped aside to allow Lopez and Cross entry into the room.

Skipper said, "I hardly know you, fella. But from the vibe you're giving off, I don't think we have a straw short enough for *you*."

Duncan pulled the door shut. Eyes narrowing, he fixed the crew chief with his best intimidating stare. Once he had the shorter man's undivided attention, he growled, "Where you hail from, 15T?"

The last part was a reference to the crew chief's military occupational specialty.

Speaking for his crew chief, Ari said, "My *15T* is from Florida, originally. Panama City, specifically."

Chuckling, Duncan said, "And that would explain why he comes across as all hat and no cattle."

"He's solid as they come," Haynes shot, bristling at the put-down.

"I'm just yanking his chain," Duncan said, offering his hand to Skipper. "Pleased to meet you. I fully retract my ball breaking."

Skipper reciprocated, saying, "Just figured it was the senility talking."

"Touché," Duncan drawled. "I think you and me are going to get along just fine." He turned to Ari. "Now let's talk about me getting into the left seat of that stealthy whirlybird of yours."

"Over my dead body," said Haynes. Though the tone had been serious, his wide grin suggested he was ribbing his fellow aviator.

Duncan said, "So I have a chance?"

Gloves in a pile on his lap, Ari made a show of inspecting his nails. Finally, lifting his gaze to meet Duncan's, he said, "Who knows … stranger shit *has* happened."

Inside 10A, Lopez and Cross stood on opposite sides of Cade's bed.

Lopez had one gloved hand resting on his friend's shoulder and, for the umpteenth time, was retelling the story of how he and the team, with the help of a couple of squads of Rangers and a smattering of volunteers from the 10th Special Forces group out of Fort Kit Carson, had conducted the quickly concocted mission against the PLA forces who had ambushed and taken Cade hostage.

Fearing the worst, the assaulters had held nothing back. They'd gone in with orders to take prisoners. Save for a couple of squirters who got away—they did not.

"I personally popped the pendejo who did that to your hands," Lopez said. "Face shot him real good. Fucker still had bloody pliers in his pocket." Grimacing, he looked to Glenda and Raven, both sitting quietly by the window, and offered an apology.

Raven waved a hand at him. "I've heard every bad word a dozen times."

Glenda said, "I, however, would appreciate it if you watered down your language."

Voice soft and inflected with nuance from his upbringing around California surf culture, Cross said, "I caught your guards flat-footed. Bastards were a few feet away and playing Call of Duty on a big screen. Gave them both a new eye in the back of their head, if you know what I mean."

Feeling Glenda's gaze on him, Cross patted Cade on the shoulder and told the fellow Pale Rider he would keep his seat on the Ghost Hawk warm for him.

Lopez edged around the bed and approached Raven. Slipping an iPhone and white earbuds from a pocket, he said, "I want you to give this to your dad when he wakes up." He turned the smartphone over to show her the yellow sticky note affixed to the back. "Here are the instructions for its use." From another pocket came a sealed envelope. Across the flap, the word *Wyatt* was written in black ink.

Taking the items, Raven said, "Who's this from?"

"General Nash."

Sharp edge to the words, Raven said, "Freda Nash? She's a general now?"

"Has been for some time," Lopez answered.

"What's it say?"

Remembering Raven was much younger than she carried herself, Lopez swallowed the smart-ass remark lingering on his tongue. Instead, he said, "None of my business. But I think your dad would be pissed if anyone read it before he has a chance to."

Raven set the items on the shelf by the Christmas tree. And though she had already thanked Lopez and Cross more than once for settling the score with the men who'd ambushed, shot, taken hostage and beaten and tortured her dad, she did so again. "If it wasn't for you two and the rest of the team, I wouldn't have my father back." Tears welling in her eyes, she went on, saying, "Thank you so much for putting your lives on the line."

Glenda looked on as the two rough men in camouflage and body armor stooped to receive long, crushing hugs from the girl.

A couple of minutes after Lopez and Cross had entered, Axe and Griff were in their places and telling war stories of their own.

"The PLA are sure to mount an offensive in the spring," Griff said. "So we're going to need you to rub some dirt on those nails and work on getting your stamina up."

"Yeah, mate," added Axe. "Sooner you slip on your gun belt and helmet, the better."

Though Raven didn't know these two like she knew Lopez and Cross, she treated them to the same thanks and hugs.

Not one to follow rules and regs, Ari came in with Haynes and Skipper. After exchanging pleasantries with Raven and Glenda, he bent over and whispered something into Cade's ear. Finished, he hinged up and caught Raven trapping him with an expectant stare.

Raising his hands in mock surrender, Ari said, "Just telling Wyatt a joke. One that is *not* suitable for mixed company."

Without missing a beat, Glenda stood and said, "OK then, gentlemen. Glad you stopped by. Visiting hours are now over."

After the men filed out, Duncan entered, Stetson trapped under one arm and a hangdog look on his face. Regarding Glenda, he said, "Doc already filled us in out in the hall. Figured this young whippersnapper would already be up and doing calisthenics. Looks like I was mistaken."

"It's going to be a trudge for him to get back to where he was before …" Suddenly the tears were back, and Glenda couldn't finish her thought.

Duncan placed one hand atop the covers at the foot of the bed. Giving Cade's foot a soft squeeze, he said, "You'll be back to whippin' commie ass in no time," and turned his attention to Raven. "We'll leave you alone with your dad, Bird. Anything you need from us before we go?"

Raven shook her head.

Glenda said, "We'll be in the hall if you need us."

Raven said nothing. As the door clicked shut behind her new grandparents, she took her dad's hand in hers, pulled a chair over from the wall, and settled into it.

Sleep had Raven in its full embrace moments later.

The cacophony the Black Hawk created as it launched and thundered off to the east didn't register. However, a few seconds later, the muffled *whoompf* and shockwave that followed it had her wide awake and off searching for Duncan and Glenda.

Chapter 17

On the heels of the distant explosion, Raven burst from room 10A. Meeting the couple's startled gazes, Raven led them down the hall to a south-facing window, where Duncan jerked the horizontal blinds out of their way and stepped aside.

Raven placed her palms on the window and, in direct response to seeing the nest of flames and roil of black smoke lifting into the sky, drew in a sharp breath.

Hands resting on Raven's flagging shoulders, Glenda gasped, "Did the boys just crash?"

Duncan pushed his aviator glasses up on his nose. "Too far south," he noted. "They flew off to the east, toward Peterson." Squinting, he added, "That's a mile or so out. Looks like something's burning near the motor pool. Maybe someone's negligence touched off the fuel dump."

One hand over her mouth, Glenda said, "I thought for sure that helicopter had crashed." She paused for a few seconds. Finally, hands clasped and shaking terribly, she went on, "I can't take losing any more of my boys. I just can't take any more loss."

"There, there," Duncan said, corralling her in his arms. "Let's go down and get some coffee." Regarding Raven, he said, "That'll give you some alone time with your dad."

Emergency lights strobing with great urgency, a fire engine roared down a sidestreet. As the siren wail diminished, Raven nodded. "That'll be fine."

Duncan said, "Come on down when you're ready for a ride back to the Antlers."

Fixated on the ever-growing smudge blackening the horizon, Raven said, "I need the exercise. I think I'll hoof it home." With that, she turned and started walking back to 10A.

"You have a change of heart," Duncan called, "you come find me."

Back in 10A, with the door closed and heavy curtains fending off the flat light of the rising sun, Raven pulled a chair near the head of her dad's bed and sat down.

No sooner had she taken her dad's hand in hers than his eyelids snapped open and he was fixing her with a questioning look.

Excited to see more than just a brief glimpse of the whites of his eyes, Raven accidentally increased pressure on his hand. Feeling some reciprocal input, the last vestiges of bitter doubt that had been building for weeks inside of her finally began to crumble.

Tears welled in her eyes. "I thought this day would never come."

Cade seemed to smile, though the apparatus down his throat made it look more like a grimace.

"Your entire Pale Riders team was here. Lopez, Cross, Griff, and the British guy ... Axe." She rattled off the names of the air crew, too, then said, "They all just left in one of the noisy Black Hawks."

Cade's eyes widened. Then he glanced toward the window and added a subtle head roll that Raven took to be a nod.

"We're in Colorado Springs, again. They were going back to some place called Peterson."

Again with the head movement.

Raven palmed her forehead. "You heard the explosion?"

He blinked once. *Yes.*

"You're wondering if they crashed."

Again he blinked one time. *Yes.*

She said, "Sorry, Dad. I thought I woke you up by rushing in here. That boom you heard came from the motor pool. At least that's what Duncan said."

Cade's head sank back into the pillow. Straining to lift his free hand off the bed introduced him to the fact he was in restraints.

"Doctor Cole says those are on so you don't rip out your IV lines. He also said you will need that intubator thingy to stay in your throat until you can breathe on your own. Do you understand?"

Cade nodded and blinked once. *Yes.*

"Want me to take them off?"

Again with a lone blink. *Yes.*

"Are you going to do what the doctor said? Rip out the medical stuff?"

Cade blinked twice. *No.*

"Promise?"

Cade simply stared at his daughter, who instantly viewed the question in an absurd a light as he must have. For if there was one thing binding them together beyond the love they shared for each other and the blood coursing their veins, it was the fact that, where matters of life and death were concerned, he always told her the truth.

As Raven worked the buckles on the left side restraints, she went on to describe how much Colorado Springs had changed since they were here last. Once she'd moved to the opposite side and started to repeat the process, she told him about Lev and Jamie staying behind at Eden. "We had to leave Black Beauty. You should have seen all the bullet holes in her." With one buckle to go, she paused and pinched away tears. "Some of the bullets got by your armor and hit *you,* Dad."

Finished loosening the final buckle, Raven slipped the restraint from his wrist. Before she could look up, his arms were encircling her neck and she was being drawn forward ever so slowly.

Raven lay her head on his chest, listening to the steady cadence of the heart beating inside the parent she thought was lost to her forever.

***

Ten minutes had passed when Raven felt her dad's arms go limp around her neck. Certain the short time they'd spent communicating had worn him out, she positioned his hands at his sides and adjusted the pillow behind his head.

It took her a few seconds to find the rectangular box with the red button that she knew, if pressed, would bring a nurse or doctor running.

Raven thumbed the button and sat back in the chair.

A few seconds passed and Cade's doctor and a nurse she didn't recognize came barging into the room.

Marveling at how the response had been way faster than she'd anticipated, Raven waited for the unlikely duo to finish giving her dad the onceover before she related their conversation and told on herself for removing the four-point restraints.

"That's reckless," said the doctor. Shooting the petite brunette nurse a worried look, he ordered the restraints to be put back on.

"I wouldn't recommend that," Raven said. "But you do what you have to do. I'm pretty sure my dad has already accomplished all that he set out to do today."

Chapter 18

January 1, 2012

The new year slinked in the door with little fanfare and six inches of fresh snow. There really wasn't anything *happy* about the forward march of time to justify banging pots and pans together, let alone setting off fireworks to mark it. With the Chinese PLA forces now enjoying established footholds on both coasts, and multiple credible reports of civilian survivors coming into contact with their foraging parties hundreds of miles inland, Colorado Springs was beginning to look like the unlucky kid picked to play monkey-in-the-middle with the two tallest kids in class.

Though the breathing tube had been removed forty-eight hours after Cade's emergence from the coma, a week later the simple act of walking ten feet to the bathroom and sitting on the toilet had left him a little winded.

Finished doing his business, he stood before the mirror, hands gripping the edges of the granite sink, and scrutinized his clean-shaven face. Running along the orbital bone outside of his left eye was a half-moon trail of pink scars caused by bullet fragments and flying automotive glass. The day he'd crashed the Ford F-650 and received the wounds to the face, he'd also caught two bullets in the back. One, a through and through that had somehow missed nerves and bone and, most importantly, his spine, was healed entirely. Only thing pointing to the fact he'd been struck by that particular Chicom round was the pair of inchworm-looking wounds where it had entered and exited. The scars were separated by a hand's width and still a little tender to the touch.

Fragments of the second bullet were still lodged in his back. After punching through the F-650's sheet metal, it had struck the edge of one of the ceramic plates protecting his back, broke apart, and the rest was history.

The surgeon said that had the bullet been tracking a fraction of an inch left, if it hadn't killed him, he'd have spent the rest of his days in a wheelchair.

"Maybe you should get a floppy hat like Wilson's," he said to his own reflection. "It'd be better than having to answer to kids wondering how the Hubba Bubba bubblegum got stuck on your face."

Someone knocked on the pocket door at the far end of the shared bathroom.

Cade paused the program playing on the iPhone, took the buds from his ears, and wrapped the cord around the device. Setting the phone on the shelf along with his toothbrush and straight razor, he said, "Come on in. I'm decent."

The door slid open a foot or so and Raven poked her head through the gap. "Talking to yourself again, eh? Isn't that what crazy people do?"

"*Bú.*"

Raven made a face. "Huh?"

Cade said, "*Bú* means 'no' in Mandarin Chinese."

She pushed the door all the way open. Hands planted on her hips—a classic Brook pose—she said, "Why are you learning Chinese?"

"To increase my value to the teams. At least that's what I gathered from Lopez leaving the iPhone for me at the hospital."

"I'm guessing you're using some kind of a learning app. Like Rosetta Stone, or something?"

"*Shí de.*"

Smiling, Raven said, "How long have you been studying?"

"I just listened to the app for the first few days. Started whispering the words as soon as the good doctor removed my breathing tube."

"That's less than a week. What else can you say?"

"There's so many different ways to say many of the words. It's pretty complicated. However, I think I have some of the colors dawn pat. I can introduce myself. Ask for directions." He shrugged. "Just the basics so far."

Brows lifting, Raven said, "What phrase do you really, really want to learn to say first?"

With no hesitation, Cade said, "Get the hell out of my country."

"That would be nice."

"The day is coming," Cade replied. "This is the first time an invader has set foot on American soil since the Japanese took Kiska Island in the Aleutians. I'm sure President Clay and her Joint Chiefs are planning a robust spring counteroffensive."

"Will you be deploying again?"

"Let's not get ahead of our skis now, Bird."

Gesturing toward the iPhone, she said, "Then how do you explain that? I saw the sticky note that was attached to it. The one from your team leader."

"You read it?"

Raven shook her head. "Nope. That's your private business. Doesn't mean I don't have a gut feeling about it."

"I'm glad you're listening to your gut."

"Is it telling me something I want to hear?"

Cade looked at himself in the mirror. As his gaze slipped back to her, he said, "For now, it's just something to get my mind back up to speed. Mental pushups, if you will."

"You did real well on all the mental acuity tests the doctors made you take."

Grateful his daughter was the one to steer the conversation elsewhere, he said, "Scores weren't as good as I'd hoped for."

She folded her arms across her chest. Sounding every bit like her mother, she said, "Baby steps, Dad." Again changing course, she asked, "How about the tingling in your right arm? The headaches? The back pain?"

Though Doctor Cole had assured Cade all of that *should* get better or disappear altogether with time, he said nothing.

Parroting something she'd heard both her mom and Glenda say, Raven asked, "On a scale of one to ten, if ten is the worst pain ever, and zero is nothing, what's your pain level?"

"Ah, a junior nurse in training," he said, chuckling. "Been hanging around Glenda, have we?"

Raven lowered her chin toward her chest. If she had been wearing glasses, she'd be looking over top of the lenses. Eyes narrowing, she repeated her question.

"A seven or eight for the back. The pain I can handle with aspirin and Ibuprofen. I just think of the pain as weakness leaving my body. But these"—he paused and raised both hands—"the way these nubs for fingernails itch as they're coming in is a *million* times worse than dealing with my back. If I hadn't been awake to feel the pain when that Chicom bastard started ripping them out, I'd do it all over again just to stop the damn itching."

"Maybe I could take a champagne bucket outside and fill it up with snow for you. You could take turns icing them down in it."

"And have pins and needles *on top* of the itching?" He shook his head. "Thanks, but no thanks."

"Don't be a baby. It might help."

Pick your battles, thought Cade. He made his way back to his room, stepped to the window and opened the curtain. For as far as he could see everything was blanketed in white. The streets north of the Antlers. The Red Zone beyond the curving stretch of I-25 bordering the city's west wall.

Down below in the park, splashes of color on a low brick wall stood out in the sea of white. Though he couldn't make out much detail, it was similar to the graffiti he'd seen sprayed on big-city subway trains.

The glare having less of an adverse effect on his eyes than he'd anticipated, Cade left the curtains parted and turned to face Raven. "I'll go down and fill the bucket with snow if you think it'll help."

"I think it will," she said.

"Couldn't hurt me to walk a bit more," he responded. "And the fresh air will do me good." He paused, then delivered the bad news. "Someone desecrated your park."

Raven made a face, then edged past him. Placing both hands on the glass, she walked her gaze across Antlers Park.

"They sure did. Bunch of buttholes. Can't have anything nice, even during the zombie apocalypse. Don't know how I missed that earlier."

Cade said, "We'll paint over it."

Raven shook her head. "Then I'll have to stare at a blotch on the wall every time I walk by it."

A series of thumps sounded out in the hall.

A beat later there came a knock at the door.

Cade said, "Who is it?"

"It's me, Daymon. I come bearing gifts. Open up."

Knowing precisely what "gifts" were arriving, Raven turned away from the window. On the way to get the door, from the dresser top she took a chewed-on rubber ball and the curved device designed for chucking it. When she opened the door, Daymon was looking down on her. "Bird!" he exclaimed. "Where have you been keeping yourself?"

Raven shrugged. "Here, mostly."

Presenting his knuckles to Raven, Daymon said, "That's all about to change now that the hard-charging Captain America is home."

The two bumped knuckles, then Raven slipped on by him. After urging Max to join her in the hall, she met her dad's expectant gaze and pointed to where she'd placed the ice bucket.

Wearing a mock frown, Cade asked, "Where are you off to?"

"I'm taking Max to the park to do his thing." She paused. "I might walk him some, too."

"How long do you think you'll be gone?"

"An hour or so."

Two birds, one stone, Cade thought. He asked, "You have a radio and your pistol?"

Daymon was watching the exchange. Addressing Cade, he said, "That girl goes nowhere without that little Glock of hers."

Cade nodded. A tilt to his head, he said, "What's up?"

"Eventually," Daymon interjected, "your heartrate and lung capacity will be." He made brief eye contact with someone in the hall, then fixed Cade with a bug-eyed stare. "I'm not a vampire. You going to invite me in, or what?"

Cade made a sweeping motion with one arm.

After disappearing for a short while, Daymon's back filled up the doorway. In his hands was one end of a high-dollar treadmill. As he tucked his elbows to his sides and reversed his way into the room, he said, "Three brothers and a sister moving … at your service. Where would you like your delivery?"

Though he thought he knew the answer, Cade said, "First tell me whose idea this is and where you got them."

"It was Glenda's idea," Daymon said. "We lifted it from the hotel's fitness room."

Backing up from the doorway, Cade said, "Does it work?"

"I didn't test drive it," admitted Daymon. "If it doesn't, there's seven more where this came from." When he tilted his end to fit it through the doorway, the treadmill's metal frame chunked off a six-inch-long piece of walnut trim.

"There goes your tip," quipped Cade as he moved aside to let Daymon maneuver the bulky piece of equipment past him.

On the other end of the treadmill was a woman who gave up maybe an inch in height to Daymon. Her hair was red and full and equally as unruly as Daymon's. She fixed Cade with her green-eyed stare. "Where do you want it … Captain Grayson?"

"How rude of me," Daymon gushed. "Captain Sonja O'Neil, meet Captain America. AKA Wyatt. AKA Grand Poohbah of the world-famous Eden compound."

Ignoring Daymon's attempt at humor, O'Neil said, "I've heard all about the Castle Rock mission." Shaking her head, she added, "Two nukes?"

Wearing a sheepish expression, Cade said, "Cover blown. Pleasure is all mine."

Sweat was beading on Daymon's brow. Still holding his end of the treadmill, he said, "Where do you want this monster?"

Cade said, "Put it in front of the window."

Daymon slipped past Cade, crabbed around the corner of the king bed, and set his end down near the corner of the room. "We'll put them on either side of the window."

"*Them*?"

In answer to Cade's one-word query, Wilson backed his way into the room. He was a bit hunched over and obviously burdened with the lion's share of the load.

The *"load"* was an upright exercise bike. And it wasn't one of the sexy easily stowable jobs sold on television by hard-bodied fitness models sweating to a bass-heavy soundtrack. This thing was a dinosaur and nearly as big and cumbersome as the treadmill.

Carrying the back end of the bike by its adjustable seat was a kid Cade last saw on the day everything went dark.

"Peter Dregan," Cade said. "So good to see you among the living. I want to thank you for—"

Shaking his head vigorously, Peter said, "I will accept no thanks from you. I did nothing. It was your daughter who saved us. If not for Raven, I would be with my family in Heaven."

Cade didn't know how to respond. Until now he'd assumed escaping the Chicoms and getting to safety had been a joint effort between the kid and his daughter.

Peter said, "Where do you want the bike, Captain Grayson?"

Patting Wilson on the shoulder, Cade instructed them to take it into the adjoining room and leave it beside Raven's bed.

With Wilson taking the lead, more fine millwork was lost as the world's clumsiest movers did Cade's bidding.

Chapter 19

"Hard to believe we were ankle-deep in snow just a few hours ago," Griff noted. "And now, here we are … in the middle of the desert watching heat waves rise off the blacktop."

"It's only a thirty-five-degree swing," countered Ari as he eased back on the stick to bring Jedi One's airspeed closer to the seventy-mile-per-hour limit posted on the signs a hundred feet below them.

Doing the honors, since he'd won immunity by drawing short straw last mission, Griff made even the tops of the pair of straws clutched in his fist and presented them to Cross.

"I hate going first," lamented Cross. "I always lose when I do."

Having already volunteered for one of the two slots the ground mission required, Lopez said, "Fifty-fifty is not great odds, mi amigo." He swung his gaze to Axe. "You feeling lucky today. Nigel?"

"I predict it'll be me and Griff on overwatch, mate."

Cross let his hand hover over the straws for a beat. Then, as if he was conducting some kind of Haitian voodoo ritual, he waved it in a clockwise circle, palm down over the straws, all while uttering some indecipherable incantation.

"Get it over with, already," Griff mumbled. "My hand could be put to better use."

Over the shipwide comms, Ari said, "Griff, Griff, Griff … please spare us the sordid details of your miserable sex life."

Griff put the middle finger of his free hand to use, flashing the cheeky pilot the bird while mouthing, "Blow me" in the direction of the curved mirror arcing over the cockpit glass.

After blowing on his hands and briskly rubbing his palms together, Cross plucked a straw from Griff's gloved fist.

The crew chief formed an L with the thumb and pointer finger on his right hand. Holding it in front of his visor, he said, "*Looooser.* Now get over here so I can rig you up."

Shaking his head, Cross said, "We're not baiting the hook today. Boots on the ground, baby."

Axe had already removed the high-tech sniper rifle from its case and was in the process of assembling it.

"Just pulling your leg," Skip said. "Griff put me up to it." Reaching under the seat, he came out with a collapsible aluminum pole resembling a dog catcher's tool and a black nylon bag containing a half-dozen tracking collars.

The stretch of Interstate 15 below the Ghost Hawk was occupied by a slow-moving zombie horde. Having originated in Southern California, and just recently gained the numbers sufficient to deem it a threat to anything in its path, the ambulatory mass of decaying flesh and bone aptly dubbed *Sierra Charlie*—or *SC* for short—was barreling straight for downtown Las Vegas.

Ari said, "Nash's team has been tracking this one via drone and satellite off and on for two days now. Intel says two fighting-age males on motorcycles are somewhere out ahead of the pacesetters." Addressing Haynes, the left-seater for this mission, he added, "Bring up the FLIR."

"Roger that," Haynes said. "Bringing up the FLIR."

"Overtaking the column in thirty," Ari said calmly. "I want all eyes on our flanks. The PLA bikers could be hunkered down in the desert."

The tail of stragglers was stretched out a mile or so behind the main body. Roughly sixty feet across at its widest, the main body was a conga line of doddering death that seemed to go on forever. In the far distance was a smattering of low hills backstopped by medium-sized mountains. In the middle distance, rising up from the flat basin, the glass wrapped multi-story casinos of Las Vegas sparkled like pirate's treasure abandoned on a desert island.

Peering out his port-side hip window, Lopez said, "Ari, now that you have eyes on, how does this compare to Nash's satellite imagery?"

"My gun-toting friend," Ari answered, "Sierra Charlie has doubled in size since it left the valley. I'd guess it's now a good three miles from tip to tail."

Lopez whistled. "How many *demonios* is that? Sixty … seventy thousand?"

Shifting his attention from reinspecting his M4 carbine to the undead horde below, Griff said, "A hundred thousand … at the least."

Adept at crowd-size estimation thanks to his time spent in the Secret Service, Cross looked to Griff and jabbed his thumb at the helo's ceiling.

Skipper had just punched a button, starting the flush two-foot by three-foot starboard-side gun port to slide out of the way. Right away the cabin was invaded by a blast of air ripe with death and tinged by jet exhaust. Once the crew chief had swiveled the Dillon Aero minigun into place and locked it down, he took a long hard look at the horde. Finally, shaking his head in disbelief, he said, "You mean to tell us that's more than a hundred thousand dead heads we're looking at down there?"

All business, Cross said, "Double that and add another fifty thousand."

Incredulous, Skipper said, "A quarter of a million? You've got to be kidding me."

Ari said, "What you're looking at there, boys, streamed straight out of L.A.'s Inland Empire a little over a week ago."

Speaking into the boom mike affixed to his comms headset, Lopez asked, "Any sign of the Pied Pipers?"

Haynes manipulated the FLIR pod controls, sweeping the high-resolution camera across the front third of the horde. "Negative," he responded. "I just see a train of death. Zero breathers."

Ari said, "See if anything presents on thermal."

"Copy that. Going to thermal and increasing magnification." After a dozen or so seconds, during which the Ghost Hawk had halved the distance to the horde, Haynes said, "I'm not picking up any hot spots. Nothing mechanical moving ahead of the leaders."

"Doesn't matter. The damage is already done," Ari noted soberly. "My guess is the PLA scouts peeled off and are already on the hunt for another horde to redirect inland."

Lopez said, "Pipers or no, we still have a job to do." He tightened the chin strap on his ballistic helmet, made sure his plate carrier was snugged tight, then verified by feel that the pouches on his chest each held a full magazine and all were secured should he have to go to ground quickly.

Following Lopez's lead, Cross gunned up and got his gear squared away.

Haynes said, "I have the lead element on standard optical. Piping it back to you, Lopez."

In the cabin, Lopez studied the high-res image. Finally, he said, "Not much separation. With the speed they're moving, going boots on is going to be risky."

Ari said, "If Mother Nature isn't going to freeze them—"

Interrupting, Lopez said, "You think that thing we did to the Houston herd would work with these kind of numbers?"

"Only way to find out is to try it," Ari answered. "Question is: What's on the playlist?"

"I think it's one you'll approve of," Skipper responded.

While the crew chief cued up a song on his iPod, Ari had swung a wide turn to port, maybe a quarter-mile out over open desert, then looped back around so the Ghost Hawk was tracking parallel with I-15, coming in low and slow out of the north, straight for the front of the mega-horde.

As the first guitar riff of Lynyrd Skynyrd's *Sweet Home Alabama* blared from the Ghost Hawk's external speakers, a wide grin materialized below Ari's smoked visor. The second Van Zant's famous admonition rode over the guitar work, the SOAR pilot repeated along, hollering, "Turn it up!" as his helmeted head bounced in time with the drums.

Once the lead element was in Jedi One's turbulent wake, Ari added power, dropped the stealth helo's nose, then worked the stick and pedals so that the aircraft traced a tight serpentine path as it skimmed a dozen feet above the undead procession.

"Is it working?" Ari asked.

Skipper wedged his body against the minigun and stuck his helmeted head partway into the slipstream. Confident the safety line would keep him from an unexpected flying lesson, he craned hard to his right and saw exactly what he had hoped to see. "Dominos away," he crowed. "I think it's safe to bring us back around."

Lopez braced against the bulkhead and let his eyes roam the cabin as Ari threw the helicopter hard to port. Across from him, eyes closed and looking as serene as could be, Griff was sitting upright with his rifle propped muzzle down between his legs. If the shooter had any fear of Ari plowing the bird into the Nevada hardpan, the SEAL was hiding it well.

Sitting across the cabin from Skipper and wearing a wide grin that showed off his artificially white teeth, Cross was busy playing air guitar to the catchy rock anthem that had captured the dead's undivided attention.

Axe, on the other hand, was a little more pale than usual. His gaze was locked on something outside his window. Lopez figured it likely the man was just searching the ground for a point of reference to anchor to in order to get his equilibrium in check. "You going to be all right, Axe?"

Lips pursed, Axe nodded an affirmative.

Always the smartass, Griff handed Axe one of the airsickness bags Ari had made by a printing shop before everything went to shit. "If you're about to earn yourself a puker patch," he said, "better uneat your breakfast in this."

Axe waved off the bag with an extended middle finger.

In his headset, Skipper heard Ari order him to cut the music and ready the minigun. As soon as the former task was completed and Skipper had ahold of the Dillon's twin grips, Ari was back and telling him to "thin out" the lead element as soon as they were broadside to it.

The lead element consisted of about fifty robust specimens, almost half of them just becoming aware of the returning helicopter. A few hundred yards of open interstate stood between them and the front echelon of the main body, which, at the moment, was either already splayed out on the roadway in full repose, or in the act of toppling over. Looking skyward in unison and then tracking the rock-

and-roll emitting helicopter as it performed its high-speed low-to-the-ground flyover had started a chain reaction in the mega-horde that was still resulting in bodies far off in the distance falling atop one another, arms and legs akimbo, a decaying drift of death inextricably linked, some already struggling to rise.

Out of the blue, Griff said, "Ari, have Skipper save the ammo for the Dillon." He looked to Lopez. "I want to go boots on, too. I'll thin the herd while you two work."

"We're short a man, Griff."

"Axe can handle overwatch. He's a helluva shot with that tack driver of his."

Lopez hesitated a second, then agreed. "Once we're out of the bird, you engage the lead element. We'll flank right. Make sure you leave us some strong-looking Zs to work with. Once that's done, you watch our six."

Griff said, "Roger that," and proceeded to give his M4 a final onceover.

Chapter 20

With the patch of I-15 that was to be their landing zone coming up fast, over the comms, Ari said, "Wheels down in ten."

A whirring noise followed by the solid *clunk* of the landing gear locking in place ran through the troop compartment.

Wearing a serious expression, Lopez said to Griff, "If the horde gets back to moving and gains even an inch of ground … you call for our immediate exfil."

Smiling, Griff said, "Good copy, Sir."

Ari's landing was as smooth as they came, the helo barely moving after its wheels contacted the interstate.

Lopez glanced out the port-side windows. He saw that the main body was dangerously close—a couple of hundred yards distant, at most. As he led Cross and Griff through the open starboard-side door, he found the distance to the lead element to be a hundred yards, at best.

Lopez was hearing Ari saying, "Boots on!" even as the turbines were spooling up and the Ghost Hawk was getting light on her gear. He was up and running with Cross toward the freeway shoulder when he sensed the bulk of the chopper cleave the air directly over their heads. In his side vision, two things registered at once. To his left, he saw Griff's shouldered carbine jerking subtly, the brass casings tumbling through the air. To his right, coming across his field of view, the helicopter was banking hard to port and climbing into the blue morning sky.

If the maneuver that took the Ghost Hawk directly over the lead element was planned by Ari, it was brilliant and came at the right time. Because out of the thirty or so creatures that had gotten back to standing after the initial pass, nearly half of them were blown off their feet by the down blast from the scything rotor blades.

By the time Lopez and Cross were perpendicular to the lead element, Griff's accurate fire had already granted a large number of the Zs their forever death.

Leave us something to work with, thought Lopez as he jogged through a thin haze of exhaust left behind by the helicopter's low pass.

Cross followed close behind Lopez with the dogcatcher's pole clutched in one hand and bag of tracking collars in the other. Halfway to the lead element—only a handful of the Zs aware of the meat flanking them—he began to call out targets.

"Copy that," responded Lopez over their shared channel. "Adult male, red shirt, one shoe." He leveled the suppressed M4, sighted on the emaciated first turn to One Shoe's immediate left, and pressed the trigger twice.

Nothing. The first round cleaved a V-shaped chunk of decaying flesh from the Z's face but did nothing to slow its advance. The second round, he surmised, had missed and continued out over the desert.

Cursing himself, Lopez slowed his pace, drew and held the breath. Exhaling, he pressed the trigger once more. The old adage *the third time's a charm* held true. The screaming hunk of lead made a mess of the first turn's face, imploding everything from brow to septum in on itself. As the creature fell, he shifted his attention to the Zs on One Shoe's right flank. Five rounds fired in quick succession dropped three of them.

Cross was saying "One to go" at about the same time the female Z coming up on One Shoe's six was cut down by a round fired by Axe in the hovering helo.

"Owe me a pint, gents," said the SAS shooter over the open channel. "And it better be a proper pint. Not one of those fourteen-ounce pours in a wanker glass."

Cross said nothing. He had already handed the bag of trackers to Lopez and was busy extending the cable noose and maneuvering the pole near One Shoe's bobbing head.

"Right here," bellowed Lopez, freezing the Z in its tracks by waving one hand eye level to it. "Want a piece of me?"

As Cross was lassoing One Shoe, in his ear he heard Skipper warning that Zs were peeling off the lead element and dozens in the main body were beginning to rise.

One Shoe had a half a head advantage in height and weighed maybe thirty pounds more than Lopez. The recent turn also enjoyed a three- or four-inch reach, which, as Cross struggled to control its sporadic lunges, made it very dangerous and difficult for Lopez to get close enough to apply and activate the tracking collar. To mitigate the latter problem, Lopez drew the matte-black Gurkha Khukuri from the sheath strapped to his leg. Taking hold of the fingers waggling at the end of One Shoe's right hand, he swung the knife on a downward arc, the fierce blow from the twelve-inch recurved blade instantly severing the ashen limb at the elbow.

After removing One Shoe's other arm with a similar downward chop, Lopez went to work fitting the collar. Bobbing his head side to side like a boxer to avoid being bludgeoned by the flailing, bloodless stumps, he chose an opening, came underneath a scything left-cross, and swept the Z's legs.

There was a solid thud as One Shoe face-planted on the unforgiving blacktop.

Without pause, Lopez placed a boot on each stump. Then, using a process practiced countless times on a CPR dummy, he leaned over and fastened the tracking collar around One Shoe's neck.

After making sure the collar's embedded solar panel was unobstructed by hair or clothing, he cinched it tight. Lastly, to keep the Z from interfering with them as they worked, he cinched a zip-tie around the Z's ankles.

Cross loosened the noose and worked it up and over One Shoe's craning head.

Target two was a teenaged female with multiple bite wounds on both arms. The tee shirt clinging to her emaciated frame was emblazoned with the PINK logo. It was also punched through with multiple bullet holes and stiff with dried blood.

The holes bore powder burns around the edges, leading Lopez to believe the shots had been fired up close and personal.

"That's got to be the last one," Ari called over the comms. "Sierra Charlie is Oscar Mike. Initiating immediate extraction. Jedi One inbound."

Demonios on the move, was what Lopez heard. The words alone caused an electric current to trace his spine.

As Griff's rifle fire cut down the last of the lead element, leaving Pink all alone on the interstate, Lopez issued Cross a silent command.

Understanding the hand signal for what it meant, simultaneously Cross waved the catcher's pole in front of Pink and crabbed to his left in order to bring the Z around so that it faced the inbound helicopter.

Attention momentarily drawn from the fresh meat to the baffled whine of turbines and bass-heavy *thwop* of Jedi One's rotor blades thrashing air, Pink froze mid-shuffle.

Taking full advantage of the diversion, Lopez approached Pink from behind, wrangled her pustule-covered arms behind her back, and trussed them together with a pre-looped zip-tie. Keeping his gloved hands free from the undead teen's snapping teeth, Lopez fitted a tracking collar around her pencil-thin neck. After activating the tracking package, with the Khukuri he chopped a sizeable clump of greasy blonde locks away from the collar's rear-facing solar panel.

Hearing the announcement "Wheels down" come through his headset, Lopez glanced over his shoulder in time to witness Griff boarding the settling chopper. As he turned back and commenced cutting through Pink's cuffs, he felt something encircle his right ankle and tug backward.

Seeing the pale hand reach out from the stack of bodies felled by Griff, Cross immediately dropped the pole and rushed toward a falling Lopez. On the run, Cross drew his Sig P226 from the drop-thigh holster and brought it to bear on the pile of corpses.

Aware of his predicament, Lopez twisted around and drove a knee into the sternum of the dead thing pulling him off balance. As one hand arrested his fall—the gloved fingers plunging through the parchment-like skin covering a sunken belly—the other was swinging the Khukuri at the attacker's upturned face.

Simultaneously, as the recurved blade buried inches deep into the Z's left eye socket, a single round fired from Cross's Sig punched a quarter-sized hole into its right temple.

Cross reached Lopez as he was keeling over. Seeing the damage from the dual death blows, he holstered the Sig and then yanked Lopez to his feet.

Bellowing, "Go, go, go," Cross took the black blade from Lopez and finished slicing off Pink's cuffs. Then, like a bouncer jacked up on adrenaline, he tossed the hissing monster away from him.

With the Ghost Hawk's turbines spooling up behind him, and Skip's call that the herd was "Danger close" sounding over the comms, Cross stalked through the sea of bodies to get to One Shoe.

To escape the encroaching wall of walking dead, Ari was forced to launch and start Jedi One sideslipping toward the lone man still on the ground.

Cross had just cut the zip-tie from One Shoe's legs when the helo's shadow eclipsed the sun and he was caught up in its vicious down blast.

With gloved hands reaching for Cross from above, and a multitude of pallid, bony hands straining to get ahold of him, he dropped the Khukuri and thrust both arms skyward.

As his feet were yanked off the ground and someone was clicking a carabiner to his chest rig, the reaching hands of the dead gained purchase and he felt his boots and pants being pulled from his body.

In the end, as the Ghost Hawk powered safely into the sky, the thin nylon line and brute strength of friendly hands won the life and death game of tug-o-war with the surging mega-horde.

Seeing that the cabin door was still fully retracted, Cross contorted his prostrate body so that he was lying on his chest. Grabbing hold of the metal lip his helmet had come to rest on, he pulled himself forward and peered groundward. What he saw chilled him to the bone: One second there was a helicopter-sized patch of gray interstate separating the advancing mob from the accumulation of twice-dead corpses. In the next, like angry surf blitzing to shore, walking corpses overran the fallen, completely filling the void.

As the column of death poured over the forty or so head-shot corpses—their pounding feet punishing flesh and bone alike—Pink and One Shoe found their footing, performed clumsy pirouettes, and fell in lockstep with the new leaders of the procession.

Chapter 21

Max's number *two* was at the bottom of a hole in the snow and still steaming when Raven finally located it. "You couldn't have taken a dump a little closer to my bench, could you, *Max*?"

The dog had chosen a patch of ground underneath a copse of trees where the snow wasn't very deep. He was sitting on his haunches and directing his multi-colored gaze at her.

"You want me to throw the ball for you, or would you rather go for a walk?"

Raven readied a poo bag. Breathing through her mouth, she stooped over and mined the rapidly cooling clump of dog crap from the brown-rimmed oval hole in the snow.

As if Max understood his options, he jumped up and sauntered toward the park's south exit.

A walk it is, thought Raven. *Only question is: Who's walking who?*

After tossing the bulging bag into the trash can near the park's southeast entrance, Raven hustled to catch up to the shepherd, who had ranged ahead and seemed to know exactly where he was going. With the threat of encountering a zombie inside the walls near to zero, Raven kept her pistol holstered. Her gun hand, however, remained empty, the gloved fingers in constant movement and just inches from the Glock.

Max paused now and again to sniff at bushes and poles before halting completely and showing great interest in a solitary fire hydrant.

Having finally caught up with Max, Raven paused and checked her surroundings. Seeing only a lone CSPD Tahoe slipping by a block north, and rising over her the squat Exelis building with its perpetually darkened windows and empty parking lot, she clucked her tongue. Having gained Max's undivided attention, she said, "Smell a doggo you know?"

In response, Max lifted his leg and painted the snow around the base of the hydrant the color of banana Slurpee.

Raven said, "Claimed!" and they moved on.

***

After passing by the rear of Pikes Peak Center, with its chain-link-enclosed loading dock and boarded-over doors, Raven and Max entered the shadow of a four-story parking garage once used by desperate survivors as a temporary refuge from the dead. Knowing it was still home to abandoned vehicles and tents and the mummified corpses of the lucky few who had died of exposure, starvation, or illness caused Raven to shudder. Knowing that those same people did not come back hungering the flesh of the living offered her little solace.

The screech of what sounded like car-door hinges in dire need of lubricant rose over the subtle squelch of snow being compacted under her boot soles. It came from far away, likely somewhere deep in the bowels of the garage.

Hackles raised and teeth bared, Max stopped in his tracks. Remarkably, the shepherd made no sound. He just sniffed the air, then directed a glance toward his master.

"Good boy," Raven whispered. Looking up at the third level where she thought the noise had originated, all she saw was the multitudes of tarps strung up by survivors to cover the open spaces between floors. Some were blue. Some were red. Most were earth tones represented by several different shades of green, brown, and gray. With every errant gust of wind, the tarps rippled and went taut, straining at the corners where they'd been secured to what looked to be overhanging sprinkler pipes.

Hand going to the butt of her Glock, Raven stepped onto West Vermijo Avenue, Max by her side and still casting furtive glances at the looming garage.

"Just the wind," she said in a soothing voice. In her mind's eye, however, she pictured a horribly rotted first turn the reclamation crews had somehow missed on their final sweeps after the last of the freeway panels had gone up. It was belted in a car parked deep in the shadows and waiting for someone with their guard down to get near enough to grab hold of.

Shoving to the back burner the unlikely scenario conjured up by her very vivid imagination, she crossed the avenue on a diagonal.

Old habits die hard. Favoring the sidewalk bordering a wide-open parking lot, versus the one crowded by trees and the office building attached to the garage of the dead, she trudged east.

Kitty-corner from the snow-covered parking lot, rising up over South Cascade Avenue, was the former El Paso County Judicial Building. Now being used in a federal capacity, housing the offices of a fledgling government struggling to rise from the ashes of the near Extinction Level Event nobody saw coming, the bunker-like cement structure bearing the name Bureau of Eradication Reclamation and Restoration was accepting a steady stream of people looking to either procure tickets to go outside the city walls or exchange harvested ears for credit to be spent in any number of places within the walls.

One block beyond the BERR building, its bell tower rising up over a mishmash of FEMA trailers, single-wide mobile homes, and recreational vehicles set up on every available patch of ground, was the Colorado Springs Pioneers Museum.

Since most of the government buildings had been lost in the conflagration that left the no-man's land just outside the east wall, the three-story building dominating the center of the block had become the place where city government conducted its business; and business was certainly booming. A line of restless people Raven guessed to be Snowbirds—the surge of survivors who showed up after every new snowstorm—snaked down the steps and out of sight around the nearest corner.

Turning the corner, she muttered, "Get used to it, people. Freedom isn't free."

Raven's destination was the single-wide Fleetwood mobile home bordering the walkway at the Pioneers Museum's southwest corner. It was positioned at a forty-five-degree angle and sitting on a foundation of concrete blocks. Aside from an OPEN sign ablaze in one of the windows, and the mountain of empty cardboard boxes drooping under the weight of new snow, the only thing pointing to the fact that the place was a store was the hand-painted LOLAMART sign perched above the handprint-stained front door.

A serious-looking African American man Raven knew from her time spent at Schriever was the gatekeeper for the day. Buck was a few inches taller than Daymon, maybe six foot five, and sported a full beard streaked with gray. Though she didn't know if he was a SEAL, Green Beret, or member of Delta Force, she did know he was a year or two older than her dad and had fought beside him in Iraq and Afghanistan.

Dressed for the weather, Buck wore all black outdoor gear that would be considered top shelf in most ski shops. Only thing on his body that screamed *Army Surplus* were his scuffed combat boots and natty black watch cap, the latter pulled down low enough on his bald head so that it covered his ears.

Slung diagonally across Buck's barrel chest was a stunted rifle that resembled an AK-47. Raven thought for sure the smaller model was called an AKS Krinkov. She knew this because her dad had pointed it out when one of Bin Laden's recorded interviews was showing on the History Channel. The same type of rifle had been leaning against a dirt wall and within arm's reach of the now-dead terrorist.

Buck's Krinkov was positioned on his body so its metal stock rested near one shoulder and the worn pistol grip rode above his belt line, just inches from his dominant hand. The setup told Raven that bringing the AKS to bear on anyone coming at LOLAMART with bad intentions would require a simple shrug of the shoulder and quick upward sweep of the weapon's stubby muzzle.

Bad news for them.

Money well spent by Lola.

Looking up from the SKILLSET magazine cradled in his mitt-sized hands, Buck smiled wide and said, "Well hello, Miss Raven. Pleasure to see you this fine morning. Buying or selling, today?"

"Pleasure is all mine, Buck," was the only adult sounding salutation she could conjure up on the fly. "A little of both, I suppose," was her answer to his question.

Buck descended the short stack of stairs and met Raven beside a bank of scratched and dented metal lockers that looked to have been scavenged from a school or gym. "You know the routine," he said, doing the *gimme* motion with his gloved hands.

Raven drew the Glock from its holster. She removed the magazine and racked the slide, intercepting the ejected round with her free hand as it tumbled to earth.

"Impressive," Buck declared. "Nowhere close to flagging me with the muzzle, and your booger hook stayed off the bang switch the entire time."

Handing the pistol to the man, butt first, she said, "I learned from the best."

Voice gone soft, the big man said, "Speaking of your dad … how is he?"

"He's home now and getting better by the day." She paused. "Apparently he's well enough to start learning how to speak *Chinese*." She had screwed up her face as she said *Chinese*.

"Damn," said Buck. "Good ol' Nash has him on the fast track to ordering from the menu without going to the numbers."

He placed the Glock and magazine in the locker numbered 3, snapped a padlock shut on the handle, then turned to present the key to Raven. When his gaze fell on her, he saw that her smile had been replaced by a look of confusion.

"Order by the number?" Raven asked, head adopting a slight tilt. "Like at McDonalds?"

Stepping away from the entry, Buck chuckled and then explained how, to keep the layperson from butchering the names of the dozens of available dishes on their menus, as well as for ease of ordering, many Chinese restaurants put a number next to each item.

Brow arched, Raven said, "I see." Having never ordered from a Chinese menu, she took Buck at his word. Ordering Max to stay, she mounted the stairs and pushed through the door.

Chapter 22

"What we need is a couple of Pied Pipers of our own," Griff said. "Lead that horde over the edge of the effin Grand Canyon."

Holding the sniper rifle vertical between his knees, Axe looked to Griff. "You still in the volunteering mood, mate?"

"Someone's got to do it, overwatch boy." Griff smiled to let Axe know his chain was being yanked.

"I'll have you know, Griff, *Overwatch Boy* dropped a pair of Zeds creeping up on your six." Axe glanced at the interstate below the Ghost Hawk. Off the starboard side, rising up beside the old highway, was the iconic *Now Entering Las Vegas* sign.

The closer they got to downtown, the more outbound vehicles they saw stalled out on the interstate. Similarly, side streets and boulevards around the interstate were clogged with unoccupied vehicles, nearly all of them loaded down with belongings.

"Lots of people left their rides behind," noted Cross.

"Your ride almost left *you* behind," quipped Griff.

"Wasn't even close," Ari shot.

"Closer than I would have liked," Cross admitted. "I have the rips in my pants to prove it."

"But did you die?"

Deciding to let Griff have the last word, Cross went back to taping up his torn pants legs.

Up front, Ari was still scanning the west/east-running streets. Imagining that the PLA scouts had to resort to backtracking or even dismounting their motorcycles to get through the particularly nasty blockages, he said, "Where oh where are our Chinese friends?"

Haynes said, "What would you want to do if you had been riding a bike across the desert at slow speed for hours on end?"

"Shoot myself," Griff joked. "Motorcycles are meant to be ridden fast and with a hot babe on back."

"Seriously," Haynes pressed. "Once you saw that beacon in the distance, besides the obvious air-conditioned casino or seafood buffet, where would you go first?"

"I'd find me a brewski and a swimming pool," Lopez said. "And not necessarily in that order."

Ari slowed Jedi One and brought her to a hover above a cloverleaf being negotiated by a small herd of dead. In twos and threes, as the down blast from the main rotor swirled their wispy hair and tugged at clothing gone threadbare from exposure to the elements, the Zs paused and looked expectantly skyward.

Flanking the boulevard cutting underneath the interstate was a pair of gas stations. Both of the attached convenience marts were just metal shells, the windows devoid of glass, the shelves emptied. Snaking off from the fueling islands and into the road were six lines of inert vehicles. Each line held a dozen or more cars, SUVs, and pickups, some of which were loaded down with personal belongings and all manner of home furnishings.

Ari said, "Folks didn't get far. Which begs the question: Where are the riders? I have a feeling they're laying low somewhere and waiting for Sierra Charlie to shuffle on down the road."

"What makes you think the dead won't deviate?" Lopez asked.

"I-15 is a natural conduit," Haynes stated. "So unless a majority of the pacesetters take an off-ramp, maybe to chase something living they think they can eat, I bet the whole stinking lot of them will pass right on through."

Still holding the bird in a hover, Ari said, "Anyone in the cheap seats have an idea where they might have gone?"

Silence.

"Don't all you ladies speak up at the same time," Ari continued. "Where would you go?"

Griff spoke up. "Think like a Chinese tourist. Say you're visiting New York. What's the first thing you go and do?" Answering his own question, he added, "You go see Ground Zero."

Struck by an epiphany, Lopez said, "Everyone who goes to Vegas *has* to see the fountains at the Bellagio. I bet the riders are no different."

Haynes said, "Nail on the head. Though the fountains are likely just standing water, you'd still be killing two birds with one stone."

"And that water can be purified for drinking," Cross added.

"Even if it was full of duck shite," Axe said, "I'd still take my boots off and dip my feet."

"They're riding, not marching," Griff said. "Still, I like the way you're thinking. They have an hour, maybe two lag time before the horde reaches the Vegas sign. The cars on the interstate will slow them down some."

"Only until the main body gets to them," Cross said. "Then, *bang* ... cars will be tossed aside like toys."

Ari said, "We better move it, then." He nudged the stick forward and applied right pedal. As the helicopter went nose down and started a slow turn to starboard, he went on, saying, "The riders are here. I'm sure of it. They stopped somewhere and are likely taking catnaps in shifts. And I agree, they're probably set up near some water." He regarded Haynes. "High Tower, you know this city better than any of us. Where do you think we should start our search?"

With no hesitation, Haynes pointed to a regal-looking building off in the distance. "Start at the Bellagio." For the benefit of the team in back, he targeted the hotel with the FLIR pod and fed the live feed to the troop compartment monitor.

As Ari kept the Ghost Hawk tracking north, three hundred feet above Interstate 15, everyone aboard was afforded a bird's-eye view of a number of landmark hotel/casinos.

The south gatekeeper was Mandalay Bay, a stout wedge of concrete rising to nearly eye level with the helicopter. Curtains hung through jagged holes punched in many of its windows. On the ground below, debris pushed by the desert wind danced over mirrored shards of glass glittering in the sun.

Next came the Luxor's pyramid. It was seemingly untouched, the intact glass panels streaked with dirt.

Behind the Luxor, its faux skyline nearly as impressive as the real thing, was the New York-New York Hotel and Casino. In the distance, the 1149-foot-tall needle-like Stratosphere Hotel rose above it all.

"At the clover leaf," called Haynes, "make a ninety-degree turn to starboard."

"Copy that," replied Ari, beginning the task of bleeding airspeed and swinging the bird around to the right.

"Bellagio dead ahead," Haynes stated. He tapped the glass cockpit to enlarge the image.

Rising up behind the palms fronting the Bellagio, maybe two blocks distant, stood a replica of the Eiffel Tower. Though it was considerably smaller in scale than the real deal, the amount of detail put into its construction was impressive.

The palms dotting the Bellagio grounds were in dire need of attention, their fronds brown and drooping. In the middle distance the burned-out hulk of a super-stretch limousine sat across the main driveway. It was ringed by twice-dead corpses ravaged by decomposition.

Closer in, blocking the exit spilling onto a wide thoroughfare, was a red double-decker sightseeing bus. BIG BUS LAS VEGAS was splashed in gold across both sides.

Chain-link fencing anchored by cement footers and fronted by Jersey barriers ringed the property. Just outside the barriers, sitting amongst a sea of brass shell casings and dead bodies, was a trio of desert tan Humvees. Though the squat vehicles were fitted with top-mounted cupolas, they had been stripped of their heavy weapons.

Trapped inside the perimeter were dozens of zombies in varying states of decay. And since the hotel's main doors were thrown open, it was clear to Ari and Haynes that the walking dead had free reign of the place.

Seeing the same images on the rear monitor, Lopez said, "Looks like someone put up a helluva fight trying to hold it."

Ari tapped the image. Sounding disappointed, he said, "All that aside … it looks as if our hypothesis is shot. And to add a kick in the nuts to it all, the fountains are as dead as those things walking the grounds."

"Looks like the duck pond at my *abuela's finca*," commented Lopez.

A usually reserved Cross said, "Tijuana called ... it wants its drinking water back."

Axe said, "Bugger. If the wankers did visit the famous Bellagio *fountains*, looks as if they popped a selfie and moved on."

"You think?" Griff chided. "The entire property is compromised. Nothing to see here. Move along."

Ari flipped up his visor and looked a question at Haynes.

Shrugging against his shoulder straps, Haynes said, "We do have enough fuel to grid search the strip north to south one time. Caesar's Palace is pretty well known, too. Remember that movie The Hangover? It's where they filmed it."

Ari didn't need convincing. Nor did he ask Lopez for input. The urge to see the place where one of his favorite comedies was filmed was motivation enough to add a few more minutes' stick time to what was already one hell of a long mission. Firm set to his jaw, he threaded Jedi One between cross-competing multi-story hotels, turned to a northerly heading, and grabbed some altitude.

Chapter 23

The inside of LOLAMART smelled of cigarette smoke and mildew. A space heater worked hard to warm the still air. Gutted from floor to ceiling, chest-high shelves crisscrossed the floor where interior walls used to rise. Only thing in the popup store that spoke to it once being someone's dwelling was the thick brown carpet underfoot and the dark wood paneling behind Lola's makeshift checkout counter.

The stock on Lola's shelves changed constantly. One day after the arrival of the contents of a previously looted convenience store, the shelves burst with whimsical items and toys—most made in China. Another time a foraging party had returned with U-Haul trucks filled with goods salvaged from an untouched sporting goods store. The guns and ammunition were first to go, with the camping and fishing gear not so hot a commodity. Last time Raven had visited Lola's, the odds and ends from that haul were still languishing on the shelves. As the bell over her head signaled the door closing at her back, she hoped that was still the case. However, like Forest Gump's take on life, Lola's inventory was the chocolates in the box and you never knew what you were going to get.

The woman behind the counter rose from her chair and directed her gaze toward the door. Greeting Raven by name, she began to rattle off the recent arrivals and the stores they'd been liberated from.

Making her way to the nearby counter, Raven asked, "Got anything left from the Outdoor N' More haul?"

Cigarette bouncing as she talked, Lola said, "Moved all that to the back forty and marked it all down more than half." She pointed a crooked, arthritic finger toward the area of the store she regarded the *back forty*.

Looking to the rear of the store, Raven spotted a middle-aged couple perusing the aisles. After waiting for the shoppers to vacate the aisle she had her sights set on, Raven made her move, passing shelves brimming with alkaline batteries, disposable propane canisters, wooden matches, and propane stoves.

The item Raven had come looking for was indeed on a lower shelf at the back of the rectangular trailer. And true to Lola's word, it was priced to move.

Once the couple completed their business with Lola, Raven made her way toward the front, along the way grabbing a pouch of bacon treats for Max off a low shelf.

Lola was dressed head-to-toe in surplus BDUs in woodland-pattern camouflage. On her feet were Sorel snow boots with wool liners showing. On her hip was a compact pistol, the make foreign to Raven. She was lighting a new cigarette with the stub of the previous cigarette as Raven approached the counter.

Close up, it was crystal clear the woman was somewhere in age north of Duncan and south of dirt. Calling her seventy was probably being generous. Her features were angular, like a granite escarpment sharpened by water and time. Eyes the color of river rock, set deep within wrinkled folds of skin, had tracked Raven's every move.

Raven met the woman's stare and thrust out her chin. "Do you have any spray paint?" she asked politely. "Or some kind of solvent that removes it from wood and cement?"

"You can get something that'll remove it over at the fuel depot. Talk to Jon Lang. Tell him I sent you and he'll cut you a fair deal. As for spray paint"—she took a drag off her cigarette and held it in— "the paper pushers at Reclamation intercept all that comes through the gates. They're using it to mark doors after they clear the homes and businesses of corpses and roamers. I hear they're just getting started on the east side of Aurora." Lola paused and her gray eyes roamed the merchandise spread out on the counter before her. Coughing and releasing the trapped smoke through her nostrils, she said, "What're the game cameras for?"

Raven set the Beggin' Strips on the counter. Digging out the card loaded with credits earned from lopping ears and scrambling brains, she said, "We have *pests* outside our place."

Looking over top of her bifocals, Lola said, "The big, two-legged type, I presume."

Raven nodded. "Since they're breathers, I can't just hide out and put a bullet in them next time they turn up."

"Too bad you can't." She laughed. It was more of a wet rasp, really. "What makes you think you're dealing with more than one *pest?*"

"Gut feeling."

"Always good to listen to your gut. That's why I'm still breathing."

Barely, thought Raven as she dodged the swirling smoke.

Lola finished bagging the goods and reached for Raven's card. Drawing the card back, Raven looked a question at the woman.

"Five credits," said Lola, eyes unblinking and locked with Raven's. Either Lola's habit had rubbed off on Buck, or vice-versa, because those crooked fingers started doing the same *gimme here* waggle.

"I'll pay two credits," shot Raven, voice firm and unwavering.

Lola sighed. Hands going to her bony hips, she said, "That barely covers the dog treats."

"Who's going to buy a game camera *inside* these walls? Out there you might get lucky and get three credits for them. Inside the walls"—she shook her head—"that is *not* gonna happen."

"People are going soft," Lola conceded. "Three credits for the treats and information. I'll throw in the cameras. Besides, I've still got a half-dozen where these came from, don't I?"

Lips curling into a half-smile, Raven nodded and relinquished her card.

The transaction occurred like any other before the dead started coming back to life. One quick swipe and the credits were removed. Where they ended up and who was keeping score didn't even register on Raven's give-a-crap radar.

Lola said, "You got batteries for the cameras?"

"Plenty," Raven answered. "Do you have any muscle cream?"

"Like Ben Gay?"

Raven chuckled at that.

Barely able to contain her own laughter, Lola said, "It's a brand name, young lady … not a punchline." Tone turning serious, she added, "We've all gotten wound up so damn tight as of late. What with all this surviving and stuff." She paused. "You want one tube or two?"

Raven nodded. Holding up the requisite number of fingers, she said, "Three." Pointing at an item on the counter behind Lola, she said, "And I need one of those."

"Is it all for your dad?"

Again with the nod, only this time Raven was biting her lip.

Lola set the silver and red can beside Raven's purchases. Next, she reached under the counter and came up with a handful of white tubes sporting red letters. "This is all on the house." She dumped everything into the bag. "Least I can do after all your dad has done. He *was* involved in the operation that stopped the Denver mega-horde from getting here, wasn't he?"

"That's my dad," said Raven, an *aw' shucks* tone to her voice. As she scooped up her purchases, she skipped over in her mind all the things he had done for the country so far. And the list was long, rescuing scientists from the Canadian research lab the most important among them. As Raven walked out with her bag in hand, she wondered if the search for a cure was still ongoing, or if the previous antiserum failures—such as the batch that killed her mom—was a portent that Omega would remain forever unchecked.

Max was sitting next to Buck's muddy boots and staring at the trailer door when Raven emerged. As if he had x-ray vision and could see the bacon treats in the bag, his gaze locked on the item in her hand and his stub tail began to twitch.

Hand out, Buck said, "Get what you need?"

Relinquishing the key, Raven nodded. "Everything but the cure for Omega."

Buck met her gaze and handed over the Glock and magazine for it. "I hear Mother Nature isn't cooperating."

"We shouldn't have tested her in the first place."

Jaw taking a granite set, Buck said, "No *we* about it. The Chinese are the ones to blame. We're just trying to clean up their mess."

Raven ripped open the treat bag and gave Max a full strip. As the dog played with the fake bacon, tossing it around like an injured mouse, Raven probed Buck for more information. "Why aren't you out on a mission with the teams?"

"I will be soon," he said. "Chinese are no doubt taking advantage of the cold weather same as we are. Only they're trying to gain ground on us. We, on the other hand, are taking ours back from the dead. This"—he spread his arms—"is me using my mandatory stand-down time to earn a little extra scratch."

Pleased she had ferreted out that Buck was in fact a Delta, just like her dad, she wished him well and set off back toward the BERR building, hoping to chat with whoever was in charge of paint procurement.

Chapter 24

Las Vegas

Reaching the north end of the initial search box, Ari downed a five-hour energy drink, settled into the comfy wool seat cover Duncan had recovered for him, and nosed the helicopter east.

On the helo's port side, Treasure Island Hotel and Casino's full-size galleon sat in silent repose atop an expanse of oil-slicked water clouded with blooms of green algae. Once engaged in a constant state of mock battle, the wooden ship now looked forlorn, its multiple cannons silent and streaked white with bird droppings.

Ari took his eyes off the casino attraction and initiated the search on a southern tack that had them riding over a dozen or so hotels bordering Las Vegas Boulevard.

A minute after beginning the search, they reached the south end of the first leg of the pattern and were afforded a second viewing of the Bellagio as well as a good look at the mega-horde. It was hard to miss, even from several miles out. And from the looks of it, the column hadn't made much progress since they wrapped up their tagging op.

"We still have plenty of time to go boots on the ground if it comes to it," Haynes said.

"Copy that," responded Ari as he banked Jedi One hard left and gained enough altitude to afford the FLIR pod an unimpeded view of Caesar's Palace as well as the surrounding hotels and side streets.

Holding Jedi One in a solid hover, Ari glanced at the screen and saw that Caesar's had received the same chain-link and Jersey-barrier treatment as the Bellagio. However, Caesar's perimeter looked to be intact. Dead giveaway was the solid run of fencing with no breaches and that the grounds were free of walking dead and the fountain pools contained no festering corpses.

Over the comms, Lopez said, "I just picked up on some movement on the portico below the Caesar's sign."

Griff said, "You mean the sign that goof Alan was holding onto for dear life in the movie?"

"I don't know about that," responded Lopez. "But I'm certain there's someone hiding in the shadows."

Haynes announced he was zooming on the portico and going thermal with the FLIR. A tick later, both of the helo's screens went black for a split-second. When the new image popped up, there was a distinct human form where only shadow had been.

The form was represented by orange and red and yellow and was swaying nervously from side to side.

"That's a person, all right," Ari said agreeably. "And he's armed with some type of handgun."

Haynes said, "I concur. Shall we make contact?"

Ari said, "Affirmative. I want to do the talking." He peered into the troop compartment. "Skipper, you need to be ready on your gun. Lopez, volunteer someone to man the port side minigun. Axe, you get set up behind that rifle of yours."

"What do you want *me* to do?" Cross asked.

Ari said, "Keep eyes on our breather. Watch for muzzle flashes. If we do start taking fire, note the location and start a play-by-play so our gunners can return fire."

Not quite the glamorous job he'd envisioned, Cross thought as he cozied up to the port-facing window.

Meanwhile, Lopez had opened the cabin door for Axe and moved gear around so the SAS man had room to work. Next, he deployed the port-side minigun and took it by the handles.

After hearing a trio of voices confirm they were ready, Ari started the helo creeping forward. As he did so, he slowly dropped the bird to an altitude that put them eye to eye with the stocky man on the covered patio.

"Be advised," Cross warned, "the tango sees us. He's coming forward, now. Be advised: His weapon is down. Repeat … weapon is down."

"Copy that," Lopez responded. "I have him painted."

"Cycling out of thermal," Haynes said. "Three times magnification coming online."

The second the feed refreshed, Ari flicked his gaze to the new image appearing on the glass cockpit. Voice rising in pitch, he said, "I can't believe who I'm looking at. First person who confirms my hunch gets himself a case of beer when we return to base."

Incredulous, Haynes said, "No way that's him. I agree he looks a lot like—"

"That's him, mates," Axe interrupted. "I have him in my crosshairs. And from the looks of it, he's not fallen victim to the apocalypse diet."

"Damn," said Cross. "You're right. He's looking fit. What was his old fighting weight? Two, maybe two-thirty?"

"He could be pushing three hundred pounds for all I care," Axe declared. "There's no mistaking that face tattoo. Ari, you can go ahead and make that case Adnams Bitter if you can find it. Guinness, if you can't."

"Closing," called Ari. "Watch his hands. No doubt they're still pretty damn fast."

"That's a given," Lopez said. "What are you going to do?"

"Communicate," Ari said. "Switching to personal address."

As Ari brought the Ghost Hawk broadside to the portico, the former Heavyweight Champion of the World wove between a phalanx of planters full of dead flowers, then stepped up to the waist-high stone railing.

The helo's rotor wash whipping the dead plants into a frenzy was also playing havoc with the champ's silk pajama bottoms.

His voice amplified and coming from a flush-mounted external speaker, Ari said, "I'm going to need you to holster your weapon, Mike."

The man smiled, exposing a picket of gold teeth. Running a palm over his bald pate, he holstered his pistol. Smile fading, he placed both hands on the cement railing and looked a question up at the hovering helicopter.

"Do you require assistance?" Ari asked.

"As if Iron Mike needs help surviving the zombie apocalypse," shot Axe. "He can probably punch his way through a herd of zeds without breaking a sweat."

Iron Mike shook his head.

"Have you seen anyone pass through here?"

The champ nodded enthusiastically. Then he released his grip on the rail and held up two fingers.

Haynes zoomed the FLIR camera in on Tyson's head. "Anyone good at reading lips? He's saying something and pointing at the ground."

Cross said, "I got it. He's saying there's a pair of riders downstairs. Not sure if he means inside the building, though."

Ari thanked the champ over the PA as he applied pitch and powered the helicopter away from the casino. Then, speaking over the shipboard comms, he said, "I'm going to bring her around the building real close to the deck."

Haynes said, "Want me to search the lobby for heat sigs?"

Ari said, "Affirmative, High Tower." Addressing Skipper, he added, "I'll leave you a good aspect for the starboard gun."

Lopez set Axe up in the open starboard door with the explicit order to drop any squirters. "Try not to kill them," he implored as the helicopter reached the end of its clockwise orbit and began to descend.

Ari hovered Jedi One over an intersection cloaked in the shadows of two opposing buildings. From the standoff position, roughly a block and a half south of Caesar's Palace, the scope of view was narrow, leaving just the most important slice of the white building showing in the distance.

"Thank God the fountain's not working," said Haynes as he worked the FLIR controls. "It'd make a visual search of the valet area and lobby impossible. And I'm not so sure thermal would pick out anything through the spray."

Under the nose of the helicopter, the pod housing the advanced optics suite panned slowly left to right. Directly below the pod, maybe a dozen feet clearance between the helo's nose and the tips of their straining fingers, a crowd of walking corpses was gathering.

"Stepping up magnification," Haynes said.

On the starboard minigun, Skipper was at high alert. It'd only take one missile fired from the shadows to ruin their day. Whereas Ari had had lots of room to maneuver evasively and dispense flares the last time they'd come under fire by a heat-seeking Chinese missile, here, with nowhere to go but up, the helo was pretty much a sitting duck. Gloved fingers kneading the weapon's grips, he said, "I have a wide field of fire. All clear visually."

"Copy that," Ari said. He glanced at the screen and saw the covered drive he remembered from the movie. It looked to be all marble, or maybe it was plaster painted to look the part. Beside the hotel's closed glass doors was a valet stand. Behind the doors the lobby was nothing but a black rectangle devoid of movement and detail. He thought, *Anything could be hiding in there.* He said, "Go to thermal."

Haynes said, "Going to thermal."

The once pitch-black screens in the cockpit and troop cabin came to life with a flash of warm colors. Anyone watching the change saw four distinct heat signatures inside the lobby. Two were vertical, man-shaped blobs made up of yellow, orange, and red. The other two were horizontal to the floor and consisted of two distinct hot spots glowing at different intensities.

"We've got two tangos," Haynes warned. No sooner had the words crossed his lips than his screen erupted with twin blooms of red. Directing his gaze out the cockpit glass, he saw the gunfire directed at them as star-shaped orange and red winks of light. "Taking fire," he bellowed.

"Weapons free," Ari called even as he was pulling pitch and applying pedal.

In reaction to Ari's input, the turbines shrieked and the ship began a slow counterclockwise rotation. Skip's "Copy that!" was nearly drowned out as the minigun, belching fire, sent a lethal lead storm downrange.

Chapter 25

While Raven had been inside Lola's place, a small line had formed on the steps of the BERR building. Bypassing the majority of the people, Raven stopped on the covered landing and commanded Max to stay there.

With the people at the head of the line looking on bitterly, Raven entered the building through the revolving door, crossed the soaring marble-appointed atrium, and took the stairs to the second floor.

Located in a rectangular room on the BERR building's north side, the Department of Reclamation, with its waiting room full of cheap furniture and year-old magazines, was no different than the handful of government concerns Raven had visited with her mom and dad before Omega had rendered most of them irrelevant.

As indicated by the writing etched on the brass plaque on the entry door, this particular space was formerly home to the Colorado Division of Youth Corrections. Nothing inside the drab rectangular room led her to believe correcting Colorado's youth was an easy job. Posters set at intervals on the walls featured happy shiny people spouting slogans that, at this point in a delinquent's journey, Raven felt amounted to too little, too late. By the time one had contact with the law and ended up here for adjudication, how real of an impact could a bunch of PSAs have on their future?

Not much, was her guess.

In the spaces between the former tenant's messaging, someone had taped up posters reminding visitors of rules that at this stage in the survival game, should already be common knowledge to anyone who had come this far since that Saturday in July when the world changed forever.

One poster read *Be Sure It's Dead — Put Two In The Head.* Another: *When In Doubt: Scramble The Brain.* A third bore the grim message: BITTEN? — A.C.T. FAST — AMPUTATE - CAUTERIZE - TELL.

Shifting her attention from the walls to the dingy orange chairs set out haphazardly around the room, Raven noted that the half-dozen people already waiting to be seen by the thirty-something with the high-and-tight cut in the wheelchair were all spread out around the room.

The government worker, who seemed to be holding down the fort all by himself, was a blur of motion as he made his way to a far cabinet, filed some papers, slammed the drawer shut, then retook his post behind a waist-high counter fronted by a thick pane of ballistic glass.

After adjusting the laptop hinged open in front of him, the man bellowed, "Eighteen," and walked an expectant gaze over those seated about the waiting room.

Tearing a numbered paper chit from a dispenser, Raven chose the seat farthest from the door, where she could see anyone new as they entered, yet also keep an eye on the people waiting to be called ahead of her.

***

Fifteen minutes into the June 2011 issue of Seventeen magazine and quickly tiring of reading about long-dead celebs who had no clue of the meat grinder they'd soon be facing, Raven heard her number called.

Taking one last look at the glossy full-page spread on which a pair of teen heartthrobs were standing hip-to-hip and smiling as if the world was truly their oyster, she tossed the mag aside, then rose and adjusted her gun belt.

While civilian establishments still reserved the right to exclude open carry, inside the walls of the new capital the Second Amendment was alive and well. Furthermore, due to the extraordinary circumstances brought on by China's sneak attack on several American cities, and the rapid nationwide spread of the virus they had introduced into the population, gone were all of the other stringent rules pertaining to when and where one could exercise their 2A rights.

Taking a circuitous route through the room that had her walking by a huge fish tank thick with green algae and putting off an odor that would gag a maggot, Raven made her way to the window, coming in at an angle that let her see the clerk, yet remain in his peripheral and out of sight. He was wearing a MultiCam blouse and matching pants. Though he wore black chevrons pegging him as a sergeant, and the name tape on his chest read *Chambers*, Raven knew he preferred to be called Brian.

Swallowing hard as she stepped before the window, Raven silently petitioned God to forgive her for what she was about to do.

Seeing a shadow fall across the counter in front of him, Sergeant Chambers glanced up from the paperwork he'd been looking over. Expression taking a sudden turn from half-way-welcoming to one that all but screamed *Not you again,* he said, "You were here less than a week ago, Miss Grayson. I doubt your paperwork is anywhere near to landing on the Arbiter's desk. It's not that we don't care ... it's just that we don't have the manpower we need to move these things along." He paused and lifted his hands into a position of surrender. "I'm doing all I can for you. I promise you that."

Duly noted, thought Raven. But that wasn't why she was here.

She said, "I know you're not a miracle worker, Brian. I have other business. If you're interested, that is."

The *miracle worker* statement had caused Brian to bristle. Though he was confined to a wheelchair, he was still the man *all* things in this department *had* to go through. He rolled his chair back a foot or so and crossed his bulging arms over his chest. "I may be interested. What kind of *business?*"

"Spray paint," Raven said. She had uttered the two words in a manner that allowed them to be interpreted as either an answer or question.

Leaning forward, brows coming together, Brian said, "You have some for me?"

She nodded. A lie.

"I struck the motherlode over in Yoder." Another lie. "And it's probably enough paint for the clearing crews to tag half the houses in Aurora. How many cases will you take and how much is the bounty?"

"Speaking of bounty," Brian said, "Kim from Eradication was bragging on you the other day. Said you brought in more ears from one trip than most adult cullers bring in after a week outside the walls."

Nodding, Raven said, "Praise doesn't pay the bills. How much paint can you use and how many credits is it worth to you?"

As if he'd just been delivered a dose of bad news, Brian slumped in his chair.

"What is it?" Raven asked, voice full of manufactured concern.

Speaking slowly, Brian said, "What color is your paint?"

"Six cases of glitter-infused gold, six of teal, and a couple of cases of canary yellow."

Brian's head began a slow side to side wag. "People way above my pay grade say that red, black, and white are the only acceptable colors. Bring me those and we'll talk."

"This is *Aurora* we're talking about," Raven said. "Your boss isn't going to leave the walls and risk being irradiated just to check on what colors his men are using to mark those doors."

Still shaking his head, Brian said, "Can't use it if it isn't regulation. It's just how the Army works."

Leaning toward the glass, Raven said, "All right then, Sergeant Chambers. Where *do* you unload the stuff you get in that isn't regulation color?"

"Aside from your dreadlocked friend, who took all the puke green off my hands, the tattooists are my main customers. They snap it up as soon as it comes in. Hell, I couldn't keep it on the shelves if I had shelves to put it on."

Feigning a look of disappointment, Raven thanked Brian for letting her pick his brain.

After apologizing for his initial assumption, he said, "How is your dad doing? Is he adjusting to life in the slow lane? Took me a couple of months to come to grips with the fact that I'd never fast-rope from a helo again."

"He's a fighter," she said. "I'm sure he'll be back to fast-roping from helos in no time."

"We're all pulling for him," Brian said.

Nodding, Raven took a step toward the door. Then, just as Brian was calling the next number, she turned back and asked him who was in charge over at Reclamation.

"Ask for Trudy DeAngelo. She's short with dark hair. A real spitfire. Kind of like you, only thirty years older. Trust me, you'll hear her before you see her." After acknowledging the new person forming up to his window, Brian craned and added, "Tread lightly with her, Raven."

Thinking, *I most certainly will, real lightly*, Raven stepped back into the hall, a sly grin forming on her face and the initial elements of a plan caroming around inside her head.

Chapter 26

Las Vegas

Inside the Caesar's lobby, having just watched the thick glass doors fracture into a thousand pieces and those pieces cascade to the stone floor and bounce in every direction like dice thrown by a drunk, the rider shouldered an FN-6 Man-Portable Air-Defense System missile launcher and sighted on the spot in the sky the American helicopter was most likely to emerge. While the rider waited, what was left of the mangled motorcycle the second rider had just gotten astride was leaking different-colored liquids onto the floor. A suitcase-sized hunk of shredded flesh trapped underneath the bike and spilling internal organs was all that remained of a man who had just stopped firing on the helicopter long enough to issue the order to deploy the MANPADS missile.

Limbs trembling furiously, the second rider looked away from the patch of blue sky and regarded the multiple blood trails leading away from the limbless torso.

At the end of one bloody track was an arm. It had come to rest against a massive round column in the middle of the lobby. Bent at a ninety-degree angle to the floor, the gloved hand appeared to be waving a final goodbye.

A bare leg—still shod in a black combat boot—sat atop a white rug slowly turning crimson.

The dead rider's rifle and parts of the arm and hand that had been gripping it were now a gory jumble at the terminus of yet another jagged red streak.

The dead rider's helmeted head was nowhere to be seen.

Confident that firing a missile at the futuristic-looking helicopter would ensure a similar fate, the second rider discarded the

MANPADS, straddled the dirt bike, then kick started the engine to life.

Having swung the Ghost Hawk out of harm's way and repositioned above an intersection a block down and at an oblique angle to the Caesar's Palace entrance, Ari held the helo in a hover and watched for movement in the area where the rifle fire had come from.

"I think Skip pasted them both," Lopez said glumly. "Set us down and I'll lead a team in to gather intel."

Griff was glassing the front of Caesar's with Steiner binoculars. "Not necessary," he growled. "We have a squirter."

On the monitor, Lopez watched a lone rider atop a camouflage motorcycle bounce down a long run of stairs, make a sharp left by the fountain, and barrel toward the far fence line. The point in the fence the rider was tracking for was fronted by a handful of Zs. The sidewalk occupied by the Zs was already littered with a dozen twice-dead corpses, some of them surrounded by pools of brackish fluid.

Cross said, "No doubt they cut the fence to get their bikes inside. Look for a seam. That's got to be where he's headed."

"Closing the gap," Ari said as he side-slipped the helicopter down the street toward the rabbiting rider. "Axe, if I keep presenting you this angle, you think you can drop him inside the perimeter?"

"Certainly," Axe answered. "He's not going home to his mum."

"Unless he starts shooting at us, keep him alive," Lopez ordered.

"Copy that," replied Axe, dropping his eye to the high-powered Leupold scope atop the Remington MSR chambered in .300 Win Mag. He was sitting cross-legged on the floor, dead center in the open starboard-side door, with only a thin nylon strap to prevent a hundred-foot fall should he get pitched out.

The rider appeared to be slowing down, then all of a sudden he swerved right and accelerated rapidly toward a spot in the fence a few yards from the assembled Zs.

"I see where they came in," Griff said. Pointing out the spot for Axe, he went on, "It's only secured with a couple of zip-ties. To get through, he'll be forced to stop and clip them. Hit him when he dismounts."

Axe said nothing. He was already in the zone, everything external slowing and snapping into sharp focus. The moment the speeding rider presented his full right-side profile, the SAS shooter announced, "Right thigh. Through and through," and pressed the trigger.

The only indication Axe had just discharged his suppressed rifle was the subtle rocking back and forth of his upper torso.

Still training the minigun on the squirter, Skipper saw the spritz of blood and witnessed the rider's right leg leaving the peg. By the time the damaged leg was toe down and being dragged limply along the pavers behind the slumping rider, the bike had adopted a serious death wobble and was leaving in its wake an oil slick.

A total of three seconds elapsed between the disabling shot and the bike and rider going down hard in front of the crease in the fence. As the rider spun away in one direction, arms and legs flopping as if all control of them was lost, the bike skittered off in the opposite, shedding parts and marking the white walkway green wherever the camouflage paint came into contact with it.

The rider was arrested by the fence a couple of yards short of the opening. The bike was not. It hit the fence a few feet to the right of the unmoving rider, opening up the seam and becoming wedged there.

Lopez saw the Zs take note of the rider and begin a slow march towards him.

"Murphy just arrived," Griff said. "The fence is breached."

Seeing a few of the dead go to ground by the motorcycle and start clawing their way through the fence to get to the rider, Lopez said, "Axe, *do not* let the Zeds get to the rider."

Axe said nothing. He was busy slinging lead downrange at the prone zombies.

Addressing Skip, Lopez said, "There's more Zs on the way. Think you can eliminate them without dinging the rider?"

Skip said, "Negative."

Coinciding with rapid-fire reports from Axe's rifle, the pair of Zs clawing their way up the rider's legs went limp. More Zs fell as Axe shifted aim and emptied the rifle's magazine.

Struggling to get free of the corpses piling on, the rider lost hold of the sidearm he'd been trying to bring to bear. As he groped the ground blindly in search of the lost pistol, the already compromised run of fence bowed inward.

Cold ball forming in his gut, Lopez said, "Skipper, we need him alive for questioning. You have got to take the shot."

Considering the number of dead things drawn to the scene by the harmonic rotor thwop and initial minigun fusillade, it was a wonder the fence still stood.

"Going hot," Skipper warned a half beat before the minigun came alive with the sound of a thousand angry hornets. Aiming head-high to the gathering throng, he walked a three-second burst left-to-right across the fence. When the crew chief finally took his finger from the trigger, the sidewalk and ground opposite the downed bike and rider was littered with body parts and a couple of dozen twice-dead Zs.

Watching the surviving rider crawling on hands and knees away from the carnage, Lopez said, "Ari, how close can you get us?"

Eyes scanning the ground all around, Ari said, "I'll put down right next to the fountain."

For the first time in a long while Lopez second-guessed the ace pilot, saying, "You think there's room?"

A wide grin appeared under Ari's visor. "If Evel Knievel can land his Triumph on that postage stamp, no reason I can't squeeze this old girl in there." Then, voice all business, he said, "Wheels down in ten."

Chapter 27

Raven followed Max around a corner and saw more people and activity in one place than she had since leaving Schriever Air Force Base at the end of summer. Though she'd been in the new capital for a few weeks, this was her first time seeing the fuel depot up close. It was huge. Larger than she imagined it would be, taking up a substantial chunk of real estate on the city's west side, maybe a mile or so as the crow flies from the government offices she had just come from.

She paused on the sidewalk by the depot's northeast corner, under a sign that read *Lang and Son Travel Plaza*, first and foremost on her mind: locating the man whose name was on the sign.

The former truck stop at the center of the bustling operation featured a trio of buildings, all adorned with colorful signage. The largest of the three buildings was a glass and metal affair with a flat roof bristling with antennas and satellite dishes. The building was bracketed on two sides by fuel islands sprouting a dozen pumps each. Parked on cement pads beyond the far island was a fleet of eighteen wheelers. Most of the tractors and massive tanks pulled by them were painted Army green.

The entire facility was patrolled by soldiers wearing dark-green camouflage uniforms. Razor-wire-topped fencing easily twice Raven's height surrounded the entire facility. The one entrance she could see was manned by two more soldiers carrying heavy machine guns. Behind the soldiers, a lone Humvee blocked the entrance to a Jersey barrier chute just wide enough to accept a single fuel truck.

Outside the north fence sat the remains of a burned tank trailer. It rested on melted tires, its once-gleaming metal skin misshapen and soot-streaked. The ground and foliage all around were scorched black.

As Raven keyed in on graffiti marring parts of the tank's polished skin untouched by fire and soot, a garage door on a peripheral building rolled up and a man emerged from the gloom. Shielding his face against the rising sun, he crossed the distance toward her. The slow and deliberate gait suggested to Raven the *man in charge* may have just found her.

Wisps of gray hair wormed from under a trucker's hat bearing the truck stop's stylized L&S logo. The man's face was mostly obscured by a bushy silver beard, his nose and ears red from exposure. And though he looked to be Duncan's age—pushing sixty for sure—he wore the uniform of a much younger man: black Converse All Star high tops, distressed blue jeans sporting a sharp crease, and a puffy North Face parka one shade south of safety-orange.

"Jon Lang," said the man even as he was still a dozen feet away. His accent suggested he was from the southwest; Texas or Oklahoma was Raven's best guess.

Omitting her well-known last name, she said, "My name's Raven. Pleased to meet you."

Stopping close enough to the fence to be heard over the daily activities without having to raise his voice, Lang asked her if she was lost.

Raven shook her head. Though she hated liars and refrained from telling even little white lies, what she was about to tell Jon Lang was the type her mom would have called a *whopper.* Nevertheless, though it didn't make her feel any better, she figured her dad would put the fib into the *work smarter, not harder* column.

Pushing all that from her mind, she said, "Miss DeAngelo from Restoration sent me. I'm heading a youth group whose goal is to eradicate graffiti from every building inside the walls."

Hands going to his hips, Lang said, "DeAngelo, huh? I've dealt with her. Amazing your head is still sitting atop your shoulders. She's a—"

Interrupting, Raven said, "*Ballbreaker.* I know. Yes ma'am and no ma'am only goes so far with her."

Having vetted the interloper to his liking, Lang moved closer and threaded his fingers through the chain-link. Nodding toward the wreckage, he said, "We've been hit by the taggers. Preceded the bombing, but I'm not entirely sure they're connected."

Raven said, "Bombing? The explosion that happened just after Christmas?"

Lang nodded.

"Crier said it was a careless smoker."

Lang shook his head. "That might be the party line. But it's certainly not what the Army EOD guy told me. He said it was some kind of limpet-type explosive. It could have been attached anywhere. That it was remotely triggered suggests someone was nearby and watching when it exploded." He glanced at the blackened sidewalk to his left. "We're just lucky the driver parked it outside. Another plus … the EOD guy said that whoever did this didn't know where to place it on the tank to achieve maximum damage. Springs Fire Station is just around the corner. They had it under control in no time." He paused and returned his gaze to Raven. "Now what can I do to contribute to *your* cause?"

"All we need is something strong enough to remove paint from wood, cement, brick, and steel." She made a face, then added, "A wire brush would be useful."

"You got it," Lang said, gaze narrowing. "What'd you say your last name is?"

"I didn't."

"You're Raven Grayson, aren't you?"

"Apparently my dad's reputation precedes me."

Lang smiled. "Apparently, it does. And it makes sense what you're doing. We need more young people like you who care about the little things. Caring about the little things leads to giving a rip and acting on the big picture stuff when you get older. I bet you're going to follow right in your pop's footsteps. Do great things for this nation."

Raven said, "I just try to do my best with what I've got."

Lang regarded Max.

"Your dog made it through all this?"

Raven nodded.

Lang crouched to get to the dog's level. "What's his name?"

"Max," she replied.

Snorting as he rose, Lang said, "That's mighty original."

"He adopted *us*," Raven noted. "And he arrived with his undead human family. I put them all down and freed him from his duty. His name was stamped on his tags."

Lang smiled at that and shook his head. "Strange times we're living in. I'll collect your supplies. I think I have an old pack my son brought back from the Sandbox. He'll never use it again. Be right back."

Raven said nothing. However, the younger Lang's fate was on her mind as she watched the dad walk off toward the same garage he'd emerged from.

Chapter 28

As Ari threaded the Ghost Hawk between a pair of opposing palms, in his mind's eye, he was seeing Evel Knievel's red, white, and blue motorcycle hitting the very spot on the ground he was about to put down on. He remembered the daredevil flying over the handlebars when the bike's rear tire came up a yard short on the landing. And much like the rider Axe had just winged, when Evel and *his* bike parted, the bike continued on by itself for a short distance before gravity and inertia working together brought it down on its side and sent it spinning away, out of control, toward the gloomy maw of a nearby parking garage.

The same parking garage he could see out Haynes' cockpit glass. Doing a quick double take, he learned the garage was home to a dozen or more high-dollar supercars. There were Lambos, Ferraris, Aston Martins, and Bentleys. All were backed in and lined up contrary to the painted-on yellow lines.

Haynes whistled. Pointing to the garage, he said, "Looks like Iron Mike's been doing some car shopping."

Concentrating on nestling the Ghost Hawk on the limited real estate still a dozen feet below her wheels, Ari acknowledged that he'd spotted the shiny, multi-colored collection of rides each costing six and seven figures before money and the status that came with being wealthy lost all meaning. Craning to his right, he went on, "How's the seam in the fence, Skip? Is it holding?"

Over the shared comms, the crew chief said, "Affirmative. But barely, and more Zs are inbound."

"Cover the no-man's land," Ari ordered. "Pay attention to the blind corner at your two o'clock."

Skipper nodded, then turned all of his attention and the Dillon's still-smoking business end on the narrow slice of Caesar's Palace courtyard he was tasked with covering.

"Pale Riders are ready to deploy," Lopez said. "Egressing starboard. Griff and Cross will secure the lobby. Me and crack-shot Austin Powers will prep the rider for transport."

As they gave their weapons and gear a final once-over, Griff and Cross couldn't help but snicker at the Austin Powers reference.

"Not very original, boss," responded Axe just as the helo's wheels came into contact with the ground. "But way better than the bullshite Benny Hill remarks Griff was going on with during the Salt Lake mission."

Griff was out the door first, saying, "At least I stopped short of giving you a few fanny slaps to the back of your head."

Hitting the ground running, a severe forward lean to his upper body, Cross followed in Griff's footsteps, M4 at a low ready, head on a swivel.

M4 in one hand, medical kit in the other, Axe said, "Good thing for you, mate," and bailed out after Cross.

Patting Skipper on the shoulder as he jumped from the helo's open door, Lopez said, "Schriever TOC, this is Whiplash Actual. I have the ball."

After a brief pause, there was a short burst of static on the open net and a captain identifying herself as Jensen acknowledged the handoff.

"Whiplash Actual," came a second female voice, "this is Oracle Actual. We're working hard to get a bird in position for you. For now, though, we *do not* have eyes on you. Proceed with caution."

Recognizing the call sign as that of freshly minted One-Star Brigadier General Freda Nash, commander of the 50th Space Wing, Lopez said, "Good copy … Whiplash Actual out."

In Jedi One's left seat, Haynes divided his time between watching the fence off his left shoulder, the garage entrance, and Griff and Cross as they picked their way across the courtyard fronting Caesar's Palace.

Now and again, as the two-man team covered the hundred yards or so to the short stack of stairs fronting a covered valet area, they would stop and take cover behind the trunk of a palm tree or one of the massive stone planters dotting the property and conduct a hasty visual recon of their entire surroundings. To say the pair of Pale Riders were methodical in their approach would be a vast understatement. And though Skipper's short burst from the Dillon had likely killed the other rider or injured him so severely that he was knocked out of the fight, Griff and Cross were taking no chances as they made their way to the covered drive.

Weapons shouldered and horizontal to the ground, the Delta shooters entered the shadow of the covered area and pressed themselves flat to a supporting column. Haynes watched the point man, Cross, communicate something to Griff using only hand signals. After Griff nodded in agreement, he fell in behind Cross and together they set off across the covered drive.

The two shooters moved in unison, rapidly covering the twenty feet or so across ground littered with broken glass. After a barely discernable pause at the threshold to the gloomy lobby, one at a time, their movement fluid and smooth, the men poured through the opening nearest to them and disappeared from sight.

In Jedi One's right seat, Ari's attention was focused on Axe and Lopez as they closed in on the fallen rider. Though their options for cover diminished greatly the closer they got to the fence-lined sidewalk, Alpha Team's carbines were always aimed at the prone form atop a rapidly spreading pool of blood.

Eyes never leaving the men on the move, Ari smothered his boom mike with a gloved hand. "You know," he said to Haynes, "after Evel cleared the fountain, he came down on this very spot."

Seeing Lopez and Axe reach and quickly strip a rifle from the fallen rider's back, Haynes swiveled his head in Ari's direction. Covering his boom mike, he said, "It's also the spot where Evel almost *died*."

"C'mon," Ari shot, "he *only* broke just about every bone in his body and lapsed into a month-long coma. I'd hardly call that"—he made air quotes with his free hand—"'*almost dead*'."

152

Back to watching the hotel entrance, Haynes said, "The coma rumor was just a promotional stunt. Saw that in a documentary a few years back."

The coma talk steered the conversation to Cade Grayson and started a back and forth about how resilient the man was.

"They say guys like him are just hard to kill," Ari said.

"Even though I've known Wyatt for only a short while," Haynes replied. "From all I've seen, I agree with you one thousand percent." He took his eyes off the hotel entrance long enough to fix Ari with a concerned stare. "I've heard grumblings amongst some of our customers about him not being fit enough to return to the teams."

Looking side-eyed at his left seater, Ari said, "Not these guys. They've bonded. There is a true brotherhood about them. If Wyatt wants back in, he *will* make it happen." He paused. "And they will accept him. Of that I have zero reservations."

Haynes said nothing to that. He didn't know all the history the two men shared. So he kept his mouth shut and focused solely on his slice of the pie.

As Cross entered the lobby, the stink of feces and metallic tang of spilt blood hit him full on. It rocketed him right back to an op gone bad. Only thing missing was the snap-crackle of incoming rounds and moans of the gut-shot breacher taking half a dozen enemy rounds that could have just as easily struck him.

Breathing through his mouth, Cross swept the foyer with his eyes and rifle and found it clear of immediate threats. While the pillars to their fore were not wide enough to fully conceal an average-sized human, the sofa to his left and adjacent chest-high check-in counter could be providing someone with pretty good cover. Keeping his rifle trained on the former, he flicked his gaze left.

First thing Cross saw—besides the destroyed motorcycle and bloodied remains of its rider—was the yard-long MANPADS missile launcher.

Nodding at the unfired air-defense weapon, Cross said, "Looks like we just dodged a bullet."

Griff quipped, "We caught Murphy sleeping, is what happened."

On the floor next to the MANPADS was an oval puddle of vomit. Before Cross could point it out to Griff, the bearded operator was stepping in it.

"Christ almighty," Griff exclaimed. "I don't know what's worse… having to look at the contents of this dead Chicom's bowels or stepping in his buddy's fresh yack."

While Griff dragged the partial corpse from underneath the bike so he could search the tattered uniform for anything of importance, Cross was peeling off to search the rest of the lobby.

Finding only a length of what looked to be large intestine on the floor behind the sofa, Cross moved on to the combination concierge/check in counter. Muzzle cutting the plane first, he peered over the counter. Seeing only brochures and office supplies littering the floor, he called out, "Clear."

"Found a small notebook and laminated surrender card on this one," Griff called. "Can't believe the dumbass wasn't wearing body armor."

Finished negotiating the colorful miasma of human detritus to get back to the twisted bike, Cross said, "Stupid is as stupid does. Anything in the saddlebags?"

Griff shook his head. "This one was bingo on supplies. Probably another reason they let the horde go on autopilot."

Eyes roaming the lobby, Cross hailed Lopez. As he was relaying their findings, an out of place sound echoed from the far end of the foyer. Hinges in need of lubrication was his first guess. As he brought his suppressed M4 to bear on the spot in the dark he figured the noise emanated from, a stocky form, hands raised over its head, materialized from the gloom.

"Look what you did to my beautiful floors," called the man as he emerged into the light.

Griff had raised his M4 and grabbed some cover behind a marble column. Upon seeing that the man was unarmed, he relaxed, dropping his rifle to a low-ready position. As if on the outside chance there was another person with the same face tattoo and golden grin, Griff called across the distance, "Champ? That you?"

"I was at one time," said the man, chuckling. "How about you call me Mike." He turned to face the dark hall he'd come out of and clucked his tongue.

"I don't like this," Cross said, his M4 never leaving the stocky survivor.

"It's OK," Mike said as an adult tiger, its coat shiny and well-groomed, padded from out of the gloom. "He's domesticated. Harmless as a church mouse." He pointed at a hunk of meat on the floor and whispered something to the big cat.

The tiger stretched, then sauntered over to what looked to be a chunk of human thigh. It sniffed the item once, then trapped it to the floor with one big paw and started to chew on it.

Stomach going queasy on him, Griff said, "Have you seen these riders before?"

Nodding, Mike said, "Oh yeah. All the time."

Cross looked a question at the champ.

Griff asked, "How often?"

"Once a week I hear engine noise on the 15." He gestured to the boulevard. "And I've seen them from my balcony four or five times since late November when we all moved in."

The cat finished with the meat, licked the blood off the floor, then took a few tentative steps in Cross's direction, stopping only when it came across another substantial piece of dead Chicom.

"We better go now," Cross said. As he backed away from the feeding tiger, he mentioned the revival of Colorado Springs and invited the champ to relocate there if things went south here.

"We're staying here," said the former champ. "You should see the penthouse."

"I have," Griff replied. "In the movie."

"So much nicer in person," Mike said. "I've got enough supplies to last a year or two."

"Are you alone? Just you and Tigger, I mean?"

Wide smile revealing the picket of gold teeth, Mike said, "Got an uncle, a cousin, and a couple of Harrah's dancers upstairs. We'll make it." Looking to the tiger, he added, "His name is Buster. But I like Tigger."

Obviously awed to be in the presence of the former champ, Griff said dreamily, "What I wouldn't give for a selfie."

Lowering his rifle, Cross said, "You have got to be shitting me."

Griff shrugged. "If I had a phone. Just saying."

Calling Buster back to his side, Mike said, "I'm going to need you and your buddies to mend the fence before you all leave."

"I'll see what we can do," Cross said. "No promises." Shaking his head at the surreal encounter, he tucked the intel into a pocket and struck off for the rectangle of daylight.

Chapter 29

Lopez went to work removing the rider's helmet. It was a matte-black full-face number with a smoked shield.

Axe quickly checked for a pulse. Feeling the flutter of a heartbeat, he drew his blade and sliced through the strap to the rider's bullpup carbine.

As soon as Lopez peeled the helmet off the rider's head, he found he was staring down into the almond-shaped eyes of a twenty-something Asian woman. Her face was angular and flexed with equal measures hatred and pain. Her lips were pressed into a thin line, rimed with blood and quickly turning blue. "Holy shit!" he exclaimed. "This ain't no man."

"Doesn't matter," Axe shot, tucking the woman's combat knife into one of his own pockets. "She's still our enemy." He dove into the medical pouch. "I'm going to patch her up so we can take her in and wring her for intel."

Lopez said nothing. He was busy cinching a tourniquet above the entry wound high on the agitated woman's thigh.

Our enemy, thought Axe as he worked hard at holding the thrashing form to the ground on the growing pool of her own blood. *I've become a bloody Yank.*

Exasperated, Lopez said, "She's bleeding out. I think you nicked an artery."

Axe worked the glove off his left hand. "Let me check." As he probed the wound with two fingers, his face screwed up and he shook his head. "It's retreated," he said soberly. "I can't save her, mate. Only one way left to do this."

Axe rooted around in the gaping wound until he found what he was looking for.

As soon as the SAS man found the nerve and applied pressure, the Chinese soldier's body went rigid and her eyes rolled into the back of her head.

Having watched Cade Grayson do something similar to a renegade former SEAL at the lake house in Idaho, Lopez started firing questions at the woman in Mandarin.

Though Axe had one knee planted on the rider's shoulder, the other knee on her ribcage, and the hand not currently touching nerves pressing hard on her sweat-slicked forehead, it was all he could do to stay in control of her.

Lopez went quiet and nodded toward Axe, who understood the silent command and released pressure on the out of sight nerve cluster.

Body going limp, the rider's face worked into a wicked smile and a sharp retort spewed from her twisted mouth.

"Press again," Lopez said to Axe, and he switched to Mandarin and resumed the battlefield interrogation, saying, "I'll save your life if you answer me."

Body arched off the ground, the rider spilled her guts to Lopez.

"That was a good start," Lopez said to the rider. "Where?"

The rider went on with Lopez shooting back follow-up questions and Axe watching the nearby fence flexing under weight of the dead things pressing into it.

"You lied to get her to talk," Axe said.

"You're the one two fingers deep into her thigh and pressing the live wire," Lopez replied. "Got no room to talk, bro." In his ear he heard Ari report that Cross and Griff had just returned and were aboard the helo. Peering back at the dying rider's ashen face, he made a decision that would prove to haunt him for some time.

Rising with one arm around the rider's neck and the other hooked around her narrow waist, Lopez clean-jerked her off the ground. "Brace the fence with your rifle," he bellowed and hoisted the hundred pounds over his head.

Without question, Axe rose and shored up the chattering chain-link with his rifle's collapsed buttstock. "Fence is failing, mate. We have got to go."

Thinking only of the survival of the crew in the waiting chopper and the trio of Pale Riders under his command, Lopez fed the PLA scout to the dead.

With the screams of the doomed rider competing with the rising turbine whine at their backs, Axe and Lopez each searched a saddlebag for any useful intelligence. Coming up with a map and some papers scrawled with Chinese characters, the pair rose and began the long trudge back to their ride, which was already going bouncy on its gear and blowing fronds on the nearby palms into a frenzy with its rotor wash.

Chapter 30

The Antlers

Cade quickly learned the thirteenth floor of the Antlers was nothing like the tenth floor of Penrose. In place of the dim lighting, hushed voices, and occasional squeak of orthopedic shoes against vinyl flooring was a frat-house atmosphere where leaving doors wide open and yelling between rooms to communicate seemed the norm. Though he had never set foot in a frat house, Cade imagined this was what it would be like.

In less than an hour, Cade had become a recluse, opting to take his meal away from the others, in his room, where he could keep the shades drawn shut and allow his hearing to adjust to this new environment.

Now, an hour later, the vegetable omelet whipped up by Tran was not sitting well in Cade's stomach. While he'd been eating solid food for some time now, the meal consisting of powdered eggs and homegrown vegetables was a far cry from the tapioca pudding, Jell-O, and off-the-shelf protein drinks Glenda and the other nurses had been shoving down his gullet at Penrose. If he hadn't known any better, he'd have thought they were fattening him up for slaughter.

The vigorous workout on the exercise bike, he guessed, was not helping matters.

Cade removed his right hand from the tepid water, moved the champagne bucket aside, and dried the hand with one of the Antlers' monogramed towels.

While Raven's suggestion worked wonders once his hand was numb from prolonged immersion in the slushy snow and water mix, once the water rose above freezing, the tingling and phantom pinpricks returned. He made a mental note to give her credit for thinking of it once she returned from walking Max.

As the invisible hornets renewed their attack on his fingers, Cade's attention was drawn to the cold plate of food he'd set aside for Raven. Wondering what was keeping her, he threw on a fleece jacket, grabbed a long-range radio and his binoculars from his bag, then made his way to the Founders Suite's west-facing balcony.

Strangely, the communal living area was quiet. On one chair, both legs draped over its overstuffed arms, was Sasha. The top of a book and her mane of red hair was all Cade could see of her as he threaded through a maze of high-end furniture to get to the French doors leading to outside.

Closing her book, Sasha craned around. "You need anything, Mr. Grayson?"

"It's Cade. And thanks, but I think I'm good." He paused, hand on the door handle. "Where is everybody?"

As if reading from a pre-prepared list, Sasha said, "My brother and Taryn took Tran to get a tattoo. Glenda is at Penrose. Peter is down in the weight room, why is anyone's guess. He's already a catch and pretty buff. And I believe Duncan is downstairs with your daughter and Max."

"What are they doing downstairs?"

Sasha sighed and rolled her eyes. "Who do you think I am?" she shot. "Your secretary? Raven called on the radio while we were eating. She spoke with my brother, then asked to talk to Old Man. They *all* left pretty soon after that. Duncan took his pistol and a radio. Oh … and he also had his toolbox with him. That's all I know."

As the teen buried her face in her book, Cade stepped out onto the balcony and powered on the radio.

"Raven, Dad here. How copy?"

After a few seconds the radio hissed static and Duncan replied in her place. "Her hands are dirty, Wyatt. You still on restriction? Or did Mommy say you can come out and play?"

Having missed his friend's sense of humor, he stifled the urge to laugh. Instead he asked, "Where are you two?"

"In the park."

"Which one?"

"Your daughter's park," Duncan said. "She's adopted Antlers Park and is in the middle of a beautification project."

"I'm not following." Cade lifted the Steiners and glassed the park, left to right, stopping at the bench he knew Raven favored. Seeing that it was vacant, he said, "I don't see either of you."

"Wait one," Duncan said.

While Cade waited, he aimed the binoculars on a spot outside the west wall. Frozen mid-trudge, on the road between two boarded-up buildings, were about a dozen Zs. Though the cold had gotten to them, nobody else had. They all still possessed their right ears. Which meant he was staring at free credits for someone willing to break the two-mile rule and go and collect them.

Seeing a flash of movement near the park's northwest entrance, Cade panned the binoculars and spoke into the radio. "I got you, Duncan. You know, you waving your arm at me like that reminds me of the old cowboy sign in Vegas."

"Vegas Vic," replied Duncan, relaxing his arm. "He towered over the Pioneer Club on old Fremont."

"I don't know why it came to me," admitted Cade. "Ever since my emergence, I keep recalling the strangest stuff."

"I know the Pioneer well, amigo. All the money I gave to them over the years, figure I could have bought a house … or two."

Cade said, "I'm coming down," and strode back to his room to put on boots and gun up.

He had the elevator to himself for the ride to the lobby. The doors opened and he stepped out onto the gleaming tiled floor. Though he'd been in and out of the former hotel on several occasions, he was having a hard time remembering whether he needed to go left or right.

Seeing the woman security guard whose name he couldn't recall, he strode in her direction. After offering the woman a subtle nod, he hit the panic bar and pushed through the door to outside.

Hunching his shoulders against the sudden chill, Cade grabbed the handrail for stability. Eschewing the short run of stairs, he followed the wheelchair ramp to the sidewalk.

Navigating the recently shoveled sidewalk, Cade made his way to Antlers Park's northeast entrance.

Halfway to his destination, two things happened. First, legs going a little wobbly underneath him, he wished he would have checked his pride at the door and brought along the cane Dr. Cole insisted he use when venturing outside. Oh the ass-chewing he'd get if the doc could see him now, in the snow, one slip away from possibly finding himself back in ICU.

As Cade stood on the sidewalk, pausing to catch his wind and give his overtaxed leg muscles a moment's respite, Max ripped around the corner at full speed. Seeing his master, the dog skidded to a halt on the sidewalk.

Cade said, "Show off."

Max rolled his head left and right and back again.

"You'd make a damn fine owl."

Tongue lolling, Max just stared.

"Take me to your other master."

As if he understood fully, Max spun a one-eighty and sauntered back the way he'd come.

Chapter 31

After a short walk that seemed much longer than it actually was, Cade came upon a scene even Norman Rockwell would have a hard time transferring to canvas. Still, he interpreted it immediately. And if he had the chops to paint the scene himself, he'd call it "Foreman."

Duncan was seated on a bench in front of an antique locomotive and coal car. He was sipping from a thermos and watching Raven scrub graffiti from a low brick wall.

Looking up from her task, Raven braced her hands on her knees and flashed a wan smile.

Cade said, "Couldn't that energy be applied to something more important? I think a foraging mission outside the walls while the Zs are mostly immobilized would be a better return on investment."

"No wheels," Raven said. "Daymon's on a *date.*" Though she was wearing yellow rubber gloves and holding a scrub brush in one hand, she still made air quotes around the word "date."

Max had chosen a spot on the walk equidistant to the three humans and seemed to be following the conversation.

Duncan said, "Good to see the gimp out and about."

Ignoring Duncan's sad attempt at humor, Cade regarded Raven. "What about him?" he asked, hooking a thumb at his friend. "Can't he drive you in the Jimmy? You need to capitalize on every opportunity you get to work on your skills."

Duncan said, "Nope, muchacho. Glenda took my wheels to 'work.'" Mimicking Raven, he made air quotes around "work," because, clearly, he was doing nothing of the sort. "And speaking of your daughter's skillset ... you should see how she wields that Gerber pig-sticker of yours. Like a chip off the old block, this kid."

164

Cade shuffled through the snow to get to the bench. Taking a seat next to Duncan, he looked long and hard at the graffiti. It was obviously painted by a person with some kind of background in art. It consisted of a turntable, a glossy black vinyl record in motion, and a disembodied hand in the process of manipulating it.

A gold four-finger-ring with the word PAIN running across it hovered over the knuckles.

Below the turntable was a long string of archaic writing. If falcons, cats, dogs, and boats were interspersed with the strange characters, a person might think he was looking at ancient Egyptian hieroglyphics.

The longer Cade scrutinized the script, the more he felt as if he'd seen it before. Filing it to the back of his mind, he said, "Why are you doing all the work?"

Raven said, "Oh, I already put Duncan to work. He just finished a couple of minutes ago."

"I'm not the only one," Duncan muttered. "She's got people all over town doing her *bidding*. Raven's a crafty little lady. Go on," he said with a nod, "tell your dad about all the balls you currently have in the air."

Cade said, "What work were you doing, Old Man? Drinking coffee?"

"I was making sure your daughter didn't run out of paint remover."

Looking sidelong at Duncan, all business, Cade asked, "That is *just* coffee in the mug, right?"

Duncan raised his right hand. "Scout's honor," he said. "No more booze for this guy. Glenda promised to have Daymon and Wilson toss me on the street if I so much as *look* at a bottle of Jack Daniels." He took a sip of coffee. Steam wafting around his face, he lowered the thermos and said, "I believe the old gal's every word. You could say I'm a pole cat who, at this very moment, is livin' out life number nine."

Noting the toolbox under the bench, near Duncan's feet, Cade made a slow visual recon of the park, picking out a couple of things along the way and making some mental notes on other things that piqued his interest. Finished, he said, "If the person or people you hope to catch in the act know a thing about surveillance, they're likely going to spot those trail cameras." He regarded Duncan. "Great placement if you're dealing with Bambi or Zs."

Offering Cade his coffee, Duncan said, "Well, my eagle-eyed friend, what would Cade do?"

Now sitting cross-legged and fully invested in the conversation, Raven said, "In Duncan's defense, I didn't see them right away. And I knew what I was looking for."

Cade sipped from the thermos. Wiping his lips, he said, "I'm acting on the assumption the people who are doing this are the ones who tagged the tanker at the fuel depot. You did say the graffiti was, using your words, 'super similar,' right?" He handed the thermos back to Duncan.

Raven nodded. "It *was* the same color. Same line quality, too."

Duncan capped the thermos and set it by the toolbox. Regarding Raven, he said, "Was it this same …" he paused as if he was searching for the right word.

Speaking in unison, Cade and Raven said, "Gibberish?"

Raven smiled, pointed at her dad. "Jinx," she blurted. "You owe me a Coke, Dad."

"At this point," Cade replied, "after having been on a Diet Coke desert island for so long, I'd have already sucked down that Coke if I had it."

Smiling, Raven pulled her new backpack close to her. She dug around inside it and came out with something cupped in both hands.

Cade's eyes got big. "You didn't."

Duncan said, "If that's what I think it is, you know what the doc said about those."

Raven tossed the item across the divide.

Catching the silver and red can one-handed, Cade regarded Duncan. "Now who's being the mommy?" Again going real serious, Cade said, "If the people responsible for this vandalism also knew enough to build the bomb used to blow up the tanker, you need to let the authorities in on whatever you find out." He stared at Raven for a long three-count. "I don't want you taking things into your own hands. Are we clear?"

Raven nodded.

"I'm not saying you can't hold your own," said Cade. "Especially if it came to a gunfight. Mom trained you well. It's just that confronting them by yourself puts all of us in their sights. Wilson, Sasha, Tran … "

"My money is on our little Bird of the Apocalypse."

"No betting," shot Raven. "You know how Glenda feels about that."

Muttering something about being a grown ass man, Duncan rose from the bench, both of his knees sounding like popcorn popping as he did so.

"That's how I feel all over," admitted Cade, whose radio decided to come alive with a burst of squelch.

All at once, Tran's voice was coming from all three radios.

Duncan lifted his radio to his lips. Once Tran had finished informing them that he and the others were home and dinner would be ready within the hour, Duncan asked the man about his new ink.

"Long story," Tran replied. "I'll show you at dinner."

Duncan grimaced. "Copy that." Releasing the Talk key, he looked to Cade. "Hell, I could have used a good belly laugh about now. No doubt Tran chose something off their flash sheets. If I was still a betting man … my money would be on Yosemite Sam or the Tasmanian Devil. I'm sure he didn't get anything as prescient as that infidel tat across your back. Considering all that was going on at the time, that was a well-thought-out piece."

Not at all interested in what Tran decided to have added permanently to his body, nor the tattoo he got between one of his many deployments, Cade rose on creaky legs. "If I can make it upstairs before dinner," he joked, "I'm going up to squeeze in a quick nap."

Raven pushed herself up off the ground. "I'll walk you to the elevator."

Shaking his head, Cade said, "I got it. Besides, I'm taking the stairs."

Smiling wide, Duncan said, "That's the Cade we all know and love. Remember what you told me, amigo?"

Cade looked a question at the man.

Smile fading, Duncan went on, "Pain is just weakness leaving your body."

"That it is," agreed Cade.

"I may have a remedy for that," Raven beamed. She rooted around in her new pack and came out with two tubes of Ben Gay. Passing them out, she said, "Compliments of Lola."

Cade said, "Lola?"

"Keeper of the shop near the square," Duncan said. "And if Glenda didn't already have her meat hooks in me …"

"Ewwww," said Raven. "She's way older than you."

"Way older? I beg to differ," Duncan said. "Besides, nothing wrong with a man having a sugar mama."

"Well, she's a bit older than you. And you better take back the meat hooks comment, or I'm telling Glenda."

Cade stood there, head panning between Duncan and Raven. He couldn't lie, he was finding amusement in the old wiseass veteran being dressed down by his tween daughter.

At Cade's feet, Max had been doing the same.

Showing his palms, Duncan said, "Cool your jets, little lady. I was just jaw jackin'. I meant nothing of what I said. Consider it stricken from the record."

Cade loved the immediate capitulation on Old Man's part. And he really loved how his daughter had brought it about. Sowing a healthy dose of fear every man had of hurting the feelings of the woman they truly loved.

Suppressing a grin, Cade started off for the sidewalk, the hitch in his giddy up more pronounced than ever.

Weakness leaving my body.

As the banter behind Cade continued, the tug-o-war inside his tired mind was back, with the neat handwriting on the yellow sticky note in his pocket winning out over the Siren's call of the pillow-top mattress awaiting him on the thirteenth floor.

Chapter 32

Before entering the Antlers' lobby, Raven clomped her boots on the drive to remove packed snow from their lug soles. Pushing through the door, she held it open for a trailing Duncan.

"Thank you, Bird. I'm taking the elevator. If I don't make it to dinner, send out a search party."

Raven nodded, then regarded the guard on duty.

"Temperature holding?" asked the man she hadn't seen before. She didn't immediately answer. Instead, she slowed her gait and sized him up.

She figured the man was about her dad's age: somewhere between thirty and forty. That was where the similarities ended. While her dad was about five foot ten and a hundred and eighty pounds, this man was several inches shorter and looked to be carrying an extra hundred pounds.

Survivors with similar attributes had been showing up with increasing regularity. While news of the formation of the new capital was old, the overwhelming numbers of zombies migrating from the eastern seaboard and points south had made getting to Colorado Springs a deadly endeavor during the summer and fall in the heartland and high plains.

Small groups of survivors arriving on foot early on had told horrific tales of starting their treks east and north and west in convoys dozens of vehicles strong only to be winnowed down after coming up against zombie hordes and roving pack of marauding breathers.

Some who had shown up alone told of losing entire families. Adults, kids, pets—the ravenous dead did not discriminate.

Other survivors who had made it through the initial attacks, scattered into the winds, and then banded together down the road, had fared much better. These were the people showing up armed and driving liberated vehicles filled with food and supplies. And these were the people Colorado Springs needed if it was to become the place the President said it could be: a shining beacon of hope on the high plains.

What the once-dead city needed now, thought Raven, was to have a replica of the Statue of Liberty built and erected in the badlands outside the eastern wall.

What Colorado Springs didn't need at this point, was more survivors like this marshmallow squeezed into a rent-a-cop uniform two sizes too small for him. It was people like this Daymon called "Prestons"—named after the pudgy lawyer who'd damn near gotten him and her dad killed in Hanna, Utah way back at the start of the apocalypse.

With the Zs slowed or stalled out altogether, the chance of inadvertently running into the path of a mega-horde greatly diminished, survivors like the rent-a-cop, *Prestons* who had previously bugged-in, were coming out of the woodwork—so to speak.

Word on the street was that the population of Colorado Springs was likely to double or triple before spring.

Not happy with the delayed response, the man whose nametag read *Dagwood* rose and repeated his inane question concerning the weather.

After answering the man with a simple nod—more than she felt was warranted—Raven followed Max as he padded along the length of narrow, red carpet rolled out from the entry to the elevators.

Where is President Clay going to get the food to feed all the arriving mouths? was on Raven's mind as she left the carpet and made her way to the stairwell.

As if wondering why they weren't taking the elevator, Max paused by the stairwell door and glanced up at Raven.

Seeing the side-eye look directed her way, Raven said, "If my dad climbed all these stairs a week after emerging from a coma, I'm sure you can handle them." Half-expecting a yip or growl in response, and getting neither, she opened the door and shooed Max through.

Ninety minutes after launching from Caesar's Palace, Jedi One was making 180 knots and just forming up with a flight of two prototype RAH-66 Comanche helicopters. Recently rescued from a climate-controlled warehouse at Fort Rucker's U.S. Army Aviation Museum, the black helos were designed with stealth in mind and painted with radar-absorbing paint. Internally stowed weapons and landing gear blessed the two-seaters with a radar signature that rivaled the much larger Ghost Hawk.

With noise signatures nearly that of their big brother, the AH-64 Apache, their rotor hum and turbine whine could be heard inside Jedi One.

"I always wanted to strap on one of those," Ari stated. "I was angling for my shot all the way up until the day they axed the program." He shook his head. "That bird sure is easy on the eyes."

"Yeah," said Axe sullenly. "I always wanted to meet Mike Tyson. Give the cunt a proper verbal thrashing for beating Frank Bruno. My dad was devastated that our mate lost. Never saw him as angry as he was that day. School boy Nigel was affected by it all. Got into two or three fights over it before the school year was out. All due to an outcome I couldn't change."

Griff said, "That happened twenty-three years ago, Axe. Old history. Let it go, bro."

"What was he like?"

"Once he got over the mess Skip made of the lobby, he was pretty soft-spoken," Cross replied.

Axe shifted in his seat. Settling his gaze on Cross, he said, "Just like he was in the Hangover. Lisp and all."

Lopez had been looking out the ship's hip window, his attention divided between listening to the commentary and ogling the beautiful landscape hundreds of feet below the speeding Jedi ride. The wide-open expanse—Arizona, he guessed—was broken up by plunging canyons, debris-choked arroyos, and mesas bristling with brush and the occasional cactus.

Seeing a feathery ochre plume rising off the desert floor a good distance off the ship's starboard side, he broke in over the shipwide comms.

"You seeing that, Ari?"

"Roger that. Probably another mega straying over from the Plains states." Addressing Haynes, he said, "Get the FLIR on it."

"Copy that," Haynes replied.

A few seconds, later an image of the plume was filling up the rectangular partition centered on the glass cockpit.

Ari said, "Zoom, please."

Haynes complied, the action revealing a knot of Zs trundling across a barren landscape. Because the horde was coming straight at the optics, and the dirt kicked up was rising and spreading like the Haboob sandstorms Ari had encountered in the Sandbox, only the lead element, numbering in the tens of thousands, was evident on the helo's monitors.

Switching from shipwide comms to a secure channel shared only by Haynes, Skipper, and the Comanche pilots, Ari alerted the latter of his intent to break formation and get eyes on the horde.

The Comanche flight came back at once, the female aviator in the lead bird saying she would like to accompany Jedi One on its short jaunt east.

Though he didn't want to have to constantly monitor the ships on his flanks, Ari agreed, saying, "Form on me echelon right. Rolling in."

Both pilots acknowledged the order and the three-ship flight banked to starboard and dove for the deck.

Closing the distance at near maximum speed and barely a hundred feet off the desert floor, they covered the handful of miles in just a matter of seconds. Now within visual range of the mega-horde, Ari hauled back on the stick and applied left pedal. As his actions were relayed to the rotors, the bird slowed considerably and nosed around ninety degrees to port.

What was once a dot on the horizon trailing a dirt cloud was now a hundred yards to the fore and presenting as a seemingly never-ending train of flesh and bone in full locomotion. The desert soil kicked up by the pounding feet rose and roiled, the prevailing wind pushing it the length of the column.

Speechless, Ari spun the helo parallel to the horde, dipped the nose, and proceeded forward at a crawl, counter to the horde's direction of travel.

As the undead procession marched on, its ultimate destination a mystery to all aboard the three helos, it left in its wake trampled cacti draped with scraps of dirty fabric, bent and broken corpses leaking organs and black fluids, and a long, wide swath of churned-up soil a shade or two darker than the rest.

In the troop compartment, Lopez said to Cross, "What kind of numbers are we looking at?"

The former Special Agent to the President didn't look away from the window. Small Town Boy probably couldn't tear his eyes from the train of death, thought Lopez.

The helicopter hit a pocket of turbulence and jounced everyone in their seats.

Shaking his head, Cross matched Lopez's gaze. "I've seen nearly a million bodies packed between the Capitol Building and Lincoln Memorial. There were so many people on the mall at one time that some people resorted to wading into the reflecting pond to get from point A to point B." He regarded the mega-horde, stared hard for a beat, then said, "There's at least a million down there. Hell, maybe two million."

"That's a lot of credits," noted Griff. "Enough down there for us all to have anything we want. It'll be like having an open line of credit at the PX. Open bar. All the Rip Its you can drink, boys." He laughed at the thought of trading ears for the energy drink staple prevalent in the Sandbox. He could already see every operator billeted back at Peterson grimacing at the prospect.

Ari broke in on the comms. "You're crazy, Griff. I'm not taking this bird anywhere near that buzz saw of gnashing teeth."

Lopez said, "Ari, think you can just get us a little closer so we can better gauge their heading and nail down a GPS coordinate of their current location?"

"We're as close as we're going to get," Ari said. "As for the other stuff ... it's already done."

"What did you tell Nash as far as size estimate?"

"I sugarcoated it. Told her we're looking at enough deadheads to ruin the day if they find their way to Springs." Turning to Haynes, Ari said, "When we put down at Bastion, I get to piss first."

Nodding in agreement, Haynes pulled up the navigation pane, inserting it on the glass cockpit where the shocking image of the mega-horde had been.

Enjoying a tailwind since leaving Vegas had helped save fuel, which, in turn, made their stop at FOB Bastion to top off their tanks—and empty bladders—a relatively quick affair.

Forty-five minutes after leaving FOB Bastion, as the three-ship flight neared the southern end of the Rockies where the craggy mountains separating the high desert and high plains of eastern Colorado began to tail off, Ari ordered the Comanche pilots to tighten up their echelon-left formation.

After seeing the two ships suck in closer, he banked right and put Jedi One into a steep dive.

For the remainder of the flight, as the trio of black helos traversed the well-known danger zone where PLA scouts had once deployed MANPADS against Jedi One, Ari flew low and fast toward Springs, all of his senses on high alert.

Chapter 33

Raven stepped into the hall on the thirteenth floor of the Antlers with the Gerber in one hand and her free hand hovering near her holstered Glock. Though she knew that her dad and most of her people were home and getting ready for dinner, four months of surviving outside the wire had taught her that throwing caution to the wind sometimes came with a death sentence.

The noise filtering through the open door to the Founders Suite was not what she'd expected. Knowing that her dad was recuperating from his first full day home from Penrose, she figured the others would be mindful of that and keeping mostly to themselves.

When Raven broke the threshold, she saw that a long table had been moved into the shared room. It sat parallel to the bank of west-facing windows and was set with fancy service and smartly folded linen napkins. In the center of the ash table were bowls and plates loaded with the type of foods that—before normal was set on its ear by the Omega virus—used to grace the table for a normal Sunday dinner at the Grayson home.

Seeing Raven come through the door, Sasha held up a spoon heaping with pasta. "Smell that? That's *real* Kraft macaroni and cheese." She made a show of licking her lips. "I'm going to eat real slow and savor every bite."

After nodding and flashing the teen a half-hearted thumbs up, Raven took stock of who was present and who was not.

Duncan had taken the elevator up and staked out an overstuffed chair facing one of the many floor-to-ceiling windows overlooking Antlers Park. From the way his head was positioned, chin nearly touching his chest, she couldn't tell if he had immediately nodded off or was reading a book opened up on his lap.

Tran had commandeered the other chair by the window. He looked up, flashed her a smile, and said, "Just in time for dinner, Miss Grayson." As he rose from the chair, his gaze dropped to her hands and lingered there for a beat.

Regarding Tran, she said, "Dinner can wait. What'd you find out?"

"One of the tattoo workers had the same color paint on her hands as you do on yours."

"You sure it wasn't tattoo ink?"

"Positive," Tran replied. "Though my Chinese is rusty, I heard them talking about their artistic conquests." He made a face. "They didn't call it graffiti, though."

Duncan rose from the chair. Setting aside the hardbound copy of *War and Peace* he'd been reading, he said, "The artists don't wear gloves while they're doing their work? That's got to be some kind of health code violation. Hell, the way the new mayor is reconstituting bureaucracy in this town, if they don't have a law on the books, it's soon to come down the pike."

Tran stirred whatever was in the largest of the half-dozen pots of food arranged randomly in the center of the table. Finished, he said, "I saw her fingers when she changed gloves. They do that between clients."

"I'm convinced," Raven said. "If there isn't a Mandarin word for graffiti, what do they call it?"

Tran said, "Oh, they do have a way to say graffiti. It's *tu ya*. But they didn't refer to it as such. They called it *xiao xi* which translates roughly to 'messaging' in English."

Sasha regarded Raven. "Any idea why they just don't call it graffiti like we do?"

Raven shrugged, deferred the question to Tran.

Tran said, "Maybe it's a cultural thing. But I think it's just young people being lazy."

Believing Tran's "young and lazy" theory to be a dig at her and the others in the under-thirty crowd, Sasha shot the man a sour look.

Duncan spared Tran the teen's wrath. "What's really on my mind," he said, "is what kind of tattoo you chose to take to the grave with you. I'm guessing you got something off their flash wall. A cartoon character?"

Smiling, Tran shook his head.

With a cock of the head, Duncan said, "Barbwire?"

Tran said, "Go fish," and stirred the food in another one of the pots.

Throwing his hands up, Duncan said, "Just show me the darn thing, already."

Tran hitched his sleeve up. He picked the corner of a bandage, then pulled it away, exposing a toned bicep with fine black markings on it. Some kind of salve slathered on it really made the line work pop.

Duncan moved in to get a better look. Lifting his aviators, he smiled and fixed Tran with a look of incredulity. "Is that what I think it is?"

"Yep," Tran said. "It's Buddha. Just the outline... for now. I almost passed out when the needle touched my skin."

"Should have gotten a badass samurai warrior or a Sun Tzu quote," proffered Duncan. "'Cause Lord knows you're no longer a pacifist."

"Maybe on the other arm," answered Tran. He winced as he smoothed the tape back down on the angry red skin bordering the tattoo. "I'll have to get through this one first."

The door to the hallway opened. Wilson and Taryn walked through wearing matching Black Diamond backpacks, pistols on their hips and compact black submachine guns in hand. He took her pack and coat, then shrugged his gear off. The coats went in the closet along with the packs and pair of identical Heckler & Koch MP5 submachine guns they'd found in the back of an SUV abandoned on a side road southeast of Bear River. The vehicle had been one of three brand-new Tahoes left parked in a neat line on the shoulder, their gas tanks bone dry. Given the amount of camping gear and sentimental items—photo albums, family portraits in frames, stuffed animals and the like—that had been left behind, it looked as if the owners expected to return with fuel and resume their journey.

The accumulated grime on the windshields and side windows had pointed to failure.

Wilson had taken the red Tahoe for himself, leaving Taryn alone with Sasha in the Raptor for the remainder of the overland trip to their new home.

Taryn pulled her fleece sweater over her head and tossed it on a nearby chair. Both of the nineteen-year-old's arms, from wrists to biceps, were wrapped with white bandages. Looking to Tran, she said, "You almost blew our plan out of the water with your passing-out routine."

"Wasn't a routine," Tran admitted. "That needle hurts real bad. When the girl asked if I wanted to lie on their couch and gather my strength so she can finish, I figured it would allow me to be a fly on the wall. To listen to them talk with no angry machine buzzing in my ear."

Looking to Taryn, Wilson said, "Give the man credit. It worked out as planned." Addressing Tran, he added, "Way to improvise."

Duncan shot Wilson a questioning look.

Wilson said, "Taryn already had the appointment to get some color added to her old tats. It was Raven's idea to have Tran tag along and try to find out if any of the artists were involved with bombing the fuel truck. It was Tran's plan to actually go ahead with the Buddha tattoo."

Taking a seat at the table, Duncan said, "I have a feeling Bird has an ulterior motive." He glanced sidelong at her. "Perhaps she wants to bring her taggers to justice, too."

Raven shook her head. "After talking with the nice man who owns the truck stop, I want to help catch whoever is responsible for destroying one of his trucks." She thought, *And then I'll follow the trail to the taggers, who are probably one and the same.* If Murphy stayed away and it all worked out as planned, she would—as her dad liked to say—be killing two birds with one stone.

Tran said, "I'm sorry, Miss Raven, but I have nothing else for you."

Duncan picked up his fork and knife. Pointing the knife at Raven, he said, "Connecting the tattoo crew to the spray paint was a good start. Now you've just got to catch them in the act. You do that

… get their ugly mugs on one of the trail cams, then you can get Chief Riggleman involved. Tell her all about your theory and let her run with it." He turned his attention to the pot on the table. "Now that that's sorted—can we eat?"

Raven wasn't hungry. Planting her elbows on a chair by the window, she looked out over *her* park. Nothing moved down there. She saw only the tracks in the snow left there by her, Duncan, and her dad.

The sun cast the park in a warm orange glow as it slipped behind the craggy outline of Pike's Peak.

Fixated on a clutch of rotters just outside the west wall, Raven said, "Where's Daymon and Glenda?"

"A young woman just arrived from San Francisco went into labor," replied Duncan. "She's only seven months along. Glenda volunteered to stay and help out in the NICU in any way she can."

"She's a good lady," Raven said. "Always thinking about others first." She made a face. "My mom was like that."

Making her way to the table, Sasha said, "Daymon knows what time we're eating. He even asked if he could bring his new squeeze."

"That kid rebounds fast," Duncan noted. "Heidi's been dead what … a month at most?"

Pinching away fresh tears, Raven said, "Anyone seen my dad?"

Sasha said, "Not since he came back from downstairs with a *Diet Coke* in hand. Been real quiet over there for an hour or so." Regarding Raven, she asked, "You know where a person can find another one of those? And don't tell me to check the vending machines."

Flashing a half-smile, Raven said, "For the tenth time … I was joking. I pulled that on you last week. Let it go, Sasha."

Wilson had already nabbed a seat at the table next to Taryn. Taking advantage of the opening, he said, "The last time Sash truly let something *go*, I was in the middle of changing her diaper."

It started with Duncan—just a semblance of one of his trademark cackles. After Taryn buried her face in her hands and snorted, the flood gates were open and everyone present—save for Raven and Sasha—had a laugh at the teen's expense.

Mouthing "Sorry" at Sasha, Raven closed the blackout curtains, then left to find her dad.

Chapter 34

Cade stood in his room at the foot of his bed, staring intently at an interior wall. The four-by-six mirror that used to hang on the wall above the waist-high walnut dresser was now tucked away underneath the bed. In its place were a dozen pages torn from a 2012 Antlers Hotel calendar. There were no pictures featuring the hotel, its amenities, its once-manicured grounds, or the Colorado landscape one could expect to see outside one of its many windows. Instead, Cade had torn out only the pages representing each individual month and pinned them to the wall with pushpins taken from the bulletin board in the Antlers' employee breakroom.

On the dresser top was a handful of different-colored Sharpie pens he'd liberated from a drawer at the front desk.

The page for the month of January was at eye-level to him and had already fallen under the pen.

After consulting the 2012 Farmer's Almanac open on the dresser before him, he selected a red pen and made some additional marks on the page. Moving on, he circled days in February, March, and then April.

There was a knock at the door between the adjoining rooms.
"Who is it?"
"Boo."
"Boo, who?"
"Don't cry, Dad. It's me, Raven."
Cade said, "That was a groaner," and threw the lock.

Raven entered the room, slipped past her dad and stepped over the treadmill. Immediately her eyes were drawn to the wall to her right.

Closing the door, two things occurred to Cade. First, having just gotten a good whiff of whatever food was being consumed in the nearby Founders Suite, his stomach growled and he remembered he hadn't eaten for some time. Then, seeing the last rays of the westering sun playing across the treadmill's chrome supports, he realized he was no longer at Penrose and that nobody would be coming around to serve him dinner. It also dawned on him, in order to not draw the ire of the handful of other tenants calling the Antlers home, he needed to close the blackout drapes before the sun slipped entirely from view.

The former didn't break his heart. Though the skeleton crew keeping Penrose running meant well, not a person among them knew how to cook. Cliché as it may be: Bad hospital food had survived the zombie apocalypse.

The latter set him somewhat at ease. Because—walls or no—going from living in subterranean quarters at the secluded Eden compound to a penthouse in the sky was going to take a lot of getting used to.

After pulling the curtains together, Cade regarded Raven. She was standing as he had been moments ago: hands on hips, head tilted back and scrutinizing the items on the wall. Eyes still roaming the months of the year, she said, "Did you eat?"

"I got sidetracked with *this*."

Sounding a lot like her mom issuing one of her edicts, Raven said, "You need to eat, Dad. And you should be sitting down while you're doing whatever *this* is."

Cade told her about the message from Nash he'd found scribbled in the fold on the rear of the sticky note.

"So you're going on a mission?"

Cade shook his head. "Not as far as I know. Nash was just being courteous. Giving me a heads up in case things get hairy around here."

"So a spring offensive by the Chinese. That's when the dead are supposed to get real active again, too. That would really suck having to deal with a determined enemy *and* a mindless flesh-eating enemy all at the same time."

"Couldn't have said it better myself."

"So Lopez nudges you into learning Chinese. Who's to say Nash isn't behind it? She's always dragging you back in."

"Can't blame her. I'm always a willing participant," admitted Cade.

Pointing at three dates circled at the end of January, she said, "What's so special about these days?"

"When is the best time to attack your enemy?"

Raven answered with no hesitation. "Zero dark thirty. The hours between midnight and dawn when their senses are dulled, or, better yet, when they're all asleep."

"Exactly. I call it throat slittin' time."

"Zero dark thirty happens every night. Why did you mark those specific nights?"

Cade sat down on the end of the bed. He looked to Raven. "Give it some thought."

"It has to do with the lunar cycle, doesn't it? And the farmers knew their stuff and put it in that book."

Cade nodded. "The lunar phase is the shape of the illuminated portion of the moon as we see it from Earth. I'm just consulting the Farmer's Almanac to find out what day of the month the night sky will be darkest." He studied her face. Could see the gears working inside her head. He asked, "What's the opposite of full moon?"

Raven bit her lip. After a beat, she said, "Sliver moon?"

"Close, but not exactly. You're thinking of the crescent moon. The opposite of full moon is called new moon. That's when it's not visible from our hemisphere. During the days bracketing the new moon, it goes from waning crescent to new moon to waxing crescent. After those three days, the moon is in a waxing phase. Which means each night it shows up a little brighter than the last."

"Which means night vision isn't as much of an advantage as it is during the new moon."

Cade said, "Bingo. How about we get some dinner?"

Raven stood on her tiptoes. Placing a finger on the letters B and M, both written in green ink in the top right corner of New Year's Day, she said, "What's this mean?"

Cade said nothing.

Looking questioningly at her dad, Raven tapped her finger on the tiny letters.

Shrugging, Cade said, "Bowel movement."

"Ewwww," said Raven. "TMI."

Now Cade was the one wearing the quizzical look. "TMI?"

"It stands for *too much information*," she explained.

Cade hitched his eyebrows to show he understood.

Raven asked, "These other markings between new moons look like Lucky Charms marshmallows. What do they all mean?"

"They have nothing to do with cereal. These are all training days I hope to get in. I just chose the symbols at random." Pointing at week one and two, all the days marked with black capital letter Cs and red hearts, he said, "The first two weeks I've been told to take it easy, so I'm just doing cardio. I'll alternate between bike and treadmill."

Raven cocked her head as if to say *Slow your roll, Dad.*

Taking the body language to mean she was worried her personal space may be in jeopardy of a dad invasion, Cade said, "If I need to go in your room to ride the bike, I'll knock first."

Raven shook her head. "That's not the issue. It's just that I think you need to relax for a bit. At least until the headaches stop."

Ignoring Raven's misplaced concern, he pointed at the different symbols packed firmly into week three. "Blue moons are leg days. Yellow diamonds are low-impact cardio days: stairs, swimming, walks around the hotel. Red hearts are high-impact cardio days: running, medicine ball, weightlifting."

"What about the black spades?"

"Those are days I'll be away training at the team facilities."

"So you're back?"

He shook his head. "Not officially. I'll be working out on my own. Range time, mostly. If I do run some kill-house evolutions with them, it'll only happen when they're between missions."

You will be back was what she was thinking as she said, "Seeing you so motivated has me wanting to up my own exercise routine."

"Going to hit the stationary bike?"

Raven shrugged. "That or take Max on a walk."

"Sounds good," Cade said. "And the bowel movement thing." He paused for a beat. "Let's keep that in house. Just between you and me. OK?"

Giggling, Raven said, "Of course, Dad. Mum is the word." She gave him a firm hug and was out the door.

Part 2

Chapter 35

Antlers Hotel

In tune with her internal clock, Raven awoke just as the unseen sun was chinning itself over low mountains somewhere in the east and turning golden the high plains of Colorado.

As she had done every morning since her father's emergence, she moved Max off of her legs, rolled out of bed and padded across her room.

Arriving at the west-facing window, she gently parted the blackout curtains and dropped her gaze to the park below.

Shit!

Someone had painted up her park again. This time the graffiti marred the newly erected granite wall. It looked to be a portrait of a man, the face red and yellow and in profile. Below it was more of the strange writing she felt she had seen somewhere before, yet still couldn't place where or when.

"Fuck! Damn it all to hell!" she cursed under her breath. The eff word just slipped out. The rest was a saying of Duncan's that had rubbed off on her over the previous months. She cast a quick glance at the door separating her room from her dad's. Seeing that it was closed gave her a bit of relief. Though her mom was gone, and she was closer to thirteen than twelve, cursing was still the one thing her dad did not take well. Even if he didn't always comment when she slipped up, his displeasure was evident on his face every time she did.

After all her dad had gone through over the last few months, the last thing she wanted to do was heap more worry on his plate.

She threw on the clothes from the previous day. Dressed in all black, she donned her coat and laced on her boots.

She pulled open her door to the connected rooms and knocked softly. "Up yet, Dad?"

Stupid question. He didn't sleep much. And nearly every waking hour was spent getting his mind and body into what he called "fighting shape."

"Coming in," she warned as she pushed through the walnut door. It was never locked. Nor was hers.

First thing Raven noted was the soft hiss of running water. Not wanting to see her dad naked, she turned to exit the room. As she did, she couldn't help but notice the pair of Asics running shoes. They were identical in style to the first pair he had worn out on the treadmill. However, pointing to all of the miles pounded out within Colorado Springs' walls, these runners were dirty and scuffed.

With daytime temperatures average for early spring and the snow gone until autumn rolled around again, Cade had been doing his running exclusively outside.

After giving the shoes a cursory glance, her eyes roamed the wall. The calendar pages were no longer just marked up with icons denoting daily workouts her dad intended to complete. The days gone by all bore writing detailing his progress along the road to full recovery. Improvement or decline—it was all there.

Standing out starkly, due to the day-glow ink used to mark the string of days, were January and February's lunar cycles. Her dad's satellite phone had remained silent as those windows of missed opportunity had come and gone.

All of the previous days in March, save for the 13th, were outlined thickly with black ink.

On today's date were three icons: a red heart, a yellow diamond, and a black spade. The shoes on the floor were a good indication the former was finished. That her dad was taking a shower told her the yellow diamond was completed, too. He would never waste the water unless he had already finished his daily laps in the Antlers' pool. That left the black spade. Seeing as how training at Peterson usually happened in the afternoon, once the active Pale Riders had finished their own physical therapy regimens, it was likely her dad's next order of business.

Strangely, though, her dad hadn't noted the true significance of the day. If he didn't broach the subject first, she decided to stay mum and ask him about it before day's end.

Exiting the room, Raven's eyes fell on the gear laid out on her dad's crisply made bed. Both Glocks were present. Threaded onto the Glocks was the pair of suppressors made specifically for them.

The scent of gun oil hitting her nose all but confirmed he would be visiting the kill house on the nearby airbase.

The distinct sound of the pocket door sliding open reached her ears and she turned away.

"It's OK," Cade said, "I'm already dressed."

Stepping back into the room, a sheepish look on her face, Raven said, "I'm sorry to intrude. I just poked my head in."

"Mi casa es su casa."

Raven tilted her head and looked quizzically at her dad. "That's not Chinese."

He shook his head. "It's Spanish. Means my house is your house." Rubbing a towel over what passed for hair on his nearly bald head, he added, "What's on your plate today? More exploring on the north side?"

She shook her head. "I'm going out with the boys."

Cade made a face. "You see what they did to the park?"

"They sure did a number this time."

"Apparently your chat with Chief Riggleman fell on deaf ears."

Another of Duncan's sayings spilled from her mouth. "She's worthless as tits on a boar."

Grimacing, Cade said, "You watch your six out there. Don't go letting that little bit of paint left there by what I suspect were drunk teenagers take you off your game. Clear your mind and stuff those feelings before you leave the wire." After a short pause, he fixed her with a hard stare. "Understood?"

Nodding, Raven said, "Looks like you're training with the team today."

Waving a dismissive hand at the calendar, Cade said, "I'm just trying to keep the rust off, that's all."

Raven thought, *That's a load of bullshit!* She said, "How are your nails?"

Gazing at one hand, he said, "These old turtle-shell-looking things? They soften up after a long swim. Stay pretty tender for a while afterward. Won't be long until they're back to the way they were before all this."

Raven made a face as she took his hand in hers.

"Relax," he said, "your dad is going to be just fine."

She inspected the regrowth without saying a word.

Sensing the change in her demeanor, he said, "Besides, I always wear gloves when I go out."

Raven released his hands. "Aha!" she said. "We have confirmation. Does that mean you got *the call*?"

Cade shook his head. "I feel another swing and a miss coming up."

Shifting her gaze to the calendar, Raven said, "*Relax*, there's still ten days until the New Moon."

After a quick glance at his recently acquired Suunto, Cade started to lace up his newish Danner boots.

Though Raven thought she would never hope for the call for him to go to actually happen, she did now. Seeing her dad with nothing to do other than work on his recovery and learn new languages was beginning to weigh on her. For she now understood the need for the rush of adrenaline he was missing. She could feel herself going soft, her senses being dulled by monotony, even after just a few days of inactivity inside the walls.

For someone like her dad, a hard charger used to being downrange and riding the razor's edge, how it felt to be cooped up for as long as he had must be a thousand times worse than what she was experiencing.

Looking up, Cade said, "Want to help me stow my gear?"

Raven put a hand on his arm. Took ahold of the MultiCam blouse and drew him near. Brown eyes searching his, she said, "They'll take you back. After all you've given, all you've sacrificed … they have to. They have no choice *but* to have you back."

Cade said, "Whatever happens, happens," and drew her near and hugged her tight.

Unable to hold it in any longer, Raven said, "Do you know what today is?"

Smiling, Cade nodded. "I'm amazed you remember." He unfastened the chain holding his dog tags and took from it Brook's white gold wedding ring. He turned Raven's hand over and placed the ring on her open palm. The diamonds sparkled as they settled there.

Raven's eyes misted up.

"Would have been fourteen years today. Second best day of my life."

She looked a question at him.

"First best was the day we met you." He paused for a long while. "That's yours now."

Biting her lip, she nodded and threaded the ring onto her necklace.

"Now help me bag up my kit."

As if on cue, they both felt deep in their chests the subtle harmonic thrum signaling the arrival of the stealth Ghost Hawk.

Looking at the window, she said, "You're going now?"

"No," he answered. "The team's returning from an op. I'm just hitching a ride to Peterson."

"Why aren't you driving? You could take Wilson's Tahoe."

Wearing a sheepish grin, he said, "Houston, we have a problem. I left Wilson's rig there the other day."

"Why?"

"We were field testing a new fast attack vehicle. Lopez shanghaied me ... all of us, really, and tooled nearly to Pueblo. Since it was getting dark, and we were closer to here than Peterson, I had him drop me at the South Gate."

She said, "So this is his way of making it up to you?"

"Either that, or he has something else up his sleeve."

Frowning, she said, "Where are they going to land?"

Cade slipped on his pack and zipped shut his range bag. "They aren't. You know Ari ... always a flair for the dramatic. I'm getting picked up on the roof." Flashing her a smile, he said, "Please tell Wilson he'll get his baby back tonight."

I may just let him sweat it for a bit, was what she was thinking. She said, "Will do." Then stabbing a finger at the ceiling, she asked, "I don't think there's room enough for a helicopter to land up there."

Cade said, "Where there's a will, there's a way."

Rolling her eyes, Raven said, "Dinner at five?"

He said, "Wouldn't miss it for anything," and was out the door and heading for the stairs.

Raven waited until the door snicked shut, then picked up a pen and on the calendar drew a big red heart around March 13.

Chapter 36

To say Raven was pissed upon seeing the true extent of damage done by unknown entities stealing in during the night would be a vast understatement. In fact, she was livid. For the first time since her dad had emerged from his coma, she wanted to break something. For after having gone to Chief Riggleman more than once to voice her concerns and received from the no-nonsense forty-something with the soft drawl a promise to "put a clamp down on whose hands the paint ends up in" once again someone had desecrated her park.

It had been five minutes since the helicopter had plucked her dad off the roof. Though her vantage from the park hadn't been the best, she could have sworn the wheels hadn't even come out of the fuselage as the black aircraft hovered above the portion of roof where Tran's garden was to go in. One second her dad was standing on the parapet, the next a pair of men clad in camouflage and wearing helmets were hauling him aboard.

The smell of kerosene-tinged exhaust was just beginning to dissipate when her two-way radio warbled and Daymon informed her he was running late.

With time to burn, Raven decided to check on the trail cameras Duncan had installed for her weeks ago.

The first camera was secreted in a bush near the southeast entrance. She walked the short distance to where the path intersected the sidewalk. She found the camera on the ground underneath the bush, but it had been moved and stripped of its batteries. The person responsible had made a point of leaving the camera where it could only be found by whoever had placed it there.

Doubting the camera captured anything useful before being disabled, she inserted fresh batteries and powered it on. When the small screen came to life, the only captured image was the distinct outline of a hand flashing the camera the middle finger.

"Eff you, too, buddy," she said, powering the camera off and stuffing it into her pack. Adjusting the SBR on its sling, she rose and walked her gaze around the park. At the far corner was a light standard. Protruding from the pole was a metal box containing a *Walk/Don't Walk* signal. It was clear straight away, even from this distance, that someone had found the camera Duncan had mounted atop the box. Having come out of the factory with black, brown, and green leaves—a camouflage pattern she thought was called Mossy Oak—the camera now looked like it had been shit out by a unicorn. Painted in every color of the rainbow, the rectangular device stuck out like a second middle finger being directed at her.

In the middle distance, a pair of workers were already scrubbing paint from a wall they'd been working on for days. Only recently had the stonemasons resumed their work on the ornate base. By engaging them in small talk, Raven had learned the twenty-year-old twins were among the handful of lucky travelers who had survived the tragedy at the wall. They had been at the tail end of what had come to be called the Pueblo Diaspora and were literally snatched from the hands of the dead and dragged aboard a black helicopter returning from a mission somewhere southwest of Springs.

A week ago, when the temperature had finally crested sixty for the first time since November, Raven had spent an hour watching the young men encase the cement base in sheets of Italian marble and line the edges with rounded tile Duncan called "bullnose."

In the week since, even with the temperature dipping back into the forties and fifties, she had seen them out here on hands and knees, every daylight hour of every day, putting to use what they had learned in the family monument business. But instead of chiseling names and dates on individual tombstones, they were adding to the wall the names of hundreds of fellow travelers killed by the ravenous dead, taken all together that day the Pueblo Diaspora met two walls, one static and erected by workers, the other mobile and coming at them, relentlessly, with claw-like hands and gnashing teeth.

Still fuming, she struck off diagonally across the park, toward the tree she knew held another one of her cameras.

Chapter 37

The tree holding the third trail camera rose up over the antique locomotive on display on the west side of Antlers Park. Nearby, the workers kneeled on brick pavers, backs arched and scrubbing furiously at the fresh paint. If they had seen Raven take down the first two cameras, they didn't seem at all interested.

"'Clamp down on where the paint ends up' my ass," she growled as she eyed the camera perched on a branch high over her head. "Thanks a million, Chief Riggleman."

To get the camera set up on the branch a dozen feet off the ground, Duncan had climbed a ladder borrowed from the Antlers.

Raven was standing and staring up at the camera, wondering how she was going to get the ladder and carry it here by herself, when from behind her came the soft scuff of leather on stone.

At once the lizard part of her brain came alive. Honed from months of living one breath to the next, her first instinct was to go for the Glock on her hip and turn in the direction the noise had originated. Halfway through the turn, the Glock already clear of the holster, she heard a disembodied male voice say, "Need some help?"

By the time she'd finished the quick one-eighty, the Glock was pressed to her hip, its deadly end aimed where she guessed the man's midsection to be. Recognizing the man as one of the twins, she said, "Matt … Michael, whichever one you are … you *can't* go sneaking up on people like that."

Raising his hands, the man said, "Sorry. I'm Matt."

Lowering her pistol, Raven said, "What the heck were you thinking?"

"I wasn't," he admitted. "Guess I'm starting to forget how things are out there." He paused long enough to let his gaze roam the park from one end to the other. "It's this place," he went on. "It's special. Takes me back to the way things used to be. Back to when we didn't have to be so, so *vigilant.*"

"I get it," Raven said. "More than you probably know." Directing her gaze to the trail cam, she accepted his offer.

That brought a smile to the young man's face.

Holstering the Glock, she asked, "Do you have a ladder?"

Making a stirrup with his calloused hands, Matt leaned forward and presented it to Raven.

"You want me to step there?"

He nodded. "It's how me and Michael got into our tree house back home."

Raven remembered one of the twins mention that their home had been in Indiana but couldn't recall where. Instead of asking, lest it dredge up bitter memories, she braced one splayed hand on his muscled shoulder and planted her right foot on his clasped hands.

"Ready?" he asked.

"Ready as I'll ever be."

He bent his knees and counted down from three.

On "One" Raven put some bend in her knees. When she felt him rise up, she pushed off with her right leg and tilted her head backwards. Arms outthrust, she focused on the branch the camera was on.

Getting ahold of the branch with both hands, she chinned herself up and hooked one arm over the top. To find the leverage to pry the camera loose, she shimmied up and draped her upper body over the branch.

The camera came off easily.

"Drop it," Matt urged.

"Uh, uh," she said. While the thing did have a sort of armored exterior, she didn't want to risk losing any evidence.

He said, "I'll catch you, then."

"I can do this myself," she insisted.

"It's twice your height."

She thought, *So was the play structure at Creston Park back in Portland.* She remembered jumping from the top of that and surviving. Only, as she suddenly recalled, there had been several inches of bark shavings to brace her fall. In a split-second her thinking about the play structure brought back another memory: her first F-bomb. She'd been four or five at the time and was simply reading graffiti off the bottom of the play structure. The look on her dad's face had scared her at the time. The quick recovery on his part—a wide smile and the promise of an ice cream cone if she never said it again—instantly rocketed him back to exalted status.

Bringing her back to the present, Matt said, "I won't drop you. I promise."

"Move it," she growled and let go of the branch.

The landing was perfect. Maybe even something a table full of Olympic judges would award a mess of perfect 10s.

Matt was going on about how impressed he was with her display of courage when his twin laid into him for taking too long of a break.

"My break's over," Matt said. "Let us know what the camera picked up, if anything."

Raven followed him back to the monument and saw that the taggers had hit the hewn stone base that would eventually accept the statue honoring the Pueblo refugees who had gotten trapped between an overwhelming surge of living dead and the fledgling capital's newly erected walls.

As Matt rejoined his brother, Raven sat with her back to the wall between the two. It was wild how much alike they were: short, dirty-blond hair. High, wide brows over dark brown eyes. Both were average size, maybe five-eight, and dressed for the work they were doing: red flannel shirts, Carhartt coveralls, rubber knee pads.

"Hey," Michael said. "Sorry I lost it on Matt."

Returning the greeting, Raven said, "You ought to tell him you're sorry."

Matt said, "It's OK. I know he didn't mean it like it sounded."

The interaction between siblings called to mind a saying Raven heard often from her parents: *What's the most important thing?*

The expected reply: *Family.*

In response to Matt's earlier request, Raven said, "Since we're all affected by these tagging buttholes, I'll check the camera right now."

The brothers stopped what they were doing and sat against the wall, flanking Raven.

Pushing the camera's recessed *On* button brought the screen to life.

Matt was looking over her shoulder as a black smudge filled up the screen. He said, "Bad angle."

Peering down on the device from the opposite side, Michael said, "Bad light, too."

Raven said. "These things *never* capture anything useful."

Matt said, "This is what? Third time they hit the park?"

"Fourth," she spat. "And this time I got nothing but a middle finger, one camera painted like an Easter egg and this"—she tapped a finger on the screen—"image that would get me laughed off one of those ghost hunter television shows."

Michael shook his head. "You already took it to the law, didn't you?"

She nodded. "They don't care about property crimes."

Matt said, "Then I think you need to take the matter into your own hands."

Stowing the camera in her pack, she said, "My dad forbids it."

"Then send your dad after them," Matt said, smiling wide at the prospect. "I'm sure he knows how to sit still for awhile."

"Not funny," Raven shot.

"Not because of the coma," Matt said, his cheeks flushing red. "No, no, no. Not even what I meant. I was thinking about his profession. His … *certain set of skills*."

The *Taken* reference delivered with a terrible Liam Neeson impression earned Matt a questioning look from Raven.

"Everybody in Springs knows *who* your dad is. And what he does … or, did," Michael said. "I bet he even has night vision goggles."

I have NVGs, Raven thought as Matt stood up and regarded Michael. "We still have a lot of names to etch today."

Michael rose. "He's older by three minutes. I better do what he says."

Raven shrugged on her pack and slung the SBR. She followed Matt to the spot where there used to be just a cement pad. It had sat there forlornly in the center of the park, the only evidence pointing to its existence while the snow blanketed the ground the four lengths of rebar jutting skyward.

Seeing the full extent of the damage done by the taggers, she thought, *Man, these two must want to murder the people who did this.* Lord knows she did.

Speaking to Michael, she said, "Who is the guy they painted on there?"

Matthew said, "We think it's that old Chinese leader, Mao Tse-tung."

Not knowing a thing about the communist dictator, Raven said nothing. Instead she was hoping the twins were fed up with the tagging. *Maybe,* she thought, *this will be the straw that breaks the camel's back.* If only she could somehow convince them to go with her to Chief Riggleman's office in the BERR building.

Strength in numbers. And they could snap pictures of the damage and present them as evidence.

Yeah, that might get the chief to take her seriously.

As far as she knew, the brothers weren't getting paid. Not with credits, at least.

When Raven had first met them and asked why they were devoting so much time to the memorial, Michael had said with no hesitation that it was not only out of respect for the people whose names they were carving on the wall, but also for all of the family and friends they had lost during the early days of the outbreak.

When pressed about how they were able to work such long hours with no compensation, Matt had said that they were being put up in the Antlers and getting three squares a day at the BERR building chow hall.

They seemed to have all they needed. Which begged the question: How to get them on board?

In her head she heard her mom say: Just ask them.

So she did.

Chapter 38

Daymon had pulled up to the curb fronting Antlers Park five minutes after Raven had finished laying out her plan to Matt and Michael. Now, after a short drive north on Cascade Avenue, which took them through the Old North End residential district, past Penrose Hospital, and onward to the northernmost stretch of freeway barriers, they sat in the idling Bronco, eyeing the north gate and the stern-faced soldier walking their way.

"Whole nine yards," said Duncan. "You all know where that saying originated, right?"

The soldier arrived at the Bronco's driver's side window and asked for credentials.

Anticipating the request, Daymon had rolled his window down and was dangling his Golden Ticket at the soldier even as the man was still speaking.

His previous question unanswered, Duncan said, "I always forget about the *rules*." Muttering under his breath, he unbuckled and started to search in earnest for his pass.

After jabbing a hand into every pocket of his woodland-camouflaged jacket, then doing the same to his like-colored BDU pants, Duncan located the folded square of yellow paper in one of the cargo pockets.

"Got it," he said, passing the document over to the soldier.

"Here's mine," Raven said, thrusting her pass out Daymon's open window.

Wearing a bored expression, the soldier collected the slips and started back for the Airstream trailer he had come from.

Poking her head between the seats, Raven regarded Daymon with a puzzled look. "We're going outside the wire *first*?" she asked.

Busy watching the final undulations of the hula girl on the dash, Daymon nodded and killed the engine.

Crossing her arms, Raven sank back into the rear seat.

"Well," Duncan said, "anyone know the answer to my question?"

Great, it's trivia hour, Daymon thought. Shooting a sidelong glance at Duncan, he proffered a guess. "Something to do with football?"

"Close, but no cigar."

From the backseat, Raven said, "During the Second World War, linked ammunition for some airplanes came in lengths of twenty-seven feet. If a pilot used all of his ammunition on a strafing run, he gave the enemy *the whole nine yards.*"

The soldier emerged from the trailer with their papers clutched in his hand.

Struck speechless, Duncan remained quiet through half of the soldier's walk back to the Bronco. Finally, having processed Raven's lengthy answer, he turned slowly in her direction. "X gets a square, little lady." He paused for a beat. "How did you know that?"

The soldier was nearly to the window when Raven said, "Because, since I've known you, that's the fourth or fifth time you've asked the same question."

Wearing a sheepish grin, Duncan said, "I'll have to try and stymie you with a new one, then. Just you wait. I've got plenty more where that came from."

Daymon took the papers from the soldier and handed them to Duncan.

"What's it like out there?" Raven asked the soldier.

The soldier, whose name tape read *Prosser* and rank insignia put him very low on the 4th Infantry Division totem pole, quickly ran down the frequency of zombie sightings by zone, then warned that, given the absence of cold weather, encounters with "Glowers" outside the wire was happening with increased regularity.

Daymon said, "Bunch of little entrepreneurs up there. What's it like on the other side of the gate?"

Prosser said, "It'll be cleared of Zs before we let you out."

Raven leaned forward and looked out the front windshield. The angle wasn't good, so she pressed her face against the fixed window to her left and lifted her gaze to the walkway running atop the north gate.

A couple of dozen kids and teenagers stood shoulder-to-shoulder on the crowded walkway. They wore stocking caps and winter clothes and were armed with slingshots of many different designs. Most were the homemade items for sale in Lola's: surgical tubing affixed to crude wooden handles. Others were the type with bent metal tubing, foam grips, and extended forearm braces.

Many weeks ago, while culling dead outside the wire south of Springs, Daymon had mentioned having a slingshot of that type when he was a kid in Utah. He had called his a "wrist rocket" and had used it to such great effect against starlings and other nuisance birds that his mother's vegetable garden didn't require a scarecrow.

While rocks were plentiful here due to the excavating done to seat the cement walls, Raven assumed the kids were instead using the same tiny ball bearings she'd seen Peter shoot with his slingshot.

As Prosser about-faced and began the hundred-foot walk back to the Airstream, he barked an order to the kids on the wall.

At once the kids rose up, leaned over the parapet, and let projectiles fly. The action was so fast and furious that Raven imagined the sounds she would be hearing if she were on the wall with them: The *sproing* of taut elastic being released. The static-like *whizz* of ammo rocketing groundward. Hollow *thuds* as the stricken rotters fell in place.

Like the rimfire cartridges for the little Ruger 10/22 she had first learned to shoot with, these projectiles would be easy on the corpses. Upon entering an eye socket, they might bounce around a bit and destroy the brain, but there would be no splitting of skulls, no blood and brains to clean up afterward, and, most importantly: no loud reports capable of carrying for miles across nearby Austin Bluffs' Open Space.

There was no "stand-down" order delivered by Prosser as he neared the trailer. One second the kids were firing down off the wall, the next they were all turned inward and staring expectantly in his direction.

Slowing his gait, Prosser removed a radio from a pocket and lifted it to his lips. A beat later, a soldier in the guard tower was giving the rampart kids a thumbs up.

All clear, Raven thought.

"Putting the hurt on the deaders," Duncan said in front of a soft chuckle. "Never woulda thought we'd be revertin' back to Medieval-times tactics so quickly."

Prosser's go-ahead call started a flurry of activity. The bigger kids put down their weapons and hauled up the pair of ladders used to access their perch. In perfect unison—as if they'd done this many times before—they nosed the ladders over the parapet and allowed gravity to take them to the opposite side of the wall. Once the ladders were set, the smaller kids scrambled over the parapet and disappeared from sight. Done bracing the ladders for the first wave, the older kids followed quickly after.

Cracking open a bottled water, Duncan said, "Efficient little buggers, ain't they?"

Firing the Bronco's V8, Daymon said, "They're all orphans. They have to be industrious or they don't eat."

Duncan said, "Everyone's got to pull their weight."

Raven shot him a sour look. "That's harsh."

Daymon put Heidi into gear. Speaking to nobody in particular, he said, "This *world* is harsh."

"Well," Raven said, "I hope they're getting what they need."

Duncan craned around. "You of all people, *Bird of the Apocalypse*, should know that *hope* isn't a plan. Like you, these kids have a plan. And they and others like them are going to be the ones who pull this country back up by its bootstraps."

A few seconds after the majority of the kids had disappeared, the ladder tenders were back on the wall and hauling the ladders up.

The north gate doors began to part. As the vertical seam widened, it was clear the outer doors were already open.

Taking a cue from another soldier on the ground near the trailer, Daymon popped the clutch and drove through the gate in first gear, maybe five miles an hour, fast enough so that they all missed seeing the blood trails on the two-lane, but still slow enough so that everyone got a good look at the orphans' handiwork.

The scene outside the wall was far different than Raven had imagined. The kids were a blur of motion, stabbing and hacking away at the twice-dead Zs. There seemed to be a hierarchy, with the littler kids collecting ears and the bigger, stronger teens dragging and stacking the corpses.

They worked from the outside in. Now and again the stackers would pause long enough to let a girl, who looked to be ten or eleven, run a Geiger counter over the prone bodies not yet pounced upon by the ear collectors.

Following behind the slicers and stackers was another work detail comprised of the littlest boys and girls. Some were stooped over, hands on knees, and staring at the ground. Others were on all fours and probing the bare dirt with spades and screwdrivers.

By the base of the wall was a teen girl. She walked slowly away from the gate, sweeping a metal detector over the ground with metronomic precision. Following in her footsteps was a redheaded boy of about ten. He stopped when she did and went to work tilling the soil with a rake.

Raven tapped Duncan on the shoulder and pointed. "They're working together like a well-oiled machine."

After a brief pause, Duncan said, "Still looks to me like a bunch of chickens peckin' for feed."

"That's what I'd be doing if my dad—" She bit her lip and looked away.

"But he didn't leave us. And you're going outside the wire. Unlike the kids back there, you're free. Free to come and go. Free to *choose* your work."

Dabbing a tear, Raven said, "I feel bad for them."

"Don't," Duncan said, "because they're on this side of the grass. And there are untold millions of us who ain't."

Chapter 39

"Yep ... there's that smell." Eyes narrowing, Duncan grabbed the collar of his tee shirt and covered his nose with it.

The air just outside the gate was heavy with the stink of death, the main contributor the massive dump truck parked upwind from the killing grounds. Filled with way too many Z corpses to count, it sagged low on its heavy-duty suspension.

Daymon rolled up his window. It was no help. The old girl had rolled off the Detroit lines more than four decades ago and was a sieve compared to the newer, nearly air-tight rigs. Only way to fix the problem was to get away from the gate. So he grabbed second gear and matted the pedal.

Continuing down a two-lane lined by mature trees and cement Jersey barriers, he upshifted again and drew in a much-needed breath of fresh air.

Uncovering his mouth and nose, Duncan said, "Much better," and cracked his window a few inches. He remembered developing an immunity to the stench not too long after the dead had started to walk. It had been the same for him once he arrived in Vietnam. First thing he saw upon setting foot on the broiling tarmac was the multitude of body bags being loaded onto the 707 that had just arrived full of fresh meat for the grinder.

Now, after a few weeks on the inside, during which he was rarely exposed to the sickly sweet smell of death and decay, his gag reflex had seemingly been reset.

Heidi lurched on her long-travel suspension as the chute of Jersey barriers they had been following narrowed and the paved two-lane gave way to an unimproved dirt track. It was a newly graded access road put there to skirt the northside Red Zone.

The hula girl threatened to take her act elsewhere as the track curled around the west side of what was once a lush green oasis within the city. Unlike the No-Man's-Land bordering the east wall, where the countermeasures consisted of mostly just tripwire-activated flares, the parkway's rolling grounds was peppered with obstacles constructed from welded steel, hewn wood, and barbed wire.

What Raven was seeing reminded her of old pictures of D-Day her grandpa had once shown her. However, the dozens of bodies stuck in the wire and impaled on traps here were not wearing waterlogged uniforms and slack-jawed death masks. Instead, they were mostly naked and struggling mightily against the objects piercing their rotting flesh.

As the Bronco passed by, heads panned and dead eyes tracked it.

The unimproved road came to a sheep gate secured with a length of chain. It was rust-streaked and being pressed upon by a pair of badly decomposed zombies.

Raven lost the game of Rock, Paper, Scissors to Duncan and had to dismount and open the gate and wait outside while Daymon pulled Heidi through.

The short run of dirt track on the back side of the gate fed to a boulevard shaded by trees and being encroached upon by overgrown lawns fronting two-story homes with darkened, grime-streaked windows.

The streets here were still garbage-strewn, and leaves and fallen branches had coalesced into little organic speed bumps Daymon showed zero care in avoiding.

"Why didn't you tell us the place you got the paint is *outside* the wire?"

Deadpan, Daymon replied, "You didn't ask."

Raven flashed him the bird.

As Daymon laugh-snorted, Duncan said, "I saw that."

"I don't care," Raven shot. *Back to the drawing board* was what she was thinking. That her plan just got altered was the real source of her anger. Daymon's quip only added fuel to the fire.

Duncan said, "Why do you care so much about that park? They're turning it into a monument, anyway. Let the graffiti cleanup be their problem."

Why? Raven thought. She didn't want to go into the thing about the initials on the bench matching her parents' initials. They didn't need to know how she had drawn strength from those symbols. Strength that she had needed at the time just to put one foot in front of the other. So instead of airing all that, she said, "You know those signs you see every so often on the road passing by the Eden compound? Those 'Adopt-A-Highway' signs?"

"Yep," Duncan said, "I remember seeing them. Patriotic groups like the Freemasons and Veterans of Foreign Wars seem to be doing all the adoptin'."

"Mothers Against Drunk Driving, too," Raven noted. "Anyway, that's what made me think of adopting the park. Just wanted to do something to keep my mind off all the waiting. All those days with no news one way or the other about whether I'd ever talk to my dad again."

"Sometimes no news is good news," Duncan proffered. "We didn't hear from Lev and Jamie until just recently. And they're doing just fine. Matter of fact, if things pan out, they'll be here in a few weeks."

Daymon said, "I thought Lev wanted to stay there."

"He does," Duncan said. "Problem is, he doesn't know how to deliver a baby."

Taking his eyes off the road, Daymon said, "Jamie's pregnant?"

"Logan if it's a boy. Brook if it's a girl. Once the roads around Eden clear of snow, they'll be Oscar Mike."

Daymon ran his window down and braked. He craned around, examining the street signs and nearby homes.

Raven made a face. "I wasn't worrying about them. Neither of them was in a *coma*."

One hand pinching the bridge of his nose, Duncan said, "Point taken."

"Quit with the jib-jab," Daymon said. "We're burning fuel." He turned to regard Raven. "You want to do your thing now? Because if you still do, tools are on the floor behind my seat."

Raven dropped her gaze to the floor. As she did, she heard coming in through the open windows the first telltale moans and rasps of dead things, no doubt coming to investigate.

Seeing the same street signs Daymon had noted, she gave the homes flanking the Bronco a quick visual recon.

"This will do." As she rose up from picking the tools off the floor, in her left side vision, she detected movement outside.

Hefting the Saiga semi-auto shotgun off the floor by his boots, Duncan said, "Zs on our four o'clock. Whatever sneaky snake thing you got in mind, Bird, you better make it quick."

"He's right," Daymon agreed. "We're drawing a crowd."

Elbowing his door, Duncan said, "I'll take care of them."

Daymon put a hand on the Saiga. "We're still in the EZ. We have to do them quiet. We get caught discharging weapons out here, they'll tear up our tickets."

"The man has a point," Raven said. No sooner had her words trailed off than the noisy pack of dead burst from between two squat bungalows off her right shoulder. The low ground-hugging shrubs and tall grass between the homes were whipped around as the head-lolling pack forged ahead on wobbly legs.

After a quick headcount, Daymon said, "Stay here, Old Man. I got this." Looking to Raven, he added, "You go to work on your thing. Don't mind me unless I call for help."

She thought, *That'll be the day*, and nodded in agreement.

Plucking Kindness and Mercy from the floor, Daymon met Raven's gaze in the rearview. "I'll need my bow as well."

Chapter 40

Daymon had been out of the Bronco all of ninety seconds when he ran out of bolts and dropped the crossbow. He was standing in the center of the road, a dozen feet from his rig's left front fender, and dragging his two machetes from their leather sheaths.

On the sloping lawn fronting the pair of bungalows between which Zs were still spilling lay the victims of his initial flurry of silent missiles.

There were nine total. Counting the three missed shots, he had averaged roughly one good hit every ten seconds. Not bad for a BLM firefighter from Utah.

Stumbling and falling over the splayed-out corpses, the next wave of dead things, maybe twenty strong, trundled down the lawn and poured across the sidewalk.

Clutching Mercy in his left hand, Kindness in the other, Daymon backed away from the Bronco on a diagonal tack that was meant to lure them away from the opposite corner where Raven was doing her thing.

One glance over his left shoulder told Daymon where he stood timewise.

Immediately after slinking out the door behind him, Raven had shimmied up the nearby sign pole. At the moment she had the uppermost sign removed and was furiously wrenching on the opposing sign. Figuring the girl required another minute, two at the most to finish her task, he led the Zs west, down the sidewalk, toward a bird-crap-spattered big Mercedes Benz sitting on four flat tires.

Long strides affording him a good lead on the pack of snarling dead, he leaped onto the hood, stepped over the glass moonroof, and took up station in the center of the car's wide, curved roof.

About to engage in a deadly game of whack-a-mole, Daymon crouched down, kicked a leg out for stability, and eyed his pursuers.

"Step right up," he crowed as a single right to left swipe of Kindness, tracking a flat plane head-high to the first two to arrive, sent both of their skull caps—wispy, bug-matted hair and all—spinning into the faces of the follow-ons.

It amused him that the dead didn't blink. Not even in the face of airborne fluids and hurtling brain tissue. Shark-like stares fixed on him, locked on him, and devoured him as the dead kept on coming. And there were far more of them than he'd anticipated.

Creating a deadly wall of steel, the pair of razor-sharp blades flashed the air. Gnarled dead hands that breached the plane were instantly relieved of fingers. Living corpses within striking range lost their heads.

Daymon stole a glance at the Bronco. Saw Duncan sitting in the passenger seat, Saiga's muzzle stabbing skyward out the open window, eyes locked on the row of homes on his side of the street.

Raven was no longer up the pole. She was now standing on the porch of a sky-blue Craftsman. From the looks of it, she was just commencing the last of her tasks.

There was a loud *pop!* and Daymon felt the roof buckle under his weight.

During the half-second he had spent looking up the street, the dead had amassed near the Mercedes' front end. Adjusting his stance and taking a spot nearer to the sloping rear window, he drew a deep breath and went back to work with the aptly named blades.

Slashing with Kindness and chopping with Mercy, he pared the threat down by half. In a matter of seconds, the pile of twice-dead Zs had grown to the height of the car's headlights. Tall enough for the dozen or so that still remained to use as a means to drape their bodies over the blood-slickened hood.

The screech of nails raking sheet metal raised the hairs on the back of Daymon's neck. His breathing was becoming labored due to the high altitude. As a result, his biceps and triceps were afire. Each new swing of the machetes brought him closer to exhaustion. He was beginning to question his willingness to become the bait in this crazy side trip of Raven's when a suppressed weapon's hollow reports reached his ears.

The beginning of a grin was quickly erased by the *snap-crackle* of bullets slicing the air dangerously close to his position. This continued for a few seconds, with the intermittent sound of bodies falling, shell casings striking pavement, and his racing heart all combining to drown out the fading rasps of the creatures surrounding him.

When the shooting finally stopped, the drift of dead bodies in front of the sedan completely obscured its bumper, grille, headlights, and hood. A twenty-something male Z had taken a head shot while on the hood and had come to rest face down and spread-eagled. One arm was twisted grotesquely behind its neck. The other was riddled with old bite marks and hung limply over the fender facing the street. Slow runners of brackish, black blood leaking from the twice-dead corpse traced vertical lines on the exposed paint. Clumps of brain tissue and shards of hair-covered skull on the bullet-pocked windshield created a gruesome archipelago stretching from one window pillar to the other.

Looking left and right, Daymon saw more of the same: corpses two and three deep blocked all four doors. Heart still jackhammering, he said, "You could have shin-shot me."

"Better than the alternative," answered Raven as she stalked around the car, SBR in one hand, Geiger counter in the other.

Daymon leaped to the ground. After wiping the gore from Kindness and Mercy, he sheathed the pair and drew his dagger. "Any of them hot?"

Returning from her counterclockwise orbit of the car, Raven shook her head and switched off the device. "Nothing to worry about." She changed mags and slung the SBR over one shoulder.

Seeing movement through a tangle of interlocking limbs, Raven knelt down beside a child-sized corpse that had become trapped underneath the weight of three others. Its one visible eye doing a crazy dance in the hollow socket was what she had seen.

Bracing the drift of corpses with a knee, Raven drew her Gerber. Hinging over sideways, she located the roving eye in the gloom. As she maneuvered the dagger through the warren of cold flesh, her stomach clenched, and an icy chill tickled her ribcage.

It's the right thing to do she thought as she buried the tip of her blade into the roving eye and put all of her weight behind the killing thrust.

Finished stilling the handful of Zs that had eluded blade and bullet, she went to work sawing a heavily pierced ear from one waifish corpse. The thing was flat-chested and looked to have been dead since summer. Random tattoos running up and down both stick-thin arms were now just blobs of color in a pallid sea of wrinkled skin and no help in identifying its gender.

"You can't do that," Daymon said. "We're in the Exclusion Zone and half of them have your bullets in them. Someone finds out this was our doing, we can all kiss our Golden Tickets goodbye."

Raven said, "If we don't take 'em, someone else will."

"If we take them," Daymon pointed out, "we can't deny it if they ask us. At least not with a straight face and a clear conscience."

An old memory triggered, Raven heard her mom in her head. *Do the right thing even when nobody is watching.*

Shaking her head, she regarded Daymon, a sullen expression on her face. Through clenched teeth, she said, "You have a point."

"Quit yer jawin'," Duncan called. "We've got some more deaders on the way." He was out of the Bronco now and hooking a thumb in the direction from which they'd just come.

Without exchanging another word, Raven and Daymon hustled back to the Bronco.

Holding his seatback forward for Raven, Duncan said, "Mighty fine shooting, Tex."

As he fired the V8 and searched for first gear, Daymon said, "Ought to call her Wyatt Junior."

"Not yet," Duncan said as he climbed in and slammed the door shut. "She's got a long way to go before she bests her dad with a rifle, let alone a pistola."

Daymon drove a few blocks west, then turned left.

"Why are we heading back toward the wall?" Raven asked.

Finding another gear, Daymon said, "Not only is the house where I got the paint *outside* the wire—"

"—it's in the Exclusion Zone," Duncan finished. Looking to Raven, he went on, "When have you known our friend here to do things the easy way? Dropping a few dozen trees across I-89 instead of just blowing the bridge like *I* wanted to do. Then he went and moved into a new place outside the wire, drawing the attention of Adrian and her ilk. I could go on."

Daymon said nothing. Just continued to drive until he reached a corner three blocks south of where he last turned.

Craning, Raven asked, "Which one is it?"

Slowing, Daymon said, "Next intersection, look to your left. It'll be on the south side of the street, second house in from the corner. Look, but don't be obvious about it."

"Side-eye it," instructed Duncan. "Do *not* turn your head in that direction."

"Understood," Raven said, making herself one with the backseat.

Though the Bronco was rolling achingly slow as it crossed the intersection, Raven didn't get a great look at the house. From the two-second-long glance, she determined only its color, that it had only one level, and that there were no vehicles in the driveway or parked at the curb.

Daymon said, "You see it?"

Duncan said, "Yellow single-level bungalow, right?"

"I got it," Raven said. "Yellow one-level. No cars on the street or in the driveway."

Duncan said, "Don't discount that garage."

"Yeah," Daymon said sarcastically, "that's where I'd park my rig if I had the balls to squat in the EZ."

Raven said, "Really, Daymon? *Balls* and *squat* in one sentence?"

Red began creeping up from the man's collar.

Regarding Raven, Duncan said, "Seen enough?"

Angry at herself for not picking up more of the surroundings during the slow drive-by, Raven said, "Now on to the next stop. What's it called?"

Duncan chuckled. "You forgot already?"

Raven said nothing.

"House on the hill. That's your only clue."

After giving it some thought, she said, "I'm stumped."
Daymon said, "You won't be for long."

Chapter 41

The next stop whose name had eluded Raven was *Ray's Restaurant*. A shingle under the sign read: *Home of the Mile-High Stack*.

A greasy spoon breakfast joint just outside the EZ, Ray's was formerly a property owned by a West Coast restaurant chain known for its powder-blue metal roofs, quaint white window trim, and wide-open floorplans.

Now the place looked nothing like those shiny beacons on the hill offering pancakes slathered with any topping one's heart desired and crowned with a veritable Matterhorn of whipped cream.

Having endured the initial wild days of the flash zombie outbreak, had its windows boarded over as a result, and then sat through months of inclement weather with no upkeep, Ray's looked more like a Detroit foreclosure than the family magnet it once was.

"Here it is," Duncan said. "I'm told that this place holds the motherlode of ears."

"I ate here once," Daymon declared. "We were fighting a big fire on the backside of Garden of the Gods. After eating orange dust and cutting scrub for ten days straight, I needed something besides the MREs and pork and beans we were being served. Talked the crew into making the short drive down here during a mandatory twelve-hour stand-down. Best damn blueberry pancakes a brother has ever had."

"Ray's," said Raven. "How'd I forget *that*? Ray and Helen were such nice people … at least once you got beyond Helen answering the door and saying, 'Ray's got a gun on you. What do you people want?'"

Starting a three-point-turn that would leave the Bronco facing back the way they'd come, Daymon asked, "What's so special about this place?"

Eyes roaming the mostly empty parking lot adjacent to the restaurant, Duncan said, "Rumor has it that early on in the Omega outbreak, some people from the surrounding community used it as a depository for their Omega-infected relatives."

As Daymon shifted into Reverse, he cast a skeptical look at Duncan.

Duncan said, "Look at it this way, ye of little faith. Hospitals those first days were full to capacity. With talk of a cure spreading faster than the outbreak, doesn't a little roll of the dice make sense?"

Raven said, "It made sense until it didn't."

Daymon finished the turn and set the brake. Regarding Duncan, he said, "Since your source came through last time, I'm willing to hear you out. Tell us how you heard about this and, most importantly, how much the person you heard it from wants for sharing the info?"

Clearing his throat, Duncan said, "A male nurse at Penrose shared it with Glenda. Apparently, some well-to-do families in the Old North End paid Ray a lot of cash to house them here. By the time President Odero requested that citizens shelter in place, Ray had disappeared. Nobody knows where he went. Just chained the doors and stopped coming by. Phones were down by then."

Raven said, "Where do they think he went?"

Daymon said, "He probably let the dead go in the middle of the night then chained the door and skipped town. Took the cash with him."

Nodding, Duncan said, "And laid low and let things blow over."

"Or he got greedy and was bit. Maybe he's in there with the loved ones. Maybe even his own loved ones," Raven said matter-of-factly.

Silencing the motor, Daymon said, "He's gotta' be a real Harry Houdini type, then."

"What do you mean by that?" Raven asked.

"He means," Duncan offered, "that the doors are still chained and padlocked. Houdini made a living escaping from straightjackets and padlocked chains."

"If you could bet with me," Daymon said, his gaze directed at Duncan, "ten credits says there's nothing but rats and spoiled food in there."

"Well, Mister Glass Half-Empty," shot Duncan. "I can't bet with you. So that means there's only one way to find out what's inside there."

Daymon unbuckled his seatbelt. "Inquiring minds need to know."

Flashing a half-smile, Raven said, "We're doing it?"

Still staring at each other, the men in the front seats nodded in unison.

With a certain electric giddiness filling the Bronco's cab, weapons and magazines were checked and then rechecked.

"Good to go," Daymon said, fetching the bolt cutters from underneath his seat.

Regarding the man, Duncan said, "You're going in with just the two blades and that?"

Daymon regarded Duncan with a look that seemed to question the older man's sanity. Brow furrowed, he pulled a Beretta from his door's side-pocket and press-checked it. Seeing a glint of brass in the chamber, he dumped and inspected the mag. Reinserting the mag, he threw off the safety and tucked it in his waistband.

"Actions speak louder than words," Duncan quipped. "Do I get to tag along this time?"

"It's your intel," Raven said. "Hope the dude knows what he's talking about."

Daymon stepped from the Bronco. Letting the door hang open, under his breath, he said, "Careful what you wish for," and strode off for Ray's, Kindness in one hand, bolt cutters in the other.

Elbowing open his door, Duncan looked to Raven. "Who put the burr under his saddle blanket?"

Instead of answering the question, Raven cast a glance at a white van sitting in the lot off the Bronco's left fender. It was a European model with a tall roof, entirely windowless behind the cab. Ray's Catering was emblazoned on its side in the same yellow font as the lettering on the sign towering over the lot.

Fingers worrying the Saiga's nylon strap, Duncan said, "What is it?"

Smiling, Raven said, "I think I have a plan that won't require us to go inside."

Though she'd only eaten in two of the restaurants belonging to the same chain whose signage Ray's used to wear, she still had a good picture of their floorplans in her head. She also remembered the pancakes and all the toppings and always looked forward to going there after church on Sundays.

If Ray had left things the same inside, she had told the others earlier, they could expect to see a waiting area with two opposing benches right inside the front doors. Facing the waiting area would be a low counter used by the cashier. On one side of the cashier's stand would be a head-high case used to display pies. On the other would be a long, low counter fronted by a dozen fixed stools.

Behind the cashier stand would be the kitchen, which took up a good chunk of the restaurant.

Flanking the kitchen would be two wide-open dining areas. It was there she figured they would find the undead loved ones.

Now Duncan was standing before the door, face pressed against the weathered plywood, trying to peer through the seam where the two doors met. "I've been inside dozens of IHOPs in my time," he said, "and for the life of me I can't picture the layout in my head. And I sure as hell can't make any of it out looking through this narrow gap."

"That's why they call you Old Man," Daymon said. "You probably have that *Old Timers* disease." He'd already cut the padlock but had left the chain wrapped around the handles. Setting the bolt cutters down, he went on, "All joking aside, I think Raven is right. I do recall eyeballing a banana crème pie in some kind of a case just inside and to the left."

Duncan said, "OK, if you say so, Rain Man. But do you remember seeing a counter full of solitary diners?"

Nodding, Daymon said, "We *all* sat there. A bunch of smelly dudes packed in elbow-to-elbow. If I'm remembering things correctly, it *was* off to the right of the cashier's stand."

Duncan said, "Time to get the formalities out of the way." He looked to Raven. "Ready?"

Raven nodded.

"You ready, Daymon?"

His shoulder-length dreadlocks bounced as his head bobbed. "Ready as I'll ever be."

Making a fist, Duncan banged on the door.

Nothing.

No shuffling sounds. The usual hissing and moaning that preceded hungry deaders slamming into a door did not rise.

After a long ten-count, and the only sound Duncan could hear was the beating of his own heart, he flashed Raven a thumbs up.

Seeing the signal, Raven backed away from the door, counting the steps off in her head. Reaching *fifteen,* she stopped on a faded blue wheelchair symbol painted on the parking lot, took her iPhone from a pocket, then thumbed it alive and tapped away at the screen.

Duncan and Daymon were now stacked to the right of the door. The former was crouched behind a newspaper box and brandishing the Saiga shotgun. In the black semiauto's mag well was a twenty-round drum loaded solely with shells containing rifled lead slugs.

The latter held the coiled chain one-handed and looked to be ready to bolt at a moment's notice.

Raven placed the iPhone on the ground by her feet, then signaled the men with a splayed hand held high over her head. Starting a countdown from five in her head, she turned and ran for the catering van.

As soon as Daymon heard the first bars of Joan Jett and the Blackhearts' *I Love Rock and Roll* issue from the iPhone, he tugged on the chain with all his strength.

Nothing.

The pair of doors flexed in the middle but didn't part.

"Again," Duncan urged through clenched teeth.

Daymon's second effort saw the right-side door bow and the window glass pop. A tick later, tiny glass pebbles spilled from behind the plywood sheets.

"Gimme' some of that." Duncan rose and grabbed hold of the chain. "Together on one, two, *three*."

Their combined efforts bore fruit.

The right door popped free of its hinges and toppled toward them, abruptly coming to rest against the bank of newspaper boxes. With nothing to keep it latched, the left door swung slowly outward, the rubber stop drilled into the concrete finally halting its slow-motion sweep.

Jett was making a plea for another coin to be put into the jukebox at the same time Daymon and Duncan were ducking back out of sight behind the boarded-over door.

For a full minute they stayed crouched down, waiting.

Duncan took a deep breath and held it. Full of nervous energy, he looked to the van where Raven was waiting. Only thing giving her away was her boots showing behind the van's opposite side rear wheel, and her shadow, which was stretched out to twice her size due to the sun's low azimuth.

Again, nothing happened.

A few more seconds crawled by. There was no sound of bodies jostling against each other inside the restaurant. The anticipated squelch of feet treading on broken glass never came.

Only thing to emerge from the blue-black gloom behind the yawning doors were a couple of bloated houseflies.

Exactly two minutes and fifty-seven seconds after Raven set the iPhone on the ground, Joan Jett's teen-angst-fueled ditty ended and the device stayed quiet as the music app shuffled the available songs.

When the intro to Metallica's *Enter Sandman* emanated from the tiny speakers, Daymon rose and poked his head past the door's edge. "Looks empty to me."

Raven's plan had been equal parts divide-and-conquer and stand-your-ground. It was to have them allowing the dead to march out of Ray's. Once the things were spread out in a long line, their attention—hopefully—focused on the music, the trio were to attack from the left with blades and bullets.

Releasing the air trapped in his lungs, Duncan said, "You're pretty trusting, Daymon. I was half-expecting you to come face-to-face with one of those trussed-up deaders with its voice box cut out."

Then one of us would have to cut your hair to free you from its grip." He shivered. "I *do not* miss coming up against those silenced fire-and-forget death missiles."

"Me neither," Daymon said. "Who's going in first?"

As Duncan was saying "I'll take point," a faint rasp sounded somewhere deep inside the restaurant.

Daymon said, "Still want to go in first?"

Though the hair on his arms was at attention, Duncan nodded an affirmative.

"Need to water your balls?"

"No," Duncan said, "but since they're *sooo* big, I'll need you to tag along and carry them for me."

Cringing at the thought, Daymon beckoned Raven over.

In response, she sprinted from behind the van and picked up the iPhone on the move. She was just getting the device silenced when she formed up next to the lanky man.

"We're going in," Daymon informed her. "Old Man is running point."

Shaking her head, Raven said, "I need the experience. Let me go first."

Daymon said, "W.W.C.D.?"

It took Duncan a second to decipher the acronym. Finally he said, "At this stage in the game, considering how she saved Peter's bacon back in Utah, and all I've seen her do outside the wire since then, I do believe Cade would let her decide."

"I'm going in," she insisted. "Move aside guys."

Chapter 42

Utilizing a technique her dad taught her, Raven heel-and-toed it over the glass and into the cramped waiting area. The stale air inside the restaurant carried on it the faint stink of rotting flesh.

Alone inside the entry, her eyes still adjusting to the low light, she let her gaze roam her immediate surroundings.

Opposing benches wrapped in red vinyl flanked her on two sides. Wood-paneled walls plastered with dozens of missing persons notices rose up behind the benches.

Aside from the wall full of head shots of people and their accompanying heart-wrenching messages, a bare coat tree tucked into a corner to her left, and the wire-frame display holding all kinds of brochures touting activities available in and around Colorado Springs, Ray's waiting area was no different than the ones she'd seen in similar restaurants in Portland.

Daymon's memory of the area just inside the entry was spot-on. To Raven's left, partially blocking the darkened dining area beyond, was a pie case. Head-high to her, the glass case was home to only empty shelves and wraparound mirrors, the latter of which were reflecting back at her tiny versions of Daymon, Duncan, and the small rectangle of daylight behind them.

Thumbing on the compact tac-light affixed to her SBR, Raven swept its cone of light over the restaurant's interior.

Shadows danced against the vibrantly papered back walls. Fresh air introduced from outside moved gossamer strands of spider webs back and forth. To Raven, they looked like inverted kelp beds. Dust motes skated across the stark-white beam as she raised up onto her tiptoes and aimed her rifle at the area beyond the pie case.

There were no booths along the walls. Just clean and unworn spots on the carpet where they used to sit. All of the tables and chairs had been stacked and pushed away from the front of the left-side dining area. Creating a head-high wall of turned wood and iron table legs, the warren of furniture cut off a third of the room and blocked entirely a short hall leading to a pair of swinging doors.

As Raven dropped the beam to the ground, she keyed in on some movement behind the furniture. Just shadows at first. Then a pustule-riddled arm made an appearance. It was small and was quickly joined by more.

Slender fingers at the end of tiny, pale hands kneaded the air.

Her light picked up a flash of red and glinted off something metal.

Causing Raven to start, Duncan said into her ear, "More of the same on the other side. Seven or eight kids. Look to be mostly tweens and teenagers."

She crouched and painted a cherubic face with the light beam. The eyes staring back at her were as dead as the pallid face they looked out of. Seeing that the leather straps bracketing the undead girl's cheeks were attached to a red ball, she said, "What's that thing in its mouth?"

Duncan looked a question at Daymon.

Clearly disgusted, Daymon said, "It's a fuckin' ball gag."

In unison, Duncan and Raven said, "What's that?"

Meeting Duncan's gaze, Daymon said, "You didn't see Pulp Fiction?"

"I did. I was drunk. Don't remember much of it." He paused for a beat. Then, face lighting up, he went on, "The Timex in the keister bit was pretty damn funny."

Daymon recounted the scene in which Ving Rhames' character, Marsellus Wallace, and Butch Coolidge, played by Bruce Willis, were in a basement and trussed to chairs with like items strapped to their faces.

Duncan said, "It's coming back to me now. Seems pretty elaborate since the ones on the other side just have Ray's napkins jammed down their throats."

Duncan said, "Who uses ball gags?"

Daymon looked to Raven. "Earmuffs, young lady."

Duncan pretended to cover his ears with his hands.

Raven flipped both men the bird. "You see what's all around us? Death and destruction everywhere. That being said, I don't see the issue in me hearing about how people torture other people."

Duncan made a face.

"It's a sex dominance thing," Daymon said to Raven. "Shall I go on?"

She waved him off. "Why the gag balls?"

"To keep them from making too much noise," he answered. "And that's why I doubt Ray skipped town."

Eyeing the kids, Raven said, "Where'd he go then?"

Daymon said nothing.

Eyes widening, Raven looked toward the swinging doors. "You think we're going to find him in the kitchen?"

"That would explain the need to silence the Lord of the Flies gang," Duncan theorized. "Wonder where he got the gag balls."

Raven said, "Maybe Ray had a dark past."

"Or maybe," Daymon said, "he raided an adult toy store and cleaned out their inventory."

Raven made a face. "That's gross," she said.

"Are we doing this or not?" Duncan asked. "Because if we're not, I want to get back and have an early dinner."

Intrigued, Daymon said, "Where ya thinking?"

"That stand on Cascade and Pikes Peak that does up the awesome teriyaki chicken skewers."

"I'm down. I say we do this. I still need gas money." He looked to Raven. "The credits you promised if I took you by to get the stuff for your—"

"—Art project," she said. "I'm working on something special for my dad."

"How is your dad?" Daymon asked.

"Doing better. He's training with his old team right now."

Duncan prickled. "Once you're on a team, you're always a member. Just because what happened, happened, doesn't mean he's a pariah. Or been excommunicated."

"I *know*," Raven said. "It's just that I'm afraid he's going to be disappointed if he doesn't get back—"

"—in the saddle," Duncan finished. "I know the feeling. Joined the army at seventeen and got in on the tail end of the war. Flew helos in and out of countries we weren't supposed to be in. Had relations with all kinds of lovely ladies." He paused. "Damn, I miss those days."

Hands on hips, Daymon said, "Enough with the trip down memory lane. How are we doing this?"

After a bit of deliberation, which was all right by Duncan, he and Daymon left to go to the other side of the restaurant to take care of the teens.

Determining she would be little help dismantling the "Great Wall" of overstuffed vinyl booths, Raven volunteered to put down the ball-gagged kids.

Now, with grunts and groans and the noises of furniture being moved filtering over from the east-side dining room, Raven stood before the tables and chairs, counting heads.

Seven.

Seven unfortunate kids who had once been the apple of some mom or dad's eye. Their reason for being. Their sole focus in life.

Seven more souls to add to the hundreds she had already released from their earthbound shells. Or Hell on Earth, as her mom had described the walking dead's existence.

Purgatory was how her dad had once described the plight of the undead.

There was no need for Raven to move anything to get to the faces staring back at her. She just snaked her arm past the spindles and chair legs and killed them one-by-one by introducing the Gerber to those dead, staring eyes. Unblinking, the black orbs presented her easy targets.

Finished, she found a linen napkin and cleaned the blade.

The sound from the other side was ongoing. So Raven removed a couple of chairs blocking entry to the short hall. Standing on one of the chairs she'd left behind, she looked through one of the porthole windows in the pair of swinging kitchen doors.

The kitchen—if that's what was beyond these doors—was pitch black.

Steeling herself for what might await her, she raised the SBR horizontal to the floor and shined the tac-light beam through the right-side window.

Chapter 43

Raven had been correct in her initial assumption. Beyond the swinging doors lay a massive open kitchen. Revealed in the beam lancing from the SBR's light were dozens of feet of stainless-steel counters, industrial-sized glass-fronted ovens, utensils and pots hanging from the ceiling, and, to the right, a long, narrow cooking line that tested the reach of the encroaching beam.

She jumped off the chair and squeezed through the doors, the suppressed SBR's business end leading the charge.

The stench of death tailing Raven through the doors was quickly nullified by the eye-stinging odor of disinfectants.

To her left, exposed by the light spill, was a cramped office. It contained a small desk, filing cabinets, and a paper shredder. Its windowless door was open and resting against the right-side wall.

On the other two walls were corkboards papered with official-looking documents.

Above the desk was a framed article from the *Food Scene* section of the local newspaper. It was full of praise for Ray's. The article's author noted how pleased the community was to see a locally owned concern move into a property vacated by a big chain.

The man and woman in the picture accompanying the story looked to be Duncan's age—maybe sixty years old. Big smiles painted their faces. The American Dream.

Something banged against the wall, causing the picture frame to vibrate. Raven looked closely at the couple, studied their faces, then moved on.

A legal pad on the desk was covered with the names of people Ray had taken in. Next to the names were dollar amounts and contact numbers.

The evidence was mounting that the rumors were true. Raven didn't know how she felt about it. Was Ray taking advantage of the families' emotions? Or were the families taking advantage of his kindness?

Instead of chewing on it further, she filed it as yet another mystery of the apocalypse never to be told by those involved.

Again, something heavy impacted the wall at her back.

As Raven left the office to investigate, her light splashed across a massive steel-skinned door. It was just to the right of the office door and inset into a wall clad entirely with shiny, white tiles. Emblazoned on a plastic plaque below the door's lone window were the words: WALK IN FREEZER - KEEP CLOSED! Under the plaque was a handwritten sign: DANGER! DO NOT OPEN DOOR!

The admonition only served to pique Raven's interest.

Looking closer, she saw that the window glass was clouded by something smeared on it from the inside. Judging by the noises she had heard coming from within, she guessed the "something" was bodily fluids. That guess was confirmed when another "something" slammed against the door from inside.

Then a face filled up the window. It was bloated and gray and wore a full beard just like the man in the photo. The eyes darted in the sockets as it mashed its broken teeth against the glass. That the cataract of fluids on the glass didn't smear as the dead thing dragged its tongue across it suggested to her it had been trapped in there for some time.

Raven had little doubt "something" number two was Ray.

But was he alone? Was the woman from the picture in there, too?

Parroting Duncan, she said to herself, "Only one way to find out, young lady," and pulled a chair from the office and placed it before the walk-in door.

Raven climbed onto the chair, cupped her hands beside her cheeks, and pressed her face to the glass. She could feel vibrations through the glass as Ray's corpse went into a frenzy, banging against the door again and again.

Probing the cooler's interior with the tactical light revealed nothing. Just Ray, who she guessed had put himself in there. Pretty safe place to turn if you didn't have the stomach to take your own life.

Suddenly she felt a lot of respect for Ray. Even if the rumors were true about him charging to take in people's loved ones, he'd certainly redeemed himself by this one last unselfish act.

Deeming the importance of freeing Ray's soul from his bloated corpse not as important as staying on this side of the grass herself, Raven went to step off the chair. As she leaned over and braced herself with one hand on the chair back, the banging abruptly ceased.

A deafening silence descended on the dark kitchen. Then, without warning, two things happened near simultaneously.

First, as if manipulated by a ghost, the door handle levered out all by itself. The follow-on audible click of a locking mechanism disengaging echoed about the stainless-steel-and-tile-clad walls. Then the door exploded outward and, accompanied by a blast of putrid air, Ray's reanimated corpse careened through the doorway.

The door edge struck Raven on the temple, lifted her off the chair, and sent her sprawling to the floor. She landed on her back with the chair on its side by her feet and the sharp edges of the SBR biting into her ribcage on one side.

Now at floor-level and aimed in the cooler's general direction, the beam thrown by the tactical light created ominous shadows that danced across the ceiling and walls.

Survival instinct kicking in, she went for her Gerber.

Retaining a good deal of momentum, the zombie encountered the upended chair shins first. Tripping over its own feet, the thing that used to be Ray pitched forward, arms fully extended, dead eyes locked firmly on what was likely the first fresh meat it had seen in a long while.

With the chair the only thing between being trapped underneath a couple of hundred pounds of snarling monster, Raven raised her left hand to ward off Ray and yanked the black dagger free of its sheath with the other.

Ray's knees impacted the floor at nearly the same instant his upper body hinged over the upturned chair. The sharp *crack!* of bone striking tile was followed immediately by the distinct noise of fabric tearing.

As Raven grabbed a fistful of neck flesh with her left hand, she felt something heavy fall across her knees and shins and pin them to the floor. In the next beat, with cold hands pawing at her face and her lungs coming under assault from the sharp acidic stink of feces, she extended her left arm and locked the elbow.

With just the chair and weakening arm muscles keeping the snapping teeth from tearing into her neck, she buried the Gerber into the thing's left eye. A quick twist of the wrist stilled the corpse for the last time.

Releasing her grip on the loose skin hanging off its throat, she kicked and squirmed her way out from underneath the dead weight.

After getting her wind back, Raven lifted the rifle and trained the light on the scene she'd only been privy to small snippets of.

The cooler door was wide open. Protruding from it about midway up was a six-inch-long metal shaft. Capping the shaft was a red plastic disc. Tracing the curvature of the disc were the words EMERGENCY LATCH RELEASE.

Thankfully Ray had been alone. Only thing she could make out in the cooler were a couple of metal beer kegs and a dozen or so white buckets.

Just outside the door, Ray lay sprawled over the chair, his ample midsection punctured through by both chair legs.

Explaining the pressure and spreading wetness Raven had felt on her legs, his guts and other internals had burst forth and now lay in a big greasy pile on the floor. Best guess was that the continuous slamming against the cooler door led to the emergency handle being depressed. Also likely was that all that slamming had contributed to the horrific horizontal gash the chair legs were buried in.

As Raven rose and went to wipe off the dagger, she heard a loud crash from the other side of the restaurant. She was on her way to investigate when the crashing noises were replaced by a plea for help. Then came the *pop, pop, pop* of a pistol being discharged. As she was passing by the pie cooler, there was a final spasm of gunfire, then silence.

All in all, from the initial crash to the gunfire abruptly cutting out, maybe six seconds had elapsed.

Staying low, she crossed the entry tiles. Poking her head around the divider separating the lunch counter from the main dining area, she called, "Daymon? Duncan? You guys all right?"

"Yeah," replied Daymon. "Some of us are more *all right* than others."

Hearing this, but still harboring a bit of trepidation, she rose and stalked the length of the head-high divider. When she entered the right-side dining area and trained the light on her friends, she didn't quite believe what she was seeing.

Chapter 44

"How about giving me a hand here?" Daymon said. He was kneeling next to Duncan, who was lying on his stomach in the center of the room.

Drained of color, eyes closed, Old Man's face was a mask of pain.

The Saiga shotgun was propped against one of many fallen booths. Arranged neatly on the floor next to the weapon were Duncan's aviator glasses and one of Daymon's machetes.

On the floor behind the men, illuminated by the beam of a dropped flashlight, were the bodies of nearly a dozen headshot Zs. They had come to rest in every imaginable position, their blood and bodily fluids already comingling on the carpet.

Spotting on the floor near Duncan a dark wet spot the size of a dinner plate, Raven blurted, "Is he bit?"

Speaking through clenched teeth, Duncan said, "My damn back went out on me."

Planting a knee on Duncan's lower back and both hands on his shoulder blades, Daymon remarked, "At the worst possible time, too."

Exhaling sharply, she said, "Went out? Is it broken?"

"Muscle spasms," answered Duncan. "Hurt it years ago tryin' to shear a big ol' sheep. First time in a long time it's done this."

Words dripping with sarcasm, Daymon said, "To quote that old thespian dude … 'timing is everything.'"

Duncan grimaced. "Shakespeare you ain't."

Biting her lip, Raven asked, "What's the wetness on the carpet?"

Continuing to apply the pressure to Duncan's upper back, Daymon switched knees and averted his gaze.

Duncan sighed. "I pissed myself." His eyes opened and he fixed a watery gaze on Raven. "Please don't tell anyone. Especially not Glenda."

Backing off the pressure, Daymon said, "You ready to try again?"

Sweat was beading on Old Man's brow. After taking a swipe at it with his sleeve, he said, "Roll me over."

With little help on Duncan's part, Daymon got him rolled over onto his back.

Raven's eyes flicked to the man's BDU pants. Sure enough, though not as noticeable as the stain on the floor, a similar-sized wet spot had spread across the front of the camouflage pants.

Nodding, she said, "Of course I'll keep this between us. It's nobody's business anyway." She shed her coat and draped it across Duncan's midsection.

Lifting his head off the floor, Duncan said, "It's not dead. I just pissed my pants. Wasn't the first time. Surely isn't the last."

Raven said, "Too late now."

Changing the subject, Daymon fixed Raven with a knowing look. "What happened with you over there? What's that slime on your legs?"

"Taking care of the kids was no problem. I still need to harvest the ears."

"Damn girl," Daymon said. "You're getting cold-blooded in your old age."

Ignoring the comment, Raven went on. "Ray trapped himself in the refrigerator."

Duncan said, "He's a real tiny guy, huh?"

"Far from it."

Having worked a couple of restaurant gigs as a teen, Daymon knew what she had meant. He said, "She's talking about the walk-in *refrigerator*. I used to sneak to the walk-in at this one restaurant and suck the gas out of the whipped cream canisters. Talk about a head rush."

"Talk about dead brain cells," Raven shot.

"Was Ray an opportunist?" Daymon asked. "Or was he being altruistic."

"I don't know what that means," Raven said. "But I do think Ray meant well. The money was in the office with a ledger. I think he thought this was all going to blow over. Looked to me like he was planning on giving the families back their money."

Daymon said, "What was all the noise I heard coming from over there?"

"Moving chairs and bodies," Raven said, straight-faced.

A half-truth, for sure. For if word of what really happened got to her dad, her Golden Ticket might just get revoked. And that was the last thing she needed, especially considering the location of the graffiti crew's stash house.

With considerable effort and a little help from Daymon, Duncan got into a sitting position.

"Pressure down there is so bad," Duncan said, "it makes me think I'm about to shit myself."

Hearing this, Raven snatched up her coat and shrugged it on.

Daymon said, "Really?"

Illuminating her own legs from the knee down with the taclight, Raven said, "Can't be any worse than Ray's gut juice."

Daymon's dreads whipped as he shook his head in amazement. "Cold-blooded." Threading his arms under Duncan's armpits, he said, "Ups-a-daisy," and clean-jerked his friend off the floor.

Raven asked, "What happened here?" Though it looked to her as if the booths had come crashing down, and the avalanche of red vinyl had led to the teenaged Zs escaping their confines—which explained the gunfire and spent brass dotting the carpet—there was no accusatory tone to her voice.

"Like I said … bad timing." Daymon pointed to the jumble of booths beside the bullet-riddled corpses. "We were lifting the last of them off the top row and *it* just happened. Old Man collapsed and took me and the booth to the ground with him."

Now sitting on a padded chair, Duncan said, "Then that booth hit the other booths—"

"And *Jinga!*" Daymon finished. "The walls, they came a tumbling down."

"I watched it all from the ground. Helpless as a blind kitten who's wandered into a coyote's den. Pissed myself watching the deaders pour out."

"Glad I brought the Beretta," Daymon conceded. "Burned an entire mag of nine-mil on them."

Duncan said, "Shoulda seen it. Damn Wyatt Jr, this one. Head shot after glorious head shot."

Raven said, "I heard it all. And it was over before I got out of the kitchen."

Duncan rose from the chair and shuffled toward his friend. Standing on unsteady legs, he wrapped the taller man up with both arms and hugged him hard. "Surprised the heck out of me."

"Surprised me, too," Daymon said. "Didn't know I had it in me."

"Don't go getting a big head, now," Duncan quipped. Then, voice all business, he added, "We're even for me rescuing you from the attic in Hanna."

Looking side-eyed at the man, Daymon said, "Really? We're still keeping tabs?"

"Just pulling your leg. Now how about you two go collect *our* ears?"

"On it," Raven said.

Feigning a scowl, Daymon said, "What are you going to be doing?"

"Keeping this chair warm and supervising."

Raven had already trooped off for the other dining room.

Alone in the room with Duncan, eyes going misty, Daymon said, "That was close."

Staring at the floor by his feet, Duncan answered back, "Way too close."

Chapter 45

The Antlers

"For the third time," Raven said, "start passing the dang *food*." She looked at her watch. Saw the minute hand click forward yet again.

Twirling a length of his blond locks around one finger, Peter said, "Your dad is *never* late."

Duncan met Peter's blue-eyed gaze. "It'll be all right," he said, adding emphasis to the words by bugging his eyes at the teen. "He's probably being held up at the gate. A technicality with his papers, or something."

Sasha said, "Maybe the Tahoe broke down. Lord knows Wilson doesn't lift a finger to keep it in good running shape."

Through clenched teeth, Wilson said, "Sore subject. Pass the potatoes, Sis."

Bumping Wilson's knee under the table, Taryn said, "We are eating. Not here. Not now."

Wisely, Wilson kept "the truck is brand new" comment to himself and instead speared a boiled spud and plopped it on his plate.

Finished shuttling food-laden serving dishes to the table, Tran crossed his arms and watched the people whom he considered family fill their plates with pappardelle noodles and canned chicken and potatoes and homemade rolls. Only thing missing was a salad and fresh churned butter. The former problem would soon be rectified when spring took a firm foothold and his first planting in the rooftop garden could commence. He had big plans for *his* garden.

The latter would take a miracle. Out of all the people he'd talked to since arriving at the new capital, not a one of them had seen a single live cow during their travels across the country.

After bowing her head in prayer, Raven took a roll and passed the basket.

"Maybe he's getting the Tahoe's oil changed," Sasha speculated. "Or having the tires rotated. Least he could do after holding it hostage for two days."

Deciding to let Wilson stew over the whereabouts of his precious rig, Raven changed the subject, saying, "Thanks for the information, Glenda. Ray's was everything you said it would be. I can't imagine being in a city this size when it all started. The choices people had to make in order to survive. Pure madness."

Peter said, "Salt Lake changed overnight. Most of our neighbors kept their kids inside. Dad's business was booming as people stocked up on gas and oil. We even opened a contract with FEMA and the National Guard."

Sasha said, "Denver sure was a shitshow. Wilson had to do some stuff he's not proud of."

Gesturing with her fork, Taryn said, "That's enough, Sash. Try working on your filter."

Pointing her fork at Taryn, Sasha said, "You're *not* my mom. Try working on minding your own business."

"I'm old enough to be," Glenda said, "and then some. So zip it while we eat, Sasha. You want to spar with your brother and sister-in-law—take it elsewhere."

That shut Sasha up.

"I transferred a few credits to your account," Raven said. "If you want, you can give some to your co-worker."

Fork poised midair, Glenda said, "That good a haul?"

"Nineteen from Ray's. Another dozen from stragglers we came upon on our way back in."

Tran said, "No Glowers?"

Raven shook her head. "Not a one. Sign on the gate said it's been a week since they've seen one arrive. Seems to me that the diversionary barriers are keeping them from entering the hot zone."

"A step in the right direction," Glenda replied. "However, I'm reserving judgement until we see a string of hot weather. That seems to get them moving about."

Finally taking his seat at the head of the table, Tran looked to Glenda. "Where's Duncan?"

"Today wore him out," she said. "Then there's the sprained back. I rubbed some Ben Gay on it. On top of that, I gave him a couple of melatonin and a mild muscle relaxant. He's out like a light."

Addressing Raven, Tran said, "Where's Daymon?"

"No idea. He dropped us off here and drove off."

"It's that new ginger flame of his," said Sasha. "Gotta strike while the iron is hot."

Peter said, "Strike what?"

"Never you mind," Glenda ordered. "Just eat your meat."

Expecting more fireworks, Raven started shoveling her food in her mouth. She had almost cleaned her plate when the main door to the Founders Suite swing inward. For a long five-count, nobody was there.

Finally, encumbered with an overstuffed pack, some new exotic-looking weapon slung on his back, and a Pelican case in each hand, her dad waddled across the threshold.

Heading the question off at the pass, Cade found Wilson and said, "Your truck rides like a dream. Whipper filled her tank and checked the fluids. Thank you for letting me use her. And I'm truly sorry I left it at the base overnight. It was kind of out of my hands."

Mouth full, Wilson nodded and motioned with his fork. "You can use it any time you need to."

"I was right," crowed Sasha.

Cade said, "If the call comes, I'll take you up on that. And I'll bring her back with a full tank."

Still chewing his food, Wilson simply nodded and smiled.

The second Cade had said *call*, Raven realized that he was wearing brand new MultiCams. Affixed to them in all the appropriate locations were distressed versions of Old Glory, captain's bars, a name tape reading *Grayson*, and the Pale Riders patch. Feeling her heart skip, she said, "What's with the new gear and uniform?"

Standing there, all weighted down, a smile wide as the room, Cade said, "I'm back in the fold."

"Bravo," Tran said, raising his glass. "It's only Gatorade, but I think a toast is in order."

Cade waved him off. "Not necessary."

"To Cade," Tran said. "May his shadow darken the doorstep of all our foes, and his blade drink of their blood."

Color spread to Cade's clean-shaven cheeks. Though he wanted to thank each and every one of them personally, he simply bowed his head.

Glasses clinked and dinner resumed.

Meeting Raven's gaze, Cade said, "Get me a plate, please. Then meet me in my room."

***

Raven was sitting on her dad's smartly made bed, eating a cherry Pop Tart and watching him inventory the contents of the pair of black, hard-side cases.

"When's your next mission?"

Looking up from his task, speaking in fluent Mandarin, Cade said, "*As soon as I get my kit straightened out. Probably early tomorrow morning.*"

Hands on hips, a half-smile forming, Raven said, "In English, *por favor.*"

Cade repeated himself, only this time he did so in fluent Spanish.

Raven stared daggers.

After flashing an impish smile, in English, he said, "You look so much like your mom when you do that." As he repeated the answer to her question, he was removing his wedding band. Still talking, he unclasped Raven's necklace and threaded one end through his band. Reversing the process with the clasps, he said, "Keep it safe for me."

Dropping the pair of rings into the front of her shirt, she said, "I haven't forgotten Mom's rituals."

"I know you haven't," he said, tousling her hair. "Doubt we ever will." Pulling her close, he whispered some instructions into her ear.

Nodding slowly, Raven pinched away the forming tears. Then, fixing her dad with a stony gaze, she said, "I'll make sure I do."

Diving both hands into the Pelican case nearest him, Cade said, "Want to help me change out all these batteries?"

Eager to learn all she could about the exotic-looking gear in the box, she plopped down on the bed between the open cases.

Chapter 46

Friday, March 16, 2012

"Early tomorrow morning" hadn't held true. When dealing with the United States Army, "Hurry up and wait" was the norm. And that was just fine with Cade. The extra couple of days had allowed him time at the outdoor shooting range located near Spring's south entrance. There he had put a few dozen rounds through the weapons he'd be taking with him on the secret mission he was to be briefed on later in the day.

The first three nights of the delay—all under scattered clouds and a waning moon—he had used the cloak of darkness to fully acquaint himself with the cutting-edge full-color NVGs the new Delta commander had procured for the Pale Riders. Sure, he had drawn funny looks from the small number of people he'd encountered during the late-night forays into the core of the darkened city. Who wouldn't gawk at a guy dressed in all black and wearing a low-rise tactical helmet with the newest generation four-tube NVGs sprouting from his face? He got it. He had studied his own reflection in the Antlers' windows that first night out and thought the new gear made him look like he'd just arrived from outer space.

After putting the NVGs through the paces, and swapping batteries three times, he knew their strengths and limitations and had a firm grasp of how long he should expect the batteries to last. Which wasn't long. The new goggles sucked batteries dry in about half the time as the white-phosphor devices he wore during the raid on Adrian's Bear Lake compound.

Now, in his room and dressed in the black fatigues he would wear for the coming mission, he stood by the window, looking down on Antlers Park as the first light of day began its steady creep over the single canopy below.

Deep in thought, he strapped his newly repossessed Gerber to his left leg, snugged his trusty Glock 19 into the drop-leg holster riding on his right side, then turned and began the arduous task of muscling the single full-size Pelican case to the door, all while being careful to be quiet and not wake Raven.

Nothing doing.

No sooner had he moved the case to where he wanted it than the door to his daughter's room opened and she materialized from the blue-black gloom.

She wore two-piece pajamas in a bright pink Tartan no respectful Scottish clan would dare claim. She yawned and stretched in the doorway. Finished, she said, "Stealing away in the early morning hours, eh?"

"Busted," he said. "Guilty as charged."

"So the call came?"

He nodded. "An hour ago."

"You weren't going to give me a goodbye kiss?"

"I did. When you didn't wake up, I decided you needed the sleep more than you needed to hear me tell you what you already know. Besides, I was thinking about your mom and feeling a little maudlin."

"Maudlin?"

"It means to get emotional. Usually when drinking. It's the only word I can think of to describe how I get to feeling when I let my guard down."

"First off," Raven said. "I can't remember ever seeing you drink. Secondly, a rock shows more emotion than you do."

Cade grimaced. "Ouch, that hurt." After a brief pause, he said, "Truth is … I didn't want to be around when you found out your park got hit again."

"It's Friday, isn't it?"

He nodded. "Did you see the preparations they're making for the President's ceremony?"

"The Jersey barriers?"

"Yep. They tagged some of those. Same weird symbols as before."

"The statues?"

He shook his head. "They left them alone."

Good, she thought. The McGregor brothers were already pissed she had put on hold her plan to stake out the house where Daymon had procured his paint. If their work on the monument suffered another setback, no telling how much pressure they'd put on her to reveal its true location. They were still traumatized from the very event their work was to memorialize. That and a handful of other good reasons marked them as the last two people on earth she wanted to be caught with inside the Exclusion Zone.

Cade said, "If it's any consolation, I did record a video message for you on your iPhone."

"What's it say?"

"Pretty much that I'll be back when I get back." He went quiet for a spell.

"And?"

"And … while I'm away, do not do anything I wouldn't do."

She smiled. Then she yawned again and strode off towards her own room, which had a better vantage of her park.

Cade loaded his gear onto one of the Antlers' trolleys and chanced a ride on the elevator. In the garage, he loaded his stuff into the Tahoe, then drove to the East Gate, where his new military ID got him through with zero waiting and even less scrutiny.

During the short drive from Springs to Peterson, Cade counted a total of ten Zs. Most he'd spotted at a distance, ambling down an arterial or side street. Especially amusing was the trio of first turns just outside of No-Man's-Land. They were paying all their attention to a fifty-foot-long string of vinyl flags beating the air over a used car lot. So enthralled were they—like infants under the spell of a noisy rattle—that they were totally oblivious to the Tahoe until it was well past them.

Arriving at Peterson's West Gate, Cade was greeted by a pair of airmen clad in crisp MultiCam BDUs.

"Identification, please," said the twenty-something female sergeant whose name tape read *Moon*. In one of her hands, she held a clipboard with a half-inch-thick stack of papers trapped under the shiny metal clip.

Cade was ready, handing the airman his ID and letting her know his business in the most general of terms.

After a few seconds of scrutiny, during which the athletically built woman cross-referenced his name against what he guessed was a list clipped to her clipboard, his ID was returned.

"We need to inspect your vehicle prior to you entering the base."

No arguments from Cade. He sat silently in his seat as she walked the four corners of the SUV, now and again bending over to pass a boxy device over the tires and running boards.

As Sergeant Moon did her thing, a baby-faced airman trailed her with a disc-shaped mirror-on-wheels, using it to give the undercarriage a very thorough looking over.

As Cade waited for the two to finish with the formalities, he took in his surroundings. On the front of the brick guard shack was a sign shaped like a shield. *Peterson Air Force Base - Home of the 21st SPACE WING* was written across the middle of the shield in navy-blue lettering. The station bristled with antennas. Hanging from the eaves were a pair of the ubiquitous black domes. They were positioned so the closed-circuit cameras within could see everything coming and going.

Parked next to the guard station was a dark blue Humvee. It was surrounded on three sides by blast-proof HESCO barriers. A third airman in the Humvee's roof-mounted turret was visible behind the Browning heavy machine gun.

Behind razor-wire-topped hurricane fencing was a secondary barrier made up of joined cement freeway noise barriers. The dirt at the base of the cement slabs was uneven in spots, suggesting they were added *after* the exterior fence.

The gate itself was wide enough to allow even the largest of military vehicles. It was wheeled and constructed of the same material as the hurricane fence. Welded horizontally to the outside of the gate were inch-thick metal rods. The rods were so close together that Cade doubted a Z could thread its fingers through to find purchase.

Finished checking the Tahoe's exterior for radiation, Moon gave the interior a cursory inspection.

Apparently uninterested in seeing what was inside the console and glovebox, checking the contents of his kit bag, or learning what the Pelican case held, she said, "You're good to go, Captain Grayson. Have a pleasant day." As she did so, she flashed him a crisp salute.

Captain Grayson, thought Cade as he returned the salute. Another affirmation this was all real, that he wasn't still in a coma and having a whopper of a dream.

The gate slid away silently, and he drove onto the base.

Chapter 47

Peterson Air Force Base

Entering the base for the first time via the West Gate, it took Cade a moment to find the road that would see him to the gargantuan hangar being used exclusively by Delta and the 160th Special Operations Aviation Regiment. The spartan living quarters sat tucked away in the rear of the hangar. Access to it was through a set of double doors facing a fenced-in parking lot. Capable of accommodating thirty or so vehicles, the lined lot presently had just two Ram pickups and a Toyota Land Cruiser taking up spaces.

Cade negotiated the sharp bend in the drive, drove onto the lot, then nosed the Tahoe in next to the white Land Cruiser.

Leaving the gear in the truck for the time being, Cade approached the door with empty hands and a nagging suspicion that he was going to have to use the Iridium sat-phone to call someone to let him in.

Each door had a stout handle that looked to be fashioned from some kind of exotic alloy. Recessed in a tamperproof panel next to the left-side door jamb was a black ten-by-ten square of glass. A shroud of clear plastic protected the panel from the elements.

Biometric lock.

Which explained why he hadn't been issued a key or supplied with a password.

Feeling a little better about his prospects for getting into the facility, he slipped his hand under the shroud and placed it palm-down on the glass.

Though his name didn't show on the panel, there was a beep and an audible click.

Success.

He cracked a rare smile.

I'm back on the team.

Standing there all alone on the landing, flush with the knowledge he was being trusted by not only his peers, but also by Freda Nash and Cornelius Shrill and maybe even President Valerie Clay, Cade felt as if he'd just summited Mount Everest. Or at least his own personal version of that incredible feat of extreme mountaineering. Especially after being captured by the Chicoms then having the entire Pale Riders team, including Rangers and SOAR assets, risk their lives to rescue him.

His initial failure had him thinking his days of riding the razor's edge were behind him.

Long gone.

Sayonara.

A rush of cool air hit him in the face as he opened the door.

Skylights on the ceiling and windows high on the walls let in just enough light so that he could see the contents of the hangar. What he saw was far from what he'd expected. Instead of a couple of C-130s or a single C-5 Galaxy filling up the space, shoehorned in with their maintainers' equipment were nearly a dozen black helicopters.

Instantly recognizable in front of him were the bulky forms of the pair of twin-rotor CH-47 Chinook heavy-lift helicopters. Beyond the 47s, four MH-6 Little Birds sat side-by-side. Lined up near the "Killer Egg" recon helos was a trio of angular black stealth helicopters, one of which Cade recognized as Jedi One—the lone surviving Ghost Hawk in the Special Operations Aviation Regiment's possession.

The other two helos were harder to place. He'd never seen anything like them in person. Best guess was they were single-seat Comanche attack helos, or perhaps a stealthy reincarnation of the venerable Bell AH-1 Cobra attack helicopter.

Lastly, taking up the front third of the hangar, near the massive rolling doors, their sharp-edged black fuselages and twin rotors glinting in the ambient light, was the pair of stealth Chinook helicopters Cade had seen in action on more than one occasion.

A hallway branching off to Cade's right led to another gray door and yet another biometric scanner. *Bunker* was stenciled in red on the steel door.

Cade pressed his hand on the pad. The audible *click* of the door locks retracting was loud in the enclosed space.

The door swung out smoothly and he was hit by conditioned air a few degrees cooler than that in the hallway. He reached around the jamb and flicked the pair of light switches.

A soft hiss sounded, and the new environs were bathed in the stark light cast off by two dozen overhead fluorescent bulbs.

Entering the room, Cade found himself standing before a very large wooden table. Ornate carvings of skeletons and mythological creatures covered every square inch of the tabletop. All four of the table legs were wrapped by carved serpents. Someone had spent a lot of time carving the thing. He'd heard there was a long-running debate among the different teams as to who procured the table, and what conflict region they had brought it back from.

A dozen utilitarian-looking stackable chairs were positioned at equal distance around the table. On the table were briefing papers, Bic pens, thick manuals for communications gear he wasn't familiar with, and a lone ashtray. In the ashtray was the chewed-on stunted corpse of a Cuban cigar. Seeing the stubbed-out nub brought back memories of running operations in Iraq as a newly minted Ranger. His first commander, Don "Smokey" Blake, was never seen without a cigar either protruding from a BDU pocket or clenched between his teeth. And since the West Point grad, now a four-star general, was back and helming United States Special Operations Command, Cade hadn't seen him without at least three Cohibas in his possession.

Standing out amongst the papers scattered about the table was a yellow sheet bearing his name. Taped to the sheet was a key. Scribbled on the sheet in black Sharpie: **Briefing 1300 hours ... 21st Space Wing Tactical Operations Center**. He turned the sheet over and found a map of the base with the TOC circled for him.

While Schriever and Peterson were similarly appointed, the latter had residential neighborhoods, fast food restaurants, a bowling alley, and many more luxuries within its rambling perimeter.

Peterson was crisscrossed by tree-lined streets and featured a large dining hall near the building in which the TOC was housed.

Cade removed the tape and examined the key. NSN was the only marking on it. He recognized this brand from his days on the teams. It was pretty much standard Army-issue.

Looking around he saw that the team room was much larger than he first thought it to be. The table and chairs were surrounded on four sides by chain-link floor-to-ceiling fencing. The fencing was shiny and new and had been apportioned into seven similar-sized cages. Each cage was roughly forty feet on each side and accessed by a single man-sized gate. Each gate bore the name of a different team operating under the USSOCOM umbrella and fitted with a smaller version of the biometric scanners found on the outside doors.

Internally, each team cage housed eight smaller cages. Each identical enclosure had its own man-sized gate emblazoned with a team member's name and secured by a boxy brass padlock. Inside the individual cages was a single waist-high workbench, racks for weapons, and multiple shelves bursting with all manner of gear.

The Pale Riders' cage was right of the door. A locker with his name on a plate was dead ahead from him. Even from a distance, he could see it was stocked to the gills.

Cade returned to the Tahoe and retrieved his kit bags and Pelican gear box.

Moment of truth.

With his belongings on the floor at his feet, Cade placed his thumb on the small biometric pad. A beat later, there was a click and he was in.

Once inside the Pale Riders' cage, he faced a final test, which he hoped wasn't a cruel joke being perpetrated on him by Lopez or Ari, or maybe even the entire team.

The lock was indeed an NSN model stamped with *U.S.* on one side and *Master Lock* on the other. The plug accepted the key straight away and the key worked the pins and counter pins, unlocking the NSN with a solid *snik*.

Standing there on the threshold to his locker and smelling the sweet odor of Hoppe's Number 9 gun oil brought the past screaming back at him. Starting with his first day as an Army Ranger, on to being hand-picked and promoted to Delta by the concerted efforts of Mike Desantos and Greg Beeson, he relived it all.

In Mike Desantos' voice he heard the oft uttered phrase: *Back in the saddle again.*

In his late wife Brook's voice he again heard her give him her blessing. For she knew better than anyone that he wasn't truly alive unless he was downrange and in harm's way, doing the difficult things normal men were no longer raised or expected to do.

Chapter 48

Raven selected a beach-cruiser-style bicycle from the Antlers' subterranean storeroom and walked it past a long row of trucks and SUVs nosed against the building's cement foundation.

Instead of riding the bike up the ramp and then going through the time-consuming process of running the gate up manually, she angled the Schwinn into the waiting elevator and wedged herself in after.

Elevator doors opening, Raven wheeled the bike out and across the lobby, being careful to keep the tires from squeaking on the floor, lest Eve look up from her book and start in on the chit-chat that much sooner.

Raven was a dozen feet from the entry when Eve's head panned in her direction. As the woman slowly lowered the Grisham novel her face had been buried in, the inquisition began.

Skipping the pleasantries, Eve said, "Where are you going today?"

"Out," Raven said.

"Did you see your park got hit again?"

Raven sighed. "I'm going to get some pictures and then go downtown and show them to whoever will look at them."

The woman shifted in her seat. Casting a glance out the double doors, she said, "You better hurry. Last time I was out for a smoke break, looked like the brothers were getting ready to roll fresh paint over the graffiti. Heaven forbid the President is forced to see that crap. You think the brats are doing that in south Springs?"

Though Raven wanted to disengage from the motor mouth, she said, "They hit the fuel depot in January. Just last week the BERR building got sprayed up with stencils of the Chinese President's face."

The SBR was biting into her shoulder, so she paused to adjust the sling.

"I didn't hear about the BERR building. Then again, since I don't trust walls to keep the hissers out, I tend to stay close to home. I actually prefer to stay in my room and watch the world slowly die."

You're the one who's slowly dying, Raven thought. After casting a quick glance at the drive that she imagined at this time of day would be choked with valet drivers delivering vehicles to hotel guests raring to get out to lunch or, perhaps, take a tour of Garden of the Gods, she said, "Did you see anything last night? Like when you went out to … *smoke?*" The word "smoke" was accompanied by a sour expression as she imagined how a cigarette might taste.

Eve shook her head so vigorously a tightly braided strand of hair sprung from underneath her watchman's cap. "Oh, *hell* no," she said. "I don't go out there at night. I do all my smoking right here when it's dark out."

Raven thought about trying to reassure Eve the walls were pretty formidable. Instead, not wanting to get into a back and forth, she simply asked Eve to help with the door.

The bike ride to the BERR building was short in comparison to the time Raven would have wasted had she not escaped Eve's chitchat tractor beam. Five minutes after mounting the mint green, seven-speed cruiser outside of the Antlers, she was parking the Schwinn in a bike rack under cover of the building's front façade.

Down the street at the Pioneers Museum block, business was booming, with long lines snaking from the trailers and onto the white cement sidewalks.

Skirting the line of people waiting to get into the BERR building, Raven slipped through the open doors and went straight for the middle-aged CSPD officer standing sentinel near the bank of elevators. He was barely taller than her and stood a little slouched over.

As she drew near, the officer stopped worrying his neatly trimmed mustache and raised a hand to slow her approach. Seeing his other hand drifting surreptitiously to the semiautomatic on his hip, she raised her hands to show him she wasn't a threat.

"Relax," she said. "I need to speak with Chief Riggleman."

He pointed to the elderly woman at the head of the line Raven had just circumvented. "See her?"

Though the officer's reedy voice made Raven want to smile, instead she kept a straight face and nodded.

"She's ahead of you."

Raven said nothing.

He cocked his head and swept one arm right to left. "See that? It's a line. How it works is you get in back of and wait your turn."

She craned to read the plastic nametag pinned to his uniform.

"C'mon, Upton," she said. "I have some information the chief needs to hear."

"Don't you all."

"It might have something to do with President Clay's ceremony on Sunday. How would it look if something was withheld that might help the Secret Service keep her safe? I can hear the Town Crier now." Deepening her voice and speaking loudly enough for all to hear, she said, "Constable Upton could have prevented—"

Interrupting her, the officer said, "It's *Sergeant* Upton. I'll let you upstairs if you agree to disarm."

Raven shrugged off the SBR and handed it over. "Safety's on."

Doing the *gimme, gimme* motion with one hand, Upton said, "Pistol and the blade."

Reluctantly, Raven handed over her Tennessee Toothpick. She paused before dragging the Glock from its holster. Instead of handing it over, she dumped the magazine, racked the slide, and let it stay locked back. Flashing the sergeant a wan smile, she made a show of proving it was empty by poking a finger into the chamber. As she picked up the ejected round and dropped it and the magazine into the sergeant's awaiting palm, she thumbed the slide catch and holstered the weapon.

Again Upton did the *gimme* motion with his free hand.

Raven shook her head. "I feel naked without it. So I'd like to keep it."

Upton thought about it for a second. While his first instinct was to pat her down for another weapon or spare magazine for the Glock, the thought of it gave him pause. Not to mention if he did so, he might have to answer to the girl's dad. And Lord knows, Cade Grayson was not a person whose bad side he wanted to be on.

So he took the high ground, telling himself, *She's just a kid.*

Pocketing the single round and magazine, he said, "Promise me this is all you're carrying."

Fingers on one hand crossed, Raven nodded.

"Make it quick, then," Upton said. "Second floor, northeast—"

Interrupting, Raven said, "Northeast corner. I know. I've been there before. And Dena knows me."

The elevator dinged to announce its arrival.

A man and woman with a small child in tow exited the elevator and brushed past her without saying a word. As they continued across the wide-open lobby, an argument erupted between the adults.

"Be respectful," was Upton's parting advice as Raven boarded the elevator.

Finding herself all alone in the elevator, Raven retrieved a spare mag from a pocket, drew her Glock, inserted the mag, and racked a round into the chamber. She was just holstering the pistol when the doors opened at the second floor.

Riggleman's office was down a corridor and to the right. On the walls were framed photos of high-desert scenery. She stopped where the gray carpet met the oak door bearing the chief's name.

Taking a deep breath, Raven pulled the iPhone from a pocket. Hearing no movement or voices through the door, she delivered a couple of sharp raps.

From within came a woman's voice. It was kind of smoky and carried a hint of a Southern drawl. "Who is it?"

"Raven Grayson."

There was a brief pause. Then, "Come in."

As Raven entered, she noticed nothing had changed. The walls were still bare. Boxes stuffed to overflowing with papers took up one corner. Standing in the opposite corner was a wooden coat rack. The pair of spare uniforms, desert-tan plate carrier and tactical helmet with *Chief Dena Riggleman* stenciled on it was causing the coat rack to list slightly to one side.

With the former police station currently a soot-blackened pile of rubble in No-Man's-Land just outside the east wall, it was clear that Chief Riggleman was just occupying this part of the BERR building until new accommodations were found.

"You again," said Chief Riggleman. "What now? Kids use too much chalk on the sidewalk outside the Antlers?"

Still standing, Raven simply smiled. Waiting for the chief to give her the respect a taxpaying citizen deserves, she crossed her arms and hitched her brows.

Riggleman kicked her boot-clad feet off the desk and leaned forward. Fingers steepled, she said, "That magazine in your Glock, is it empty?"

"Nope," Raven said. "Locked and loaded is the new gold standard."

"Who taught you that? Your dad?"

Raven nodded.

"You know there's no way to fully put that pistol on *safe*."

Raven lifted her left hand where the chief could see it. Making a trigger-pulling motion, she said, "This is my safety."

The chief dropped her gaze and exhaled sharply. Then, one hand doing the same *gimme* motion as Upton, she said, "Lay it on me. Whatcha got?"

***

Five minutes after her presentation in Riggleman's office, Raven entered the elevator feeling as if no headway had been made in rectifying her problem. Sure the chief had *oohed* and *aahed* as she examined the photos on Raven's phone. But it was all for show. At least that was Raven's gut feeling at the time.

The door slid open on the main floor. First thing Raven saw was the angry expression on Upton's narrow face.

"Chief called down ahead of you. She's blown away. Says you carry yourself like an adult."

"I've seen things."

Upton looked at the line of people. It seemed stalled out, the citizens at the front clearly agitated.

"You made me look like a fool. Next time you come here you get in line like everyone else. And leave your guns at home. Grayson or not, you pull that crap on me again, I'll personally take you on a tour of our Spring Creek Juvenile Detention Center."

Raven struggled to keep from smirking. *You made yourself look like a fool.*

"Truth is, being scolded by the chief is better than the alternative," she finally said.

Officer Upton was still processing the cryptic insinuation as Raven picked up her knife and spare magazine. In the next beat his jaw dropped, and it appeared as if he might proffer a question—or at the very least, start yammering like an imbecile.

Nothing came out of his mouth.

Pleased with the way she had derailed Upton's train of thought, Raven shouldered the SBR and made her way to the exit.

Chapter 49

Peterson Air Force Base

Cade drove straight from the Bunker to the Aragon Dining Hall, Building 1160 on the map provided by Lopez. Along the way he spotted McDonalds' ubiquitous golden arches. Though they weren't lit up, just the sight of them had him pining for simpler times. While not a huge fan of fast food, he would never turn down one of their delicious French fries. The apple pies weren't bad, either.

Aragon Dining Hall was in a mostly brick building with a center-pitched, red metal roof. Large glass windows in front looked out over an expansive, partially covered outside dining area. Nobody was eating lunch outside. Which made sense. People still alive after the worldwide Omega outbreak were conditioned to enjoy indoor shelter whenever possible.

In case the need arose for a quick egress, Cade backed the Tahoe into a space in the lot behind the hall. Flanked by a pair of desert-tan Humvees, and with mostly government-issued sedans with sensible colors and trim levels filling all the nearby spots, the red Tahoe LTZ stood out like a zebra in a herd of wild mustangs.

Stepping from the Chevy, Cade shielded his eyes against the late-morning sun. With just a few feathery clouds scudding the brilliant blue sky, and the temperature hanging in the low sixties, the day was shaping up to be a good one for the walking dead. A few more like this and once again they'd be highly mobile and arriving outside the wire in numbers not seen since early autumn.

Cade brought his M4 and a couple of fully loaded magazines with him. He took the stairs to the hall's back door and walked on in.

There were maybe a dozen people scattered about the massive room. They all looked up or panned their heads toward the door as it clattered shut.

The air inside the Aragon was heavy with the heady scent of vanilla and maple. As he passed by a counter containing silver urns and a couple dozen ceramic mugs, the earthy nose of coffee just a little past its prime stopped him in his tracks.

After drawing a mug of steaming black coffee, Cade took a tray from a tall stack of them and went through the line.

The airmen doing changeover to lunch seemed less than eager to serve him. Considering the age-old intraservice rivalries, he didn't give it much thought. Taking a big stack of the last of the pancakes left over from breakfast service, Cade set a tack for a table occupied by an older gentleman who looked vaguely familiar.

Cade guessed the man was roughly the same height as him. Though distributed differently, it looked as if they both carried roughly the same weight.

The older man wore his silver-white beard short and kept it trimmed neatly around the edges. Wispy strands of like-colored hair worked hard at concealing the man's male-pattern baldness. On the table in front of the man's tray was a navy-blue ball cap. *Strategic Air Command - March Air Force Base* was stitched in gold across the front. The cap's stiff brim was shaped just so. Placed prominently up front above the lettering was a pin memorializing POWs of the Vietnam war. Next to the rectangular pin was another enamel and gold item showing the man's support for the Wounded Warriors Foundation.

Stopping near the edge of the round table, directly across from the man, Cade said, "Anyone sitting here?"

"You are," answered the man. He was wearing Wrangler jeans and a bright red tee shirt with *World's Best Grandpa* on the front.

Cade set his tray down and extended a hand. "Your name's Dan, isn't it?"

A look of astonishment parked on the man's lined face. "Sure is." He tilted his head back and regarded the vaulted ceiling for a spell. Having dredged something from his memory, he met Cade's gaze. "Your name tape says Grayson. I remember you from Schriever. First name is Cade, if my memory serves."

"That it is," Cade confirmed.

The man rose on shaky legs, then shook Cade's hand.

Considering the man's unsteadiness, Cade was surprised by the firm grip.

Retaking his seat, Dan said, "Your fingernails ... looks like you tangled with the Devil."

"More than one," Cade conceded. "They got better than they gave."

Dan nodded. "That's always a good thing." He paused for a beat. Then: "What brings you here?"

"Business." Cade looked around the room. "Pretty slow in here considering it's almost lunch time."

Dan sipped from a can of Coke. Setting the can on the table, he said, "It was like a ghost town in here during breakfast. Like night and day from the norm. Most of the aviators and all of the techs have been either grabbing food to go, or not coming in at all." He paused for a beat. "Something big is going down. A blind man could see that."

Cade said, "Why aren't you helping to get the birds ready?"

"I was thrown some tasks at the end of summer." Dan pushed his tray to the side. Fixed Cade with an earnest look. "Apparently Whipper has no use for me now. The old bull's been put out to pasture ... *again*."

Cade paused between bites. "There's nothing for you to do in the city?"

"Last thing I want is to be back in a big city."

"It's still manageable," Cade said. "Has an Old West feel to it."

"Better than Wild West," Dan said. "To keep busy, I'm going to start volunteering at the base range. Put my NRA certification to good use."

Cade said, "I did some shooting over there." He downed the coffee in his mug and started sopping up syrup with the last of his pancakes. Looking up, he went on, "Somehow our paths didn't cross. Maybe I'll see you there in the future."

"Doubtful," Dan said. "I think I may just load up the Subaru and go find me a cabin up in the Rockies. Something small near a glacially fed lake. Stock my cupboards up real nice and ride summer out. Come winter I'll kill as many of those dead things as I can." He rose and snatched up his tray. "Wash, rinse … repeat until I can't no more."

Cade watched the man turn to walk away. He said, "Until we meet again, Dan."

Looking over his shoulder, Dan said, "Stay frosty out there, young fella."

Chapter 50

Dan's parting words stayed with Cade as he drove the short distance to the Mission Support building. His destination, the 21st Space Wing Tactical Operations Center, was tucked away somewhere inside the sprawling multi-story glass-and-steel building.

Save for the trio of desert-tan Humvees ringing President Clay's hulking MV-22 Osprey—Marine One—the parking lot east of Building 350 held nothing but American-made SUVs and lifted 4x4 pickups.

Team vehicles, Cade thought as he parked next to a jacked-up Ford Expedition at least a foot taller than the stock Tahoe. The sword-wielding half-man, half-Pegasus decal on the rear window of the matte-black SUV told him it belonged to one of the Night Stalkers.

"Looks like we have ourselves a joint briefing," he said aloud to himself. "You were right, Dan. Something big *is* going down."

Before locking the borrowed rig, Cade stowed his M4 in the backseat area and left the spare mags in the center console.

The guard at Building 350's north entrance checked Cade's credentials against a list. Amazed he was not relieved of his sidearm and dagger, and that there was no magnetometer in play, he asked the airman for directions to the TOC.

Two levels underground, the air in the corridor leading to a set of double doors labeled 21 SW Tactical Operations Center was several degrees colder than that outside.

Gooseflesh pricking on his arms, Cade rapped on the door and waited.

He stood there for a long ten-count before a mountain of a man wearing off-the-shelf 5.11 pants and a Condor polo emerged through the door. The man's attire notwithstanding, the wraparound sunglasses and flesh-colored earbud all but identified him as Secret Service—one of the President's detail, to be specific.

Cade's credentials were checked again, only this time he was relieved of his Glock and Gerber and given a wand-check by the man who failed to identify himself or even utter more words than necessary to get Cade to comply with his demands.

Feeling a bit naked without at least a pistol, Cade brushed past the unsmiling "Mountain" and stopped just inside the door. Nearby stood three more of President Clay's detail. They were all wearing navy windbreakers, the bulges of personal defense weapons presenting if you knew where to look.

The air inside the tall-ceilinged, windowless room was a bit warmer than that in the hall. It smelled of stale sweat mixed with the faint, chemical odor of hot electrical components.

Peering past the detail, Cade saw a wall of monitors and at least a dozen 21st Space Wing personnel at their respective workstations. Each station had its own computer monitor, keyboard, and pointing device. Phones, some with their red lights blinking, sat between every other station.

President Clay was sitting in a leather chair to his left and mostly obscured by her detail.

Standing at the front of the room, arms crossed and surveying the assembled aviators and shooters, was an Air Force major general Cade had never seen before. Though the two-star was above average height, the top of his head fell a full foot short of the bottom bezel of the nearest flat-panel wall-mounted monitor.

Sitting on a leather chair to the two-star's right, cigar clenched between his teeth, USSOCOM commander Don "Smokey" Blake seemed uninterested in the chatter going on all around him.

As Cade ventured into the packed room, he caught sight of the Pale Riders, minus Axe, who he knew had winged back to the U.K. weeks ago.

Panning about the room, he saw Ari, Haynes, and Skipper sitting behind a rectangular table, their attention focused solely on the trio of three-ring binders opened up before them.

Moving on, he spied three shooters whom he recognized from his time running ops in Africa with the 5th Special Forces Group. Lounging on a chair behind the larger of the three Green Berets was Captain Javier "Low Rider" Lopez. Seeing that he'd been made by his friend and fellow Delta operator, Lopez leaned forward, extended the middle finger on his left hand and feigned itching his nose with it.

Smiling at the covert bird flip, Cade hooked a thumb at Cross and Griff.

Obviously playing dumb, Lopez furrowed his brow and shrugged.

Cade pointed and mouthed, "Why aren't you over there with them?"

Lopez pointed two fingers at his own eyes, then used those same fingers to direct Cade's attention to the pair of Pale Riders.

When Cade reacquired Cross and Griff, the blond-haired operator was holding some kind of document above his head and using it to wave Cade over.

Still wondering why the team was split up, Cade crossed the room and took a seat beside Griff.

Regarding the redheaded SEAL, he said, "What's up?"

"You're up," Griff responded.

Cross flopped the manila envelope on the table in front of Cade.

The words *Top Secret — Eyes Only* and *Operation Clean Slate* were splashed across the envelope. It was sealed with a length of red tape.

The moment Cade read the words, it dawned on him that Lopez was leading a team that included the 5th Group shooters.

The brass looked as if they were about to begin what would likely be a lengthy PowerPoint presentation.

Cade's eyes were drawn to the sealed document. He could wait no longer. Besides, nothing was holding him back. So he broke the seal and removed the contents.

In addition to the cover sheet confirming what Cade already knew—he would be leading the Pale Riders on Operation Clean Slate—there was a map of Portland, Oregon and photos of places he knew all too well.

As the Air Force two-star was joined by an Army major carrying a remote control, a man Cade hadn't seen since going through Q-Course with him at Fort Bragg pulled up a chair next to him and sat down.

"Natanumo," Cade said, clapping the big Fijian American on his muscular back. "Been a long time."

"After Robin Sage I went on to 7th Group. We saw tons of action running ops out of Bagram. I was in Germany on Z-Day. Place was a shit sandwich. Didn't make it back to Carson until late August."

"Well, Nat, I'm glad you and I are going downrange together. Welcome to the Pale Riders."

The major general was about to begin the briefing, so Cade quickly introduced Fui "Nat" Natanumo to Cross and Griff and then turned his eyes to the display above the Air Force two-star.

Chapter 51

After leaving the BERR building empty-handed, Raven had paid a visit to Lola's. Now, sitting on a bus bench a block south of Colorado Springs only government-sanctioned tattoo shop, she was thumbing through the manual to the Nikon D90 in the camera bag on the bench next to her.

The tattoo shop was occupying a space on the corner of Tejon and Moreno formerly home to *Missing Link Motorcycles*. Facing west on Tejon, the recessed entry to the ground-level storefront was an inky black hole in the building's two-story brick facade.

Above the door was a sign bearing the former store's name and its motorcycle-riding Cro-Magnon mascot. Tattoos ran up and down the arms and legs of the caveman. Whether the shop's new owners were responsible, Raven had no clue. Someone had also altered the sign so that it now read *Missing Link Tattoo*.

Sun warm on her face and forearms, Raven set the manual aside and removed the digital camera from the bag. Next, she swapped out the stock lens for a telephoto item nearly the length of her forearm.

Flicking the power switch on the top-mounted dial to On, Raven felt a slight tremor in the camera body as its screen flared to life. As Lola had promised, the camera's battery held a full charge and its installed SD memory card was empty.

She hefted the camera to her eye and trained the lens on the tattoo shop. Even with the lens magnification dialed all the way in, she could only see the front door and a small slice of the sidewalk out front.

Policing up her stuff, Raven walked the beach cruiser a half block south and set up shop on an outdoor table on the sidewalk in front of a coffee shop shuttered long ago.

When Raven again framed Missing Link Tattoo in the viewfinder, she was able to see the shop's front door as well as the majority of the sidewalks and streets coming in from all four directions.

As she settled in to wait for the late risers to open up the shop, she heard a car horn sound far away to the south. Then, drifting in from the north, well beyond the wall, she detected the soft purr of a helicopter.

In the trees directly overhead, birds called back and forth, their sweet song foreign to her after a long fall and winter spent mostly inside.

Now and again she caught snippets of news being delivered by the Town Crier, positioned on a corner near the Pioneers Museum, a full three blocks away.

***

Ten minutes into her wait, Raven was struck by the fact that every once in awhile, when the wind kicked up from the south, she caught the sweet scent of colorful wildflowers growing in a planter nearby. It was the first time in a long time she could remember not being able to detect the stink of death so prevalent since that last Saturday in July when her world changed forever.

***

The first person to arrive in front of Missing Link did so at a quarter to two, riding a woman's ten-speed, and caught Raven completely by surprise.

By the time Raven had powered on the Nikon, trained it on the sunlight-dappled doorway, and snapped a dozen photos, she knew three things for sure: The pixie-like person working a key in the padlock on the door was female, she was short and thin, and she was of Asian ancestry.

Once the woman—or girl, Raven couldn't be sure—had walked her bike inside the store and closed the door, Raven confirmed her first impressions with a quick review of the shot footage.

Two more people on bikes showed up at a quarter past two. "Fashionably late" was what Sasha called it. "It's what important people do to set themselves apart from the common man" was how she had framed it.

265

All of which led Raven to believe the pair were the tattooers.

The photos she had shot of the pair arriving and dismounting their mountain bikes were way better than those of the person first to arrive. The crisp images showed that both riders were of Asian descent and likely in their twenties or early thirties. Unlike the person who'd opened the shop, these two sported a plethora of visible tattoos. One man had what looked to be a king cobra coiled around his neck, with the serpent's hood dominating one cheek and its long, forked tongue encircling one eye. Snake was well-muscled and wore his dark hair high-and-tight, like her dad.

Both men sported tight leather pants that looked like they came off the motorcycle shop's racks.

The second man's taste in tattoos centered mainly around things found at sea: multi-masted sailing ships, ornate anchors, and bare-chested mermaids. His dark hair was slicked back and glistened in the sun. A cruel mouth was framed by a neatly trimmed goatee. Both ear lobes sagged under the weight of multiple gold hoop-earrings.

After pausing in the doorway and looking down the street in the direction he'd come from, the wannabe pirate followed Snake into the shop.

Over the next forty-five minutes the shop attracted a handful of people. Most were already tatted up. All but two were Caucasians, the exceptions being Daymon and Tran—arriving together right on time.

At three sharp, her head swimming with questions, Raven packed up her camera, mounted the Schwinn, and pedaled off southbound.

In the hour since the briefing concluded, Cade had gotten a lot done. During the drive over from the Mission Support building, with call signs and tanker rendezvous times and situation reports of what to expect on the ground in his old hometown all competing for attention in his head, he had composed the body of the letter in the sealed envelope on the table before him.

Over the years he'd penned his share of death letters. Until now every one of the envelopes he stuffed those letters into were addressed to Brook.

The Sharpie seeming to weigh a ton in his hand, he wrote his daughter's name across the front of the envelope.

The Bunker was quiet, the air still and cool; nevertheless, as the pen's felt tip squeaked against paper, he felt his neck go hot.

All of the members of the various teams sharing this space— Pale Riders included—had already donned their body armor, gunned up, inventoried their rucks, and rallied to the flight line.

Alone with his thoughts, Cade rose and made his way to the Pale Riders' cage. He put the letter on a shelf in his partition and closed the door.

After ushering the escaped emotion back into the imaginary lockbox in his head, Cade hefted his ruck, slung the suppressed M4 over one shoulder, and set off to rejoin his team.

Chapter 52

Hurry up and wait.

Cade had heard the pejorative early on in his career. Maybe even as early as basic training.

The four words described succinctly what to expect as a cog among many in the *Big Green Machine*.

Today was no different. Someone down the line was having a problem getting one of the refueling birds off the ground.

Emerging from the hangar housing the *Bunker*, Cade immediately got an eyeful of the dozen or so helicopters that would take four different Special Forces teams into the fray. Stretching away to the east from the open hangar doors, the assembled machines represented the newest technology available before Omega brought the entire world to a grinding halt.

Shooters and aviators huddling in the shadow of a Stealth Chinook were busy reading briefing handouts and inspecting their weapons one last time.

Aviation techs and crew chiefs up and down the line were using the downtime to recheck avionics and square their birds away for the long flights ahead of them.

As Cade reached the Ghost Hawk—fourth from the head of the line—Nat was just finishing a set of pushups.

Ari, Haynes, Cross, and Griff were embroiled in a game of Texas Hold 'Em. Where they got the table and set of folding chairs, Cade hadn't a clue.

Wearing a flight helmet, with a spray bottle full of blue liquid in one hand, towel in the other, Skipper was polishing Jedi One's cockpit glass.

Approaching Nat, who was now standing, Cade said, "Don't you Fijians ever get tired of working out?"

"Naw, Wyatt," Nat replied, flexing one arm for effect. "One can never take a day off." He paused and a thoughtful look fell on his face. "Except leg days," he went on. "It's OK to skip those once in awhile."

Cade was about to make a crack about tattoos and Pacific Islanders' penchant for covering their bodies with them, when, out of the blue, Skipper said, "It's on, Riders. Time to kick the tires and light the fires."

Jumping up from the card table, Ari said, "Code name, *Irene*. I repeat … code name, *Irene*."

Shooting the aviator a skeptical look, Cade said, "That wasn't in the brief. Gotta be another one of your Black Hawk down references, right?"

"*Bingo!*" Skipper said, spinning a finger in the air. "We are *go* for green."

Passing by Cade, Ari said, "Nothing gets by you, Wyatt. Time to mount up."

Cross and Griff folded the table and chairs and carted them over to the hangar.

Ari and Haynes boarded the Ghost Hawk and immediately busied themselves with getting her turbines fired.

Just as the rotors started spinning, the team members were strapping in.

Five minutes after the call to "go" came through, all four flights were lifting into the air.

Crows loitering atop the hangars squawked their displeasure and, in an explosion of black feather, took flight en masse.

To keep anyone watching from getting an idea of the mission's true objectives, the helicopters all thundered off in the same southeasterly heading.

As silence fell over the lonely corner of Peterson, four miles away the gaggle of noisy aircraft was slowly splintering, each individual flight adopting the heading that would see it to the assigned objective.

Antlers Hotel

When Raven returned from her *mission*, she stowed the Schwinn behind some bushes and entered the Antlers through the front doors. As she paused to let her eyes adjust to the dim environs, Calvin Stephens, a sixty-something, former 20th Group paratrooper and retired Alabama cop, was manning the security desk in place of Eve.

"How's huntin' today, little lady?" The man's soft Southern drawl was easy on the ears. It didn't tend to echo around the lobby like Eve's shrill voice.

Since late February, when Raven had met this particular volunteer, her fondness for him had grown. Though she was technically still a kid, he treated her as an equal, never probing or prying for information she didn't feel like sharing readily. While she'd never asked if he knew of her dad, she suspected, having been in the Special Forces himself, Calvin had already put two and two together. She also liked that once the soft-spoken man initiated conversation, it was always left to her to dictate where it went. Small talk in passing or five-minute chat—Calvin always went with the flow. Never once had he been condescending or tried to talk over her. In a way, she wished more adults—and quite a few of the younger people she knew— would learn something from the man.

Parroting one of Duncan's go to lines, Raven said, "I didn't get any ears today. But I did cross some Ts and dot some Is."

"Bird of the Apocalypse is gettin' things done."

Acting as if she hadn't heard him use her new moniker, she said, "Hey, Calvin … do you remember ever coming across a computer and printer during your rounds?"

Calvin removed his watch cap. Ran a hand through his thinning gray hair and chewed on the query for a beat. Finally, eyes lighting up, he said, "Check the closet in the Food and Beverage manager's office. I think I did see some computer stuff in there." As if surrendering to an unseen enemy—perhaps a finicky memory—he raised both hands off the desk, saying, "It could be stereo equipment, for all I know. Lord knows I'm more than a bit tech-challenged."

Raven regarded the Colt revolver holstered on the man's hip. "But you can shoot straight, right?" she replied, making a pretend pistol with her free hand.

Calvin smiled and chuckled. Producing a finger-gun of his own, he said, "That I can, little lady. That. I. Can."

"Treasure huntin' time," Raven said as she continued on through the lobby.

Calling after her, Calvin said, "If you find a Western novel or some car magazines on your hunt, please grab them for me."

"You got it," Raven said, triggering the tac-light on her SBR and entering the long, darkened hallway branching off the main lobby. The hall ran about fifty in a straight line then made an abrupt ninety-degree right-hand turn.

As Raven cut the corner, muzzle leading the way, the cone of light illuminated the entire fifty-foot run of wall to her left. The beam revealed three doors leading to three separate rooms.

The plaque on door number one read: HOUSECLEANING.

VALET was on the sign affixed to door number two.

Seeing the *FOOD and BEVERAGE* plaque on door number three, Raven said, "Bingo," and dropped the beam to the doorknob.

The light revealed extensive damage to the jamb and doorknob.

Someone had been here before her. And that *someone's* crude job of breaking and entering spared her from having to shoot the lock out.

Before trying the knob, Raven tapped lightly on the door with the butt of her SBR.

Nothing.

She grabbed the knob, turned it clockwise, and pushed the door in with the toe of her boot.

The door swung in silently.

Illuminating the small office, she learned it had been ransacked. Pushing in and opening the only closet, she learned Calvin should trust his memory more often.

Slipped sideways into a cubby was an Acer laptop. The power cord for it was on the shelf beside the cubby. On the same shelf was a Lexmark combination printer/copier/fax, spare ink cartridges for it, and a few different types of paper.

The laptop and paper fit into her pack. The printer she had to carry in her outstretched arms. It was heavy and awkward and hard to get through the doorway. After stepping on the cord and almost fumbling the printer, she stopped and reeled the cord in.

For a second she thought about calling Calvin over to help. When she realized that would leave the entry unguarded, she sucked it up and continued across the lobby, the elevator her ultimate destination.

Exiting the elevator on her floor, she bumped into Wilson.

"Want some help?" he asked.

"What does it look like?" She was breathing hard and obviously struggling with the forty-pound item.

He said, "Hard to tell these days. Taryn hates it when I try to be chivalrous."

Though she wasn't quite sure what the big word meant, she gasped, "Be chivalrous, already. Take it before I drop it."

Relieving her of the printer, Wilson said, "Where do you want it?"

"In the Founders Suite, please."

In passing, Wilson asked, "What's in the bag?"

"I rented a camera at Lola's."

"Rented?"

"I negotiated a price to keep it for a few days. If I want to keep it for good, the rent goes toward purchase." She opened the door for Wilson.

"I wouldn't have thought of that."

"It was Lola's idea," Raven conceded. "She's a shrewd businesswoman." She took the laptop and paper from her bag. Set it on the table next to the printer. "Can you help me get it running?"

Wilson nodded. "That, I can do."

A disembodied voice said, "Whatcha up to, Bird?" It was Duncan. Still, it didn't quite sound like him. Looking toward the far end of the room, Raven spotted his stockinged feet first. They were inverted. Three, maybe four feet separated his toes from the ceiling. Around his ankles were some kind of cuffs. The cuffs were hooked to what looked like a cot. The cot's black frame was connected about midway to a tower that allowed it to pivot from vertical to horizontal and back to vertical, the latter position leaving the person on the cot hanging upside down.

"What is that *contraption*?" she asked.

Duncan said, "Do you know who Roger Teeter is?"

Raven moved around so she could make eye contact. Once she did, it was way weird because Duncan seemed to be standing on his head.

She shook her head. "I have no idea who he is."

"Neither do I," Wilson called. "Almost done setting this printer up, by the way."

"He invented this *contraption*."

Raven made a face. "And what is it?"

Duncan said, "It's called an inversion table. Glenda brought it over from the hospital."

"What's it for?" Wilson asked.

Duncan flung his arms forward. The inertia created sent the cot part moving. In turn, his body went with it. Now right-side up, Duncan said, "It stretches my spine out. Relieves pressure and such. An hour spent in this *contraption* lets me be up and walkin' about for a few pain-free hours."

Wilson powered on the laptop and printer. Looking up, he said, "Why don't you take something for the pain."

"He can't," Raven said. "Glenda said that if he did, in no time he'd be back to drinking again."

Duncan said, "The big boss is right. It's a slippery slope, for sure."

As he removed the ankle boots, he went on: "Did you get some pics of your perpetrators?"

"Let's see." She took the memory card from the Nikon and inserted it into the laptop's card reader.

After a short pause, during which the computer was making soft grinding noises, the screen came alive with a mosaic of photos, about fifty total.

Raven selected frontal and profile pictures of the slim female who opened up the shop, Snake, and Pirate. She printed three of each and passed them around. "Memorize those faces. If you see them near my park, let me know right away."

Wilson said, "Roger that. I can take a shift down there. Help keep an eye on the place until the President's team seals it off for the upcoming ceremony."

Raven shook her head. "They're already putting in barriers. Secret Service will be here tomorrow to sweep the building. Best we stay out of their way."

Sasha asked if she could do anything to help. Though her delivery was nonchalant, her body language told Raven the teen was looking for some excitement.

"Save your energy for dish duty," Raven answered. Making a face, she added, "Best if we let the authorities do what they do *best*."

"Bullcrap," said Peter. "You're planning something. I've seen you work."

Sasha planted her hands on her hips. A slight tilt to her head, she said, "I've known you to buck authority before. You're just like your dad ... always keeping your cards close to your vest." Lips pursed, gaze narrowing, she asked, "What are you planning?"

Raven shook her head. "Nothing to report. Besides, I made my dad a promise. I intend on honoring it."

Duncan grunted as he studied the faces on the photos. "These folks look like the kind of bipedal vermin you don't want to tangle with." He tapped a finger on the one Raven called Snake. "In nature, the colorful animals are the dangerous ones. Don't you forget that, Bird."

"Don't worry," she said, fingers and toes crossed, "I won't be doing anything my dad wouldn't do."

Chapter 53

The thrill of the multi-ship launch and subsequent fifteen-minute nap-of-the-earth dash from Peterson had worn off somewhere over the Rockies' western slope. Having been asleep since, even staying so throughout the first aerial refueling, Cade had missed seeing the landscape transition from scrub and sparsely treed expanses of high desert to fertile ground home to lush forest and brilliant green meadows.

Sensing the helo course-correct and take a slight nose-down attitude, Cade broke sleep's embrace. Cracking an eyelid, he peered at his Suunto.

He had been out of it for two hours. The nap had left him feeling groggy and had done nothing to dispel the headache brought about by the bouncing and jostling they'd all experienced as Ari steered Jedi One around the back side of the Cheyenne Mountain Complex and darted west, using arroyos and tree-rimmed canyons to keep their true course a secret.

Sitting on the helo's port-side, back to the rear bulkhead, afforded Cade a commanding view of the landscape through the window glass to his left. He was also able to observe the entire troop compartment, Haynes up front in the left seat, Ari in the right, and a good chunk of blue sky through the slanted cockpit glass.

Griff and Cross occupied rear-facing seats across from Cade. Both men were asleep, their gloved hands clutching their weapons. Facing forward, safety straps straining to keep his large frame on the narrow seat, was the newest Pale Rider, Fui "Nat" Natanumo. Nat was asleep, his Mk 46 Mod O Light Weight Machine Gun trapped between his outstretched legs. Basically a lightened version of the venerable SAW (Squad Automatic Weapon), the Mk 46, made by Fabrique Nationale, was belt fed with 5.56mm x 45mm linked rounds and equipped with a foregrip, bi-pod, and holographic sight on the top rail. With a 200-round ammo belt in the box, the weapon weighed less than twenty pounds. Child's play for the huge Pacific Islander.

Always a jovial soul, Nat wore a wide, bliss-filled smile even as he slept.

A laminated map draped across his lap, SOAR crew chief, James "Skip" Skipper, sat on the seat below the stowed starboard-side minigun. As always, the wiry thirty-something was paying most of his attention to the ground below. Now and again he would consult the map or look to the rear-facing monitor affixed to the bulkhead over his head.

Either sensing Cade's scrutiny or having detected movement reflected back at him from the starboard-side window, Skip turned his attention inward, to the troop compartment.

All Cade saw of the man's face when the helmeted head finished its right-to-left pan was a pair of coal-black eyes. They were framed by the matte-black helmet and grinning-skull facemask strapped to it. Though Cade couldn't see Skip's mouth moving, he could hear him shouting over the baffled turbines and low harmonic thrum of the Ghost Hawk's super-quiet rotors.

"We just refueled, sir." Skip tapped a gloved finger on the folded map. "Our twenty is here, northeast corner of Utah. We'll be transitioning into Wyoming airspace in five minutes."

Not far from Eden, Cade thought. He nodded and looked past the crew chief. The rest of the three-bird flight was out there somewhere; however, the viewing angle out the starboard-side windows prevented him from seeing either the lone Comanche attack helo or the stealthy Ghost Chinook carrying a quick reaction force consisting of two twelve-man Ranger chalks.

The view out his window was breathtaking, the westering sun far off and low in the horizon. In Ashley National Forest, a thousand feet below the speeding Ghost Hawk, alpine lakes glittered like jewels in a crown honed from obsidian. Far off, solitary trees on knife-edged ridges cast long, skeletal shadows across sun-dappled meadows.

As Cade watched the sun retreating to the west, in real time the forest all around was being slowly consumed by dusk's inevitable and steady creep. Flashing Skip a thumbs up, he said, "Thanks for the update. Wake me before the next refuel rendezvous."

Skip acknowledged the request with a thumbs up of his own.

Sleep when you can. Heeding the sage advice from Mike Desantos, his late mentor and friend, Cade closed his eyes and nodded off.

***

The distinct *clunk* of the drogue mating with Jedi One's telescoping fuel boom woke Cade from his slumber. As he came to, he heard snippets of conversation. In the next beat, Skip was waving at him and mouthing, "Refueling as we speak."

Mouthing "Thanks," Cade looked at his watch and learned he'd been asleep for about ninety minutes.

Inside the cabin, now awash in red light meant to preserve night vision, Nat was still asleep. Which was a wonder, because Cross and Griff were engaged in spirited conversation.

Outside the windows, night had descended on the countryside. Far off on the horizon, all that was left of day was a thin sliver of purple quickly fading to black.

Returning his attention to the cabin, Cade saw that all eyes were on him.

"Goldilocks has awakened from her slumber," Griff said, his Southie accent making the statement sound more like an indictment than an observation. "What were you dreaming about, Wyatt?"

Immediately coming to Cade's defense, Ari said, "Your *mom*, Griff. Instead of breaking the guy's balls, why don't you include him in the next round of shit-you-can't-unsee."

Cade looked a question at Griff.

Stretching his shoulder harness to its limits, Cross leaned forward and offered Cade a fist.

Bumping fists with the smiling man, Cade said, "What's the topic, gentlemen?"

Griff said, "We're talking about the strangest shit we've come across outside the wire. It's Skip's turn."

Skip had unclipped the face mask on one side. It bounced and swayed every time the helo encountered turbulence. Looking at Cade,

277

he said, "Sorry about not waking you for this, Captain. Didn't think it was your kind of thing."

Even in the dim red light, Cade could see the sheepish look on the man's bearded face. "No worries," he said. "You'll pay for it later."

Face blanching, Skip said, "It won't happen again, sir."

"Just pulling your leg," Cade said. "You're up, Skip. Let's hear it."

Skip smiled. He was obviously happy to be let off the hook so easily. Clearing his throat, he said, "So we're on the rebound leg after inserting a team of Green Berets somewhere east of Seattle. Ari comes on talking about some huge yachts docked on the Sound below us. Then, all of a sudden—as Ari's been known to do—he throttles way back and dumps altitude so he and Durant can pick the biggest boat out of the pack."

"*Yacht*," Cross said. "Last I heard a boat is twenty-seven feet or less. Anything above three hundred foot or so is a ship. Got it?"

Ignoring the SEAL, Skip went on, saying, "*Sooo* as I was saying … there's this sloop docked out ahead of a *mega-yacht* called *Charade*. The sloop's a big three-master called *Slippery When Wet*. She's maybe sixty feet stern to bow and lashed pretty tight to the dock." He pauses to scan the ground all around. Satisfied Jedi One's only company is the other two ships, he continues: "On account of the rollers and whitecaps the wind's pushing in off the Sound, she's moving pretty good side-to-side. As we go right over top of her, Ari starts his turn, and I see that some poor bastard has gone and hung himself by the neck from the main mast."

"What's funny about that?" Griff asked. "I've seen plenty of people who've gotten the Omega and offed themselves at the end of a rope."

From his seat up front, Haynes boomed, "For cryin' out loud, Griff, let the man finish his story."

Though he wasn't hungry, the words *Eat when you can* scratched at the back of Cade's mind. It was yet another of Desantos' many sayings and it spurred him to delve into his pack for an MRE.

Picking up where he left off, Skip said, "This poor bastard must not have known the *rules*. He looks to have been up there a day, two at the most. Birds had only grubbed on his eyes and lips at this point. *Funny* part is that he's spinning around the mast on the end of his noose like a damn tetherball. His arms are going all"—Skip flails his arms—"crazy like he's batting at a bee that's fucking with him. And every time this unlucky bastard gets wound up all the way in one direction, the sloop's rolling and banging on the dock starts him on a return journey around the mast." He stopped the bee-batting motion and threw a visible shudder. "Just imagine that being you up there, Griff. Spinning around again and again until either the rope snaps or it saws through your neck."

Shaking his head, Griff said, "First off, *I* would eat a bullet before stretching my neck out at the end of a rope. Much more efficient, my friend."

"You'd have to stop yacking long enough to suck on your Sig," Cross quipped. "I doubt you could pull *that* off."

Griff threw the other SEAL the bird while mouthing, "Fuck off, surfer boy."

As Cade tore into the MRE, there was another *thunk* and the KC-130 refueling bird out of the recently reopened Idaho Air National Guard base disengaged from Jedi One. A tick later, the turbine whine rose inside the helo and Ari was back on the comms. "Anvil Actual, it's your turn. Let's hear your best shit-you-can't-unsee tale."

"I'll go last," Cade said, dredging a spoonful of cold spaghetti from the foil pack. "Let's hear if Griff can top Skip's zombie tetherball."

Griff cracked his knuckles. Smile widening, he began, saying, "I'm just back stateside after nearly getting my ticket punched in Paki-land and I'm sent out and about with some Team Ten shooters. Orders are to see who's left at the Raven Rock facility. Word was some of the Joint Chiefs made it there. Anyway, we're on the ground after being infilled outside of the effective range of Rock's countermeasures. We commandeer a couple of Humvees left behind at a National Guard roadblock. Closing in on the Raven Rock facility we come across a group of moaners."

"What's funny about that," Skip mocked. "Groups of moaners are a dime a dozen."

"One of these *moaners*, smartass," Griff replied, steely gaze directed at Skip, "is totally naked. Johnson all hanging out. He's got pierced nipples and a bunch of Japanese-style tattoos… all … over … his skinny white body."

"Get to the point," Haynes ribbed.

Grimacing, Griff said, "So nipple-ring-boy is pretty well endowed."

"*Was*," Skip reminded.

As Cade drank from his hydration pack, he was struck by how (even if he didn't always show it) he really enjoyed the team banter. Amused, he looked on as Cross made the universal "*hurry it up*" motion with his hands.

"Don't know if he did it to himself, or if he came across it as he was doing what roamers do, but this fool has a rat trap on the end of his junk."

Everyone aboard, save for Nat, who was still chin-to-chest out of it, drew a breath and groaned.

Griff held a hand up to silence the peanut gallery. "It's not a little old hardware store mouse trap. This thing is an industrial-strength trap. Six inches by four, I bet."

Cade couldn't resist. He stopped chewing long enough to say: "How did this super-trap not sever the Z's member?"

A ripple ran through Griff's red beard as his smile widened. "The dude had all kinds of piercings up and down his *member*."

Incredulous, Cross asked, "Prince Albert, too?"

Nodding, Griff said, "The helmet was pierced front to back. And the whole kit-and-caboodle was bouncing up and hitting him in the gut with each step as he walked towards me. That fucking hunger in its eyes still gives me a case of the shivers."

Skip asked, "What'd you do next?"

Gloating, Griff said, "Two to the face, one to the junk." He looked to Cade. "What do you think, Wyatt? You top that episode of strange-shit-you-can't-unsee?"

Cade thought his treatment of Francis *aka* Pug outside of Schriever just might eclipse the rat-trap story. While cutting the killer's Achilles tendons and letting him get bit and turn was satisfying, watching the zombie version of Pug flop like a fish out of water every time he tried to rise from the ground fell in the category of shit-you-can't-unsee that he would take to the grave with him.

Raising his hands in mock surrender, Cade said, "You got me. No topping that gem."

Voice rising over Cade's, Ari said, "Three hours and change to Target Bravo. Next refueling will be sixty miles out. Any changes to our game plan, Anvil?"

Swallowing a bite of pound cake, Cade said, "Satellite imaging didn't tell much of a story. Can you get us close enough to Bravo to conduct a covert recon before proceeding to infil?"

Ari said, "Affirmative," then ordered Haynes to alter their waypoints accordingly.

Sleep when you can.

Cade finished the MRE and stowed the packaging. Meeting Skip's gaze, he said, "Same request."

Nodding, Skip said, "I'll wake you when we're five minutes out."

Cade returned the nod and closed his eyes.

Chapter 54

The long-range Motorola on the dresser in Raven's room came to life with a burst of static. She'd been in her room since after dinner, declining an offer from Peter and Sasha to join them on a walk.

Leaping from the exercise bike, she rolled over the bed ninja-like and lunged for the radio. Snagging the whip antenna, she cycled the volume down and pressed the Motorola to her ear just as Daymon's voice was issuing from its tiny speaker.

"She-Ra, you there? This is He-Man."

Daymon hadn't explained the meaning of the code names when he had come up with them. At the time, Raven hadn't cared enough to ask. Now, as her thumb depressed the Talk button, she was wondering what part of Daymon's childhood experience they came from. After a short pause, she answered, saying, "She-Ra here. What's up, He-Man?"

There was a chuckle on the other end, followed by: "Pirate, Snake, and Pixie are just beginning their closing duties."

The code names given the trio were Raven's doing. She'd come up with them during her long-range recon by camera. Though she didn't like using them—thought it silly actually—Daymon did have a point. While the long-range radios had more than a hundred unique channels, those channels were not encrypted; therefore, anyone with a similar radio could be eavesdropping on them at this very moment.

Incredulous, Raven said, "*What?* It's only nine o'clock!" Then through clenched teeth, she whispered, "Peter and Sasha are out and about. Plus, other people are still awake here."

Daymon said, "Changing channels," and the Motorola in Raven's hand went silent. Consulting the list, she adjusted channels and waited.

After a brief pause, a burst of squelch was followed by the same exchange of code names. Then Daymon said, "I was their last customer. As Pirate finished up on my piece, the two men started speaking amongst themselves in Chinese—*mostly*. I did hear Snake tell Pirate something that sounded like 'hurry up ... we still have a lot of *sheetrock* to hang.'"

"In English?" Raven asked.

"Broken English," Daymon replied. "At least on his part. Pirate's English is better than mine."

Enjoying the cloak-and-dagger routine a little too much, Raven said, "I think it's best we change channels again." After following the same routine, she went on: "She-Ra here ... how copy?"

"Loud and clear."

"What'd Pirate say?"

"He told Snake to 'relax,'" Daymon answered. "Then he insisted they still have nearly two days to complete their 'renovation.' 'To get everything right and in place.'"

This information started Raven's stomach to churn. She knew this was bigger than cryptic graffiti in her park and a fused-to-the-street tanker-truck. Refocusing, she said, "What about Pixie? Is she involved?"

"She was just listening and watching them at this point. My gut tells me she's part of it."

"How long until they come my way?"

"Twenty, maybe thirty minutes. That is if they don't stop for a drink on the way home."

"They're on their bikes?"

"Affirmative," Daymon said. "Same three as before."

"You did the *thing* we discussed?"

"Yep. Took a *smoke break* after the first hour. They're all in place."

Raven imagined the lifelong non-smoker (cigarettes, at least) making air quotes as he said "smoke break." She said, "Switching frequency," and rolled the channel and sub-channel to the next on her hand-written list. Finished, she went on, saying, "He-Man, this is She-Ra. How copy?"

"He-Man here. Good copy." He paused. Coming back, he said, "We probably don't need to change frequencies so often."

Raven said, "Whatever. I'm getting ready now and will be in place in ten minutes."

"Copy that," Daymon said. "I'll give you a heads-up once they're out the door and Oscar Mike."

Raven had no problem with Daymon throwing in the mil-speak. It was the same language her dad used when he needed to get his point across in a hurry. She was very familiar with it. In fact, after her dad gave the Eden survivors a crash course on the subject, everyone there, save for Sasha, had adopted the most common phrases as part of their normal vocabulary. The only downfall, however, was that hearing it over the radio made her think about her dad, who at this very moment was somewhere out there in the wild, doing who-knows-what for God and country. "Outside the wire" was how he would have phrased it if he were here.

Instead of replying verbally to Daymon's sign-off, she clicked the Talk key once to signal that she understood.

Saying a quick prayer for Daymon and her dad, she shrugged on her pack, donned the black watch cap, and snugged the NVG-encumbered tactical helmet onto her head. She clicked the plastic clasps together and cinched the chinstrap tight as it would go. She bobbed her head up and down and all around. Thanks to the stocking cap, the helmet stayed put, the movement nearly nonexistent.

Tight as it's going to get, she thought.

Raven slipped the suppressed Glock 19 into the holster on her thigh and then scooped up the suppressed SBR. She checked the magazine, reseated it, and then threw the selector to Safe. After inserting fresh lithium batteries in the EOTech holographic gunsight, she tested its operation. Satisfied her rifle was good to go, she set it on the bed next to her pack containing the Nikon and some other items taken from one of her dad's Pelican cases.

Feeling the first jolt of adrenaline stirring within her, she donned her mom's old plate carrier. Lastly, she jammed spare magazines for her weapons into her mom's old chest rig and strapped it on over the plate carrier.

The hand-me-down gear fit her pretty well. Which told her she'd grown some since October, when her mom had passed.

Wow. Dad hadn't been blowing smoke after all when he told her she was getting to be nearly as tall as Brook was when ...

Blowing smoke was one of those Duncanisms she'd adopted while her dad was comatose. While she didn't use the long version of the saying, she still got a disturbing visual from its abbreviated form. Making a mental note-to-self to purge the colorful language from her lexicon, she looked at her reflection in the mirror. Dressed in all black, she thought she looked a bit like a ninja. Which made sense, because that's what guys in her dad's line of work were often called.

She contemplated finding her dad's black face paint and finishing the job.

Don't do anything I wouldn't do.

That settled it for her.

She slung the SBR over her shoulder and flicked off the lamp. With the blackout curtains pulled shut over the windows, the room was pitch black. She couldn't make out a thing. Not even the reflection of herself she'd just been staring at.

Reaching up, she pivoted the NVGs down so they came to rest an inch or so in front of her eyes.

Finding the On switch by feel, she powered the device up and saw a robot-looking version of herself, rendered in white and soft shades of gray, staring back at her. She marveled at all the detail conveyed by the newest phosphor white technology. She could almost count the tiny hooks on her plate carrier's Velcro adjustment straps.

Keeping the NVGs deployed, she shrugged on her pack, then made her way to the door. Moving out into the dark hall, she locked her door and pocketed the key.

The hall was empty. Clear as day she saw the door to her dad's room, the double doors of the Founders Suite, and further down the long hallway, the doors to a number of unoccupied rooms.

She stood there for a beat, listening to the soft voices of her friends in the Founders Suite. It sounded like they were playing some kind of board game.

Determining her exit had gone unnoticed, she padded down the long hall, toward the elevators, the soft scuff of her boot soles on the luxurious carpet the only evidence of her passing.

Reaching the elevator, she was able to make out every little detail, from the fine detail on the wallpaper on down to the Braille on the elevator call panel.

Raven chose the stairs over the elevator, having them all to herself from thirteen to the lobby.

For just a second, as she entered the lobby's dim environs, she contemplated removing the helmet and walking by the desk with it tucked underneath her arm. While Eve and the other civilian volunteers might miss it, Calvin would not.

Thinking hard about how to stave off any questions, she flipped the NVGs up and strode toward the entrance. Straightaway she saw that Calvin was pulling an all-nighter.

As she neared the wooden desk set up just inside the doors, she heard reedy vocals and the jangling guitar of a band with a funny name. Duncan had called them Creedence Clearwater Revival. He was a big fan, too. Said he used to have a song of theirs as the ringtone for his old cell phone.

As always, Calvin was genuinely pleased to see Raven. Silencing the song having to do with someone running through a jungle, he ran the volume down and greeted her warmly. He looked her up and down. No way he could have missed the helmet and NVGs.

"I see you're going with the Johnny Cash look tonight."

"That's me … the girl in black."

"Well, you get those fools defacing our park. You catch them in the act and have them at gunpoint … call the law first, and then call me." He smiled and tapped the flex cuffs hanging off his belt. "I'll come right away and help you detain them."

"Will do." Raven threw him a quick salute, then stood there, waiting for him to get up and let her out.

Outside, the night air was cool on her exposed skin. The stairs ahead were barely discernable because the recessed lights above the covered entry were extinguished. As if gripped in a massive blackout, the city within a city was completely dark. No streetlights burned. No vehicles could be heard or seen traversing the nearby thoroughfares.

Looking up, she saw that the windows in the building rising up above her were all shrouded by curtains. The night sky was cloudless; the stars immediately above her bright and well-defined.

To the east, the waning moon was a pale-yellow sliver. It was low in the sky and pale in comparison to the swath of stars crowding it.

So this is what a waning moon looks like was echoing in her head as she deployed the NVGs and hustled off toward her park.

Chapter 55

The sun was well below the western horizon when Ari came on over the shipwide comms: "Thanks for flying Night Stalker Airways. Rise and shine, Pale Riders." After making sure everyone was awake and patched into the shared comms, he directed all eyes to the fully lit structure coming into view on the ship's starboard-side.

They'd been following the mighty Columbia River's twists and turns since leaving Idaho and crossing over into Oregon. Keeping the Ghost Hawk in the deep and wide trough carved long ago by massive glaciers on the move, Ari had led the three-ship flight on the circuitous course, never once putting more than a hundred feet of altitude between the bird's smooth underbelly and the Columbia's choppy surface.

Now, cruising along due west at about two-thirds speed, the brash pilot was pulling pitch and obviously itching to either impart knowledge to his customers or humor them with his stand-up comedy. Either way, they were a captive audience.

"Behold the shining beacon of light at our one o'clock. You may be asking yourself, 'What in the Sam Hill is that?'"

Craning to see out the nearest window, Nat said, "Besides the location of our FARP ... what are we seeing, Night Stalker?"

"That, my friends, is Sam Hill's former home," said Ari. "One of them, at least. It's been a museum for many years. Sam named the property Maryhill. Place was wired for electricity before power lines reached this far out. He also had it designed with cars in mind, well before cars were a big thing. It's sitting on a subterranean ten-car garage that's been converted to display Native American artifacts and other fine art."

Situated on the Washington side of the river, the multi-level stone and glass monstrosity—lit up entirely by solar-powered lights atop poles ringing its rectangular perimeter—was the biggest home Cade had set eyes on since the raid on Robert Christian's mansion on the hill in Jackson Hole, Wyoming. He didn't know how many square feet he was looking at, but the estate was nearly as big as the White House, with the sprawling grass- and tree-covered grounds to match.

Bordering the mansion's west flank and cast in a soft yellow glow from the perimeter lights was a massive vineyard. Dozens of rows of grapevines marched away from the mansion, into darkness.

Save for a strip of lawn on the south side that sloped away gently to a shelf of barren land overlooking the distant Columbia River, the remainder of the grounds north and east of the mansion were mostly flat and home to knee-high grass and mature trees.

A single paved drive bordered by scree and low scrub snaked away from the mansion, north by east. It climbed and switched back on itself a few times before finally merging with east/west running State Route 14 several hundred yards north of the museum grounds. Beyond SR-14, perched high atop a hill Cade could only make out the jagged outline of, were a number of electricity-generating wind turbines. Though the east wind was blowing gently, with gusts now and then topping twenty miles per hour, the massive blades atop towers hundreds of feet tall were barely in motion.

East of the honey-colored Maryhill Museum was a pair of empty parking lots. A sidewalk flanked by chest-high grass split the acre of blacktop down the middle. Wending their way past a trio of picnic tables being slowly swallowed by the grass were a couple dozen raggedy-looking first turns. As they entered the spill from the first of the overhead light standards, long gangly-armed shadows suddenly appeared in their wake.

The eerie sight reminded Cade of the scene in *Close Encounters of the Third Kind* in which first contact was made with the pale-skinned aliens.

As the entire scene below continued playing out on the monitor above Skip's head, the crew chief was busy readying one of the safety-orange diversionary devices known as a Screamer. By the time the helo was sliding in above the small herd, he'd armed the spherical device and sealed its access panel.

Speaking to no one in particular, Cross said, "That should buy us some time."

Griff said, "That woman's screaming *never* gets old."

Weighing in his mind who was better at sarcasm between Ari and Griff, Cade felt the Ghost Hawk bank and instantly lost sight of the Zs.

Hailing Ari on the comms, Skip said, "I want to drop the device in the scrub near where the drive splits from the feeder road. That should draw the Zs off the property."

"Copy that," Ari responded. In the next beat, the Ghost Hawk was changing direction. Over the ensuing two seconds, the mansion swung out of sight and the hillside filled up the cockpit glass.

Five seconds after leaving the mansion and grounds behind them, Ari had flared the near-silent Ghost Hawk and adopted a steady hover a dozen yards above the snaking drive.

The moment the helo leveled off, Skip started the starboard-side door powering back in its channels. Before the door had hit the stops, cool air thick with the stink of carrion and tinged by burned jet fuel was assaulting the cabin.

Showing no fear, Skip leaned partway out into space, his nylon safety strap stretched tight and the down blast whipping at his uniform. As the helicopter spun on its axis, with the mansion coming into view through the open starboard-side door, Skip tossed the armed device into the inky darkness.

The lifelike wail of a dying woman was blasting from the Screamer before it hit the ground.

While Ari had been working the Ghost Hawk into position for Skip to do his thing, Haynes was busy reacquiring the Zs with the FLIR pod.

With the wails from the Screamer rising above the decibel levels produced by the hovering helo, Haynes said, "Tracking the tangos."

Cade watched the whole thing play out on the flat-panel screen. In the middle distance, down the hill, rendered in shades of green and black, the zombies came to a lurching halt. As the raggedy first turns jostled against each other to get turned around, heads panned and mouths formed silent Os. Cade heard the hisses and moans in his head as the Zs turned clumsily and began a steady uphill march, toward the source of the screams.

Ari said, "Fish on! Good job, Skip." Hailing the other two ships in the flight by their unique call signs, he instructed them to orbit out of sight until the dead located the diversionary device.

Hearing the warrant officer piloting the Stealth Chinook—Jedi One-Two—come back with an "Affirmative," Ari nosed his bird around to the west and bled altitude to treetop level.

With the Screamer doing its thing, Ari looped them around the estate. As he was putting the mansion between Jedi One-One, the pilot aboard the Comanche—Jedi One-Three—came on the net to confirm that the Zs were still tracking the device.

Holding One-One in a hover below the crest of the hill south of the mansion, Ari said, "Now we wait, gentlemen."

During the initial low-level pass, Cade had spotted broken-out glass and obvious signs of smoke damage around the museum's many south-facing windows. Addressing Ari, he asked: "Any idea who burned the place?"

"Negative," answered Ari. "Intel says it was looted early on. How it got this way is anyone's guess."

Cade said, "I saw the bowser. Where's our ground personnel?"

Ari said, "Just hailed them. No answer so far."

Cade asked, "Did you pick up any movement during the pass?"

"Negative," Ari answered. "Skip?"

"Negative," said the crew chief.

"Haynes," Ari said, "switch to thermal."

"Going to thermal." Manipulating the FLIR pod, Haynes zoomed in on the mansion's northwest corner. Once the image steadied and the multi-wheeled, tarp-covered fuel bowser was framed fully on the screen, it was clear there were no human-shaped hot spots presenting in the vicinity.

Cade said, "Contact the TOC, see what they know."

Ari said, "Wait one."

Thirty seconds crawled by.

The thermal image remained unchanged, just the bowser backstopped by the mansion. Engine putting off no more heat than the rest of the vehicle, the bowser was but a dark silhouette against a much larger and equally dark silhouette.

Ari came back on over the shared comms. "The team answered last check-in ninety minutes ago." He paused and fixed Cade with a hard stare. "Unless they show their faces soon, we are on our own."

Shaking his helmeted head, Cade thought, *Eff you, Murphy.* Before he could respond to Ari, the Comanche pilot was back on the net with news that the Zs were clear of the grounds and almost to the diversionary device.

Ari ordered One-Two to refuel first. As the Chinook pilot confirmed and began to roll in, Ari said, "One-Three, One-One. You belly up next. We'll assume overwatch for you while you're wheels down."

"One-One, One-Three. Solid copy. We'll repay the favor when you're wheels down."

Once Ari finished his reply and had signed off, Cade covered his mike and walked his gaze about the cabin. Raising his voice to be heard over the turbine noise, he said, "Anyone want to volunteer to assist Skip with the hot refuel?"

Watching Jedi One-Two settle on the concrete parking pad beside the bowser, Griff said, "I'm game. Someone else has to wash the windows, though. I'm no good with a squeegee."

***

Twenty minutes after arriving at the FARP, Jedi One-One's turn at the bowser came.

As Cade watched the Comanche rise from the parking pad and its wheels tuck back up into its sleek fuselage, he felt the Ghost Hawk under him go nose down and bank hard to port.

"Wheels down in ten," Ari said over the shipwide comms. "I got good news and bad news. Which do you boys want to hear first?" Instead of waiting for an answer, he made an executive decision, saying, "OK … good news first. There *will* be enough JP left for us." He paused only long enough to again meet Cade's gaze. "Bad news is, Mister Murphy is cornholing us for the second time today. Lock and load boys, all the refueling activity has drawn the Zs away from Skip's toy."

Cade saw the bad news confirmed on the monitor. Sure enough, the entire herd was turned around and staggering down the narrow drive leading to the mansion. Wasting no time, he ordered Nat and Cross to exfil ahead of Skip and Griff once the helo was wheels down. They were to take up positions a dozen yards from the door, one at each end of the bird—their sole job while Skip worked the controls on the bowser and Griff connected the fuel hose would be to protect the helo and make dead certain nothing got near the tail rotor. For if the whirring blades suffered any damage, One-One would likely be grounded. And should that happen, only way out was an emergency extraction aboard an already crowded Jedi One-Two and a very uncomfortable ride from there on out.

Cade followed up his instructions by saying that he would trail the refueling team out the door and take up a position equidistant to the helo and bowser. His job would be to cover Skip and Griff while they worked on refueling their ride.

Ten seconds after the Comanche rocketed skyward from the rectangle of white cement barely a dozen yards west of the fuel bowser, Jedi One-One's wheels were fully deployed and the matte-black helo was taking the prototype gunship's place.

The troop compartment door hit the stops as One-One's wheels made contact with terra firma. In rushed air thick with the damp-earth smell of decaying vegetation and the ever-present nose of burning jet fuel.

Leading the Pale Riders out the door, Skip hit the ground running. Head down, muscled arms and legs pumping, Griff stuck like glue to the crew chief.

When the rest of the team's boots hit the ground, they were all business. There was no cracking wise, no ball breaking, and no wasted movement as they took up their assigned positions.

Chapter 56

Five minutes into the hot refuel, it was crystal clear to Cade that, once again, Mister Murphy was not going to cooperate. The evidence came to him in the form of an ominous report from Jedi One-Three, circling high above the operation.

Over his headset, Cade heard: "Anvil Actual, this is One-Three overwatch." The pilot didn't wait for confirmation the team leader on the ground copied his transmission. Instead, he went on, saying: "Be advised, I have eyes on multiple ambulatory dead closing on you from the west. Apologies for the short notice. The bastards didn't show up on my initial thermal sweep."

Cupping his boom mike, Cade said, "One-Three, Anvil Actual. Good copy. How long do we have until contact? How many bodies do you have eyes on?"

"They're *danger close*. I count twenty. I repeat: *two ... zero ...* tangos are just now emerging from the vineyard. They're funneling through the two rows nearest your position."

Though he knew the term "*danger close*" was never used loosely by aviators, he asked, "Can you put some ordnance on them?"

Negative," said the Comanche pilot. "Not with the hot refuel still underway."

"Copy that," Cade replied. "Anvil Actual, out."

No way he could allow this new development to affect the refueling. If they were to abort now, there was no guarantee command back at Peterson could get another tanker out to them before they went bingo on fuel. Then there were the logistics of keeping the other two birds in the flight airborne.

It was crystal clear to Cade that any way he gamed it, it was imperative that they finish what they started. Taking the bull by the horns, he got on the comms and ordered Nat to shift his focus to protecting the refueling team. Looking to Griff, he motioned the SEAL to the northwest corner of the building and told him in no uncertain terms that the Zs were *not* to advance past his position.

Hoping he hadn't just spread his team too thin, Cade ducked his head and hustled around the Ghost Hawk's angular snout. Along the way he met Ari's gaze. The aviator was not his usual jovial self. In fact, there was worry in his eyes.

As Cade proceeded to the helo's port side, he saw Haynes in the left seat. Mouth moving a mile a minute, the big man was pointing over his left shoulder.

Over the comms, Cade heard: "Zeds at my eight o'clock!" In the usually jovial man's voice were equal parts fear and incredulity. Where the Zs were coming from was anyone's guess.

Going to one knee twenty feet from the port-side cockpit door, with the tips of the whirring rotor blades but a shiny black blur overhead, Cade shouldered his M4 and sighted on the first of the Zs beginning to spill from the overgrown vineyard's gloomy depths.

Framing the twisted face of a female Z with the EOTech optic atop his rifle, Cade settled the red reticle between its eyes and pressed the trigger two times.

The shell casings flying from the rifle's ejection port were batted down by the rotor wash and sent skittering across the cement drive.

As the face-shot Z toppled forward, Cade targeted the one next in line and delivered another lethal double-tap dead-center on its forehead. Having been practicing the Mozambique Drill the day before, it was all Cade could do to keep from putting two in the third creature's chest and one in the middle of its pallid face. Reminding himself to save that technique for the enemy Chicoms, he pumped a pair of rounds between its dull eyes.

Seeing the third corpse slump atop the pair of twice-dead Zs at the mouth of the right-side row of vines, Cade tracked his muzzle left, to the pair of zombies struggling to break free of the clutching vines the next row over.

The Z in the lead was short and heavily tanned. Most of the middle-aged man's clothing had deteriorated to rags, leaving not much to the imagination. A wound stretched from ear to ear under its chin. It was bloodless and rippled like gills on a fish as the Z staggered into the open. To Cade it appeared as if someone had opened the guy's neck with a straight razor. The lack of blood on the sagging jeans and tattered polo-style shirt suggested he was already one of *them* when suffering the injury. The missing craters of flesh peppering its Popeye-like forearms, each ringed by raised, ragged flesh, all but confirmed Cade's theory.

As a long, drawn-out moan rumbled from within its barrel chest, Cade overlaid the red pip on its nose and pressed the trigger two times.

The first hurtling hunk of lead punched out its left eye. The second 5.56 hardball round hit just to the right of the first, causing a flap of pale skin to peel back, most of the left ear with it.

When the Z fell to its knees, its upper torso got caught up in the wire strung between support posts. A final moan was just crossing its lips when three more shamblers emerged from the gloom.

The first of the trio, a boy of about six when he joined the ranks of the dead, was stopped in its tracks by the gnarled roots and vines crowding in on the kneeling corpse. Since turning, the four-footer had accumulated a bird's nest of twigs in its curly mop of brown hair. With every labored step the Z took to break free of the grabby vines, the multitude of gunshot wounds stitching its torso opened and closed like so many tiny, purple-lipped mouths.

Maggots no bigger than a grain of rice wriggled from the pulsating wounds and spread out across the Z's narrow, bony chest.

That the Z was a kid didn't register on Cade's give-a-shit radar. He was a threat to mission continuity and had to be dealt with.

Cade's M4 barked twice. The pair of bullets, traveling at roughly 3,000-feet-per-second, split the undead boy's skull like an overripe cantaloupe. The kinetic energy behind the one-two punch lifted him off his feet, sending a moist cloud of maggots, confetti-like, into the air. As the ruptured head continued on the backward trajectory—trailing large chunks of brain tissue, flecked bone, and encompassed by a halo of brackish blood—the already compromised abdomen wall tore from navel to sternum, releasing a torrent of maggot-infested entrails.

The Zs following the twice-dead boy out of the vineyard's dark maw shook the vertical two-by-twos keeping the rows straight. As a result, the kneeling corpse was shaken loose and fell atop the boy.

The dam broken, Zs spilled forth, trampling the pair of corpses into the soft soil as they tumbled out of the vineyard in twos and threes.

Bodies fell left and right. Arms and legs windmilled limply.

This was the epitome of a target-rich environment.

Cade continued firing his weapon until its mag was empty and the bolt locked open.

Like lemmings over a ledge, the Zs kept coming.

Transitioning from rifle to pistol, Cade let the M4 fall on its single-point sling and dragged the Glock from its holster.

There was no time for a press check. He aimed and began to burn through the fifteen-round magazine.

The third Z to fall victim to a pair of 9mm rounds fired from Cade's Glock was still on its way to the ground when a barrage of gunfire from Cade's right cut into the female first turn following it.

Knowing that at least one of his team members had joined the fight, Cade emptied the last of the Glock's magazine into the dark void behind the face-shot female Z. As he dumped the spent mag and jammed a fresh one into the mag well, he cast a quick side-eyed glance to his right.

Spotting Griff standing a dozen feet away, MP7 shouldered and in the middle of a tactical reload of his own, Cade bellowed, "You got a SITREP for me, Griff?"

Griff responded, telling Cade the bird was refueled and Cross and Nat had their hands full with the other herd.

"I think we're getting to the end here," Cade responded.

Griff said nothing. His rifle was already doing the talking for him.

In just a matter of seconds, coinciding with Cade shooting his third magazine dry and the Glock's slide locking open, he and Nat were encircled by three dozen twice-dead corpses. The ground all around the pair of Pale Riders was littered with spent brass, rotting gray matter, and pooling, brackish blood. Leaves ripped from the vines by the rotor wash dotted the glossy black puddles.

Having just reloaded and thumbed the Glock's slide forward, his attention focused solely on the rows of vines to his fore, Cade heard Ari come on over the net and order everyone to disengage and ready for launch.

Turning toward the Ghost Hawk, Cade saw Skip manning the port minigun and the door to the crew chief's left beginning to slide open. As he started to sprint toward their ride, Nat and Cross could be seen piling in the starboard-side door.

Both Cade and Griff ducked their heads and did the same, through the port-side door, their weapons clattering on the cabin floor as gloved hands grabbed hold and hauled them aboard.

Already light on its landing gear, the turbine transitioning from a docile whine to a banshee-like howl, the Ghost Hawk shuddered once then climbed swiftly away from the blood-soaked parking pad.

"Did we acquire any unwanted passengers?" Ari asked over the shipwide comms.

Cross peered out the open door. "Negative. All clear to starboard."

Looking groundward, past the minigun's protruding barrel, Skip said, "Port-side all clear."

Fighting the loading G forces, Griff rose to his knees, grabbed hold of the nearby bulkhead, then slid his backside onto his seat. After strapping himself in, he bellowed "Go to Hell, Murphy!" and flipped both middle fingers at the scene falling away below the helo.

Flat on his back, chest rising and falling as he greedily gulped much needed oxygen, all Cade was thinking about was his daughter and the poor advice he imparted upon leaving.

Don't do anything I wouldn't do.

Chapter 57

Raven had retrieved the Schwinn from the bushes where she'd stashed it earlier. She rode around the Antlers' east side, continued a block north on South Cascade, then circled back to the west on Kiowa Street.

Pedaling the beach cruiser down the center of Kiowa, she passed by the Penrose Library, a multi-story stone and brick structure that reminded her a lot of the sturdy old Pioneer courthouse in downtown Portland. Across the street from the library was St. Mary's Cathedral—a hundred-and-twenty-year-old church designed in the Gothic Revival style. With multiple spires and lots of stained-glass windows, at night it looked to Raven more like a Transylvanian castle than a place where one worshiped God.

A run of thirty or so stairs rose from the street to an ornate stone landing fronting a pair of massive oak doors. Standing sentinel above the covered entry was a near life-sized statue of the Virgin Mary. With a demure look on her alabaster face and outstretched arms, it seemed to Raven that the statue was offering her absolution for—or maybe even embracing—what she was about to do.

Turning off of Kiowa, Raven followed North Sierra Madre Street a block south.

At the next intersection, with Antlers Park, Cascade Street, and the railroad tracks all in sight, she coasted the bike to a complete stop and dismounted.

Gaze roaming the darkened storefronts and buildings all around her, Raven stashed the bike in an alley behind a long-shuttered Caribbean-themed grill.

After a minute or so spent contemplating angles and distances to the two north/south arterials most popular with the city's growing population, Raven tried the doors to the restaurant—front and back—and found them locked. She didn't want to attract attention with a gunshot or the sound of breaking glass, so she walked her bike across the street to check out Pikes Peak Community College.

Though the modern building had many windows overlooking Antlers Park, it would do her no good because chains were wrapped through all the door handles.

Moving on, she discovered, kitty-corner from the restaurant, a small one-level building that looked to have once been a gas station. *Depot Square Railroad* was etched on the glass door. A pair of Dodge Ram pickups parked on a cement apron fronting the building bore the same name on their doors.

Though she wanted to do her surveilling from inside, she parked her bike and crouched down between the pickups where she could see the train tracks fifty yards west of her, all of Antlers Park to the south, and the intersection of Pikes Peak and Cascade a block to the east.

Remembering that the newer models of NVGs were prone to sucking the life out of batteries faster than previous generations, she resorted to watching the three avenues of approach without them.

Sound carried in a city with very few people. Especially one in which civilian motorized vehicles were banned from the roads from dusk to dawn.

Crickets struck up a symphony once Raven settled in. Now and again the low engine growl from a CSPD patrol Explorer making its rounds would echo down the side streets. Far off, outside the walls (or so she hoped) competing packs of coyotes could be heard calling back and forth.

More than an hour passed before her radio finally emitted a low burst of static. It was Daymon. He said, "Our trio of tattooers stopped off at a boarded-up hardware store a few blocks from the shop. I'm real close to the entrance and didn't want to draw attention to myself by calling you. The girl just left. She's out of earshot now. Went west for a couple of blocks before turning north. I would imagine she's now heading in your direction."

Raven pressed the Talk button. "What about Pirate and Snake?"

There was a long pause. Then, whispering, Daymon said, "They're coming out now. Looks like the tattoo bros found themselves new backpacks. And boy, do they look like they're carrying some weight inside them."

"Are they still coming on their bikes?"

"Yep," he answered. "All three are riding. You better get ready. I have a feeling they're going to regroup. Watch for them crossing Pikes Peak sometime in the next few minutes."

Raven said nothing. Instead, as her dad had taught her, she broke squelch one time to indicate she understood, rolled the volume way down, and powered on the NVGs.

***

Five minutes after stowing the radio in a pocket, Raven was dividing her attention between the three approaches. Everything she looked at was presented to her in shades of gray, black, and white. It was as if the world had been washed of all three primary colors. Still, she could make out even the tiniest of details, down to the names of the streets on the distant signs where Pikes Peak and Cascade intersected, the individual railroad ties supporting the tracks west of her, and even the terrified expressions on the faces of the statues making up the monument to the Pueblo survivors.

With Antlers Park fully ringed by Jersey barriers, and the stage erected for the President's ceremony taking up the majority of its western edge, navigating its bisecting pathways by bike wasn't particularly easy. Making a calculated decision based upon that presumption, Raven spent less time staring south, into the park, than she did at the other two directions of approach.

Swinging her gaze toward Cascade Avenue, she spied a pair of bicycles zipping right-to-left across her field of view. The riders were about the same size as Pirate and Snake, but the thing she was looking for was missing.

Quickly dismissing the riders, she panned right, pausing on the park to watch two people walking toward her on one of the paths. She watched them stop next to the monument and embrace. A tick later they were jamming their tongues down each other's throats. It was as if she was watching two ghosts. Though she was no expert—hadn't even had her first real kiss, actually—they didn't seem to know where to put their hands, nor how to coordinate the tilt of their heads to get their teeth aligned. She surmised they were new members to the lip-lock-club. Their stilted, clumsy movements reminded her of a baby foal trying to stand.

Moving on, she watched the tracks for a ten-count. Seeing nothing coming there, she walked her gaze in the other direction.

In the park, the couple was now sitting on *her* bench and still going at it hot and heavy. She threw a leg over his and ran her hands through his long, straight hair. She mashed her mouth on his, the angle of attack constantly changing.

Raven noted how the girl's hair was pulled back and tied, leaving a fuzzy ball about the size of a grapefruit out back. The way it bounced to and fro was familiar.

At once, like a lightbulb flicking on, Raven realized she was spying on Sasha and Peter—now sans the third and fourth wheels.

So much for walking Max! she thought, as the kissing moved on to second base.

Stuff is getting real!

Feeling an emotion equal parts revulsion and embarrassment, Raven instinctively closed her eyes and looked away to her right.

Skin crawling, she shook her head once, real slow and deliberate. Drawing in a breath, she lifted her gaze and focused on the train tracks. There, in the middle distance, she saw what she had been waiting for: three white dots. They were maybe a yard or so off the ground and coming at her on a diagonal. Brighter than anything surrounding them, they blinked steadily, like the beating of a heart at rest. As they grew nearer, they bounced up and down and jinked left and right. Just subtle movements that gave the impression they were crossing paths with each other.

Thirty seconds after picking up the distant strobes, they were crossing behind the converted gas station. Rising from her position between the pickups, Raven focused on a spot in space, just to the right of the building, where the riders were bound to come back into view.

Since the infrared strobes Daymon had planted on the three bicycles were visible from a great distance with the NVGs, she figured she could afford to give them a nice head start.

After waiting a long fifteen-count, she straddled the Schwinn and pedaled westbound. She rounded the rear of the Depot Square Railroad building and immediately saw the IR strobes. They were far off and didn't appear to be slowing.

She gave chase, pedaling her heart out, the backpack and slung SBR pummeling her back. She turned left, coasted west another block, then stopped on the corner, where she was flanked by a U.S. Postal Service mailbox and a low-slung car resting on four flat tires.

Looking north, she picked the strobes back up. They were still moving but seemed to be slowing.

The coyote calls could be hard over the noise of the bikes bouncing along uneven ground paralleling the railroad tracks.

After catching her breath, Raven began pedaling north, only to have to stop and dismount a block later because the riders she was following did the same.

Raven watched the trio from behind a plastic garbage can on wheels. They crossed the tracks and stopped beside the western wall. It was an old segment of cement barriers constructed before Z-Day. It was inundated by ivy and bordered by a narrow gravel lot.

As Raven looked on, Pirate peeled a section of the ivy veil aside and hid his bike behind it. From the ground behind the ivy, he dragged a ladder into the open. It was different from the one her dad had kept in their garage back in Portland. This one was segmented and folded in on itself.

While Snake and Pixie stashed their bikes, Pirate straightened the ladder and locked the individual segments into place. After leaning the ladder against the wall and issuing instructions to the others, he climbed up ahead of them. With the pack weighing the man down, every step looked to be a chore. Once on the top, he shrugged off the pack and let it fall to the ground on the opposite side of the wall.

Pixie stashed her bike and waited while Pirate scanned the freeway left to right through a pair of binoculars. Seeing Pirate flash a thumbs up, Pixie grabbed ahold of the ladder and started climbing.

Still straddling the wall, Pirate grabbed Pixie's hand and helped her up. Once she was steadied atop the wall, he helped her roll over so she was balancing on her chest. With both of her legs now on the opposite side of the wall and jutting into space, he stretched out atop the wall, hooked his knees on either side, then helped the waifish Asian down to the ground on the other side.

Snake didn't need any help. Once Pirate was over and gone from view, he climbed the ladder all by himself, monkeyed both legs over the top, and planted his butt in the middle of the wide swath of crushed-down ivy.

After hauling the ladder up and positioning it on the other side, Snake disappeared from view, whistling a movie theme song Raven knew she had heard more than once but couldn't quite place.

What amazed Raven was that he did it all while loaded down with the backpack. Pretty impressive for a guy not much bigger than she.

While Raven waited for her quarry to get a head start, raindrops began to strike the ground all around her. Soon the small drops doubled in size and were creating a sonorous cadence as they struck the garbage can's flat lid.

She endured thirty seconds out in the open, with a torrent of water inundating her collar, and, gnawing at her the entire time, the real possibility the trio might be out of sight if she waited too long.

Multitasking, she hailed Daymon, telling him all that had transpired, and assuring him she could not wait the ten minutes it would take for him to get to her.

"Be careful," was all Daymon could say at that point. As he signed off, he issued a stern admonishment: "Don't do anything your crazy Uncle Daymon would do."

Just as the squall moved off to the east, with Daymon's cryptic advice still nagging her, Raven left her bike propped against the can and set off running for the wall.

Chapter 58

By the time Raven reached the wall, barely a minute had passed since the people she'd been following had slipped from her view.

Standing in the exact spot the trio had just vacated, she looked up at the cement freeway barrier. It towered over her by fifteen feet or so and was completely overtaken by the ivy.

She swung her rifle around to her back and grabbed a handful of ivy. She tugged hard. It stretched a bit and came away from the wall. She leaned back, testing the runners with her entire weight. There was a tearing sound and most of the runners in her two-fisted grip tore away from the wall.

Suddenly she was a prime example of Newton's Law, backpedaling and windmilling both arms. The weight of the rifle and pack on her back only added to the forces trying to send her sprawling. However, thanks to good reflexes and a superb sense of balance, she remained on her feet.

Glaring at the wall while cursing under her breath, she came to the sobering conclusion that she was going to need a ladder. As she scanned the nearby businesses, thinking hard about where she might find one, she heard in her head: *Improvise, adapt, and overcome.* It was a mantra made popular by the United States Marines. And though her dad was in an entirely different part of the country, she had heard the words uttered in his voice.

The saying was usually used as a prompt to get her to think outside the box—and that's exactly what she did.

Acting on the four-word nugget of wisdom, she crossed the street and retrieved her bike.

Making a second trip across the street, she emptied the rolling garbage can.

With the rain still coming down hard all around, she wheeled the can ahead of her, bumped it over the sidewalk, crossed the gravel, and then pushed it hard against the wall. Next, she yanked all three mountain bikes from behind the ivy, retrieved the tiny IR strobes, and shoved them deep in a pocket.

Though the beach cruiser just about matched her bodyweight, she managed to get it up and laid flat on the rolling bin's wide lid. Getting Pixie and Snake's high-dollar light-weight bikes atop the Schwinn and interlocking their pedals and bars to create a stable base was a cake walk compared to lifting the ungainly steel-framed beach cruiser.

So far, Raven figured that for all her *improvising,* she had gotten less than eight feet closer to the top of the wall. Even if she stood on the stacked bikes, went to her tippy toes and reached for the sky, she guessed she'd still be a foot shy of reaching the top.

Dipping back into the well of *improvisation,* she manhandled Pirate's bike so that it was popping a wheelie with its rear tire on the ground and the front elevated and resting on the ivy. Though the mountain bike weighed only half as much as the Schwinn, it was not going to be easy to keep in this position *and* get it to where it needed to go.

She stood, bike braced on the wall, sweat from the earlier exertion mixing with rain and running down her face. It stung her eyes and tasted salty on her tongue.

Think, think, think.

Looking the length of the street, she spotted another rolling bin. It was parked on the curb near a Chinese restaurant and full to overflowing.

Leaving Pirate's bike propped against the wall, she hustled down the street to retrieve the bin.

The bin was full of rotting food whose stench would give a bloated recent-turn a run for its money.

She pressed her shoulder to the bin near the handle and lowered her hips. Using all the strength in her legs, she stood up from the crouch, knocking the can on its side. She grabbed the top of a tied bag and pulled. The bag tore, leaving her holding a slimy scrap of knotted plastic.

She took hold of one wheel and tugged on it. *Nothing happened.* Combined, the can and its contents were too heavy for her to budge. So she went to her knees and started digging the mess out with her hands. Chicken bones embedded in a gray sludge jabbed at her fingers but failed to penetrate her damp gloves.

She got the bin emptied to the point where she was able to upend it and pour most of the sludge out into the street. Gagging and on the verge of throwing up, she returned with the rancid-smelling bin, parking it next to the other.

Clambering atop the second bin, she hauled Pirate's bike up and trapped it vertically against the wall. Pressing one shoulder against the wall to give her a little added stability, she lifted the bike's knobby rear tire over the stacked bikes. To stabilize what was to be her makeshift ladder, she turned the bike flat against the wall, drove its rear tire into the frames of the other bikes, and then buried the handlebars deep into the ivy.

Beaded sweat stinging her eyes, she jiggled Pirate's bike a couple of times. Finding it stuck fast, the tip of the front tire a foot or two from the top of the wall, she placed one foot on the seat post.

Everything under her suddenly went wobbly.

She froze, every muscle in her body tensed and humming with nervous electricity.

Once the bike stopped moving, she drew in a deep breath and planted her opposite foot on its horizontal head tube.

Success.

The bike and everything holding it in place stayed still. Not statue-still, but it was good enough.

Trying to replicate the previous step, Raven grabbed a fistful of ivy, prayed to God it would hold at least a portion of her weight, then pushed off again.

As the toe of her boot found purchase on the bike's front forks, the bin underneath the bikes started a slow roll away from the wall. Thankfully, after moving a hand's width from the wall, the gravel made a popping noise and all movement ceased.

Perched precariously more than a dozen feet off the ground and really pissed at herself for not chocking the wheels with something, she froze and drew in a deep breath.

Feeling a bit like one of those crazy free-climbers scaling El Capitan with just shoes and a bag of chalk—albeit facing just a sprain or broken bone versus a seconds-long freefall to a grisly splat—she reached slowly over her head and threaded her fingers gingerly into the ivy.

After a couple more calming breaths, Raven said, "Eff you, Murphy." Simultaneously, she let go of the ivy, shot both legs straight, and thrust her hands toward the sky.

While the poorly orchestrated move propelled her vertically off of Pirate's bike, the equal and opposite reaction started the bikes and garbage can sliding slowly to her right.

Body in midair, legs and arms at full extension, everything that had been supporting Raven was rocketing toward the ground.

As the discordant jangle of bicycle chains and crash of metal frames colliding rose up around her, Raven managed to grab the top of the wall with both hands. Body stretched out fully, her gear adding to the immense strain being put on her fingers and wrists, she began to kick her legs. To get her entire body moving pendulum-like along the wall, the kicks had to be timed just right.

After the third left-to-right pass, toes carving shallow furrows in the ivy, she finally managed to get one leg hooked over the wall. From there it took every ounce of her upper body strength to get to where she was straddling the wall like the others had.

Now, balanced just so, with her fingers and arms feeling like overstretched rubber bands, she deployed the NVGs and powered them on.

As the goggle's white-phosphor display lit up, she learned she had a commanding view of roughly half a mile of I-25 in either direction. Beyond the freeway was No-Man's-Land. She saw lots of movement. A flash of a face showing itself behind a window. Pale forms flitting across a desolate street littered with husks of burned-out cars.

She also learned, save for a dozen or so dead things plodding down the freeway away from her, that she was all alone. The trio was nowhere to be seen. Which suggested to her that they rode away on bikes they had waiting for them on the ground below her.

Peering groundward, she saw the ladder. It was only partially folded up and looked like a metal insect which had gone and died on a dirty windowsill. No care had been taken to hide it. It was just there in the open atop a dirt embankment that fell gradually away from the mostly flat, narrow track of dirt paralleling the wall. Pressed into the dirt and showing as narrow gray lines were a number of crisscrossing tire tracks. The only thing the tracks had in common was that they all ranged off to the north.

Sadly, Raven didn't spot any bikes out in the open. Nor were there bumps in the ivy where one might be stashed.

The drop to the ground here was shorter: twelve feet or so, she guessed. She made sure the coast was clear in both directions then hung from the top of the wall by her fingers. This time she didn't need to do any gymnastic moves. She just dangled for a beat or two, then let go.

After landing flat-footed on the track, the damp dirt making for a soft landing, she went to one knee and shouldered her rifle.

Determining she was still alone and fairly certain the Zs across the way hadn't heard the single soft *thud* of her feet hitting the track, she struck off north, staying on the track but taking care to not disturb the tire imprints.

The tire tracks ended a couple of hundred yards north where the dirt embankment suddenly became poured cement. It was scored to look like large rectangular tiles and rough against her boot soles. Muddy tire tracks on the gradual decline told Raven that the riders had turned here and ridden down to the freeway, where all traces of them ended abruptly.

Raven walked down to the freeway and paused beside a stalled-out CDOT Ford F-450. In the truck's bed was a darkened traffic update reader board. She imagined when last it was lighted up, the words had read: DANGER - ZOMBIES AHEAD!

Looking east, she spotted a bubble of light that had to be the distant North Gate. Swinging her gaze forward, she saw a couple of dozen Zs. They had followed the next ramp off the freeway and become trapped behind the row of barricades and Jersey barriers blocking the outlet. An overhead sign told her the off-ramp in question fed the neighborhood where she expected to find the house Daymon had shown her.

In the middle distance was a small herd of zombies, maybe thirty total. They were in a tight group and trundling through a copse of trees planted along the sloped embankment. Every footfall kicked up dirt that presented as little gray-white eruptions. Viewed through the goggles, the eruptions called to mind the surface of the angry Pacific during a winter storm.

Pulling up fifty feet short of the herd, she cut ninety degrees right from the freeway and tackled the treeless end of the embankment head on.

Hairs on her neck standing to attention, she put one foot in front of the other, careful to not make any noise that could be heard over the dry rasps and moans made by the rancid pack of first turns.

The handful of times her boot soles triggered tiny mud avalanches, the dead whipped their heads in her direction. Each instance, as she went stock-still and returned the curious glares from the safety of the all-encompassing darkness, those slack-jawed skull-like faces—as presented in the white-phosphor display—added a new level of horror to a world she thought could no longer faze her.

It was as if someone had powdered their faces, gouged out their eyes, then jammed shiny black marbles in place of them. It was so disconcerting, she almost wished for the old NVGs that showed everything in varying shades of green. Halfway to the top of the embankment, she said to hell with it, took a knee, and switched the NVGs off. She told herself it was to conserve batteries, when in reality, she feared that engaging the dead in one more protracted staring contest might be enough to break her will to continue. Send her slinking back to the Antlers empty-handed.

Just as her heart rate was getting back to normal, she detected the low growl of an engine. It was definitely diesel and laboring hard. Turning in the general direction the sound had come from, she switched the NVGs back on.

The moment the display flared back to life, she saw two things that created mixed feelings within her. On the plus side, she watched a multi-wheeled truck emerge from No-Man's-Land, cross the overpass, turn down the ramp, and come to a full stop behind the Jersey barriers.

In the negative column, the dead that had been climbing the embankment, every stinking last one of them, lost all interest in the prey they were following. As the undead mob turned abruptly and fixed those shark-eyed stares on the Pikers riding in the back of the truck, any hope Raven had of them unwittingly leading her to the tattooers' house was squashed like a bug.

With the Pikers already introducing the dead to their sharpened javelins, Raven made lemonade out of lemons, climbing the rest of the way up the embankment and slipping silently into the Exclusionary Zone.

Chapter 59

Bonneville, Oregon

In the twenty minutes since Jedi One's harried launch from the parking pad behind Maryhill Museum, Cade had broken down his rifle, cleaned and oiled the important integral components, then reassembled it. Now, as the helo raced west, just feet over the Columbia River's choppy surface, he was working on reloading the magazines he'd burned through.

Adrenaline from the combat high was just beginning to dissipate. As a result, his hand tremors had gone from a ten on the Richter Scale to maybe a five. So far nobody seemed to notice. If they had, nobody mentioned it. Probably because it was normal, with everybody experiencing it to one degree or another.

While the usual adrenaline dump had sharpened Cade's senses and contributed somewhat to his performance, the severity of the aftereffects had taken him by surprise. He didn't recall ever suffering such a long-lasting bout.

Chalking the phenomena up to the fact that he was not too far removed from an actual life-or-death encounter, and that his last—being shot and then tortured by the Chicoms—actually saw him on the doorstep of the latter, he snugged the full mags into their slots on his chest rig, crossed his arms, then tucked his hands in his armpits where they'd be out of sight.

Cross leaned across the dimly lit cabin and thrust something in Cade's direction. "PowerBar?"

Cade shook his head. "I'm good," he stated. "I'm saving my appetite for when we get to where we're going." He looked up and smiled as a fond memory of home crossed his mind. Dropping his gaze to Cross, he went on, saying, "I know where all the good stuff is stashed."

Cross said nothing. He unwrapped the bar, wolfed it down, and chased it with a long pull off an energy drink.

Flashing his easy smile, Nat said to Cade, "I have a five-hour pick-me-up if you want one."

Cade was staring out his window. Though he could see only snippets of the landscape below, he knew they were overflying the spot in the Columbia River Gorge where the terrain slowly morphed from hardscrabble high desert to the rough mountainous terrain and lush green forest the Pacific Northwest was best known for.

Holding a hand toward Nat, Cade said, "I'm good. Protecting Ari's tail rotor woke me right up."

"You're not *good*," Griff shot. "Looks like Captain's got a case of the jazz hands. You always come down hard like that?"

Cade glared across the cabin at the SEAL. While the man was an equal opportunity ballbuster, Cade hadn't expected to be called out by him in public. Knowing that the DEVGRU guys pulled no punches when it came to critiquing their own, he took it as an act of affection and let it slide.

Ari unexpectedly entered the conversation. "Reminds me of a joke," he said. "An oldie but a goodie. Who wants to hear it?"

Skip had been training the red beam from his tactical light on the laminated map on his lap. Hearing Ari's question in his headset, the crew chief shook his head and made a slashing motion across his throat.

Haynes came on the comms next. "If it's the one I'm thinking of, I better take the stick."

Ari said, "Haynes has the bird."

Skip said, "Here we go," and leaned away from his window, settling the flashlight's beam on Ari in the right-front seat.

Taking his hands and feet from the flight controls, Ari lifted his NVGs up and said, "Everyone's heard of the world-famous Epileptic Diet, right?"

Crickets.

Ten seconds passed.

Finally, Griff said, "Spit it out, already."

"*Close*, but *no* cigar," Ari quipped.

Five more seconds passed.

"Five minutes out," Haynes said, banking the Ghost Hawk hard to port, overflying a sprawling business park lit up in the orange glow of halide lights that had to be fitted with solar panels.

Taking Haynes' warning as his cue to get on with it, Ari said, "The Epileptic Diet consists of a *shake* for breakfast. A *shake* for lunch. And a sensible dinner."

Cade had a perfect view of Ari as he recited the joke. Each time the aviator said "Shake" (as if suffering a seizure) he had convulsed violently in his seat. After the second put-on attack of whole-body shakes, the pilot had leaned between the front seat and fixed the customers in back with an expectant gaze.

Griff started the slow clap. Soon, everyone but Cross had joined in.

"I'd take a bow," Ari said, "but I need to retake the stick."

In his headset, Cade heard the pilots of the other two helos state their intention to break formation and vector off for their loiter LZ.

Responding next, Ari said, "One-Two. One-Three." He paused. "One-One here. Good solid copy." He signed out, saying, "Be sure to leave a light on for us."

Haynes brought the bird back to level flight and handed her over to Ari just as the helo entered a rain squall. As the bombardment on the radar-absorbing skin rose to a sonic tempest, Cade could barely hear the cockpit chatter piped into his helmet.

As per usual in early spring, Portland and its suburbs were under a near-constant barrage as storms rolled in from the Pacific Ocean some sixty miles to the west.

Driving the stealth helo deeper into the airspace over Gresham, Oregon, Ari came on the shipwide comms. "No sense in doing a recon of Target Bravo in this," he reasoned. "We'll have One-Three gather photo and video intel as soon as this weather breaks."

If *it ever breaks,* thought Cade. He knew the rainy season in his former hometown: it stretched from roughly Labor Day weekend until July 4th, when Mother Nature saw fit to begin the usual two-plus months of solid sunshine. Sure, there were nice patches of weather bookending "summer", but they were few and far between. He said, "Will this rain be adequate cover for you to get us closer to our loiter than the LZ in our original plan?"

Skip looked up from the map but said nothing. Clearly his job would be changing if the plan deviated in the slightest bit from the one already on the books.

Ari said, "I put Blue Thunder here in *whisper-mode*, I can insert you smack-dab on General Jinlong's ball sack and he wouldn't be any the wiser."

Cade was well aware of Ari's penchant to sometimes overstate the Ghost Hawk's performance envelope. The aviator was also known to embellish his stories with pop-culture references—with *Blue Thunder*, an '80s television show featuring a high-tech helicopter, a favorite often revisited.

Cade asked, "*Close*? As in *three* blocks from the initial loiter, *close*?"

Ari answered, "Where *exactly* do you want to infil?"

The helicopter began to descend while Ari put it into a shallow turn to starboard. As he did so, he began to bleed airspeed, too.

"There's Creston Park three blocks from our loiter. It's roughly a quarter-klick north by west as the crow flies."

"How's the LZ?" Ari asked.

"It's a patch of grass large enough to set the entire flight down, if need be. It's about a quarter-mile around and ringed by a dozen or so hundred-foot-tall Douglas Firs. Creston School shares the park. It's on the east edge and has a soccer field out back that'll do in a pinch as a backup LZ."

"Checks all the boxes," Ari said. "What about our noise sig? Is it going to carry to Target Alpha?"

"Not with all this rain," Cade answered. "And when we exfil … it shouldn't be an issue."

"Because there won't be any Chicoms left to hear good ol' Blue Thunder," Griff added.

Bristling, Skip looked up from the map. "It'll work, Ari." Flicking his eyes to Griff, he added, "Her name's *Elvira*. Don't you forget it."

As the Ghost Hawk passed through a ground-hugging cloudbank, it shuddered subtly and lost a good chunk of altitude.

Pulling pitch and goosing the turbines to gain back some of the altitude, Ari said, "Seven minutes, gentlemen. Please return to your seats. Tray tables up. And please place all electronic devices on Airplane mode. And thank you for once again flying Night Stalker Airways."

Cade smiled at that. He really had started to miss the adult company. The camaraderie shared by men willingly throwing themselves into the grinder. There was nothing quite like the bond they all shared. Not even close.

Cross tapped the glass near him. "Portland is your old stomping grounds, huh?"

"Yep," confirmed Cade. "We are in my old stomping grounds. When we're done cutting wire and slitting throats, I'd love to be able to treat you all to a pint at the pub near my place. But I don't think it's going to happen. Their kegs are probably all dry as a first turn crossing the Mojave."

Nat shook his head slowly, side to side.

Griff groaned.

Cross clucked his tongue.

Coming back on the comms, Ari said, "Better stay in your lane, Delta. You do the face-shooting, I'll provide the stand-up."

Cade said nothing. However, he was smiling when Nat critiqued his comedic timing. "It's not on point, bro. Not even close."

"Understood," Cade said, agreeably.

Cross and Griff were a flurry of activity, both busy readying their weapons and checking gear.

Skip had unbuckled and retrieved the thirty-foot-length of rope used by the team to fast-rope from the Ghost Hawk in the event, for some reason, it was not able to go wheels down on either of the LZs.

Outside it was still pissing rain.

Cade unbuckled and moved to the front of his seat. He flipped his NVGs down and powered them on. As the full-color display lit up, he noticed that the rest of the team had followed his lead.

Extending his pointer finger, Skip silently informed the Delta Team they were one minute out.

As the *whirr* and *clunk* of the landing gear deploying and locking in place sounded in the cabin, Cade was busy crossing himself and uttering a prayer under his breath.

When Ari announced, "Thirty seconds out" over the onboard comms, the minigun was fully deployed and Skip was on high alert, aiming the six-barreled personnel shredder groundward.

As Jedi One's wheels touched down on grass Cade and Raven used to play Frisbee and Tee-Ball on, the cabin door stopped in its tracks, locked in the full-open position.

Skip said, "Out, out, out," and started calling out the contacts flooding out of the park's heavily treed areas.

Chapter 60

After avoiding the Pikers' operation on the freeway ramp, Raven had left the NVGs powered on and immediately picked up her pace.

The deeper she pushed into the EZ, the more zombies she spotted going in the opposite direction. A couple of times, as she neared the cross street that fed to the distant North Gate, she was forced to double back a block or two in order to avoid large packs of Zs drawn south to the bubble of light rising over the quiet, tree-lined streets.

Thirty minutes after making it over the wall on her *ladder* fashioned from garbage cans and bicycles, she had found the intersection she was looking for. It was lorded over by a pair of seventy-five-foot-tall oak trees facing off from opposing corners. Maybe two hundred feet due east of the intersection was the yellow bungalow Daymon had fingered as belonging to the tattoo parlor terrorists.

Keeping to the sidewalk, Raven entered the block on the north side of the street. Her search for a place to surveil the bungalow lasted all of a minute. The two-story Craftsman directly across the street from the bungalow was the only home in a row of four that had an intact front door. Like the others, the door had been marked on by the cleanup crews coming through the city early on.

Now, nearly an hour into her covert excursion, she was crouched down behind a compact Toyota Corolla across the street from and two houses west of the bungalow.

Parked out front and blocking a driveway running from the street to the one-car garage tucked behind the bungalow was a black Ford Econoline van. Painted in big white letters on its side: *Loretta Jean's Pies*. Strangely, the address to the establishment was in

Montana. Deepening the mystery was the California license plate affixed to the van's front bumper.

At first sight, Raven was certain the van hadn't been parked there the day before. She would have remembered anything that conjured up the images now taking up residence in her head. What she wouldn't give right now for a big slice of banana cream pie heaped high with the kind of whipped cream her mom used to make. Real whipped cream. With lots of sugar and vanilla. Mom's secret ingredients. Of which she had learned only recently from Tran were basically the *only* two ingredients, save for fresh cream—a commodity nearly impossible to come by in the apocalypse.

With no siblings to battle for the mixer beaters, Raven always got to lick them both clean.

Peering around the car's bumper, Raven viewed the two reasons she wasn't already inside the Craftsman and surveilling the tattooers.

Pacing the sidewalk out front of the Craftsman was a pair of Zs. While she could easily grant the recent turns a quick second death, hustle up the walkway and break into the two-story, the sudden appearance of two freshly killed corpses on a street free of corpses would *not* go unnoticed by people clearly up to no good and probably pretty good at watching their backs.

One of the dead things was a teen female with a badly disfigured face. It looked almost as bad as her dad's face following his rescue from the squad of Chinese soldiers: puffy and bruised, with lacerations on the cheeks and forehead from being slapped and punched for hours on end. Speaking to the savageness of the human animals who had done this to the Z, both arms were bound together behind its back. The rusty length of barbed wire they had used was twisted so tightly that it had cut deep fissures into the decaying flesh. Viewed through the NVGs, certain details were hard to pin down, but clear as day was the fact that both of her forearms had been removed just below the elbows. There was no splintered bone sticking out. No scraps of flesh or skin dangling from the cuts. It looked as if they'd been taken off with the type of instruments Tran and Daymon used to butcher big game.

The only solace Raven took from the arm situation was that the damage had likely been done *after* the girl had turned.

The undead teen spent most of its time patrolling the sidewalk at the terminus of the Craftsman's driveway. While Raven had no doubts she could drag the teen's body off the sidewalk and stash it someplace out of sight, it was the other Z that was literally standing in the way of her getting into the house. The *only* house on the block that would afford her a bird's eye view of the bungalow.

The middle-aged Z was nearly as tall as Daymon. It had to be at least a hundred pounds heavier. Whereas Daymon was muscled and lanky, this rotter was the opposite, with a big beer gut hanging over a pair of blue jeans barely hanging onto its wide hips.

A full beard seemed to make up for the fact it was completely bald. Coal-black, heavy-lidded eyes peered out from under a caveman-like brow.

A half-moon chunk of meat and sinew had been rent from one side of Caveman's neck. Arteries and jagged flaps of skin ringing the yawning wound jiggled with each plodding step. The resulting torrent of blood had streaked the front of its white tee shirt and continued on down its tattered pants. The blood had dried to black. When viewed in white-phosphor, the jagged runners resembled forked lightning slashing a summer sky.

Raven was tiring of watching Caveman pace. He was relentless. And tireless. He would plod away from her hiding spot, stop, make a clumsy pirouette, and then head back down the sidewalk toward her. About every other circuit the thing would pause before the walkway, its back facing the Craftsman's wide front porch, and stare longingly across the street.

To Raven it seemed as if Caveman was searching for something. Maybe it had heard the trio arrive across the street on their bikes. Perhaps the trio had made some noise when they leaned their bikes against the hedges lining the driveway. Maybe the *click* of a door closing somewhere over there had carried all the way over here.

No matter the reason, Raven was certain the Zs hadn't spied the fresh meat entering the house. For if they had, they would *not* be blocking her from entering her house. Instead, they would be across the street, banging against whatever door they saw the prey enter through.

Of that, Raven was certain.

Though the thought of trying the gate in the twelve-foot fence ringing the Craftsman's backyard had occurred to Raven, with no way of knowing if it was locked, or if the backyard held undead surprises, she was content to wait out Caveman and his armless companion.

She didn't have to wait long. Coyotes calling in the distance got the teen moving off to the east.

Caveman, however, was unfazed. He just kept on going. Like the Energizer Bunny—back and forth, back and forth.

Armless had been gone close to ten minutes when a noise piqued Caveman's interest. When the woman's laugh rolled across the street, he was in stationary mode. A second noise—a bottle breaking—resulted in him taking a few tentative steps into the street.

Finally, a door opening and closing finished what the previous noises had started.

Go, go, go, was what Raven was thinking as Caveman's head took a downward tilt and, like a fire-and-forget missile, he struck off on a laser-straight tack for the bungalow's narrow driveway.

Raven stayed behind the little Toyota long enough to see three things happen. First, Caveman reached the garage and slammed hard into the door. Then, there was more breaking glass and a hand holding a suppressed pistol emerged from one of the four tiny, square windows running horizontal across the garage door.

The gunshot was muffled but still carried to Raven's position. The crash and discordant rattle from Caveman falling into the partitioned rollup door was much louder.

Soon after the point-blank head shot, a face filled the window. It was Pirate. He looked left and right, then stared straight down the driveway. He stayed that way for a minute or so before pulling back from the opening.

The second Pirate disappeared from view, Raven was up and running for the walk leading to the Craftsman's front door. She didn't look back. Took the turn on the run, leaped the six stairs in two bounds, and skidded to a halt before the door.

Moment of truth. With no time to complete the customary "knock and wait" routine, she grabbed the knob and twisted.

Success.

The mechanism clicked and the door swung inward. Since Raven didn't have the symbols used by the cleanup crews committed to memory, she was going in blind—so to speak.

She got inside and closed the door without taking fire from the breathers or being set upon by a lurking rotter.

Lifting her gaze, she saw that she was alone on the main floor, which had been remodeled in a style that had left everything open. Which was a good thing, because it left her just one door to check. After knocking and waiting a long ten-count, she opened the door to a cramped bathroom containing only a toilet and sink.

Upstairs was arranged similar to her home in Portland: one full and one half-bathroom. Four bedrooms—one of which was used as a home office, complete with a computer and filing cabinets and a wall full of framed certificates of education. The most important bedroom was the one with a zoo animal theme. Tiger-print curtains framed a large picture window that looked out over the front lawn.

After finding the upper floor clear of dead things, she returned to the room with the zoo theme, moved a chair by the window, and took the camera from her pack. She aimed the Nikon at the floor and powered it on. Making doubly sure the flash was turned off, she removed the lens cap and trained the telephoto lens on the garage across the street.

All she could see were dim shadows and flashes of movement. Her first thought was that the focus needed tweaking. When she found that the camera's autofocus feature was turned on, it occurred to her the problem was a combination of poor angles and awful lighting.

Just like that, the wind left her sails.

She had scaled the wall, nearly breaking her neck. Come close to crossing paths with civilians on a Z-clearing operation. Then sat in hiding very close to a Z she could only defeat with a bullet—or three.

Enduring all of that and here she was with nothing to show for it. Zero effing evidence of whatever Pirate and his merry band of dipshits were up to.

Doing the first thing that came to mind, she phoned a friend, so to speak.

Daymon answered his radio right away.

Raven started the conversation with a sincere "I'm sorry." After that, she told Daymon everything that had happened up until her hitting the proverbial wall that caused her to reach out to him.

He said, "I saw the garbage cans and bicycles and knew immediately that it was your doing. I was getting ready to go over the top myself when I heard the commotion coming from somewhere down I-25. When I got to the top of the wall, I saw exactly what you just described: Pikers doing what pikers do best. No way I could have gotten past them at that point. And I damn sure wasn't going deep into East Springs on foot just to get *around* them."

"What would you do if you were in my position?" she asked. "Because I know they're up to something in there. Something bigger than burning a fuel truck or painting stupid stuff in the park. I have a feeling they're terrorists."

"I agree," Daymon said. "But you can't make contact with them all alone. Can you improve your viewing angle? Switch lenses, maybe?"

"I have one lens. I can try to improve my angle. Get a little closer to the action."

"Just be careful," Daymon urged. "You get in trouble ... help is a ways out. Even the soldiers at the gate couldn't get mounted up and rolling in less than five minutes."

Jaw taking a firm set, she said, "I have an idea," and signed off. But not before she and Daymon had agreed to switch channels on their Motorola radios to the next set on their short list.

Chapter 61

First thing Cade did as Jedi One was powering away from the LZ was to call the TOC at Peterson, identify himself as "Anvil Actual" and then confirm that he and his team were "Boots on the ground and Oscar Mike."

Though the rain had let up, the Ghost Hawk's rotor wash had not only beat the grass down all around the team, it had also sent standing water airborne, drenching them all the second its wheels left terra firma.

Looking west, across the open expanse of grass, Cade saw that the Zs flushed from the trees rising up all around the field were drawing near. They were encircling the team from three sides, the noose drawing tighter with each passing second. Instead of striking out from the LZ on a course that would take him and his team straight to the corner of 48th and Gladstone, a course that was currently blocked by several walking corpses, Cade rose from one knee and moved off north by east, toward a narrow passage bordered on the right by the rear of Creston School and on the left by a head-high chain-link fence.

Beyond the fence was a deep, bramble-choked gully. Raven was in either first or second grade when a rumor the gully was haunted circulated the school. At the time she was convinced the rumor was true. It had spooked her so badly she would go out of her way to avoid the area altogether.

Instead of worrying about ghosts, Cade was concerned they might come into contact with more ghouls. If they did, and the undead vastly outnumbered he and his team, the chokepoint would be the last place he wanted to be.

Stuck between a rock and a hard place.

If the Zs currently surrounding them and advancing from nearly every point of the compass was the "rock", so far the "hard place" was looking like their best option.

"I'll get point," Cade said over the comms. "Cross and Griff in the middle. Nat, get the rear and cover our six." Though the men replied with an "Affirmative" or clipped "Copy that," most of what he had just said was not necessary. They were all professionals and knew what was expected of them no matter the order they found themselves slotted.

Keeping a few feet of separation between each other, the team entered the passage, NVGs deployed, weapons at the ready.

Halfway along the thirty-foot run that saw them hemmed in by stucco wall and chain-link fence, Cade heard scuffing noises coming from beyond the blind corner. Dead ahead from him was the wooden play structure that had been a favorite of Raven's when she was much younger. On days when it wasn't raining—few and far between in Portland—she would beg him to bring her here to play. She especially liked to sit on the tire swing and be pushed in ever-widening circles.

It had been clear to Cade and Brook early on that their "apple" hadn't fallen very far from the tree. Like them, she was an adrenaline junky from the get-go

Ten feet shy of the spot where the passage opened up onto the asphalt playground, Cade raised a fist in the air. It was a silent signal telling the team to halt in place and observe perfect noise discipline.

After stopping and listening hard for a beat, Cade heel-and-toed it forward, keeping far left of the school gym, the suppressor on his carbine tracing a slow, smooth left-to-right arc.

Speaking softly into the mike boom, Cade said, "Contact. One tango. I'll handle it." Letting the center-point sling support his M4, he drew his dagger.

On the ground, half a dozen feet to his fore, was the saddest undead specimen he'd ever seen. The woman had been in her late sixties when she died the first time. The evidence of the attack that had infected her was clear: meat stripped from one arm. Raised bite marks on her shoulder and neck. And on the same side as the feeding had begun, the entire half of her face was missing. It was as if it had been ripped clean off. As a result, the thing seemed to be flashing the world a perpetual half-smile. Yellowed, cracked teeth aside, it was the kind of look that suggested the thing knew something the living weren't privy to.

Adding insult to injury, the Z had lost its entire right leg. A hollow hip socket ringed by fatty tissue was all there was to see where it used to be.

From continual contact with the ground, the left leg had been reduced to a short length of femur protruding from a ragged mess of abraded skin and putrefying flesh.

As the crawler looked up at him, a sad-sounding hiss crossed its thin, ropy lips.

While Cade was never one to show much empathy for the dead, thinking they were just soulless shells of their former selves, he truly felt empathy for one of them for the first time since that last Saturday in July when the entire world was turned upside down. Sure, he'd been saddened by some of the sights he'd come across. The suicides really stayed with him. Particularly the ones involving parents and their kids. He'd encountered so many of those last-resort murder/suicides that he'd started to numb to them, too.

This one was different, though. Because he had known her. Had watched her tend to her tulips in the spring as he jogged by her little one-story ranch on Gladstone. Saw her walking Gremlin, her little Boston Terrier in the spring and summer, when the weather was agreeable.

Kneeling near Bea's lolling head, careful to stay clear of her snapping teeth, he grabbed a fistful of white hair and said a quick prayer for her soul. He paused for a few seconds, staring into her dead eyes. Finally, he whispered, "I'm sorry this had to happen to you, Bea," and buried the Gerber's black blade deep into her roving right eye.

"You going to ask it to go to prom with you?" It was Nat speaking over the comms. "We've got company on our six. So if you are, better get it over with."

Cade said nothing. He rose and took hold of his carbine. Pointing the way, he set off for the empty parking lot on the far side of the playground.

Leading the team through his old neighborhood, Cade noted all the darkened windows and marveled at how some lawns had grown chest-high, while others had just died and remained barren plats of land fronting homes slowly losing a fight against the forward march of time and Portland's unforgiving climate.

Three times along the way, to ensure nobody had followed them from the LZ, Cade stopped the team and hunkered down. Each time they stayed put for seven or eight minutes. And each time the only noises they heard were the buzzing of insects and steady drips as foliage and structures shed rainwater.

One block from his two-story Craftsman, near the mouth to the alley running behind it, Cade nearly led his team straight into the midst of a large group of wandering Zs.

With mere seconds to act, using hand signals only, he ordered the team to split up and go to ground.

Acting independently, Nat and Cross peeled away to the left, entered the front yard of a powder-blue single-level ranch, and found concealment behind the cedar fence bordering the alley.

Griff opted to sidestep into the street and slink off on a diagonal that took him away from the advancing dead. Just prior to the mini-herd spilling from the overgrown alley, he reached a pair of parked cars and took a knee between them. With just the top of his helmet rising over the trunk lid of the Volkswagen Jetta to his fore, he froze in place, his suppressed MP7 shouldered and ready to rock.

Cade had only enough time to take a knee in the deep grass just inside the mouth of the alley and freeze in place. With just the impenetrable darkness of night on his side, he watched—in full color—the dead passing by in front of him. Twice his face got brushed by a cold, dead hand. And twice, he steeled himself for the fight to the death he thought was sure to come.

Chapter 62

Raven's *idea* entailed her to leave the Nikon and pack on the sidewalk beside the compact car she had hidden behind earlier. The camera, with its telephoto lens, would be no use to her where she was going. Furthermore, the backpack, prone to catching on things, would only slow her down.

For a split-second she considered leaving the SBR with the pack and camera and going forward with just the suppressed Glock and her blade.

She was working the SBR's sling over her head when, suddenly, something her dad had said to her mom back at the Eden compound popped into her head: *A handgun is only good to fight your way to a rifle.*

With that in mind, she checked the SBR's magazine and confirmed the stubby carbine held a round in the chamber.

After panning her head left-to-right, scrutinizing everything across the street with the aid of the white-phosphor NVGs, she rose up, SBR held at a low-ready, and darted for the van blocking the bungalow's narrow driveway.

On one knee beside the van's right front tire, Raven listened hard and looked the street up and down. There was nothing moving in her line of sight. However, coming from the east, maybe a block away, was a noise she attributed to shoes scuffing along a hard surface. Also, the low *thrum* of a power tool hard at work coming from the distant garage.

Figuring she would deal with the former when the time came, she rose into a combat crouch, then crossed the sidewalk and continued on up the driveway. Keeping low and moving fast, she made her way to the garage door.

Again she took a knee. Only this time she wasn't staring at the ground as she listened—she was staring into Caveman's glazed-over eyes. Even the eyes of the undead changed after they had been granted final release. Twice-dead was what Duncan called it. Threat eliminated was how her dad approached it. He was all business when it came to life and death. His only goal was to be the one still breathing after each and every encounter.

To Raven, it was the absence of that snippet of memory the dead sometimes acted on that was the difference between undead and twice-dead. Though it was far from the spark of life one saw in the eyes of the living, *something* was there.

The single round fired from Pirate's suppressed pistol had created a nickel-sized entry wound. It was equidistant to the Z's brow and hairline and weeping black fluid. How anything could penetrate that wide, high forehead was beyond her. The bone there looked to be thick as tank armor.

Thanks to the window Pirate had punched out, Raven was able to hear snippets of conversation each time the power tool went quiet.

But it was of no help to her. The dirtbags were speaking in Chinese. The dialect sounded like Mandarin—the same her dad had studied for weeks.

This is no way to gather intel.

Kicking herself for not accepting her dad's offer to use his language program, she fished her iPhone from a pocket.

Nearly as frustrated as she'd been sitting across the street in possession of a camera fitted with a Hubble-like telephoto lens and finding it absolutely useless, she thumbed the device to life.

Fingers a blur, she entered the passcode, tapped the camera icon, disabled the flash, then selected video mode. Stooped beside the garage door, she started the video rolling, swiped the display brightness all the way down, then stepped up onto Caveman's broad chest.

Amazingly, she found that the dead man provided a stable base. Way more stable than a bunch of crap with wheels piled atop a garbage can with wheels.

She waited until the power tool went quiet, then, with one hand keeping the SBR from banging the door, she rose to full extension and poked the iPhone—periscope-like—an inch or so above the destroyed window's lower lip.

Unable to see what was being captured on video, she kept her body as still as possible and moved her wrist right-to-left, in tiny increments.

Right away the conversation inside ramped back up. It went on like that for a couple of minutes, the power tool remaining quiet.

Finally, after staying in that awkward position for several minutes, her extended arm beginning to quiver, Raven stepped down from Caveman. Rubbing her cramping shoulder muscle, she swiped to brighten the display.

Nothing.

She thumbed the Power button, trying to wake the device.

No response.

The phone was dead.

Damn! she thought. The battery level had been near full charge when she left the Antlers. She hadn't taken stock of the level prior to starting the video rolling. Maybe she had forgotten to turn Wi-Fi and Bluetooth off. Having them constantly searching in a world where very few sources existed was a huge drain on a battery that had already proven to be pretty finicky.

Resigned to the fact she may have gotten only a few seconds of footage prior to the device going kaput, she stepped back up on Caveman, stretched out again, and, using the device's blank display as a mirror, stole a peek at what was happening inside the garage.

No sooner had the iPhone broken the plane than the rapid-fire Mandarin ceased.

When the power tool remained silent, a cold finger of dread stroked her gut.

The brief look Raven had gotten at the scene reflected back at her, though small and a bit distorted, told her that the trio from the tattoo shop were in fact the ones speaking Chinese. It also showed that they had a big project going on inside the garage.

The *project* had something to do with a number of metal cans. "Fifty-five-gallon drums" was what her dad called them. Four of them were sealed. Two were open and filled to the top with what looked to her like animal feed.

In the snapshot in Raven's mind, she saw the trio—Pixie, Snake, and Pirate—standing around one of the drums and pouring in *feed* from large white bags emblazoned with blue lettering and red symbols. On the ground by their feet was what appeared to be the pair of backpacks that had been weighing the men down. Though she couldn't be certain, the backpacks were empty.

The last thing that had registered when Pirate stopped talking was the sudden change in the tilt of his head. It had snapped from chin down to level and then panned in her direction.

Fearing she'd been caught spying, and with no way to get down the driveway without being seen—or worse, shot at—she withdrew the hand holding the iPhone and jumped off the corpse.

She felt her pulse rate spike as her mind raced through her options.

Ruling out the bungalow's backyard as a viable place to hide, she quickly backpedaled from the garage in the opposite direction. Reaching the hedge running the length of the drive all the way from the sidewalk to the garage, she wriggled her shoulders back and forth and wormed her way in.

Branches raked her cheeks and neck. Finally, she felt her back come up against something firm.

A fence?

The garage to the house next door?

Trapped, with the toes of her boots still on the drive, maybe an inch or so of the four-tube NVGs exposed, and fully a third of the SBR's suppressor visible to anyone who looked her way, she held her breath and pretended she was ten again and playing schoolyard freeze tag.

A beat after the branches embracing her body stopped quivering, she heard a door open and close. Then, from inside the garage, Pixie's sing-song voice: *"Shui?"*

Though her dad had been having her quiz him, she didn't recognize the word.

Pixie was repeating herself when Pirate stepped from the passage running between the bungalow and detached garage.

Boxy semi-automatic in one hand, he stopped and scrutinized Caveman.

Raven nudged the SBR's selector to Fire, slipped her finger into the trigger guard, and found the trigger with the pad of her finger.

As Pirate was looking up from the corpse, the scuffing noise Raven had heard minutes ago was back.

Snake's face filled up the broken window. He said, "*Shui?*"

Looking the length of the driveway, Pirate grunted, waved a hand dismissively, and said, "*Jiangshi.*"

This one Raven knew. Her dad had been practicing it on her a few days ago.

Zombie.

Just when Raven was thinking a Z had, for once, inadvertently paid her a favor, Pirate's gaze swung her way. As his body went stiff, her finger tensed on the trigger.

Still holding her breath, as well as a few pounds of trigger pull, Raven watched the man's head and weapon swing to face the steady scuffing coming up the drive.

Chapter 63

Portland

The Pale Riders' brush with death lasted five minutes, give or take. In the end, no shots were fired, blades remained sheathed, and, after exhaling a collective breath, each of the team members began to stir.

Rising up from the grass, Cade poked his head out of the alley and took a quick turkey peek around the fence. After getting eyes on Cross and Nat, the latter of whom was standing still as a statue and aiming his Mk 46 at the retreating dead, Cade informed them with a whisper that the alley was now clear.

Emerging from between the pair of cars, Griff hustled across 48th. When he reached the rest of the team, he sought out Cade. "That was a close fuckin' call, Captain."

Cade stared at the shooter through the NVGs. Thanks to their advanced display, he could see that the SEAL's cheeks were flushed red. The color continued down the man's neck, finally fading to pink an inch shy of the collar on his Crye Precision combat shirt. It was the first time Cade had seen the jocular SEAL show any kind of stress. It was also the first time using these particular NVGs in a combat situation. So he dismissed it as nothing.

Still, he made a mental note to keep an eye on the man. For everyone had their breaking point. You just didn't know when or where the proverbial cup would overfloweth.

The team adopted their previous marching order as Cade led them into the grass-choked alley. He moved slowly, careful to step only on the grass crushed down by the passing herd.

Every few steps Nat would turn a slow one-eighty and pause with the business end of the MK 46 trained on the mouth of the alley. He'd stay like that for a long three-count before falling back in line.

As Cade reached the beginning of the run of cedar fencing behind the fifth house east of 48th, he halted the team with a raised fist. "This is it," he said. "I'm going ahead to get eyes on. See if it's how I left it."

The team members took a knee, with Cross and Griff aiming their weapons east, and Nat covering 48th with his machine gun.

Cade ranged ahead, stopping only when he was at the mid-point of the fifty-foot run of fence.

Swallowing hard, he let his gaze roam the rear of his former home. Saw that the upstairs windows were closed. Dark curtains hung limply behind the office window on the right. The window on the left was still hung with the same boy-band curtains Brook had bought for Raven when the ones featuring Disney Princesses were no longer deemed acceptable by the tween.

All Cade could make out below the bottoms of the upper-floor windows was the top of the pergola he and a friend had erected the summer before Omega struck.

This wasn't how he imagined his final visit to the Grayson home would go down. He always imagined Brook and Raven would be left alone, without him, his final visit as ashes in an urn. He never expected to outlive Brook. Hell, in his line of work, he never expected to live past thirty.

Heavy of heart, he let his rifle hang from its sling, hooked his fingers over the top of the fence, and performed a chin-up.

The entire backyard was a jungle. Brook's prized shrubs and once meticulously manicured flower beds were now choked with weeds and migrating grass.

Cade saw his bike propped up where he had left it; however, thanks to the out-of-control lawn, only the seat and handlebars were visible. Even the wheelbarrow he'd used to get over the fence that Saturday in July remained where he'd left it: pushed against the fence a few feet from his neighbor's property line.

Still feeling a bit of trepidation over revisiting his old home, he called the team forward.

Making a stirrup by interlacing his fingers, Nat bent at the knees and nodded to Cade.

Saying, "Please don't catapult me onto the roof," Cade stepped up and planted a Danner on Nat's clasped hands.

"Contrary to popular belief," said the towering Fijian. "I know my own strength." He stood straight and, with ease, lifted Cade—all hundred and eighty pounds, plus another eighty in gear—until he was balancing on his stomach atop the fence.

Once Cade located the wheelbarrow in the thicket, he tightened his two-handed grip on the top of the fence.

"Now," he said, and with Nat's aid, he got both legs over the top of the fence.

It wasn't easy, but he got his hands turned around and managed to lower himself onto the wheelbarrow.

Apparently, Murphy was still on the clock, because the second Cade trusted the wheelbarrow to accept all of his weight, its front tire went flat and it toppled sideways, spilling him into the long grass.

Cade was a bit embarrassed, but not hurt. To spare the others the indignity, he hefted the wheelbarrow over to Nat, who took it with one hand and lowered it to the ground with ease.

One by one the rest of the team scaled the fence and joined Cade in his own backyard.

Griff turned a slow circle, surveying the fifty by fifty parcel of land. Regarding Cade, he said, "What a cheapskate, Captain. You could have at least paid the neighbor kid to cut your lawn while you were away."

Gesturing toward the sliding glass door, Cross said, "Wyatt's no cheapskate. Lookie there ... he sprang for a house sitter."

Cade had turned and stared at Griff but said nothing. Then, when Cross spoke up, he was reluctant to look and see who or what the *house sitter* was. Part of him thought the SEAL was messing with him. Then he remembered that the wholesome California surfer boy wasn't prone to pranking anyone, let alone someone who outranked him, someone he had never before shown disrespect to.

Seeing as how Cross always operated "by the book", Cade turned toward the sliding glass door, expecting to see a Z standing in his kitchen.

Sure enough, a first turn had parted the vertical blinds. It was shirtless and staring out into the backyard, its ample gut and both pale palms pressed against the glass.

"I got it," Cade said. "I'll clear the house, too. I know the floorplan and all its blind corners." In his voice, the message as clear as the wail of a police siren: This I *must* do alone.

"Understood," Cross replied.

"Two minutes, tops," Cade indicated, flashing the team a reversed peace sign.

"A second longer and we're coming in for you," Griff quipped. Voice going serious, he added, "Sure I can't help with the bloater? Get your six once you're inside?"

With a slow wag of the head, Cade shot him a look. It could only be interpreted one way: *Thanks, but no thanks.*

As Cade approached the door solo, he recalled the frantic rush to get gear and weapons loaded into his Sequoia. How the neighbor kids, Ike and Leo, were so helpful in accomplishing a task he should have done hours before fleeing the house.

With gunfire sounding across the street, he remembered hearing the noise of glass breaking then turning around just in time to see one of the dead things ride the shards of his destroyed picture window into his living room.

With all that going on at the time, he wasn't certain if he remembered to throw the sliding door's latch and replace the wooden dowel in the channel before leaving his old life behind.

Hell, he thought as he grabbed the handle and craned to see if the dowel was in place, *every door in the place could be hanging wide open.*

He was met with a mixed bag of news. The bad: the door *was* locked. The good: the person who had thrown the latch—likely Ike or Leo—had forgotten to drop the dowel in place. It was still propped up inside the channel.

Rising from the crouch, Cade averted his gaze from the bloated male Z and delivered three hard blows to the siding beside the slider.

After a long ten-count, with no other dead things joining the one grinding against the glass to his fore, Cade grabbed the handle with both hands. Simultaneously, he lifted up and jerked the handle hard to his left.

The lock giving way to brute strength produced a gunshot-like *pop*. As the door started moving right-to-left in its track, the glass sliding against the Z's fingers and face made a sound eerily similar to that of a squeegee being dragged across a wet windshield.

With the *squee* sound making the hairs on his neck stand to attention, Cade opened about a foot-and-a-half wide gap. Stopping the door's slide, he let go of the handle and took a half-step back.

The *squeee* was followed by hollow rasps as the Z angled sideways and thrust its face and both arms through the opening. Stuck between the jamb and bowed-out slider, its fingers brushing Cade's chest rig, the Z emitted a long, drawn-out moan.

Taking advantage of the Z's predicament, Cade stepped forward, wrapped the fingers of one hand in its tangled mop of graying hair, tugged up and back, and quickly buried his Gerber into one of those vacant, searching eyes.

Saying, "Allow me," Nat approached and hauled the twice-dead corpse away from the slider.

Without acknowledging the assistance, or even regarding his team, Cade stepped across the threshold. As he entered the kitchen, his gaze was drawn to the side-by-side refrigerator. On it were pictures of their family drawn by Raven when Cade was deployed. Most were in crayon and consisted of crude stick figures standing before a lopsided house. Birds and sunshine featured in some. Most had dark rain clouds hanging over the small family.

Coincidence? Cade thought not. He hated being away from them, but it had been necessary to keep them safe. It was his job and, like now, he gave it one hundred percent when he donned the uniform.

Next to the refrigerator was the whiteboard. It was still propped up on the granite counter and filled with the kind of home repair honey-dos that he loathed back then. God, what he wouldn't give now to have Brook back and telling him to "*Remember to take your vitamins.*" Or reminding him that "*Sleep is more important than the Mariners' replay.*" Or constantly nagging him to "*Drink more water.*"

As the flood of emotions accompanying the triggered memories hit him like a ton of bricks, he left the kitchen behind and gripped the handle to the door leading to the open mudroom and garage.

He tried the handle.

Unlocked.

Three hard knocks, followed by a ten-second wait, drew nothing to the door.

He pressed his ear to the door and listened hard. *Still nothing.*

Cade worked the handle, gave the door a gentle tug, and stepped back a pace.

The door swung open, real slow, and bumped against the doorstop affixed to the wall.

Setting foot in the mudroom, Cade learned two things. First, though he didn't recall hitting the remote as they drove away, the pristine condition of the garage told him he had indeed started the door closing on the way out. Second, he was relieved to see that Brook and Raven's mountain bikes were still hanging upside down from the ceiling, their front and rear wheels threaded over big rubber-coated hooks screwed into ceiling joists.

Emerging from the mudroom, Cade settled his gaze on the walnut table in the nearby dining room.

Three summer-themed placemats still sat before their predesignated *spots* at the table.

Realizing he would never share another breakfast with his family intact, his eyes glazed over with the threat of tears. Blinking away the tears, he willed open the lockbox inside of him and stuffed everything back down in it. Every ethereal thought that had slipped out. All of the pangs of regret he still harbored for not accompanying them to Myrtle Beach. His resentment of those who still had a partner in whom they could confide, whose embrace they could get lost in, and whose unconditional love they could expect no matter what happened in this crazy, ruinous tangle of circumstances life had become to him.

He told himself there would be a time and place to process all he was seeing and feeling.

He reminded himself that the time was not now.

All business, he whispered "Clear" and pushed deeper into the Grayson residence.

Chapter 64

Raven had remained stock-still, finger on the trigger, while Pirate stalked the length of the driveway. She finally exhaled and drew a breath once she thought he was out of earshot.

The dead weight crashing to the ground, somewhere out of sight, was louder than the report from Pirate's suppressed pistol.

The stocky man tromped back up the drive, muttering to himself in Mandarin. He paused for a tick before reentering the breezeway. Head down, he spent a few seconds standing there alternating between pressing his thumbs into his temples and massaging the back of his neck.

Clearly Pirate was carrying a huge burden.

Pixie's high-pitched voice finally spurred Pirate into action. Once he was back in the garage and work with the power tool had commenced, Raven stepped from the hedges. Seeing nothing but garage rafters through the broken garage window, she trained her weapon on the rectangle where a person's face was likely to show and backpedaled down the driveway.

Coming to the face-shot rotter prone on the sidewalk, she looped around the van and made a beeline for her pack.

Now, some thirty minutes after her near-death experience with the man who she figured needed to see an eye doctor, really, really bad, she was back at the spot where she had scaled the wall.

The Pikers were gone. The overpass was an above-ground cemetery awash with too many twice-dead Zs to count. A dead sled would eventually arrive and take the corpses to one of the massive graves dug into the hard high-plain soil.

With several hours to go before the first dark-purple band of dawn showed on the eastern horizon, the probability the people stuck on cleanup detail arriving anytime soon was next to zero.

Dragging the radio out, Raven hailed Daymon.

"Daymon here."

"Where are you?" she asked.

"Here," he answered.

"Where's here?"

"Stand with your back to the wall."

Raven stuffed the radio into her pocket and pressed her back to the wall. A tick later, a thick, knotted rope appeared in her peripheral. It looped high over the wall then came back to earth a couple of feet to her left. After bouncing off the wall a couple of times, the rope came to rest, hanging laser-straight, the unattached end a couple of inches off the ground.

Swinging her rifle around to her back, Raven climbed the rope, hand over hand.

Waiting on the other side, Daymon helped her to the ground.

NVGs still deployed, Raven noticed that Daymon had already rolled the garbage cans across the street and nosed them both against the restaurant.

The beach cruiser was propped up on its kickstand.

Daymon said, "Welcome back, Captain America Junior."

Raven made a face she doubted he could see. Gesturing at the three bumps under the ivy, she said, "You put the bikes back wrong."

"Do I get an A for effort?"

She said, "Thank you, Daymon. Now give me a hand."

Working together, they got the tattoo crew's bikes put back in proper order.

Daymon untied the rope from the storm grate he'd used to anchor it. As he reeled it back in, he said, "Well? What'd you find out?"

"I'm not sure."

"Did you get pictures? Video?"

Raven said nothing.

Grimacing, Daymon said, "Tell me you got some video."

"I ... *think* I got some video."

"Elaborate."

Raven flipped up the NVGs and powered them off. She turned the bike around and pushed it into the street. Still tight-lipped, she straddled the seat and pedaled off into the dark.

A few seconds passed before Daymon caught up to Raven, pedaling a bike way too small for him. Knees jutting to the sides and hunched over the bars, he fixed her with a hard stare. "Well," he repeated. "What'd you find out?"

Breaking her silence, Raven told him what she had seen with her own eyes. Then she mentioned the fifty-five-gallon drums they were filling with feed. The second she mentioned the van, Daymon said, "We need to get that phone of yours charged. Whatever you got, Duncan and Tran need to see it right away."

Nodding in agreement, Raven said, "I have a bad feeling about this."

Saying, "Me, too," with a certain sense of urgency in his voice, Daymon put his head down and pedaled as fast as he could.

Chapter 65

Portland, Oregon

Keeping his gaze lowered lest he see the pictures on the walls, Cade cleared the rest of his home, alone, and heavy of heart. When he exited the house through the slider five minutes after he had entered, half-a-dozen Snickers bars were clutched in one gloved fist, a couple of Star Trek novels bulged his pants' cargo pockets, and a treasure trove of photos were tucked safely away in his ruck. He had succeeded in finding in the clutter of his office all of the wedding photos, several of he and Brook on their honeymoon, and dozens of photos memorializing Raven's birth and each of her "firsts". He'd even struck gold, finding a few yellowed black and whites of grandparents and some color photos of his mom and dad.

Cross elbowed Griff. "See," he said, "Wyatt's word is always bond. He got into the stash of *good stuff.*"

Acting on the not-so-subtle cue, Cade passed out the candy bars, giving two to Nat.

"Thanks for clearing the deader from the door. I was in kind of a dark place at the moment."

"I figured as much," Nat said, smiling. "You didn't have to give me an extra treat for doing it."

"Consider the extra an upfront thank you. I'm going to need your help to move another stiff outside. Then we have to shore up the living room window with the sofa and love seat."

Already swallowing the last of the two Snickers bars, Nat said, "I'm on it," and entered the house through the sliding door.

"Come with me," Cade said, motioning to Griff. "Leave your ruck."

Looking up from what he was doing, Nat asked, "Where you going, boss?"

"Around the block," Cade replied. "To my old neighbor's house. It's close. We'll remain in constant contact over comms."

Cross was peeking out the sliding door, through the vertical blinds. Letting the slats fall back into place, he said, "Doubt if any deaders followed us. I'll watch the alley, just the same."

Cade said, "Zs are the least of my worries. Keep an eye out for foot mobiles. Though Target Alpha is three and a half miles out, we need to stay frosty. Last thing we need is to lose the element of surprise."

Cross said, "Copy that," pulled a chair up next to the slider, cracked it open a couple of inches, and sat down.

Cade removed the wooden dowel from the slider channel. Handing it to Cross, he said, "If for some reason you have to get up, use this. Damn locks on these are useless."

Peering through the peephole, Griff called, "Street out front is clear. You ready, Wyatt?"

Nodding, Cade made his way through the dining room and paused by the front door to radio the TOC back at Peterson, as well as the QRF waiting at their loiter a few miles northeast of Portland's city limits. After letting them both know he was leaving the team's loiter to conduct a ten-minute recon of the immediate area, he led Griff out of the house, down the steps, and paused on the sidewalk fronting the gray Craftsman.

After powering on his NVGs, Cade walked his gaze left-to-right down Boise Street, from Rawley's old home to the intersection with 48th.

Maybe because it just so happened to be *his* street, for the first time since he'd scrambled from Jedi One, Cade noticed accumulations of windblown trash, scattered drifts of leaves huddling around storm drains, and that most of the cars left at the curb sat on semi-flat tires.

The neighborhood has gone to the dogs.

The second he thought it, Cade heard a hound baying to the south—the same direction off 48th he and Griff would be turning.

The hound's call was soon joined by others. They seemed to be communicating.

While Cade loved dogs, he had no desire to see if these ones held humans in the same regard. Left alone to fend for themselves, no matter their previous training or dispositions, dogs were usually very quick to get back to their roots, so to speak. To run in packs. Hunt in packs. Cade had seen the results of a lone person caught out and about and descended upon by a hungry pack. In that instance … good ol' Fido was *not* man's best friend.

"That's not a good sound," Griff noted.

Rounding the corner at 48th, Cade said, "We're not far. House is fourth from the next corner, on this side of the street."

"Color and style?"

Cade replied, "Blue? Maybe green? It's a two-story. Detached garage is on the left side at the end of the driveway. Side door should be open."

"What were their names?"

After a short pause, during which Cade stopped at the corner of Cora and 48th to scan the street east to west, he said, "Ted and Lisa were their names. Me and Ted were known to share a pint at the local brew pub. Take in a Mariners or Blazer game."

"You don't talk sports much," Griff said. "Don't really strike me as a drinker, either. Hell, Wyatt … you're as by the book a leader as any I've come across."

If only you knew the gray areas I've visited, Cade thought. He said, "Here it is," and peeled off to his left.

Viewed with the full color NVGs, Cade learned that Ted and Lisa's house was white. He also saw that the dark green British sports car Ted had been constantly tinkering on was still sitting on jacks in the two-car garage.

After stalking around the car and giving the garage an *all clear*, Cade's eye was drawn to the bare hook on the wall where he'd taken down the axe he'd used to put down his neighbors. What a baptism by fire that had been. Surreal, to say the least.

Ted and Lisa's twice-dead corpses were on the floor, too. Fused to pools of their own dried blood, arms and legs bent at odd angles, the pair reminded him of the horrors created by the Vesuvius eruption.

But this was not Pompeii. And he wasn't here seeking closure or to make amends.

What was done, was done.

What Cade had come for was hanging from the rafters, a yard from his grasp, and wrapped in cobwebs. In fact, Ted was the one who had given Cade the idea of suspending his family's bikes from the rafters.

Filtering in through the open side door: the raucous sound of dogs barking. This time the noises seemed to come from somewhere south of the garage. While seemingly scattered when first he'd heard them, it now sounded as if the hounds had coalesced into a roving pack.

"Lend me a hand," Cade said. Standing on an upended five-gallon bucket emblazoned with Home Depot and drowning warnings, he lifted Lisa's bike from the hooks.

Griff took the woman's lavender ten-speed from Cade and propped it against the project car. Suppressing a chuckle, he said, "This one has Cross's name written all over it."

"He isn't vain," Cade said. "He'd ride a unicycle into battle if need be."

"No single wheels for this Southie. I'd rather ride a Big Wheel into battle."

Manhandling Ted's Kona mountain bike off the hooks, Cade said, "That can be arranged." As he handed the eighteen-speed to Griff, he went on, "Don't mistake my quiet demeanor for weakness. If you bust my chops in front of the others again, you'll find yourself legless and pushing yourself into battle on a skateboard."

Griff took a step back, put his hands on his hips, and hung his head.

Cade said, "Are we good?"

Looking up, Griff said, "I meant nothing by it. I'm just used to busting Lopez's balls. That's all."

Cade smiled and nodded in agreement. "He thrives on the abuse. I think he wouldn't know what to do with himself if everyone kissed his ass all the time."

"This purple rocket is just his speed," quipped Griff.

Cade shook his head. Still smiling, he said, "If Lopez was here, I'd try and stick him with my daughter's bike. At least at first. Just to see his reaction."

"You're all right, Wyatt. Maybe a little stoic at times … but you're all right, just the same." He paused and let his gaze roam the garage. Finally, fixing Cade with the four-lens-stare, he said, "I'm sorry. We're good."

The dogs were back at it again. A cacophony of yips and growls, punctuated now and then by the deep-throated baying. It almost sounded as if they were staking out the end of the driveway.

Cade tested the air pressure in the bike tires by pressing his thumb on each one. While he couldn't feel the rims when he applied pressure, all of the tires could use some air.

"We better go," Griff said. He pulled the woman's bike to the open door. "I'll take this one."

With no reason to argue with the SEAL, Cade rolled Ted's Kona into the breezeway. He was throwing one leg over the seat when he heard throaty growls. It sounded nothing like that of the dead, but he detected hunger in there, nonetheless.

Griff said, "You have an MRE? Cereal bar? Better yet, a bone?"

"In my ruck back at the house," Cade answered. He dismounted the bike, then unslung his M4 and threw the selector to Fire.

If the dogs knew the cover of darkness was not on their side, it didn't show. They were emboldened and advancing up the drive. Leading the pack was a full-sized standard poodle. Its black coat was grown out and home to twigs and burrs. Teeth bared, it looked left and right. As if on cue, the bloodhound and chocolate Lab flanking the poodle advanced.

Though he didn't want to expend one round, let alone burn half of a magazine to put down the fifteen or so mutts facing them, Cade shouldered his M4, drew a bead between the poodle's eyes, and let a round fly.

The suppressed report from the M4 was no louder than a book dropped flat on a hard surface. To the dogs, though, it was like the backfire from a car and came wholly unexpected. They all started. A couple of the smaller dogs yelped and cowered.

To Cade it was apparent the pack had had the run of the neighborhood for some time and wasn't used to push back from the living.

The 5.56 hardball round skipped off the poodle's long, slender snout a fraction of a second prior to drilling the alpha male squarely between the eyes. The poodle didn't yelp or whimper. It simply collapsed to the driveway, unmoving and no longer holding sway on the pack.

Primal instincts driving them, the rest of the pack gave up ground.

To add an exclamation point to the encounter, Cade snapped off a second shot, the round crackling like an angry hornet as it passed harmlessly over the pack. Then, as the mongrels began to fully disperse, he skipped a couple of rounds off the driveway.

"Let's go before another one goes alpha and they regroup."

Though it was unlikely the reports of the suppressed gunshots had carried past the end of the driveway, to be safe, Cade contacted Cross on the comms. After telling the operator to expect them in a couple of minutes, Cade hopped on the Kona and followed Griff, already slow-rolling the ten-speed past the dead poodle.

Chapter 66

In the Founders Suite, back at the Antlers Hotel, Raven had just started her iPhone charging.

After stowing their bikes in the bushes outside, Daymon had ridden the elevator up with her. Instead of tagging along to see what kind of footage—if any—was captured on the dead device, he had padded off to see if waking Duncan at this hour was in the cards.

When Raven had inserted the charging cord and saw the iPhone's screen remain black, she had assumed the worst: that the thing had finally gone *brick* on her. That it was a useless slab of metal and glass and any footage in its memory, unrecoverable.

Now, a couple of minutes later, on a black background on the screen was a battery icon. It was an ominous shade of red and flashing intermittently.

Coming through the door ahead of Daymon, his shock of silver hair suffering a serious case of bedhead, Duncan said, "Little lady … didn't anyone teach you that a watched pot never boils?"

Mockingly, she asked, "If a tree falls in the woods and there's no one around, does it make a sound?"

"Touché," said Duncan. "Bird of the Apocalypse knows her idioms."

"Duncanisms," she corrected. "You used the forest one a dozen times back at Eden."

Changing the subject, Duncan said, "Leave that thing alone for a minute and it'll charge faster."

"I'm just grateful it *is* charging. A minute ago I was worried it had bricked on me."

Arching a brow, Duncan said, "Bricked?"

Daymon was busy getting water for coffee going on a single burner stove. He looked up. "It means your phone has died and it ain't coming back. Even the techs at the Apple stores say they can't resurrect a *bricked* phone."

Nodding, Duncan asked, "So … what does that flashing red battery mean?"

Coming through the door Daymon had left open, Wilson said, "Means it's taking a charge but doesn't have enough juice to power up. If you want to keep this from happening again, you should find a solar charger and a couple of those backup batteries like Taryn uses."

Daymon spooned finely ground coffee into the French press. "Lola might stock something like that. Shit … she has everything else."

Obviously exasperated, eyes still glued to the device, Raven began popping her knuckles.

"I wouldn't do that if I were you," said Glenda as she entered the room. She wore a white flannel nightgown dotted with canary-yellow daisies. It stopped at her knees and clashed mightily with her fuzzy, hot-pink slippers.

Glenda's hair was the polar opposite of Duncan's. It was cut short but still looked as if she had just returned from the stylist.

Assuming the woman slept with a nightcap on, Raven crossed her arms but said nothing.

Glenda asked, "What are you all up to at this ungodly hour?"

Demeanor softening, Raven brought Glenda up to speed. She left out nothing.

Playing Devil's advocate, Glenda said, "I don't think your dad is going to be very happy when he learns you went outside the wire."

"It's not the first time," Raven said.

"First time alone," reminded Glenda. "Last time you and Sash got an extended tour of dish duty."

Wilson cleared his throat. "I'm thinking the backpacks had bolts and ball bearings in them. Add those to a homemade bomb and you got an assload of shrapnel flying around." He removed his boonie hat and scratched his head. Fixing Raven with a hard stare, he added, "You have to take this to the law. You also need to get your dad involved so he can tell his people to warn President Clay."

"First things first," said Duncan with an added wink. "One step at a time. We need to see what's on Bird's phone. If there's no evidence, Chief Riggleman won't listen to a word Raven has to say. She goes blabbing everything with no evidence, at best she'll have to speak to a juvenile judge about her leaving the wire alone. Best case … she'll come away with a slap on the wrist. Worst case … she loses her Golden Ticket *and* the right to open carry inside the wire. Can't risk all that on a bunch of assumptions." He paused for a couple of seconds. "What's that your dad says about assuming?"

Without missing a beat, Raven said, "It makes an ass out of you and me."

"Exactly," Duncan shot, waving his hands.

Thinking the man looked a bit like a crazy version of Gandalf the Grey, or, better yet, crazy Doc Brown from Back to the Future, Raven cracked an ill-timed smile.

"What's so funny?" Duncan asked. "For all we know, based on your description of what was happening in that garage, the Tattoo Gang are brewing beer. I feel like I'm stuck in a gosh darn episode of Scooby Doo."

Daymon finished pouring boiling water into the press. Meeting Duncan's gaze, he said, "C'mon … you and I both know that's not gonna happen … no matter who she tells. She's Captain America's kid, for Christ's sake."

Raven clapped her hands together. "We have signs of life."

"The zombie phone is *turning*," quipped Duncan. "What do you got?"

After swiping and poking at the screen, Raven's shoulders slumped. "I got the driveway outside the garage. I got the garage door. Then as I was reaching up to film the inside of the garage, right before the stinking battery died … I got some noises that *could be* power tools … or a blender or—"

"A radio control car," interrupted Daymon. "You're going to need more than that to convince Chief Riggleman to investigate."

"I agree," Duncan said. "How about we all use our Golden Tickets and go have a look-see for ourselves?"

Daymon started pouring coffee into Antlers' mugs.

Glenda waved him off, declaring, "I'm going back to bed before I share my opinion and get myself in trouble. You all have fun playing Nancy Drew and Hardy Boys."

Gladly accepting a mug of coffee, Wilson said, "I'm game."

Lower lip jutting, Raven said, "Half a cup, please."

Doing the *gimme* hands thing, Duncan accepted a full mug.

Sitting down at the communal table with a mug of his own cradled in his large hands, Daymon said, "So what's the plan?"

Raven was about to give Duncan the floor when the Iridium sat-phone in her room emitted its unique electronic trill. She said, "Only person who would call that phone at this time is—"

In unison, Duncan, Wilson and Daymon said, "Captain America."

Portland, Oregon

Cade was sitting at his dining room table, elbows resting on a laminated map of Portland, working the beginnings of a plan over in his mind.

The air in the main floor no longer reeked of death and mildew. It had been usurped by the sweet nose of Hoppes Number 9 gun oil.

On the table beside the four-by-four map of Portland, surrounded by the remnants of a Spaghetti and Meatball MRE, was a similar-sized image of Target Alpha. Taken by a KH-11 Keyhole satellite the previous day, the overhead of the main target bore a number of markings put there by Cade.

The first, a black square beside Target Alpha, denoted pens constructed by the Chicoms to hold prisoners. In the pens were an unknown number of American civilians as well as a former soldier very important to President Clay.

Denoted by a number of purple Xs positioned in a semi-circle west of the holding pens, essentially turning the prisoners into human shields, were the multiple components of a Chinese HQ-9 Red Banner Long Range Air Defense Missile System. It was this piece of hardware that had to be rendered inoperative before the chopper carrying the QRF could get anywhere close to the target.

North of the holding pen, arranged side by side, was the pair of singlewide trailers the thirty or so PLA soldiers were said to be housed in.

Cade moved the satellite image aside and arranged the Portland map so that it was front and center.

Snaking vertically across the map, cobalt blue and maybe half an inch at its widest point, was the north-flowing Willamette River.

At the bottom of the map, near the first of three bridges crossing the visible stretch of the Willamette, was where the team was to rendezvous with assets knowledgeable of both the target and how best to approach it without drawing enemy contact.

In order to remain ahead of the curve in the event the Chicoms had recently changed their patrol times or moved prisoners or personnel around, Cade had sent Cross and Griff downrange to perform as advance recon of Target Alpha.

With ten minutes remaining until Cade was to wake Nat, he plucked one of the Star Trek novels from the table.

Examining the cover on which the USS Enterprise was squaring up to engage a Klingon Bird of Prey, he had a sudden epiphany.

Casting the novel aside, he pulled his Iridium sat-phone from a pocket and placed a call to Raven.

Chapter 67

Colorado Springs

Saturday, March 17th, 2012

At 7:07 a.m., just as the sun was breaking the horizon to the east, Raven was poking her head out the Bronco's window and imploring the gate guard to return their papers.

"It says on the tickets that we are allowed outside the walls from sunup to sundown." She pointed east. "That big orange and yellow thing is on the rise."

Already taking his own sweet time returning from the guard shack with the group's four Golden Tickets, the wiry specialist responded by slowing his gait and taking a long, hard look at his watch.

Under her breath, Raven said, "Come on, dumbass. We don't have all day."

Approaching the Bronco from the passenger side, the baby-faced soldier, whose name tape read *Fogle*, waved a finger menacingly in Raven's direction.

"I heard that," he said, stopping a foot from the SUV and tucking their papers under his arm.

Having none of it—mostly because her "half a cup of coffee" had become two cups before they had left the Antlers—Raven waved a finger back at the soldier. "You're being a jerk," she insisted. "If you don't stop yanking our chain, I'll have my dad come and pay you a visit."

A question ghosted across Fogle's face.

Turning toward the backseat, Daymon said to Duncan, "Remind me to never again offer her coffee."

"I kind of like to see her in *spitfire* mode," Duncan replied.

"I'm new to this post," admitted Fogle. "Who is your dad?"

"Cade Grayson."

Though Fogle said nothing, his demeanor changed. Wearing a put-upon smile, he handed the papers back to Raven and motioned to the crew manning the gate.

Raven stared at Fogle as the gate swung open.

Before Daymon could pull through, the gate guards allowed the truck full of Pikers to enter.

"Long night," noted Daymon.

"Good thing," Wilson said. "Means it should be smooth sailing through the EZ for us."

Looking to Daymon, Raven held her hand horizontal near his face. It was vibrating almost as much as the hula dancer on the dash. "Does coffee do this to you?"

The gate guard waved Daymon through.

Catching second gear, Daymon said, "Not like that. Then again, a cup and a half is barely enough to open one of my eyelids."

"When will it wear off?"

Wilson said, "Four … maybe five hours."

Raven made a face.

"Relax," drawled Duncan. "They're giving you a rash of crap. You'll be fine in an hour or two. Since you stayed up all night, when you do come down you're going to be tired as all get out."

Brows meeting in the middle, Raven said, "How am I going to shoot straight?"

Daymon wrestled the wheel and steered the Bronco onto the newly graded road skirting the greenspace. Getting the rig tracking straight, he met Raven's gaze. "Let's hope it doesn't come to that. If we get into a gun fight, chances are none of us will be shooting straight."

"Adrenaline will do that to a fella," Duncan added.

"Adrenaline or no," Wilson said, "my hands always shake."

Raven said, "I feel like I'm going to throw up."

Daymon said, "We're almost there. Can you hold it?"

Raven nodded. Pressing a finger to her pursed lips, she hung her head out the window.

Daymon braked and downshifted. "Almost there." Regarding Duncan in the rearview mirror, he said, "You sure rolling up all hard and acting like we're undercover agents or some shit is the right approach?"

Duncan shrugged. "You got a better idea?"

Now a block from the house and approaching from the opposite direction as Raven had, Daymon noticed there was no van out front. He said, "Looks like the Norma Jean pie van is gone."

"Loretta Jean's," Raven corrected.

Suppressing a chuckle, Duncan said, "Daymon, my man … Norma Jean was Marilyn Monroe's real name."

Shaking his head, Daymon said, "Still can't believe Nixon and Babe Ruth both hit that."

In the backseat, Duncan and Wilson made eye contact. Neither had the heart to correct their driver.

The house was on their left and coming up quick. The hedges rising up beside the drive cast a shadow over the bungalow and blocked everything from view save for the lawn and front porch. On the former, a van-sized rectangle of grass was mashed down. Deep furrows that could have easily been made by spinning tires bracketed the disturbed patch of lawn.

As they drew even with the house next door to the bungalow, Daymon slowed the Bronco to walking speed.

Craning to see past Wilson, Duncan said, "No van in the driveway."

Raven said, "It could be *in* the garage."

Daymon said, "Only one way to find out," and pulled the Bronco hard to the curb across the street from the bungalow. He was cutting the engine when Wilson began to protest.

After stilling the hula girl with the customary finger atop her head, Daymon twisted in his seat until he was facing Wilson. "Water your balls and gun up, Red. 'Cause I'm over this not knowin' bullcrap."

Wilson said, "What if they're in there right now loading the van? Raven said the pirate-looking guy had a hand-cannon fitted with a suppressor. That tells me he knows how to handle himself. I really think it would be better if we let the police handle this."

"If they're in there loading a bomb onto the van," shot Daymon, "we need to put them under citizen's arrest and hold them at gunpoint until we can get the authorities on the radio."

With his bad back still acting up, it took Duncan a little longer than the others to extricate himself from the Bronco's cramped backseat.

Looking like gunslingers in a Spaghetti Western, the four of them stood in the street and watched the bungalow for nearly a minute. When nothing moved behind the windows and no sounds arose from the garage, Raven raised her rifle to the ready position and advanced toward the driveway, head on a swivel and exuding all kinds of frosty.

Moving slower than a tree sloth with bad sciatica, Duncan made it to the garage a minute after the others.

"No twice-dead rotters," noted Wilson.

Breathing hard and bracing a hand on his back, Duncan pointed out dark spots on the ground in front of the garage door. "There *is* blood here. Tells me part of Bird's story wasn't lost in translation."

"I know what I saw," Raven insisted. "Daymon, you're tallest. Take a look in the window and tell us what you see."

Saying, "I'm not going to get my head blown off," Daymon stalked toward the breezeway, Beretta in hand.

Seeing him go, Duncan trained his semiautomatic shotgun on the house rising up on their right.

Daymon took a quick peek around the corner, then slipped from sight.

He was only gone for a few seconds, returning with a hangdog look on his face.

"Bullcrap," Raven said. "Nothing?"

Daymon holstered his gun. Shaking his head, he said, "No van. No cans. No Pirate mans."

Resting his Saiga over one shoulder, Duncan said, "Thanks for nothing, Dr. Seuss. Is there *any* evidence?"

Raven made a face. "If they were using fertilizer, like Duncan suggested, shouldn't there be some that had gotten spilled on the floor?"

357

"Just a couple of stains on the floor. Could be oil or diesel. My nose isn't good enough to tell the difference."

Duncan said, "It's a garage. Unless it's Richard Petty's garage … there's bound to be some oil drips on the floor."

"Great," Raven shot. "Now all we have to go on is my dad's theory."

Nervously shifting his weight from foot to foot, Wilson said, "Cade pushed it up the chain of command, right?"

"That he did," confirmed Duncan. "If that graffiti was in fact Klingon, or whatever he called it, it's got to be in a database somewhere."

Raven said, "A show I watched on Nickelodeon mentioned that every book is supposedly recorded into the Library of Congress."

Daymon said, "Sounds legit." He looked the length of the driveway, then regarded dark clouds forming overhead. "We better go before we draw a crowd."

Chuckling, Duncan said, "What? Big bad rainstorm going to flatten your hairdo?"

"I'll be cranking up Heidi's heater before the first drop strikes the ground." Daymon started down the drive, adding over his shoulder, "You, Old Man, will be the only one of us who gets rained on."

Chapter 68

Working efficiently, the nurse and soldiers manning the infection checkpoint had Daymon and the others scanned for spikes in body temperature and inspected for bites in record time.

When Daymon finally pulled Heidi up to the gate, papers in hand, he had a story in mind to tell anyone who asked why they had only spent an hour outside the walls.

The gate guard, a tall Hispanic sergeant whose name tape read *Flores*, was cordial with them as he collected their Golden Tickets and IDs. He said, "Wait one," and strode off for the trailer.

The sergeant exited the trailer five minutes later. As he walked back to the Bronco, documents and clipboard in hand, nothing about his body language or gait told Daymon he was going to have to tell the man that "car troubles" was the reason for their trip being cut so short.

Instead, he received their papers and IDs along with a green light to drive forward.

Having lost her shotgun position to Duncan on account his back was acting up again, Raven had gotten stuck sitting behind Daymon. Poking her head past the Bronco's headrest, she called the sergeant by name.

Shaking his head, Duncan said, "No ... no, no, no. *Do not* show him your cards."

Raven made eye contact with the sergeant. Her mouth opened, but instead of posing her question, she withdrew from the window and slumped back into her seat.

A confused look landed on Sergeant Flores' face. After a beat, he craned and said, "Is she OK?"

"Bad clams," quipped Duncan.

"In all seriousness," Daymon answered, "she's been wondering how one goes about joining the Army. She aspires to be a gate guard one day."

Flores smiled. "It's no glamourous post, Miss Grayson. This is just a stop on the road to where I really want to be. Why not go the Ranger route like your dad?"

Under his breath, Duncan said, "Drive, Daymon."

Speaking loud enough to be heard through Daymon's open window, Raven said, "That's some great advice, Sergeant. What I really want to know is if you saw a black van come through here shortly after we left? Loretta Jean's Pies was written on both sides … in white, I think."

"You were the early birds this morning." He glanced at his clipboard. "And so far, only one other group has gone outside the wire after you. They definitely weren't rolling a pie shop van."

Raven asked, "Does your clipboard show anyone missing over the last couple of days?"

The soldier shook his head. "No missing persons in the last two weeks."

Now that the box was open, Daymon said, "Any new arrivals come in this morning through one of the other gates?"

"Friends of yours?" Flores asked.

"Sure," Raven lied.

"Well," Flores said, "if they made it here this morning, they would have been processed. You know, checked for infection. After that they would have been taken to see Chief Riggleman for photos and fingerprints. You should probably check with her."

Daymon said, "That's exactly what we'll do, right, Raven?"

Wilson looked to Raven. "BERR opens at ten today. That's ninety minutes or so. I'll go with you."

Raven shook her head. "Thanks, but no thanks. I work best alone."

"Like father, like daughter," Duncan said.

Pressing a radio handset to his mouth, Flores said, "Good to go. Open the gate."

Slow-rolling the Bronco for the open gate, Daymon threw Flores a mock salute. "Thank you, Sergeant. Have a nice day."

Slapping the Bronco's side, the soldier wished them well.

***

Ten minutes after questioning Flores at the gate, Raven was squeezing her small frame from the Bronco's backseat.

As Daymon retook his place behind the wheel, Wilson asked Raven, "You sure you don't want a wingman?"

"Positive."

Duncan said, "Remember, all you have to go on is the Klingon graffiti thing. In my experience, that's not much of a leg to stand on. Desecrating a park is a jerk move. But I'm afraid it isn't enough to start a manhunt for these folks and their van. I believe ... we all believe that you saw what you saw. However, Riggleman, she's not going to be as open-minded."

Standing on the curb, the BERR building looming over her, all Raven could offer up in response was a shrug and a smile.

Duncan said, "If Riggleman wants to talk to one of us, have her call the house sat-phone. I'll make sure the ringer's on."

Raven nodded.

Waving "bye" out his window, Daymon signaled and pulled away from the curb.

After watching the Bronco wheel away to the north, Raven looked up the stairs. Lined up under cover, snaking from the building's tall double doors, was a line already twenty or thirty people deep.

Figuring each person would take five minutes to plead their case or air their grievance, and that Chief Riggleman would likely need the same to answer and offer solutions, Raven was looking at, maybe, best case scenario, getting her face-to-face sometime between two and three in the afternoon.

Not acceptable considering all she'd seen and learned in the last twenty-four hours.

Offering credits to swap places in line didn't work.

***

CSPD Officer Upton poked his head from the BERR building at ten sharp. He looked the length of the line that had doubled in size over the ninety minutes Raven had been waiting.

361

A tick after showing his face, Upton ushered everyone inside on account of the worsening weather.

As Raven filed by Sergeant Upton, careful to not deviate from her place in line, she remembered the admonishment she'd received from the officer last time she was here: *You made me look like a fool. Next time you come here you get in line like everyone else. And leave your guns at home. Grayson or not, you pull that crap on me again, I'll personally take you on a tour of our Spring Creek Juvenile Detention Center.*

Currently, the SBR was slung across her back, the Glock was holstered on her hip, and her trusty blade was sheathed on her hip. *Ooops.*

If the fact she was armed registered with Upton, he didn't immediately acknowledge it. Instead, he seemed to be ignoring her.

After showing the middle-aged woman at the head of the line where he wanted her to stand, Upton straightened the rest of the line along a wall behind her. Coming back down the line, the sergeant stopped next to Raven. Whispering in her ear, he said, "Chief is expecting you. Come with me."

Taken entirely by surprise, Raven patted her Glock and tugged on her rifle's sling. "What about these?"

Acting as if he'd never issued the detention center threat, Upton said, "What about them?"

Feeling the eyes of those still in line boring into her back, Raven followed Upton into the elevator.

Remaining tight-lipped, Upton led Raven out of the elevator on the second floor, down the gray carpeted hall, and to the northeast corner of the building, where he left her standing before the door to Chief Riggleman's office.

Before Raven could raise a hand to knock, the door swung inward and she was literally face-to-face with Chief Riggleman.

"Come on in, Raven. Make yourself comfortable."

Raven entered the room, stopped and turned to face the chief. "Take a seat."

Both chairs in front of the desk were piled high with papers and manila folders. Looking around the room, Raven saw that the only place to sit was on the Native-American-themed area rug on the floor in front of the desk.

Though Raven was crashing as the others had warned, she said, "I'll stand. Thanks all the same."

Chief Riggleman sat on the leather chair behind the desk. Steepling her fingers, she said, "Suit yourself." She stared at Raven for a long three-count. "Do you know why you're here?"

"The messages I left on your voicemail?"

She shook her head. "No."

Even as Raven was thinking, *Because I snuck over the wall?* she was saying the first thing that came to mind. "The Klingon graffiti?"

"I heard about it. Crazy that your dad, of all people, put that together. Who knew someone took the time to create a fictional alien language? Hell, they even wrote an entire book on it."

"My dad knew," Raven said. "He made me watch a couple Star Trek episodes with him." She made a face. "Not my thing, though."

"I want to know about this pastry van."

Word travels fast.

"It's a pie van," Raven corrected.

"Pies, pastries … same animal as far as I'm concerned. Spit it out."

Raven started with the long-range recon from the bus stop on Tejon. She described the bad actors then told the entire story, from soup to nuts, leaving nothing out.

Once Raven had capped off her retelling of the events with a plea for Chief Riggleman to issue an all-points bulletin, she whispered, "Please don't tell my dad I went outside the wire. If anything comes of this, you go ahead and take all the credit. My guys will be quiet."

"You mean Duncan, Daymon, and Wilson, right?"

The chief rattling off names of people Raven knew sent a shiver down her spine.

"Let me get this right. There was *zero* evidence when you all went back to the house?"

Raven nodded.

"And the van was gone?"

Again with the nod.

"If I didn't know your dad is Cade Grayson, I'd say all this you brought to me is the work of an overactive imagination. Tell you the people you saw have graduated from selling bootleg paint to making moonshine or beer." She rose from her chair. "But you ... you I have to believe."

Exhaling sharply, Raven asked, "What are you going to do?"

"I'm going to put out a BOLO for the people and their van."

"Bolo?"

"Be on the lookout."

"Shouldn't you put a stakeout on the house?"

"Not my jurisdiction. I'll run it up the chain, though." Chief Riggleman pushed her chair out of the way, then walked around the desk.

Raven stood her ground. Regarding the chief, who was kind of invading her personal space, she said, "Do you *have* to tell my dad I went out alone?"

"You did good." The chief shook her head. "But I'd be derelict of duty if I let it slide. Plus, I'd hate to get on your dad's bad side. I've heard what happens to those who do."

Raven said nothing, her mouth tightening.

Chief Riggleman went on, saying, "If they haven't already, the Secret Service are going to put the Antlers on lockdown. I suggest you curl up with a good book and let them do their thing. Let *us* do our thing. And come this time tomorrow you'll have one hell of a view of the ceremony from where you and yours are staying."

Extending a hand, Raven said, "Thanks." She met the chief's gaze. Held it as she added, "I don't blame you for reporting on what I did. It's the right thing to do."

Older beyond her years, thought Riggleman. She said, "Now get ... before I cite you for bringing weapons into my office."

Raven didn't need to be told twice. She let herself out, the possible repercussions from her jaunt outside the wire growing larger with each step she took down the long carpeted hall.

Chapter 69

Cade had slept through dawn and a good chunk of morning. The noise of rain pummeling the skylights had woken him from a deep slumber a few minutes before he heard Griff and Cross coming in through the sliding door.

Good job, he thought. Coming back by way of the east/west-running alley system lessened the chance of them having been followed on the ground. Separately, the mature trees in the backyards, brambles and weeds crushing in on back fences, and the city's powerlines running parallel to the alley all made it very difficult for someone operating a drone to keep tabs on them.

He also had no doubt the pair, exercising caution, had stashed their bicycles elsewhere and approached the loiter on foot.

Cade stretched and looked around the room. Waking up in his old bed was surreal to say the least. Doing so wearing boots and fully clothed, *without* Brook by his side was something he could have never envisioned.

"Wyatt ... come on down. You gotta see this."

It was Griff. He sounded like a miner who'd just found the motherlode.

Cade grabbed his M4 off the bed and hustled downstairs.

The three shooters were sitting around the dining room table. Mud was tracked all over the hardwood floors. Combined with the fluids that had leaked from the restless Z, the yellow-green sludge looked a lot like baby shit.

Ignoring the mess, Cade planted his hands on the table. "What'd you get?"

On the table was a hand-drawn map of the target. It was two-by-two and multicolored. In one lower corner was a key to help decipher the many symbols scribbled on it. Beside the map was the satellite image of Target Alpha.

Eyes flitting between the two items, Cade said, "Who's the artist?"

Cross tapped his chest. "Learned all this at Rowley. Put it to work when I was assigned advance detail. Reports had to be very thorough. For me, this is easier than drafting a long report."

Tapping the map east of the target buildings, Griff said, "We found a perfect overwatch spot ... *right here*. It's on an elevated boulevard. Two lanes each way. Southbound lanes are blocked with vehicles. Shooter has clear fields of fire to the target's east side, the holding pens, and the troop trailers."

Cade said, "How about the missile battery?"

Griff shook his head. "It's mostly shielded by the holding pens." He indicated a red X south of the RQ-9 battery. "This is a vacant gravel lot. The building materials concentrated on the west edge leads us to believe a project got squashed by the outbreak. It's ringed by chain-link fence. The fence is shored on all sides by Jersey barriers."

Cade said, "Set Nat up behind one of the Jersey barriers and you'll kill two birds: Nat has cover and concealment and you get a nice crossfire using minimal assets."

Cross looked to Griff, then swung his gaze to Cade. "Our first thoughts when we saw the place."

Wearing a curious expression, Nat said, "How many Zs are hanging around?"

"You sound like Lopez," noted Cross. "Are you as afraid of the *demonios* as he is?"

"Not to that level," Nat said. "Cross is going to be in an elevated position. Me, I'm going to be pretty damn exposed."

"You might encounter some Zs on your way in," Griff answered. "Where there's fresh meat, there's always biters."

Cade put his finger on the overwatch spot. "What's the viaduct look like, Z-wise?"

Cross said, "They're mostly grabbers reaching out from windows that're broken out or had been left cracked open. Nothing I can't handle."

Nat said, "With no air support or QRF until the battery is nullified, we're going to be sitting ducks if we are compromised."

Cade said, "Don't get compromised." He paused. "I asked for a couple more shooters and was denied. With four ops happening simultaneously, they say we're stretched real thin. I need you alone on that lot with your LMG."

Nat said, "What's the distance?"

Cross said, "Perfect for suppression and direct fire," then flipped open a notebook and started rattling off locations and the respective distances to targets.

"Enough chit-chat," Cade said. "Let's get into this." He glanced at his Suunto. "We have six hours until dusk. The quicker we get this drilled down, the more beauty sleep Cross and Griff are going to get."

Feigning a flip of the hair, Cross said, "This chiseled Adonis doesn't need any."

Griff said, "You should see me without the beard."

Cade regarded the man. "I'm thinking you would look like a ginger Matt Damon."

Griff shook his head. "Try again."

With a tilt of his head, Nat guessed, "Ginger Brad Pitt?"

Griff said, "Negative. Strike two," then shot Cross a challenging look.

Cross unbuckled the chinstrap and removed his helmet. Stroking his chin, he said, "Zach Galifianakis? He's a ginger. His mug might be pretty if he ever shaved."

"Too late for that," Griff said. "He's zed chow."

Cade cracked a smile at the thought of a zombie Wolf Pack being led down Rodeo Drive by the comedian. "Enlighten us, Griff. We got work to do."

Cross started an impromptu drum roll, tapping his fingers on the tabletop.

Nat began to chant. "Spill, spill, spill …"

Totally serious, Griff said, "Hugh Jackman."

Nat stood up from the table. Doubled over and slapping both hands on his massive thighs, he said, "Ginger Wolverine. *That* I'd pay big money to see."

In the worst put-on Australian accent Cade had ever heard, Cross said, "Hey, Bub … you want a taste of me adamantium claws?"

"I can see it," Cade lied. "Now about these patrol patterns … you have them all timed and noted?"

Red creeping out of his collar, Griff nodded. Flipping open his notebook, he shared his findings.

Antlers Hotel

Raven had been in her room for less than an hour when there came a knock on her door. She was wearing gray sweatpants and a matching sweatshirt—both two sizes too big for her. Lowering her dad's copy of Sun Tzu's *The Art of War*, she said, "Who is it?"

Expecting Sasha or Peter—maybe even the two of them together—to try to goad her into being social, she instead heard a person in the hall say, "United States Secret Service. Agents Woodson and Lowell."

Raven said, "One second," and rolled off her bed.

Opening the door, Raven saw two men in dark suits. Like her dad and the men he *worked* alongside, these two had no-nonsense gazes that she knew had already sized her up and were on to cataloging the contents of her room. Hard to miss were the flesh-colored ear buds and coiled wires diving under stiffly starched shirt collars.

They were both in their thirties. They were also very fit—former military, no doubt. It was clear these men meant business. If their stoic demeanors and how they carried themselves wasn't enough of an intimidation factor, they carried compact submachine guns in addition to the pronounced bulges *underneath* their jackets.

Opening the door fully, Raven made a sweeping motion with one arm.

The blond agent calling himself Woodson, said, "To ensure President Clay's safety, we will have to secure everyone's weapons. Yours included."

Visibly stiffening, Raven said, "The heck you will. I might want to exercise my right to go outside the walls tomorrow. My Golden Ticket is only good for a couple more weeks."

The dark-haired agent Raven presumed to be Lowell said, "That's not possible, Miss Grayson. The gates will be closed at dusk tonight. Then for the following twenty-four hours they will remain closed to new arrivals and outside excursions."

Woodson said, "I understand how being disarmed could be disconcerting—"

Interrupting, Raven said, "*Disconcerting* is spotting a huge spider on the ceiling directly in line with my face. You disarm me and you might as well strip me naked, too. Because that's how it feels to me when I don't have at least a Glock on my hip."

"Understood," Lowell said. "I can sympathize. However, even taking into consideration who you are, who your father is—we have no wiggle room on this."

Raven said, "I'll get them back, right? This isn't the start of the big *gun grab*, is it?"

As if he'd been a Boy Scout, and old habits remained, Woodson raised his hand. "I promise you'll all have your weapons returned to you as soon as Marine One is wheels up with President Clay safely aboard."

In the end, after the agents informed the others and had policed up their weapons, Raven relinquished hers. Though while she did so she was protesting fiercely in her head, she didn't kill the messenger. She was sure it was exactly how her dad would handle it. Seeing as how she had already stepped in it once, rocking the boat with these two guys would only deepen the hole she'd already dug for herself.

Chapter 70

Portland, Oregon

The sun was to set in Portland at 7:17 p.m. With a dark-gray sky and driving rain working in their favor, Cade decided to have the team roll out a bit early.

With backpacks cinched down tight and rifles strapped to their chests or slung across their backs, one by one, the Pale Riders scaled the fence behind the Grayson home.

In the alley, as Cade was straddling his mountain bike, he took one final, long look at the Craftsman. Stripped of the family photos, it was no longer a home. It was now just a shell of its former self with a certain future: to be beaten down by changing seasons and the relentless march of time.

"Ready to go, boss?" Griff asked. He was straddling Brook's bike and looking in Cade's direction.

Covertly wiping a rogue tear, Cade nodded. Saying nothing, he pedaled by Griff, Cross, and Nat. Where the alley spilled onto 48th, he cut a left.

Keeping a few yards of separation, they rolled past Ted and Lisa's house.

Where the standard poodle's corpse had been now lay only an elongated skull, some rib bones, and scattered tufts of fur.

The sight caused Cade to recall the Johnny Cash lyric: *It's Alpha and Omega's kingdom come.* Though bereft of Cash's gravelly delivery, the words bore the same weight, reminding him that all of them were mortal—even the top dogs.

While mostly uneventful, to Cade their ride south through the Woodstock neighborhood was depressing as hell. Once clean and navigable, the streets were now strewn with the remains of twice-dead Zs. At the end of nearly every driveway sat rolling cans spilling forth with putrid bags of trash. Every couple of blocks they came across a citizen lucky enough to have died and stayed that way. Most looked to have either been shot or beaten to death, all no doubt victims of the agelong struggle between the haves and have-nots.

A block didn't go by in which they didn't see at least one home burned to the ground. Some homes with boarded-over windows looked as if they might still harbor the living. Like his Craftsman, many more showed signs of a life and death struggle: broken-out windows. Zombie corpses splayed out on rain-slickened driveways. Brass shell casings reflecting the failing light of day.

Nothing Cade saw during their ten-block ride between Boise Street and Woodstock gave him hope that any of his former neighbors had escaped with their lives.

More than once, as they got closer to Woodstock, with its many bars and storefronts, they were set upon by sizeable herds of first turns. To conserve ammunition, as well as lessen the possibility of alerting a Chicom patrol to their presence, Cade simply reversed course and led the team to a passable street.

At the end of a short ride made long by the handful of detours, with the last light of day revealing a thoroughly looted Safeway and fire-ravaged Bi-Mart, Cade came to the conclusion that, at least where inner southeast Portland was concerned, T.S. Eliot had missed the mark. His old neighborhood did not go out with a whimper *or* a bang; rather, evidence told him it had died from a combination of the two.

Maintaining radio silence, Cade rode out onto Woodstock—an east/west two-lane that once bustled with the cars of locals doing their weekly shopping, or college kids from Reed wheeling their way to Mickey Finn's for a pint or to Otto's Delicatessen for one of their world-famous sausages.

All of that had changed. Woodstock was now lined with vehicles streaked green with algae. Some had become tombs for the living dead, the auto glass streaked inside with their own dried bodily fluids.

Storefronts whose plate windows had survived the initial madness invariably teemed with emaciated walking corpses, their stark white palms and gaunt faces ghosting across sullied glass.

Leaves and sticks clogged most of the storm drains. The result was twin rivers of turbid water flowing westward down Woodstock. Due to hours upon hours of non-stop rain, the water was inches deep near the curbs. So swollen were the mini-rivers that they nearly came together in the middle of the two-lane.

Keeping to the yard-wide strip of visible blacktop in the center of Woodstock, Cade led the team west.

Coming to a halt at the intersection with 39th, where Woodstock took a steep dive toward Reed College, Eastmoreland Golf Course and the once rough-and-tumble Westmoreland and Sellwood neighborhoods, Cade witnessed the dull blob of a sun slipping behind Portland's tony West Hills.

Coinciding with the sun's rapid departure, the rain tapered to a slow drizzle. Then, as if a switch had been flicked, a shroud of darkness enveloped everything.

With the darkness came a sharp drop in temperature that added exponentially to the sand-paper-like chafe wrought by drenched fatigues.

Flipping down and powering on his NVGs, Cade rolled his front wheel over the hill's apex, stepped onto the pedals, and positioned his butt behind and below his seat. It was the technique he used when tackling his favorite single-track trail along the Lewis River in nearby Washington state.

What Cade hadn't taken into consideration was how wet bicycle rims affected brake performance. While the drizzle did little to alter how the NVGs portrayed the environment as the team streaked down the hill in single file, it kept the rims wet, which in turn caused the rubber brake pads to screech like a dying mallard whenever brakes were applied.

Cade became aware of this phenomenon seconds after they were all committed. Riding Ted's Kona, Nat, the largest member of the team, had braked to keep from plowing into Cross from behind. The noise rose over everything. Caused every rider to search for the source.

Yelling to be heard over the slipstream, Cade said, "It's just the wet brakes. Use them sparingly."

But it was too late. The dead had heard the noise, too.

Where Woodstock began to level out, maybe a quarter of a mile distant, Cade saw movement. At first, it was just one Z rising up from the bus shelter on the right. Then, one at a time, a dozen Zs hanging around the entrance to Reed College became acutely aware of the fresh meat bombing downhill in their direction.

By the time Cade was nearing the intersection where the Reed feeder road branched off to the right, zombies were stepping off the curb. Behind him another set of brakes started wailing away.

Griff's? It made sense, seeing as how he'd gotten stuck riding a bike a little too small for him.

Hands swiped at Cade. One caught him on the elbow, forcing him to make a high-speed course correction. As he did so the brief contact started the bike into a death-wobble he feared he wasn't going to recover from.

Simultaneously, Cade shifted more of his weight over the bars and tapped both brake levers. As his quick actions brought both tires back in line with his former trajectory, he shot a quick glance over his right shoulder.

In that split-second full-color snapshot in time, he saw Nat, shoulders lowered and blazing by the same pack of Zs that had nearly been his downfall. Due to the extra weight—body mass and weaponry—the big Fijian had already overtaken Cross and was alongside Griff.

Like an offensive lineman creating a seam for his back, Nat delivered a vicious hit on the Z nearest to him.

Having already turned his eyes forward, Cade didn't get to see the chain reaction the single glancing blow of Nat's muscled shoulder had started.

Cross inadvertently broke radio silence. "Hang on," was his admonition to Nat. "Lean into it, big guy. Reel her in," came next. Finally, the SEAL said, "Clear."

It was the one-word declaration that told Cade all he needed to know. He'd barked the word hundreds of times in dozens of different scenarios. And each time he had, it conveyed one singular message: Immediate threat eliminated. Carry on.

So he did, without looking back.

A quarter-mile further, Woodstock came to a T. Cade led the four-bike procession left, keeping to 28th Avenue, a winding two-lane bordered on the left by million-dollar homes and on the right by Eastmoreland Golf Course.

An army of greenkeepers couldn't bring the municipal course back from the dead. They'd need a John Deere combine to harvest the fairway grass. The greens were overgrown, too. Just swampy-looking patches of green as viewed in the color night vision. Had Cade been wearing old-model NVGs, he guessed the image transmitted to him would be eerily similar.

After a long climb up Bybee Boulevard, the team wheeled into Westmoreland, a neighborhood close to downtown that still retained a small-town feel.

As a result of the zombie apocalypse, Westmoreland was now more downtown Beirut than downtown Mayberry. The Starbucks on Milwaukee Avenue looked as if it had absorbed a direct hit from a Hellfire missile. The massive windows facing Bybee and Milwaukee were now just shards of green-tinted glass flowing across the sidewalk.

Across the street from Starbucks, the wooden door to Kay's Bar was propped open by a moldering corpse. While the team rolled on by, a pair of zombies doddered from the once-popular watering hole, further trampling the decaying doorstop.

Old habits die hard.

Sellwood was more of the same: a half-dozen restaurants faring no better than the Starbucks they'd just passed. County-owned window glass had apparently been an enemy of the people here, too. For every single window in Sellwood's Multnomah County Library had either been bashed in completely or shattered to the point that only jagged shards held tenuous purchase in the frame.

A closer look told Cade the place had been picked clean, its dozens of shelves as bare as those in the Woodstock Safeway. Someone's appetite to read had been sated.

Seated at a computer station in the library, its forehead pressed against a darkened monitor, a lone zombie stirred, then moaned as the bikes whizzed by.

Leaving the business district behind, Cade led the team west, through a residential neighborhood consisting of mostly older homes. As in his neighborhood, the homes showed varying degrees of preparation as well as destruction. Being the epicenter of infection, Portland was as ravaged a place as Cade had seen during his travels all across the devastated nation.

Holding a fist in the air, Cade brought the team to a halt just outside the parking lot abutting the northeast corner of Sellwood Park. It was full of mostly civilian vehicles, with a few Homeland Security SUVs and military Humvees thrown in the mix.

Wet down by the steady drizzle, dozens of tents making up a thrown-together FEMA facility sagged and swayed every time the east wind picked up.

Twelve-foot-tall, razor-wire-topped hurricane fencing fully encircled the camp. There wasn't a single inch of the entire run that didn't have a zombie crushing into it. The undead trapped inside were a mix of civilians and soldiers, with a few still clad in biological containment suits. The fence quivered and groaned as the Zs craned and leered, trying to see in the dark the source of the mechanical sounds made by the bicycles.

After a couple of minutes of hard listening, during which Cade heard only raindrops battering everything within earshot, the discordant jangling of the fence, and soft moans of the dead, he got on the net and reported their progress to the TOC at Peterson.

Receiving the green light to proceed to the rendezvous, Cade called the team into a loose huddle. With the wind blowing at their backs, he detailed how he wanted to make first contact with the mysterious two Davids—their local FBI-connected assets.

Chapter 71

The rendezvous point was a city park on the east bank of the Willamette River. Nestled between the Sellwood Bridge to the south and Oaks Bottom Wildlife Refuge to the north, Sellwood Riverfront Park was once popular with bicyclists, joggers, and anglers.

Nearly nine months of neglect had left the park largely indiscernible from the wildlands next to it.

Slated for replacement before Omega changed everything, the two-lane Sellwood bridge connected the Sellwood neighborhood with John's Landing—an up-and-coming neighborhood due south of Portland's downtown core.

Still astride his bike, its front tire pointed at the park's only access road, Cade did a quick visual recon.

To the left of the park, in the shadow of the Sellwood Bridge, was a gently sloping boat ramp. A mix of pickup trucks and SUVs, many with empty boat trailers still attached, had been abandoned on the ramp. Somehow a few Zs had found their way into the warren of vehicles and become trapped. Constantly on the move, they would go one way, bump into a trailer or vehicle, then reverse course.

The park to the team's fore was occupied by a hundred or so walking dead. Most were concentrated in one large group just inside the parking lot's barricaded entrance. Solitary Zs could be seen patrolling the grassy expanse beyond the parking lot. More were mired in the marshy area at the refuge's southern border.

The floating dock the team needed to get to was a few hundred yards dead ahead. It was L-shaped, with the foot of the L attached to shore by a short ramp. The run of the dock paralleling the bank was roughly fifty feet long and unoccupied.

While Cade didn't like the fact that once inside the park they would be surrounded by Zs and left with only one egress point should things go sideways, it wasn't his call to make. The location had been chosen by the assets on the ground and then approved by people way above his pay grade.

Because Cade would never ask something of his men that he himself wouldn't do—a leadership tenet learned from his late mentor, Mike Desantos—he declared he would be taking point.

After stashing the bikes in the grass beside the road fronting the park, Cade stepped off the drive and struck a diagonal course through the park. His first goal: to find one of the cement paths in the *jungle* and be free of the soup of mud and standing rainwater sucking at their boots.

Finally feeling his boot come into contact with something solid, Cade signaled to Cross, the next man in line, to halt and maintain noise discipline. He parted the grass with the M4's suppressor and looked at the ground. Instead of seeing his toe up against a cement lip bordering one of the paths, a hairless skull stared up at him. The impact with his Danner had dislodged the jawbone and tilted the skull a full ninety degrees in relation to the rest of the decaying corpse.

Dragging his gaze from the Joker-like grin, Cade did a quick headcount.

Cross, Griff, and Nat.

All present.

Pointing the corpse out for Cross, Cade took a step to his right and resumed the same steady pace forward. He led the team another twenty feet into the park before sensing the ground under his boots go firm. No sooner had he paused to investigate what direction the footpath would take them than, over the steady patter of rain striking the grass all around, he heard something moving through the grass off to their right—the same direction the path wanted to take them.

Panning his head toward the sound, Cade saw a Z—or rather, just the top half of a Z's head. And it was coming straight at him.

As the Z crashed through the tall grass to Cade's fore, its dead eyes flicked left and right and back again, searching longingly for prey in the dark. The absence of splashing water and the accompanying sucking sounds told Cade the thing was likely sticking to the footpath he was on. Hell, he thought, they were known to follow roads and freeways. He'd seen them acting out other rudimentary actions. It was no secret the scientists thought the dead still retained snippets of memory from their past life experiences.

Cade just hoped the rest of the roamers he'd seen from the road weren't acting on the same embedded impulses. If so, the Gerber was going to be releasing a lot of souls in the near future.

Standing statue-still, he drew his blade from its scabbard. Letting the M4 hang from its sling, he turned his body sideways and stepped off the path.

As the Z parted the tangle of grass overgrowing the path, Cade saw that it had been a boy of no more than ten when it had succumbed to Omega. Cause of first death wasn't immediately evident. However, the thing seemed to sense that prey was somewhere close by.

Those eyes continued probing the dark all the way up until Cade whispered, "I see you."

The three words froze the Z in its tracks broadside to Cade. Instantly its eyes flicked left and its head followed.

As the first guttural moan started to resonate deep in the undead boy's chest, the razor-sharp tip on Cade's Gerber was silencing it.

Twisting the black blade as it entered the eye socket nearest him, Cade locked his wrist and accepted the weight of the corpse. With his free hand, he grabbed hold of the wet hair plastered to the Z's skull. Steering the corpse with the hand still clutching the embedded dagger, Cade deposited it in the grass beside the path.

Between Cade's first encounter with the undead boy and the time the team reached the ramp connecting the dock to land, he'd put the black dagger to good use a dozen more times.

While he had grown callous to taking the lives of the enemy, putting down fellow Americans never got any easier. They didn't deserve the death sentence meted out by the Chinese due to their reckless handling of a superbug of their own creation. While Cade believed in God and that each human possessed a soul, the only tangible result derived from each thrust of the blade or press of the trigger was that each individual Z could no longer spread Omega.

The team waited near the top of the ramp to the floating dock, muzzles aimed outward, covering all three directions from which enemy breathers or the walking dead might approach.

Cade padded down the ramp, head constantly on the move and rifle at the ready.

At the bottom of the ramp, he looked the length of the dock. If the two Davids were already here, he didn't see them.

Thinking they might still be en route, he cast his gaze out over the river.

Raindrops striking the swift-moving water reminded him of incoming rounds. Affected by the river's eddies, debris scudding along bobbed and spun in crazy circles.

He had fond memories of picnicking here with Raven and Brook. Something about the river usually centered him. That was not the case tonight. Tonight the Willamette was angry and swollen and only served to make him long for that first dose of combat adrenaline.

Good things really did come, he reminded himself, *to those willing to wait*. For the closure within reach tonight, closure he could almost taste, no amount of time was too long to wait.

Speaking softly over the comms, Griff asked, "Where are these … Two Davids?"

Fairly certain Griff was looking his way, Cade merely shrugged.

As if on cue, coming right on the heels of Cade's attempt at non-verbal communication, a split-second flash of light pierced the dark to his right. It had come from somewhere near the end of the dock and was in the IR spectrum—visible only to someone wearing NVGs. After a short two-second pause, the light began flashing out the complicated sequence Cade was expecting.

Though he craned and took a few steps along the dock, all he could make out was a gloved hand holding a device he guessed to be an IR torch. From the new viewing angle it appeared the person signaling him was actually *in* the river. His best guess was that the person was wearing a wetsuit and likely holding on for dear life to the underside of the dock.

Utilizing the IR designator riding atop the M4's Picatinny rail, Cade responded with a predetermined signal of his own.

Nearing the end of the dock, Cade learned the truth about the person who had signaled him. Instead of being *in* the water, the man was kneeling on the floor of a rigid-hulled inflatable boat and was currently tracking his approach with a suppressed Heckler and Koch MP5. Chambered in 9mm, the MP5 was a close-quarter battle weapon favored by SWAT and special operations units the world over.

Cade made a patting motion with one hand and turned his muzzle away from the man.

The man did the same.

Cade said, "The chair is against the wall."

The man replied, "John has a long mustache," which confirmed to Cade he was staring at one half of the Two Davids. Which one, he wasn't certain.

"You're FBI?" Cade asked.

The man nodded. "David Feather. Special Agent In Charge … Portland Division."

Feather looked to be mid-fifties and very close in height and weight to Cade. Instead of the ubiquitous navy windbreaker emblazoned with *FBI*, he wore olive-drab rain gear. On his head was a woodland camo boonie hat. Partially hidden by the hat's floppy brim was a weathered face crisscrossed with a roadmap's worth of lines.

Feather asked, "Any issues getting here?"

As Cade started to bring Feather up to speed, in his ear, he heard Griff say, "We've got company. Some of the pusbags from the parking lot followed us down."

Regarding Feather, Cade said, "We have to go, now." With Feather working to untie the RIB, Cade summoned the rest of the team to the dock, and they all piled in, Nat nearly sending them all spilling into the river as he stepped on the gunwale.

Gesturing toward the RIB's outboard, Cross said, "What about the noise? It'll carry like a mo-fo out on the river."

Working to untie the bow line, Feather said, "Grab a paddle. We'll be staying close to shore. The safe house is less than a klick downriver."

Tone even and measured, Griff said, "They're on the ramp, Wyatt. Permission to engage?"

"Negative," Cade said. He grabbed a paddle and, thrusting the blade end to the dock, pushed with all his might.

On the port gunwale, behind Cade, Cross was doing the same.

Having taken a seat on the starboard side near the bow, Griff tracked the pack of undead with his suppressed MP7A1. A dozen or so of the reeking, waterlogged corpses were now setting foot on the dock. Behind them, twice their number jostled for position at the top of the narrow ramp.

When the bell-cow, a first turn twenty-something female, reached the midpoint of the dock, Griff repeated his request.

Knowing how fast and far even a suppressed gunshot would travel over water, Cade again shut Griff down. In the next beat, two things happened back to back. First, with maybe five feet of separation between the RIB and dock, the combination of the paddle shove-off and the river's current started the RIB's bow moving in a clockwise circle.

Then, as Cade and Cross stabbed their paddles into the roiling water, the first of the dead to make it to the end of the dock fell in. Like so many lemmings, the rest followed.

The water beside the dock, in the exact spot the RIB had just vacated, now looked like the shallow end of a public pool on the hottest day of summer. As the Zs continued to spill from the dock, a large number of them failed to sink.

For a few seconds pale hands beat the water to a froth. Then, slowly but surely, the foundation of corpses under the surface was swept away by the river's strong current. As the foundation went, so did the flailing bodies it had been supporting.

Barely ten seconds had elapsed between the shove-off and the last of the dead disappearing from view.

Knowing that fifty or sixty dead things were in the depths below the RIB, tumbling and clawing reflexively for the fresh meat that had drawn them to the water, Cade locked his gaze dead ahead and put his back into the job at hand.

Chapter 72

The safe house was a floating home half a mile downriver. It was fifth in a row numbering thirty or more. There was a thirty-foot-wide channel between the strung-together homes and shore. Shore was a sandy beach backstopped by a picket of mature dogwoods. Beyond the trees was Oaks Amusement Park. Cade saw the top of the Ferris wheel rising up over the trees. Between the branches, he caught fleeting glimpses of the twisting and turning red tracks of the Mad Mouse rollercoaster.

With two levels and a rooftop deck, the safe house was more mini-mansion than the image of a floating home Cade's mind conjured up.

The lower level was ringed by black rails and home to a half-dozen planters containing long-dead palms and other assorted plants. Pool furniture with faded padding sat helter-skelter on the open-air portion of the home's riverside deck.

Weathered wood-shingle siding, like the kind found predominantly on beach homes, wrapped the safe house from top to bottom.

Like the majority of the other floating homes, the safe house's roof was flat. Two-thirds of the roof was home to twenty or so solar panels. Mixed in with the panels were a number of small oval satellite dishes.

Everything was staggered and angled south. A yard-high parapet shielded all but the top edges of the nearest panels. Cade wouldn't have noticed the setup had Feather not mentioned it.

Each floating home in the marina had a floating boat garage out back. Most were empty. The safe house's was not. The rear end of some kind of vessel stuck out a half-dozen feet. It was covered by a black tarp, which made identifying the craft next to impossible.

As Feather guided the RIB through the channel and past the garage, Cade caught a fleeting glimpse, through the structure's cloudy windows, of the sleek enclosed cabin of a totally blacked-out boat.

They paddled the RIB between the safe house and the floating home abutting it to the north.

David number two came out and offered a hand up to Cade and the team.

Standing on the deck, with Feather securing the RIB a few feet away, Cade introduced himself and the team.

"David Lee Cox," said the man, shaking hands all around. He was wearing a black windbreaker over brown Carhartt coveralls. Holstered high on his right hip was a Colt .45 Model 1911.

Cox's gray beard, rosy cheeks, and abundance of smile lines suggested to Cade that the man was in his late sixties. Though he was carrying a few pounds north of two hundred and had a slight limp, he moved about the deck with ease. Even shod in scuffed cowboy boots, Cox struggled to rise to Cade's height.

There was a hint of the southwest in the man's voice when he spoke. Which Cade didn't find strange, considering the Pacific Northwest attracted people from far and wide, like moths to a flame.

Strange thing was: Cade couldn't quite place the accent. Interest piqued, he asked, "That accent ... where're you from originally?"

"Northern Louisiana. We tend to sound more like Texans than Cajuns."

Cade said, "Got it. Makes sense, now. Care if we call you Cox? It'd cut down on the confusion."

After a hearty chuckle, Cox said, "That'll be fine. I've been called worse."

Hand resting on his holstered Glock, Cade said, "What about neighbors? Anyone we need to be concerned about?"

Cox shook his head. "They all moved out long before Dave set this place up. I've poked around the other homes. Nothing much to see. Just a few biters and some long-dead corpses. I put the biters down ... left the rest for the river rats. Except for the bourbon, that is." He smiled, revealing a straight picket of pearly whites. "I'm slowly drinking my way through that."

Moving closer to the outside wall to get out of the rain, Cade said, "You're not worried about this place attracting squatters? Or maybe people coming back to retake their homes?"

"Evidence says most of them left by boat early on. Relocated to somewhere downriver from the city. Far, far downriver from the city if they were smart about it. Dave and another agent disconnected the gangway a few months back. Anyone who's shown up here since … just two or three small groups, really, proved pretty easy to run off."

MP5 at the low-ready, Feather interrupted. "Let's get inside. We've got lots to go over and very little time in which to do it."

A certain sparkle in his eyes, Cox made a sweeping motion before Cade and the team. "Age before beauty, gentlemen."

The safe house's interior was more bunker-command-center than what the rustic exterior would lead one to expect. The concept was entirely open, with the kitchen and bathroom at the dock-side end of the home. All of the furniture was pushed up against the walls. Dark curtains were strung up over the massive west-facing windows. The smaller windows on the safe house's other three elevations were papered over with pages culled from an *Oregonian* newspaper.

In the center of the living room, completely inundated with electronics, was a pair of eight-foot-long folding-tables. Though the outside temperature was hovering near sixty, inside the safe house the communications gear and computers and their assorted monitors had the place feeling like a hot-yoga studio.

Indicating the electronics, Cade said, "All of this runs off of solar?"

Feather shook his head. Pointing to a spot on the floor near the kitchen, he said, "Come over and stand there."

Cade humored the man.

"You feel anything?"

"A little vibration. It's not the river, is it?"

"That's our generator. It's in an insulated, sound-proofed box. Exhaust is purged through a hose that runs underwater and then snakes up onto the bank. The end where it vents is partially buried. A person isn't going to just stumble across it. They'd have to be looking for it to find it."

Griff said, "The head G-Man has got all his ducks in a row."

As Cox set up a third table, Feather retrieved the intel packet he and his operatives had collected over time.

"Let's get this show on the road," said Griff. "I can handle the coldest of surf. Sugar cookie evolutions doled out by a dickhead BUDS instructor, no problem. Sleeping in the open in the Hindu Kush, under the stars at ten thousand feet … been there, done that. But this, this steam bath… I feel my ass cheeks melting." He looked to Nat. "Is there steam coming out from under my helmet?"

Mimicking the Wicked Witch of Wizard Of Oz fame, Nat said, "I'm melting. Melting, I tell you." He paused and winked at Cross. "Naw, Griff … all I see is your ugly mug under that helmet."

Feather cleared his throat. "Target Alpha … or, if we're splitting hairs—Oregon Museum of Science and Industry."

"I know it well," Cade said,

On the table, beside the map Cross had drawn the night before, were a number of photos taken from long-range. Some were overhead shots. The former, Feather explained, were taken from the twentieth floor of a high-rise across the river from Target Alpha. The latter were Cox's doing. He'd found a high-dollar drone in a hobby shop and captured the footage from well above OMSI.

"They didn't see or hear me," he assured Cade. "Hell, from the viaduct, maybe sixty feet higher than where OMSI sits, I couldn't hear it. I'll be the first to tell you I need another round of LASIK, but my hearing is like an owl's. No concerts … ever. I don't like headphones. When I used to drive, no radio. And—"

A glare from Feather silenced the former Multnomah County Sheriff.

Cade said, "These are new? You have video?"

"Drone footage was last Saturday. Yes, I have video, too. It's on the hard drive and shows General Jinlong arriving. Like clockwork, he shows up at the same time in the courtyard and chooses one or two from the stock of comfort girls the soldiers keep in a pen in front of the launcher."

Cade said, "We're aware of the hostages."

Cross said, "I'm overwatch tonight. The general *never* deviates?"

Shaking his head, Feather said, "Not yet. The evening patrol leaves the wire. Fifteen minutes later they escort the general's black

Mercedes G Wagon back to the gate. They wait there until he's safely inside."

Crossing his arms, Cade said, "Then the patrol resumes? They stay gone for how long?"

Eyes boring into Cade's, Feather said, "They stay out every … single … time. They patrol for thirty minutes to an hour and then return by way of the thoroughfare to the east. It cuts east/west underneath the viaduct."

Cross said, "Right about where we holed up last night."

Cade nodded. Uncrossing his arms, he said, "Does the rest jive with your observations?"

Both operators had been periodically consulting their notes taken during the recon, so they were both ready with an answer.

With no hesitation, Cross said, "Take the general out of the equation … it's exactly what I observed."

Griff said, "Ditto."

Clapping his hands, Cade said, "Then we're a go. Eat and hydrate. Square your kit away. Make sure to feed new batteries to all your gear." He smiled for the first time in a long while. "We roll out in ten, Pale Riders."

Sensing the stage was now his, Feather said, "Everyone pull up a stump. I'm going to cue up the drone video." He pulled a chair in front of a nearby computer and turned the monitor to face the Pale Riders.

Fingers attacking the keyboard, the FBI man had the footage up and running in a matter of seconds.

Chapter 73

Dressed in black fatigues, with black balaclavas pulled down and NVGs deployed, the Pale Riders looked like modern-day ninjas as they stood on the back dock awaiting the big reveal.

Going by Cox's description of the craft he had spent his entire retirement nest egg building, Cade expected something resembling the Batboat to reverse from the garage.

Cox had removed the tarp from his *baby* at 8 p.m. sharp and asked that the team remain on the dock until he could get the "systems" up and running.

Cade thought it strange that the former sheriff had taken a one-thousand-amp portable jump starter in with him. He grew skeptical when the FBI man leaned over and said, "What Cox didn't mention in there is that he spent most of his career patrolling the Willamette and Columbia. He also didn't let on that this *Croc* of his is all electric and semi-submersible."

To Cade's right, interest suddenly piqued, Griff and Cross took a step forward and craned to get a better look at the boat through the garage windows.

Cross said, "Rumors about boats like these were circulating before Omega hit. No way to confirm this, but apparently DEVGRU already had one at Dam Neck. Also heard Team 10 was slated to receive something similar at Little Creek. Trials were supposed to start in August of last year."

"Day late and a dollar short," said Nat. "Army is the same way with procurement. They have a tendency to get the goods to us *after* the fact."

Cade nodded in agreement.

Feather said, "That's Cox's competitor's electric boat entry." He winked. "It's called *Alligator.*"

Cade said, "It's still electric, though. All the electric cars I've ever seen are gutless wonders."

"Those are *hybrids*," Feather pointed out. "This fella in California sells an all-electric vehicle called the Tesla Roadster. You know, after the famous inventor … Nikola Tesla. They were very limited production and impossible to come by unless you knew someone or had fuck-you-money."

Cade shook his head. "I'll believe it when I see it." After looking at his Suunto and learning that Cox had already been aboard his floating Prius for five minutes, he added impatiently: "If he doesn't produce soon, we're going to have to commandeer your RIB."

"Give him a minute," Feather said with a smile. "He's an MIT grad. He values precision over speed." Pointing out the twin columns of reverse-turbulence at the Croc's stern, he added: "He's got the motors running."

Shooting Feather a look, Cade said, "Motors? If they're that quiet at idle, what do they sound like at speed?"

"Quiet as a ghost fart."

Cade was shaking his head in disbelief when Nat asked, "Does it have any get up and go?"

Smile fading, Feather said, "Neck snapping."

All eyes were drawn to the inky water as the sleek, low-to-the-water craft began to reverse out of the garage.

Achingly slow, its pace measured in inches-per-second, the prototype Croc revealed itself to those standing on the dock.

With its angular cabin and flush windows that could have been produced by the same factory where the Ghost Hawk got its wraparound cockpit glass, the Croc looked more like the Jedi ride than the Batboat.

Feather said, "It's got internal ballast tanks. Cox can lower her draft to the point where her windows ride just above the waterline. This cuts her radar sig to that of a … crocodile. Her black paint has radar-absorbing qualities that make her nearly impossible to track."

The Croc was entirely out in the open when Feather said, "Sitting as she is, her heat sig is nearly nonexistent. No exhaust, nothing to see here … move along."

Soberly, Griff noted, "She's got no armament."

Poking his head out of the cabin's topside entrance, Cox said, "I couldn't get permission from the pols here to arm her. Remember, this is … or was, Portland. So for now, you're her armament. Hop aboard and we'll get underway."

***

Three minutes after stabbing quietly into the Willamette's north-flowing current, with only one electric motor online and driving the Croc's powerful, twin water-jets, the houseboat marina was a mile behind them and the stealthy craft had navigated the majority of the narrow east-bank passage fronting the hundred-and-forty-acre Oaks Bottom Wildlife Refuge.

Cade crouched near the cabin entrance, head on a swivel, eyes probing the bank on both sides for any tell-tale signs of an imminent ambush.

While he'd spotted an abundance of wildlife on the east bank and quite a few walking corpses, he didn't see any human forms toting weapons.

The only sounds he heard out on the water was the constant *swish* of the Croc's prow cutting the river and the occasional muffled report of flotsam and jetsam striking the hull.

With each thunk and thud that reverberated through the hull, in his mind's eye he saw a submerged Z—the byproduct of their brief loiter on the dock—grappling to find purchase on the low-slung craft.

Though he knew it was just his imagination messing with him, the possibility was real the creatures that had fallen off the dock would emerge downriver and catch a fellow survivor by surprise.

He hoped that wouldn't be the case. Still, as always, outside the wire each and every action taken came with its own unique consequence.

With the Ross Island Bridge gliding by overhead, Cade summoned Cross topside.

Cross emerged from below decks carrying his MP7 and nothing else. He'd taken the components of his Modular Sniper Rifle sniper

389

rifle out of his pack, assembled the Remington tack driver, and left the pack below deck.

With the stock folded down on the frame and both the magazine and suppressor stuffed into his cargo pockets, the slung rifle all but disappeared into the folds of his fatigue blouse.

Stuffed into Cross's chest rig were two extra magazines for the MSR, three thirty-round mags for his MP7, and another pair of magazines for his sidearm.

Cade said to Cross, "I'm calling a last second audible. Give me the HK and the mags. You take my M4. Push comes to shove and the Chicoms are moving in on you, it'll be good for you to have the advantage of its extended range."

They traded weapons and magazines.

While Cade was giving up a third of his ammunition, he was gaining a suppressed weapon whose subsonic rounds were whisper-quiet indoor and out. Perfect for where he was going.

Cade felt the boat begin to slow underneath him. There was no change in sound save for a subtle diminishing of noise made by the prow.

Feather popped his head into the open. "Thirty seconds."

Regarding the Portland skyline made Cade yearn for the past. He saw the rocket-ship-shaped KOIN Center building rooted close in on the west bank. In the middle distance was the forty-story, 546-foot tall, Wells Fargo Building. It was all white stone save for columns of smoked, vertically aligned windows. The contrast between the recessed windows and white exterior gave the impression the tower was zebra striped.

In the far distance, rising up from within a cluster of smaller buildings, was Portland's second tallest structure. At 536 feet, US Bancorp Tower, or Big Pink—a nickname based on the color of its granite cladding—rose prominently over the nearby Pearl District.

On the Croc's starboard side was a dock nearly identical to the one at Sellwood Riverfront Park. It was held in check by telephone-pole-sized metal pylons driven into the riverbed. Pointed white cones topped each pylon. In a way, they looked like half-a-dozen ballistic missiles standing at the ready.

Beyond the dock was a flat expanse of asphalt. It was flanked on the left by a fenced-in lot that encompassed an entire city block. On the right, abutting the sea of asphalt, was a windowless two-story warehouse.

Random zombies patrolled the bank near the first insertion point.

As the Croc went lower in the water, Cross checked over the M4. Powering up the EOTech—just in case—he rose and moved to the starboard side of the stern.

The insertion was, literally, a touch-and-go affair. There were no fenders deployed. Instead, Cox brushed the floating dock ever so gently with the Croc's starboard side.

The moment contact occurred, Cross leaped from the boat. The drop was a foot or less, with him easily carrying the distance to the center of the rain-slickened dock.

While Cross did not fall, his Salomons did *squeee* when they caught purchase and arrested his forward movement.

As the Croc was powering away, Cade watched every Z ashore stop in its tracks. Next, their heads turning in unison toward the dock, they all about-faced.

Even as the Zs were beginning their slow-speed turns toward the source of the sound, Cross was up the ramp and moving swiftly toward them, about to run straight through the metaphorical *belly of the beast*.

Cade wished Cross "God speed" in his head and then said a silent prayer for his safe passage.

***

Seconds after the first insertion, with OMSI's uneven roofline visible around the next left-to-right river bend, Nat was let off at the base of a steep bank shored up by a field of jagged steamer-trunk-sized boulders. Though the monster of a man was carrying the twenty-two-pound Mk 46 in one hand, and a spare can of ammo for it in the other, he tackled the unforgiving incline with the grace of a mountain goat.

As Cade watched his old friend crest the incline, he took solace in the knowledge that Nat's path was currently free of threats and his

391

final destination was completely surrounded by fence and Jersey barriers.

Once Nat was out of sight, Cox nosed the Croc toward one of the cement pilings supporting the Marquam Bridge. With the bridge's lower deck one hundred feet over their heads, Cox pointed the Croc's bow upriver, reversed the powerful water jets, then continued upping the thrust until the boat went stationary a dozen feet abreast of the massive support column.

From a couple of hundred yards west of OMSI's boarded-up facade, with Cox doing an admirable job of providing a semi-stable viewing platform, Cade and Griff spent a few minutes watching the museum and its sprawling grounds for movement.

Cade knew OMSI well. When Raven was little, he brought her here often. When he was deployed, Brook made the trek from home several times a week.

Formerly a steam-powered electric generating plant, the cement building now contained a domed IMAX movie theater, massive planetarium, and three floors of mostly hands-on exhibits.

In the river, moored permanently to a pier adjacent to the museum, was the USS *Blueback*. Used in the filming of the movie *Hunt for Red October*, the retired submarine was open for tours seven days a week.

On any given day during the school year, the road fronting the building would be lined with yellow school busses. And on those days, its halls filled with teachers herding around packs of school kids giddy to be free of their studies, the museum was a claustrophobe's worst nightmare.

At the moment, the entire building was boarded up and blacked out, which made it impossible to tell if anyone was occupying the place.

Save for a couple of Zs standing before the wrought iron fence on the museum's left side, nothing moved. No sentries patrolled the north/south walkway skirting OMSI on the river side. No spotters milled about the HVAC apparatus on the flat portions of the uneven roofline.

Based on all that he'd seen so far, it was clear to Cade that the Chicoms felt their newest forward operating base was untouchable.

In the next few minutes, if he had anything to do with it, they were going to sorely regret their hubris.

Back to back to back, three things happened. First, in their headsets, both Cade and Griff heard a pair of clicks. It was Nat breaking squelch over the coms to let them know he was safely in position. Then, on the heels of that, a single click came over the comms. This time it was Cross signaling that he had reached the hide on the Martin Luther King Junior Viaduct and overwatch had begun.

As Cade was responding that he understood by issuing a single mike click of his own, the low rumble of a diesel engine rolled across the river. It came from the eastside industrial area north of OMSI and could mean only one thing: game on.

Before Cox had the boat turned toward shore, Cade was getting the first taste of the adrenaline dump he so missed. Catching Griff looking a question his way, Cade said, "Lock and load," and donned his ruck.

Their approach to the drop-off point was smooth and quiet. Cox steered the Croc past the ten-foot cement wall supporting the museum's viewing promontory, then pulled back on the throttle. While the Croc slowed and came broadside to the rock-strewn bank, Feather kept his MP5 trained on the esplanade looming over them.

Cade felt the deck vibrate under his boots as Cox again reversed the water jets. Once the Croc had gone dead in the water, Feather pointed to shore.

Cade said, "Go, go, go," and patted Griff on the shoulder.

As soon as Griff was on his way, Cade trapped the MP7 to his chest with one arm and launched himself off the starboard gunwale.

Though there was only a yard or so of open water for the two men to clear, their landing spot was far from ideal.

Griff hit the field of rain-slickened rocks with most of his weight, plus the forty-pound ruck, dragging him backward. He immediately released his hold on the MP7, entrusting the sling to do its job. In a futile effort to regain his balance, he threw both arms forward and clawed at the air. Arms windmilling furiously clockwise, he realized no amount of *rolling up the windows* was going to spare him from taking an unwanted swim.

As luck would have it, Cade landed on a flat spot between two rocks. If it hadn't been for him seeing Griff's flailing arms, then reaching over and grabbing hold of his chest rig, the tables would have turned, with the landlubber Delta boy diving into the drink to save a Navy SEAL.

The ribbing Cross would have rained down on Griff had the scenario come to pass would have been nonstop and merciless.

A guttural grunt followed by a sincere "Thanks" was how Griff reacted.

All business was how Cade interpreted it. No denying that the shooter was nothing but a consummate professional in the field.

With the Croc already slipping away to the south, both shooters trained their weapons on the walkway fronting the museum, then started to thread their way between the rocks.

Chapter 74

The moment Cross saw the troop carrier and black Mercedes G Wagon roll up on the parking lot and stop before the gate, he was on the comms and relaying what he was seeing to everyone listening.

Ari Silver was one of those people. He was roughly twenty miles northeast of downtown Portland and already strapped into Jedi One's right seat. As he activated the ship's APU—auxiliary power unit—there was a turbine whine and a tiny jolt raced through the airframe. By the time he was feeling the satisfying rumble of the turbines behind him firing to life, the rotors atop the other two ships in the flight were beginning to spin.

Seeing the sag leave the rotor blades as they picked up speed, Ari asked Haynes to power up the FLIR pod. Next, his hands pressing buttons and flicking switches, Ari instructed his crew chief to ready the ship for flight.

Skeleton mask in place underneath deployed NVGs, Skip punched the *Door Close* button, then stuck a thumbs up between the front seats.

Jedi One went light on her gear, lifted off the tarmac fronting a long row of rust-spotted light-blue hangars, then spun a quick one-eighty. Now facing west, simultaneously Ari increased power and pulled pitch.

Ari watched Troutdale Airport disappear behind his ship. In seconds, Jedi One was formed up with the Comanche and Ghost Chinook.

Assuming the lead position, Ari radioed ahead to inform the team their close air support and QRF was en route and on schedule.

Hearing this bit of good news made Cade eager to rush in and start slitting throats. But he couldn't. They needed to allow the general enough time to choose his girl, or girls, and then retire with them to the room Feather insisted was in the far southeast corner on the building's second floor. Though Cade had a hard time swallowing the other reason for the necessary pause, the general's goon also needed time to collect the President's man from the cell they kept him in and walk him to the second-floor interrogation room.

With Cade taking point, they picked their way up the rocky bank. Coming to an alcove between a pair of two-by-two cement pillars that were part of the building's foundation, Cade held up a fist and took a knee.

The alcove was ten feet wide and maybe four deep. Like the pillars, these three walls were also load-bearing and an integral part of the building's foundation. On the right wall, exactly where Feather said it would be, was an angled metal shroud. The shroud was attached with metal screws to a two-by-two ventilation duct. Whether the duct was for intake or exhaust, Cade hadn't a clue. What he did know was that the alcove was fenced off.

After listening hard for a few seconds, they went to work.

Griff dove into his ruck and came out with a compact fence cutter.

While Griff cut a vertical seam, Cade watched their backs.

In just under two minutes, the job was done, and Griff was stowing the tool in his pack.

Peeling the fence back, Cade motioned Griff through the tight opening.

Griff did the same for Cade, then smoothed the two halves together as best he could.

Once inside the cramped alcove, Cade took out his multi-tool and went to work removing the shroud. He was through the sixth of eight screws when Cross came on the comms with word that the HVTs were inside the building and the transport was leaving the wire.

Finished extracting the remaining screws, Cade worked the shroud loose with Griff's help.

Once the shroud was removed, they were faced with a wire-mesh grate. While the fence Griff just cut through was likely to keep the homeless from sleeping inside the alcove, this grate, Cade surmised, was here to keep vermin from getting inside the museum.

Grateful he wasn't going to be shimmying through a constrictive metal duct, Cade pushed hard against the grate with both hands. Feeling a bit of give, he concluded it was secured to the foundation from the inside. The flex in the grate gave him hope the cement, likely poured over a hundred years ago, had relaxed its hold on whatever fasteners the original builders had used.

Going back into his ruck, Griff fished out another of his breaking and entering tools and handed it over to Cade.

Trying to keep the noise to a minimum, Cade inserted the flat end of the mini crowbar into the seam between the grill and foundation. Applying a few pounds of pressure separated the bottom of the grate from the crumbling cement lip. He did the same to the sides, then set the tool aside.

One step ahead of Cade, Griff had already cut a long length of paracord from a bracelet he kept in his ruck.

Nodding, Cade threaded one end of the cord through the grate near the bottom and tied it off. Gripping the cord a foot from where it was anchored, he punched the grate near the top.

It moved, but the fasteners held.

The second punch was the charm. The grate popped off and fell away. Arrested by the paracord, the grate banged against the foundation. The *clang* Cade had anticipated was minimal. Thankfully it wasn't followed by a prolonged echo.

Sticking his head through the opening and seeing cobwebs and dust confirmed to Cade that once again Feather knew what he was talking about. This part of the foundation was left over from when the building was still a power company concern. Overhead pipes and conduit snaked east along the ceiling then took a hard left at the end of a long, narrow passage. A passage that Feather's blueprints indicated would track north for a few yards to a stairway leading up. At the top of the stairway was a door opening into a cavernous wing of the museum once home to a number of school-bus-sized steam turbines.

Cade shrugged off his pack. He unclipped the MP7 and handed it to Griff.

Fitting his legs and hips through the opening was no problem. Once Cade got to his chest, the going was not as smooth on account of the plate carrier and chest rig full of spare mags.

Perched on his stomach, with his lower extremities dangling over the floor, he had to really work hard to get his upper body through.

Finally, as his shoulders cleared the cement frame, he felt his toes touch the floor.

Griff quickly passed the packs and weapons through the opening. Being a bit bigger around the waist and chest, he needed Cade's help to make it inside.

Once they were both standing inside the museum basement, they threw on their packs and gunned up.

Still taking the lead, Cade padded down the passage. Ignoring the spider webs and insect husks clinging to his uniform and gear, he stopped at the end of the twenty-foot passage and took a quick turkey peek around the corner.

At the end of another twenty-foot-long cement corridor, every inch of it crisscrossed by cobwebs, was an open stairway. On the wall across from the stairs was a bank of electrical boxes. Next to the boxes, higher up on the wall, was a trio of boxy electrical components. That they were connected to colorful cables led Cade to believe he was looking at internet routers and alarm company equipment.

The stairs went up to a cramped landing then turned back on themselves. At the top of the second flight stood a windowless door. It was clean and new-looking and had a brushed stainless doorknob. On the door chest-high to Cade was a keyed deadbolt.

Cade paused on the landing and tried to hail Cross. He got no reply. Nat didn't answer, either.

One of his guys dropping off the net was a bad omen. Could mean big trouble, actually. But both of them going silent at the same time? And with no warning whatsoever? *Impossible*. Both men had more than a hundred combat missions under their belt. Furthermore, they were both expert at concealment and recon. No way the Chicoms would get the jump on both of them at the same time.

Cade turned to face Griff. Tapping his headset, he asked, "Did you hear me calling Cross and Nat just now?"

Griff nodded and whispered, "I heard *you* loud and clear. That's it though. Maybe try hailing Ari?"

Mentally berating himself for not thinking of it, Cade said, "Jedi One, this is Anvil Actual ... how copy?"

Nothing.

Cade tried one more time.

No reply.

Tapping the wall, Cade said, "It's gotta be structural interference."

He'd been in this situation once before.

Speed and violence of action was how he handled the problem then. And that's exactly how he intended to triumph over it now.

In essence, Cade was going to put his head down and push through the fog of war, killing every last enemy unlucky enough to cross paths with him.

With no window to peer through, Cade reached into a cargo pocket and produced a three-inch LCD monitor. From his other pocket he retrieved a directional fiber-optic cable. Attaching the flexible probe to the screen, he turned to Griff. "You smell that?"

"Fish?"

Cade nodded. Sniffing his wet fatigues, he said, "It's not me."

Bringing his sleeve to his nose, Griff shook his head. "Not me."

Seeing the building's floor plan in his head, Cade said, "Across the turbine hall is the brown-bag-lunch area. I'm thinking some of the grunts are having a late dinner."

Griff nodded. "Agreed."

Cade powered on the monitor. Forcing the camera lens under the door, he said, "Let's see if anyone's stirring."

The monitor remained mostly dark as Cade panned the micro camera lens right to left. On the far end of the sweep, bathed in flickering tones of yellow and orange and red, was a metal rollup door large enough to drive a train engine through.

Commenting on the image he was seeing on the screen, Griff said, "Looks like our grunts are dining by candlelight. How romantic."

Reeling the lens back in, Cade stood up and stuffed the device into a pocket. From the other pocket, he retrieved his trusty SouthOrd lock pick gun.

In seconds, the lock was thwarted and Cade and Griff were standing in the turbine room. From somewhere off to their right came the tinny twang of what Cade guessed to be Chinese pop music.

On their left was the rollup door they'd seen on the LCD screen. Dead ahead was the brown-bag-lunch area. The rectangular room was thirty feet across and branched off to the right. Blueprints suggested about forty feet separated the open end from the room's rear wall.

More than a dozen folding cafeteria tables crowded the room. Behind the tables, pushed up against a wall, was a row of darkened vending machines. Next came a garbage can and pair of receptacles for recyclables. On the floor beside the recycling station was a box labeled LOST AND FOUND, overflowing with kid-sized coats and sweatshirts.

Save for the overpowering stench of fish cooking, the snippet of the room visible to Cade was exactly how he remembered it.

As the music slowly faded out, Cade detected the crinkling of plastic and a low murmur of voices speaking in Mandarin.

After getting Griff's attention, Cade tapped his headset. Then, with one gloved hand pantomiming a mouth opening and closing, he made a hand gesture that meant *around the corner.*

Griff mouthed, "I hear it," then used hand signals to indicate he would go wide and take the left half of the room.

Nodding, Cade mouthed, "I'm taking one alive."

MP7 tucked tight to his shoulder, Griff said, "Copy that."

Letting Griff get a two-stride head start, Cade moved swiftly and quietly toward the right-hand-side of the wide-open entry. Reaching the wall, with Griff in his left peripheral and just beginning to make his turn to the right, Cade flowed around the corner, MP7 aimed at the center of the long room, muzzle commencing a methodical left-to-right sweep.

Five Chicom soldiers were indeed enjoying a late dinner. Four were seated face-to-face at one of the tables, the rear wall to the room just a few feet behind them. One was smoking what looked to be a hand-rolled cigarette. The others held spoons and were eating out of plastic bowls.

A green Coleman camp stove was set up on a nearby table. Tendrils of steam lifted from a large soup pot sitting on the stove.

On the table beside the stove was a tray bristling with a half-dozen candles. The flickering, sallow light lent an eerie horror-flick feel to the entire scene.

The unlucky soldier in the room, a bullpup-style rifle slung over one shoulder, was up and making his way toward the garbage can. He was Griff's immediate concern.

The other four were Cade's problem.

Chapter 75

As time slowed to a crawl, Cade heard the Chinese pop music resume playing. In the next beat, a halo of red was blooming about the standing soldier's head. Shot twice in the face by Griff, the soldier collapsed to the floor.

The four soldiers in Cade's cone were caught completely unaware. Downrange from their dead comrade, they were all hit in the face by aerated detritus.

Seated, Cade's targets were at a supreme disadvantage—and they knew it.

In Mandarin, Cade said, *"Surrender! Hands up!"*

Three sets of hands dropped what they'd been holding and shot for the sky.

The soldier who'd been smoking—the one whose free hand made a slow creep toward the sidearm on his hip—earned himself one round to the chest and one to the face. A modified Mozambique courtesy of Captain Cade Grayson.

The *hero* wannabe was a bloody mess when he slumped sideways and slithered under the table.

Finger pressed vertical to his lips, Cade stared death at the three remaining soldiers.

Far away, the twangy pop music played on. More importantly, there were no shouts of alarm or call to arms echoing throughout the museum.

It was all the proof Cade needed that the subsonic rounds fired from the suppressed MP7s had gone undetected.

Before the trio of soldiers could recover from the initial shock of being splashed with blood and brain tissue, Cade had rushed forward and disarmed them.

Taking a wad of napkins from a holder, Griff gagged the three soldiers. While he trussed them with nylon flex cuffs, Cade was dumping the mags from their weapons and clearing the chambers of live rounds.

As Griff stashed the rifles and pistols behind the vending machines, Cade dumped the ammo and mags into the garbage can.

Choosing one of the soldiers—a teen, judging by the wisps of facial hair trying to pass themselves off as a beard—Cade yanked him to his feet. Speaking in halting Mandarin, Cade asked the kid who was upstairs and what they were doing.

Replying in Mandarin, the kid said, "General Sun Jinlong and Major Li Fan ... and a whore or two."

"Is there a third man?" Cade asked. "An American prisoner?"

The kid's jaw went rigid and his eyes narrowed. It looked as if he was weighing his response very carefully.

Without saying a word, Cade dropped a knee on the back of one of the other soldiers, drew his Gerber, and proceed to saw through the man's pinky finger.

The kid watched the gagged man grimace and squirm and thrash about. A few seconds was all the kid could handle before, in rapid-fire Mandarin (almost too fast for Cade to fully grasp) the kid spilled his guts.

Cade understood enough to think the kid knew of what he spoke. Satisfied, Cade rose and made a show of tossing the severed finger into the soup pot. Flipping the NVGs away from his face, he looked the kid in the eye, saying, "*Are you being truthful?*"

The kid nodded emphatically.

Detecting none of the usual micro expressions linked with deception, Cade gagged the kid and made him sit on the floor with his comrades.

After extinguishing the candles, Griff looked to Cade. "You know," he said in a low voice, "we can't leave them here."

In English, Cade said, "We can't take them with us."

Matter-of-factly, Griff said, "Sucks to be them."

Cade swiveled the NVGs back in place. Switching to Mandarin, he said, "Look at the wall." As soon as the three Chicom soldiers complied with the order, Cade stepped around the end of the table, shouldered his MP7, and shot all three men dead.

If Griff was surprised at all, he didn't let on. He simply went about swapping mags and charging his weapon.

All business, while changing his mags out, Cade said, "Science Playground. We'll take the main stairs to the second level."

They retraced their steps to the turbine hall. Seeing nothing moving in the hall, they padded past the steam turbine, wove a serpentine pattern through several standalone science exhibits, then set a course for the southeast corner of the building, the music growing louder the closer they got.

Speaking quietly on the move, Cade tried Cross again.

At once Cross responded. "Anvil Actual?" A pause. Then finally, "Overwatch One here. Good solid copy! Damn, Anvil Actual … we thought we lost you."

Five hundred yards southeast of OMSI's fenced in parking lot, Cross was prone in the southbound lane of the viaduct. Thanks to the high-powered Leupold scope atop the MSR, he had a commanding view of OMSI's east-facing elevation, the entire parking lot, the centrally located holding pen, a mostly empty motor pool, the pair of single-wide trailers that Feather insisted were home to fifteen to thirty Chicom soldiers, and the tops of the mobile missile launcher and its command apparatus.

Sounding a lot like the little girl from Poltergeist, Griff said, "We're back."

Ignoring Griff's quip, Cade said, "Structural anomaly knocked us off the air. Give me a SITREP."

Cross said, "I have eyes on the pen. The prisoners are agitated about something. They're pacing back and forth. Constantly checking the main gate. After the general picked his girl for the night, he made some kind of speech to the rest of them. It's got to be something he said."

Cade said, "Only one … *girl?*"

"She may be a teen," Cross replied.

"Overwatch Two?"

"I have eyes on Nat," Cross said. "He's good to go."

To show he was listening in, Nat broke squelch one time.

Cade said, "Jedi Flight?"

Cross said, "On schedule."

Cade shot a glance at his watch. *Still eight minutes out.* He asked: "The barracks?"

"Just after I got set up here, two tangos used the porta-john. It's been quiet since."

"Copy that," Cade said. "Moving on the HVTs. Anvil out."

Truth was, before they ranged any deeper into the museum, there was the officer cadre to take care of. Feather's source had them billeting in the Kendall Planetarium, a domed building on the northeast end of the building.

Emerging from the Turbine Hall, they found themselves in a glass-enclosed atrium. It was maybe fifty or sixty feet from the marble floor to the enormous glass pyramid rising up over the rest of the roof.

Situated directly underneath the pyramid roof was a horseshoe-shaped desk. Behind the desk was a sign displaying the prices for admission and what movies had been showing in the theater on that Saturday in July.

Diagonal from the desk were two banks of doors, eight total. Four served a walkway coming in from the east parking lot. The other four faced the north parking lot. All of the doors were shored up inside and out with half-inch-thick sheets of plywood.

Whether the OMSI staff did this early on, or the current squatters did the shoring, Cade hadn't a clue.

Three separate wings branched off the main lobby. Straight ahead, a fifteen-foot-wide passage spilled out at the box office and snack bar serving the Omnimax-domed theater. To the right, partially shielded by the front desk, was a run of stairs going up to the second floor, where the music was currently coming from. The steps numbered about fifty and were separated by three different landings. To the right of the stairs—an ADA requirement, Cade guessed—was a stalled-out escalator.

Left of Cade and Griff was another carpeted hall. At the mouth of the hall was Guest Services—a small cubby fronted by a velvet rope maze.

Beyond Guest Services, at the end of a narrow, fifty-foot-long hall, was the planetarium lobby.

Awash in dim light thrown from a gas-burning lantern was a single guard. He sat on a folding chair, head buried in some kind of electronic device.

Cade quietly heel-and-toed it off the marble floor. With the MP7 tucked in tight to his shoulder and low-wear carpet helping to silence his footfalls, Cade slipped past the Guest Services desk. Hugging the left-side wall, with Griff close on his back and periodically checking their six, Cade picked up his pace.

With the lantern's soft hiss covering any sound of their advance the carpet wasn't already absorbing, Cade angled away from the wall. Keeping the EOTech's red holographic pip pegged squarely on the guard's temple, he cleared his throat. Then, speaking in Mandarin, he whispered, *"Quiet … or you die."*

The guard's body went rigid as he looked up from the device in his hands.

Cade had cut the angle wide and was now aiming the MP7 at the center of the man's face. He sure was glad he wasn't on the other end of this encounter. Facing two black-clad figures with suppressed weapons and tubes sprouting from their faces was bad enough. Doing so while brandishing a Gameboy instead of a weapon had to be demoralizing as hell.

Not my monkey, not my circus, thought Cade. Indicating the planetarium with a nod of his head, he asked, *"How many officers?"*

The soldier's brow crinkled. Then, eyes narrowing and lips beginning to part, he went to stand.

Cade pressed the trigger twice.

No Mozambique this time. He'd opted for two to the face. The first subsonic round smacked the guard in the mouth, shredding lips and shattering most of his front teeth on the way in. Though the suppressor helped keep muzzle climb to a minimum, Cade had pulled his aim up a degree or two for the follow-on shot.

Since the guard's head was already hinged back from the initial bullet strike, the second round entered his nose at an upward angle.

Theoretically, lacking the punch of the M4's 5.56 round, both chunks of lead fired from the MP7 had entered the man's cranium, banged around scrambling brain matter, and remained there.

The evidence supported this. Save for the pair of gory, gaping entry wounds that used to be natural orifices, the rest of the skull remained intact.

Though the guard's shorts were probably soiled, the wall behind his slumped head was clean.

Cade looked around quickly. The doors and glass in the planetarium hall had received the same plywood treatment and were no doubt locked down tight. At the end of the hall, past the planetarium's exit doors, was a coat check area.

With Griff's help, Cade hauled the corpse the twenty feet to the coat check cubby and stuffed it inside.

Back at the planetarium entry, Cade tried the door.

Unlocked.

Which is what he'd expected, considering the guard placement.

Cade took out the snake cam, powered it on, and stuffed it under the door. On the LCD screen, he could only make out the circular room's back wall, a few rows of backward-canted chairs, and faint light emanating from a couple of different unseen sources.

After a brief huddle, acting on Griff's suggestion, they tackled the planetarium entry just as they had the brown-bag area.

Chapter 76

Stealth. Speed. Surprise. Violence of action. All friends of the assaulter.

With the generator humming outside likely used solely to power the HQ-9, lights out was dictated by Mother Nature. And Mother Nature had a way of resetting a man's internal clock fairly quickly.

Acting on the assumption that most of the officers would already be asleep, or well on their way, the Pale Riders walked through the planetarium doors as if they owned the place.

In the lead this time, Griff swept to the left, aiming his MP7 down each row of theater seats he passed by.

One Chinese officer sat bolt upright from a cot arranged in the gap between aisles. Griff pumped two rounds into his head from five feet away. Moving on, he killed two more men who appeared to be playing possum on cots of their own.

As the soft coughs from Griff's weapon drifted across the planetarium, Cade was having a hard time finding tangos to kill. One of the light sources he had spotted on the snake cam screen was being held by a startled officer. The man was in pajamas and on his stomach atop a sleeping bag. He had been thumbing eagerly through a worn Playboy when Cade stepped on his neck and shot him behind the ear.

The second light source was a Petzl headlamp dangling from the muzzle of a rifle propped against an empty cot. On the cot was an open book: John Muir's travelogue *The American Wilderness*.

Cade grabbed the pillow and touched it to his cheek. *Still warm.*

Three more suppressed gunshots carried across the oval room. In his headset, Cade heard Griff declare his sector, "Clear."

Replying, Cade said, "We have a squirter. I'll try and flush him to you."

Walking in a combat crouch, Cade made his way to the row of high-backed seats running along the planetarium's outer wall. From there he struck off counterclockwise in Griff's direction.

"Got him," said Griff.

About the time Cade heard Griff in his ear, he, too, saw the squirter's head and a hand clutching a pistol crest a chair back at his ten o'clock. "He's armed and coming your way."

Griff said, "Roger that."

Seeing the lick of flame lance from the other operator's weapon, Cade said, "Clear?"

"Affirmative. Tango down," confirmed Griff.

Cade acknowledged his side was clear, then beat feet toward the exit, first and foremost on his mind: how little time they had left to secure the HVTs *and* destroy the HQ-9.

With Griff taking point, they exited the planetarium hall the way they'd come in.

Leaving the Membership Services desk behind, they hustled through the lobby and made their way to the bottom of the stairs, where they halted for a look and listen.

Down on one knee in front of the unmoving escalator, Cade trained his weapon at the open space above them and reconciled the floorplan in his head with what was before him.

Keeping his weapon aimed at the top of the stairs, the most likely place for one of the enemy to suddenly show his face, Griff said, "Up, left, then straight ahead?"

Cade said, "Affirmative. Cover me," and started up the dead escalator.

While much steeper than the stairs to its left, the viewing angle from the escalator was far superior.

Engaging the enemy from low ground always put one at a disadvantage. Doing so on a ninety-degree plane would likely get one or both of them killed.

For the fourth time since they'd first heard the music, it came to an end. The silence enveloping the place was palpable. Thankfully, in keeping with the previous pauses, this one lasted only a few seconds.

As soon as the music continued on its endless loop, Cade was on the move up the escalator, MP7 tucked in tight, eyes on a constant sweep. As he rotated his upper body left to keep the high ground in his sights, Griff covered the top of the escalator for him.

Nearing the escalator's apex, his head close to breaking the plane between floors, Cade swung his weapon forward and kept its business end trained down the narrow stainless-steel chute where an enemy was most likely to appear.

Like a well-oiled machine, upon seeing Cade swing his weapon away from covering their left flank, Griff automatically turned, crouched on the escalator, and hovered the EOTech's red reticle just above the chrome handrail, where anyone hearing their approach would likely show his face.

At the top of the escalator, Cade was again presented with three options. Straight ahead was the Traveling Exhibition Hall. Seeing as how it looked to have been between exhibits before the dead began to walk, and showed no signs of having been used since, sweeping through the room to clear it would burn time they didn't have to waste.

Left of the second-floor landing was a wide-open room full of exhibits. Above the entry, *Natural Sciences Hall* was spelled out with large three-dimensional letters.

Behind them and to the right, its double doors shut tight, was the Science Playground. It was well known to Cade. He had watched over many a play session behind those doors. Waited patiently for Raven to tire of playing with sand, or water, or blocks. It was in the nearby Discovery Lab—a windowed room within the Science Playground—that Raven had learned how to produce knockoffs of Silly Putty and Play-Doh.

The music was coming from somewhere inside the Science Playground, where Feather's inside man said the young general took his women.

Outside the doors to the Science Playground was a folding chair. An ashtray sat on the floor beside the chair. Perched on the edge of the ashtray, a thin ribbon of smoke curling off the dying cherry, was a half-smoked cigarette.

In his head, Cade saw the hall beyond the Science Playground. After a short, straight run, it curled right and continued on for a few feet to the upper floor restrooms. No doubt that was where the cigarette's owner had gone off to.

Using hand signals, Cade tasked Griff with covering the top of the stairs and the entry to the Natural Sciences Hall.

With Griff watching his six, Cade went into a combat crouch, turned the corner, and walked swiftly toward the Science Playground. While Jinlong may have recently summoned the guard into the room, Cade thought it more likely that nature had called.

After a quick peek around the corner at the end of the hall, Cade continued on, a blur of black merging with the shadows.

At the bathroom alcove, Cade had to choose a door: Men or Women? If the guard had a headlamp or flashlight, no evidence of it was showing around either of the door edges.

Listening hard didn't offer any clues.

Going with the odds, Cade pushed through the door labeled Men. At once he saw a bubble of light hovering above one of the toilet stalls. In the white-tiled bathroom, viewed through the color NVGs, the light presented as a miniature sun.

Squinting against the glare, Cade said in Mandarin: "Bad fish?"

From the stall, a deep voice: "Huh?"

Cade moved a few feet to his left, aimed the MP7 to where a seated person's chest would be, and gently pushed on the door.

Locked.

In Mandarin, the guard said, "Go away, *Zhao.*"

Stretching to full extension, Cade stuck the MP7's lethal end over the top edge of the door, bent his wrist so the suppressor was at a forty-five-degree downward angle, then quickly pressed the trigger two times.

There was a gasp and then silence. A tick later a blood-spattered roll of toilet paper came bouncing out from under the door.

Speaking into his mike, Cade said, "Tango down. Coming out."

Though Cade wanted to storm into the Science Playground and stop Jinlong in the middle of whatever deviant act he was engaging in, President Clay's man was being tortured one room over. Cade had been there. Though most of the memories of what he had gone through in that Utah farmhouse were hazy, sometimes, when he was still, he would relive the agony of it all. The white-hot pain of having blows rained down on his face. The gut-wrenching lightning bolts that had shot up his arms and legs as he lost each nail to a vicious tug of those rusty pliers.

No matter how much Cade detested seemingly untouchable men like Jinlong—cowardly men who preyed on the weak—his first order of business was to keep one of his own from having to suffer even one more second at the hands of the sadist who had arrived with the Chinese President's son.

Cade and Griff didn't wait outside the Natural Sciences Hall. They rolled right in, Cade on the left, Griff the right, MP7s covering their respective slices of the pie.

At the rear of the hall were three rooms: Life Lab, Earth Lab, and Paleontology Lab. The latter was where Feather said Li Fan did all of his dirty work. The tools were already there, so it made sense to Cade.

Keeping alive Feather's streak of solid intel, the Chicom interrogation specialist was indeed in the building. Not only was he standing in plain view and framed fully in the Paleontology Lab's floor-to-ceiling windows, in person, the toad-faced man matched perfectly the photo General Nash had included in the envelope hand-delivered to Cade at Penrose.

The entire room was bathed in the harsh white light from a gas lantern. It flickered subtly, causing the shadows on the wall to twitch. Though he couldn't hear it, Cade guessed the lantern was putting out that hollow whooshing noise that always signaled *s'mores hour* on their family camping trips.

Cade saw that Fan wore the same camouflage uniform as the soldiers downstairs. On his head was a helmet with a flip-down splatter shield. The man's black rubber gloves ended mid-forearm. Wrapped around Fan's ample waist and tied off out back was a yellow, ankle-length apron. Each time the man made any kind of movement, the flickering glow of the lantern played off its blood-streaked surface.

Two other men were inside the room with Fan. Both were well over six feet tall, which meant they eclipsed the little sadist by nearly a foot.

One man stood on the left side of the room, maybe half a dozen feet from Fan's *workspace*. The other man was back to the window and appeared to be operating a video camera mounted on a tripod.

Strapped to a chair in the center of the room, face a mess of pulped flesh, was the man the entire mission revolved around. While rolling up the commie president's kid would be one helluva coup for the intel folks, it was nowhere near as important as rescuing the man who'd been recruiting and training the small bands of men and women responsible for dozens of hit-and-run attacks on the Chicoms. Having been in sporadic contact with Springs for only a couple of months, the tough-as-nails freedom fighters operated all the way up the West Coast, from Long Beach to Seattle.

That the resistance called themselves Wolverines was not lost on Cade. Nor was it lost on the Chinese Special Forces, who had been hunting them nonstop since late February, when temperatures buoyed and the mountain passes finally started showing the first signs of opening up.

Army Lt. Colonel Ret. Remember "Alamo" Baker was a modern-day Colonel Andy Tanner. He considered the Chinese his Soviets, and this was *his* Red Dawn. Named after American Revolutionary War hero Remember Baker—a famous member of the Continental Army's Green Mountain Boys—the retired colonel was known as a hard-charger in the War on Terror. Wounded by an IED in Mosul, Iraq, he was retired and living in Washington state when the dead began to walk.

The closer Cade got to the room, the stronger the coppery odor of spilt blood became.

Though Cade had already made it clear to Griff the interrogator was to be taken alive, from across the open doorway, he mouthed "Alive" to the SEAL.

Acting on a visual cue from Cade, Griff rose from behind the picture window, aimed the MP7 at the back of the guard's head, and, from point-blank range, snapped off two quick shots.

Chapter 77

At the same instant Griff was breaking the plane where the window seated with the lower sill, Cade was also rising from his crouch. He didn't hear the two shots so much as he felt the expanding gasses and shockwave from the back-to-back discharges. MP7 tucked in tight, glass and brain matter striking the floor all around, he quick-walked through the doorway, Guard Number Two in his sights.

The guard's mouth was a silent O when Cade pressed the trigger, literally swallowing the first 4.6 mm round. The guard's head was hammered back, which as fate would have it, exposed to the second round a whole lot of important items located underneath the man's chin.

Just as the cloud of blood and splintered teeth erupted from where his right cheek used to be, the follow-on round punched a small hole in his neck, shredding trachea and severing his carotid artery. The resulting stream of crimson looked like something coming from a sprinkler. As the man fell to his knees, hands instinctively going for the gaping wounds, the blood kept coming in powerful spurts attuned perfectly with the final frantic beats of his heart.

Already wearing the blood of a true patriot, Li Fan caught a face full of his comrade's hot, sticky blood. Face shield clouded with dark red runners, the little man dropped the pliers he was holding and, with both hands, ripped the helmet from his head.

Seeing the pliers fall and Fan's hands begin their upward sweep, Cade strode forward and pressed the MP7's hot muzzle to the man's neck.

Fan flinched and cursed in Mandarin as the hot steel branded a half-inch crescent onto his skin.

Ignoring the reaction, Cade said, "*Sishén?*"

The interrogator's eyes went wide.

Face a mask of restrained anger, Cade said in English, "Thought so."

Already in the room and tending to Baker, Griff said, "He's alive."

Cade zipped Fan's arms together behind his back. Regarding Griff, he said, "See if the colonel will respond to smelling salts."

While Griff dug into his individual first aid kit, Cade was saying "Alamo" over the comms. It was the predetermined code word to let the Air Force captain manning the radio at the Peterson TOC know that Baker was alive and in friendly hands.

As soon as Griff waved the ammonia inhalant under Baker's badly broken nose, the man jerked awake. Though the retired colonel was in his late fifties, his build was that of a man a decade and a half younger. Also belying his true age, he was blessed with a full head of jet-black hair. That it was shorn real close didn't surprise Cade.

"Colonel, can you walk?"

The colonel's eyes fixed on Cade. Through split lips, he said, "My nose is busted, not my legs. And last I checked, a fella doesn't need fingernails to walk."

Cade said nothing as he sawed through the paracord binding the colonel's wrists and ankles. Helping the man up from the chair, he said, "Wait one." Regarding Fan, he asked in Mandarin, "*Jinlong ... how many are guarding him?*"

Fan smiled but said nothing.

Grabbing the man's face one-handed and plunging a thumb into his right eye socket, Cade repeated the question.

The smile faded and Fan went up on his tiptoes. Still, the man remained silent.

Dragging the Gerber out, Cade moved the tip of the blade toward the man's darting eye.

"I speak English," Fan said. "Studied at Columbia in New York."

Save for a slight lisp, Fan's English was near perfect.

Cade said, "I know you do. Jinlong's guards ... how many and where?"

Fan said, "One inside. Two at the gate."

Sheathing the Gerber, Cade regarded Griff. "Gag him and bring him with."

Reaching a bloody hand out to Cade, Baker asked for clothing, boots, and a weapon.

With no hesitation, Cade stripped the requested items from one of the dead guards. He put the pants, shirt, and boots on the floor by the colonel. "Clothes are XL. Looks like the boots are size nine."

Buttoning the shirt, Baker said, "Boots are small ... but better than nothing," and started loosening them up, wincing each time the laces whipped across his fingertips.

Cade set the Chicom bullpup rifle, semiautomatic pistol and mags for both on the floor next to Baker. "We have two friendly shooters on overwatch outside, and air is on the way."

Already press-checking the polymer pistol, Baker said, "Copy that. I'll follow your lead."

On the way out, Cade took the guards' two-way radios, the tape from the video recorder, and a small leather-bound notebook he found on a nearby table. Handing a radio to Griff, he said, "Your Mandarin is better than mine. Anyone calls, bullshit 'em as best you can."

Griff nodded, then shoved Fan out the door ahead of him.

OMSI Science Playground

The Chinese pop music had just ended when Cade and Baker pulled open the set of double doors.

The interactive displays once placed around the warehouse-like space had all been pushed to the side. In the center of the room was a canopy bed. It was a four-poster and looked to be a king-sized item, if not larger. Someone had gone to considerable trouble to get it in here. Where the PLA soldiers had gotten it from, considering OMSI was in the industrial part of town, was a mystery to Cade. A number of studded leather-items—cuffs and collars and such—hung on the end of chains secured to the exposed overhead heating- and air-conditioning ducts.

Candles burned in bottles set around the bed. Their flickering, baleful yellow light illuminated both General Jinlong and the naked woman on the bed.

Caught naked and prancing around the bed's far corner, a cognac snifter in one hand and semi-hard member clutched in the other, the general let out a surprised yelp.

Cade said, "*Sun Jinlong?*"

The man's eyes narrowed.

Jackpot, Cade thought. In Mandarin, he said, "*Do not move.*"

Baker jammed his pistol into his waistband. "Cover him." Then, thrusting a bloody hand toward Griff, he said, "Flex cuffs … I'll truss the little fucker."

Baker swept the general's legs from under him, put a knee on his narrow chest, and proceeded to zip-tie his hands together.

While Griff searched the general's uniform for intel, Cade crept to the bed, MP7 aimed at the teen girl.

In English, Fan said, "She's dead. The general likes them obedient and at room temperature."

Dragging his Sig from its holster, Griff approached the general. "You sick fuck," he spat. "I ought to shove this up your ass and double-tap your liver."

"Don't," Cade said. "He'll get his later." After checking the young brunette on the bed for a pulse, he sighed and turned toward the thirty-three-year-old rising star in the PLA's newly minted Continental Assimilation Force. "We're taking a ride." Stuffing the dead girl's panties in the general's mouth, he added, "Griff, break Major Fan's nose."

After pistol-whipping the interrogator across the face, Griff said, "Copy that," and holstered his Sig.

Over the comms, Cade said, "Baby Bird is caged. We'll be exiting through the middle fire exit, second floor … three-foot mobiles in tow." Yanking the naked general to his feet and shoving him toward the emergency exit at the rear of the room, Cade said in Mandarin, "*You anger me, I will cut your penis off.*"

Chapter 78

The fire-exit doors opened up to an elevated open-to-the air stairway. Shielded from view by the upper boughs of the picket of mature trees planted along OMSI's rear wall, Cade crossed the landing, then attacked the stairs two at a time. Struggling to keep up, Jinlong fell and left good-sized bits of flesh from both knees on the serrated metal treads.

"Come on," Cade growled, again jerking the smaller man to his feet.

The stairs doubled back twice, then spit the five of them out in an enclosed area crowded by two industrial-sized garbage bins and a trio of recycling bins. Bi-fold doors to the parking lot were closed and, though Cade couldn't see beyond the bins pushed up against them, he guessed they were locked from the inside. Next to the dual doors was a man-sized door fitted with a panic bar.

After leaving Baker in the enclosure and holding the prisoners at gunpoint, Cade informed all involved in the operation that he and Griff were about to step out into the open. In response, Ari came on over the comms with word that the Jedi flight was inbound and less than two minutes out.

"Jedi One, Anvil Actual. Good copy," Cade replied. "We'll have sterile airspace in one minute. Over and out."

Thankfully the panic bar was not locked. Seeing as how there was no power going to the building, Cade wasn't worried about an alarm sounding.

Pushing through, with Griff on his six, Cade paused long enough to regard the rebar-reinforced gate roughly fifty yards to his left. Two men dressed in civilian clothes stood near the point where two halves of the gate came together.

The men carried exotic-looking submachine guns. They also seemed more situationally aware than the others they'd encountered so far.

Jinlong's guards, thought Cade.

Sitting on folding chairs set up beneath a tarp attached to OMSI's brick wall, three uniformed soldiers were playing some kind of a game that incorporated domino-like tiles.

Drawn by the generator noise, nearly a dozen moaning Zs were crushing their wraith-like forms against the gate. Though they were staring the meat from the bones of the nearby guards, they were being ignored.

Over the comms, Cade said, "Overwatch Alpha, Anvil Actual. How copy?"

"Angel Alpha … solid copy," replied Cross.

Cade said, "Do you have eyes on the seated tangos?"

"Affirmative."

Cade said, "Angel Bravo, Anvil Actual. How copy?"

"Angel Bravo, solid copy," replied Nat.

Cade said, "We're moving in ten. Be ready. If we disturb the hornet nest, I want you to light them up. Over and out."

A single break of squelch after Cade signed out told him that Nat understood fully.

Counting down from *seven*, Cade shouldered the MP7. At *two*, he felt Griff place a palm flat on his shoulder—a silent message that he was good to go.

At *one*, already on the move for the HQ-9's Command and Control trailer, Cade heard the familiar clatter of weapons and thuds of bodies hitting the ground. A beat later, a soldier who'd been sitting at the table managed to get to his feet and call out something in Mandarin. Whatever he was trying to say was instantly rendered indecipherable as a bullet fired from Cross's MSR cleaved through the man's throat.

Unable to hear the suppressed reports of the long gun some five hundred yards to his fore, Cade put his trust in Angel One to cover his approach to the RQ-9 trailer. The impenetrable darkness adding an extra sense of security, he slipped past the mobile missile launcher's metal grille.

The moment Cade reached the middle of the launcher's big-rig-sized tractor, a door opened half a dozen feet in front of him.

Skirting right to get a better angle around the door's swing, he drew up a few pounds of pressure on the MP7's already fine-tuned trigger and overlaid the red pip on the point in space he figured the PLA soldier would emerge.

Beating Cade to the punch, the soldier sprayed a burst of poorly placed rounds in his direction.

Rounds zinged off the blacktop, one striking dead-center in Cade's chest, another carving a furrow in the flesh on the outside of his right thigh.

Kinetic energy halved from striking the ground first, the round that had struck Cade's chest was stopped by the ceramic plate in his carrier.

Though winded slightly from the sudden punch to his solar plexus, and wincing on account of the hot sting from the damage done by the second ricocheting round, Cade dropped his muzzle by a degree and let fly two subsonic rounds.

Killed in the act of placing a boot on the trailer's top stair, the shooter's body went rigid and pitched forward. Carving a steady arc over the stairs, the face-shot man looked like a felled tree. The impact with the ground wasn't as impressive; however, it did draw out of one of the dead man's comrades.

Nearly perpendicular to the open doorway, his breathing still affected by the glancing blow, Cade was afforded a frontal view of the second soldier's gruesome death. Fired by Griff, maybe six feet away and from an angle oblique to the startled soldier, the first hurtling forty-grain hunk of lead struck the man under the chin, just below his right ear. As the kinetic energy was snapping the soldier's head left, Griff's second round entered an inch above the man's turning cheek. Traveling just under 1100-feet-per-second, at an up angle, the round took the path of least resistance: plowing through the nasal cavity, crushing ethmoid bone, and exiting the skull through the nasal passage.

The partially formed look of surprise was erased from the soldier's face as his entire nose—cartilage, flesh, and dermis—

exploded outward and was taken along for the ride in front of the disintegrating hunk of tumbling lead.

To Cade's right, things were happening that caught his attention. In the holding pen, prisoners drawn from their tents by the gunfire were gaping at the fallen guards.

Beyond the pen, the agitation among the dead things outside the fence was ramping up. In the middle distance, both doors on the trailers housing the PLA cadre were banging open.

Cat's out of the bag, Cade thought. Instantly, a near-solid stream of red tracer fire from Nat's MK-46 was lancing the air far off to his right.

Simultaneously, Cade was fishing an M67 frag grenade from a pocket. Pressing his back to the right side of the door, with Griff crouching on the opposite side, Cade let the MP7 hang by its sling and pulled the grenade's pin.

On the same page as Cade, Griff kept his weapon aimed at the doorway. With his off hand, Griff grabbed the door's edge and started it swinging closed.

There was no dramatic exclamation of *Frag out* or *Fire in the hole.* Cade simply let the spoon fly and, just as the door was passing the midway point in its swing, sidearmed the tennis-ball-sized grenade into the trailer.

As the door slammed shut, Cade and Griff dove to the ground.

Three long seconds later there was a muffled *whoomp.* No screams issued forth. There were no cries for help in Mandarin or any other language, for that matter.

Just silence from within.

In the event any PLA soldiers were alive inside the trailer, Griff readied a second grenade.

This time Cade tended the door as Griff pulled the pin and rolled the grenade into the trailer.

There was another *whoomp* and the Pale Riders were up and mounting the stairs.

Chapter 79

From his position south of the lot, Nat was taking incoming from the PLA soldiers spilling from their billet. Prone behind a pair of Jersey barriers, he ignored the rounds crackling overhead and striking concrete and continued firing short bursts of suppressing fire.

Immediately following the muffled explosion of Griff's grenade, Cade opened the launcher trailer door and peered inside. The smell of blood and cordite hit his nose first. Then he saw that the grenades had turned the remaining soldier into a partially clothed corpse leaking blood and who knew what else. To ensure the twin doses of shrapnel hadn't left functional any of the electronic equipment, he fired a dozen rounds into the wall occupied by multiple flat-panel screens, all of them surrounded by dials and buttons.

As Cade swapped magazines, he called, "Clear." On the heels of the one-word SITREP meant solely for Griff, he went on, "Jedi Flight, Anvil Actual, you are green for go. Romeo Bravo is offline. Repeat, Jedi Flight is green. Fire for effect on the troop billets."

In the next beat, Ari responded, saying, "Anvil Actual, Jedi One-One. Good copy. On station in thirty."

Thirty? Too much time. However, seeing as how they were hemmed in by fire coming in from the troop billet and unable to advance due to the steady barrage spewing from Nat's LMG, they decided to stay put and wait for reinforcements.

Confident in the knowledge the IR tape on their helmets would differentiate them from the enemy, Cade exited the thin-skinned trailer and took cover next to Griff, beside the stamped-metal stairs, where he hoped enemy rounds wouldn't find them.

***

Ten seconds into what was to be the longest thirty seconds of Cade's life, he felt in his chest the familiar harmonic vibrations that could only be the Jedi Flight. It seemed to be coming from two directions: east and south. Nearby, the prisoners felt it, too. Faces turned expectantly skyward and a hushed murmur arose from the cramped pen.

Another five seconds crawled by and the rotor thrum was accompanied by the distant diesel growl of an approaching vehicle.

In the pen, chins were dropping and heads were panning in the direction of the new sound.

In the next fifteen seconds, presenting to Cade as more of a slow-rolling train wreck than the calamitous kinetic action that it truly was—all hell broke loose.

As Cade bellowed "Get down" at the prisoners who were still standing, a second chain of orange-red fire joined in with the sporadic tracer fire from Nat's weapon. Only the new incoming was lancing down at a forty-five-degree angle. Looking as if it was made of interconnected rounds, the *beam* of fire tore into the troop trailers with animalistic ferocity. The thin metal skin was no match. Nor was the flesh and bone of the partially clothed troops still pouring from the doorways.

It was over in seconds for the soldiers who were just minutes away from choosing from the prisoners their girl for the night.

Like tin cans tossed into a campfire, the trailers were quickly reduced to smoking shells, their walls and roofs buckling inward. As Jedi One broke contact and swung a tight, banking port-side turn that took it over the OMSI roofline and toward the river, Jedi One-Two came in out of the east, moving low and slow, her deployed landing gear passing just feet over Cross's overwatch position atop the viaduct.

From five hundred yards out, as viewed through Cade's color NVGs, the Ghost Chinook gliding over the fenced-in parking lot was a sight to behold. Standing on the deployed rear ramp, a lone soldier trained groundward what looked to be an M240H machine gun.

Five hundred yards east of Cross's position, rolling westbound on the two-lane passing directly underneath the viaduct, the returning troop transport was picking up speed. Gears gnashed and exhaust belched as the driver worked the transmission on the American vehicle he was not overly familiar with.

Didn't matter. Because prior to reaching cover under the viaduct, a Hellfire missile fired by Jedi One-Three dropped down from the inky black sky. Engine glowing red and trailing a swirl of white-gray exhaust, the air-to-surface missile hit the transport, dead center, at nearly a ninety-degree angle.

When the twenty-pound HEAT (high-explosive anti-tank) warhead detonated, the rig's multi-wheeled backend reared up and the dozen troops sitting on opposing benches were blown apart, their severed limbs and ruptured torsos scattered in all directions. Afire and still moving, the transport rolled out of sight underneath the viaduct, coming to a full stop only when the fuel in its tanks touched off and the driver and passenger inside the cab were engulfed by flames from the secondary explosion.

Thirty feet above the licking flames, Cross was feeling the heat—literally. Head down and pressing his prone body against the cool cement wall when the Hellfire crashed into the troop carrier, the SEAL had instantly lost both of his eyebrows, every last one of his long blond eyelashes, and all of the hair on his forearms where his rolled-up sleeves had left them exposed.

Thanking God the Hellfire had struck the vehicle just prior to it sliding underneath the distant northbound lanes, he charged the M4, rose up over the wall, and began putting the burning PLA soldiers out of their misery.

While Cross was doing the right thing, a pair of F-22A Raptors flying out of Joint Base Elmendorf-Richardson in Anchorage, Alaska were releasing ordinance on Target Bravo—the sprawling Convention Center at the east end of the Steele bridge, some two miles north of OMSI. In the process of being turned into a command and control facility for General Jinlong, the glass and steel Convention Center was seconds away from becoming a pile of broken concrete and twisted rebar.

Hearing small arms fire coming from behind the HQ-9 trailer, Cade and Griff rose up and pulled back toward the museum. Enemy fire crackled the air around them as they rounded the grille on the HQ-9's tractor. Just as the twin detonations blocks away rumbled the ground under Cade's Danners, he lifted his gaze and saw that Alamo had repositioned himself outside the door and had the prisoners prone on the ground directly below the emergency stairway. Bullpup shouldered, the resistance leader was screaming at the top of his voice and dumping rounds toward a pair of PLA squirters hemmed in by the gate.

Seeing the trapped PLA soldiers hinge over and fall to the parking lot, one clutching his gut, the other clearly having taken a couple of rounds to the head, Cade and Griff hustled back to collect Fan and Jinlong.

Meeting the Pale Riders halfway, flex-cuffed prisoners in tow, Baker said, "I'm not going back with you. My work is far from finished."

"My orders call for me to break you out … nothing more," Cade said. "However, I do have a couple of requests."

Slapping a fresh mag in the bullpup, Baker said, "Shoot. What do you want?"

"When the bird with the QRF puts down, all I want is for you to let one of the medics check you out. Give you something to help you rehydrate. Let him set that broken nose and tend to those fingers."

Baker looked off into the dark. Finally he said, "Can I have a minute alone with Torture Boy?"

Cade shook his head. "That I can't do. Know that I'll make sure he answers for what he did to you. You have my word."

"The videotape?"

Cade dug the tiny cassette out of his pocket and handed it over. "I have no use for it." He paused to pivot the NVGs up. "What are you going to do now? President Clay is going to ask me what's on your mind."

"I'm going to pick up right where I left off," said Baker. "Kicking ass and taking names. Only this time if they catch up with me, they will not take me alive. I'll go down swinging. And I'm sure as hell taking a whole lot of them with me."

Cade said, "I'll relay the message. Stay frosty out there, Alamo."

Baker shook Cade's gloved hand, then turned and limped off to meet the incoming Ghost Chinook.

Chapter 80

As Jedi One-Two touched down east of the holding pen, Cade reported over the comms that the west side of the lot was now clear. Seeing the rangers spilling down the helo's open ramp, he called Cross and Nat and ordered them to return from their overwatch positions.

While ranger medics tended to Baker and the others, two more rangers sprinted toward the HQ-9, in their hands enough C4 plastic explosives to destroy all of its components.

Cade probed his plate carrier. Finding no entry hole, just a rip in the chest rig and a dent in the chest plate underneath, he probed the hole in his pants. Coming away with a bloody finger and the knowledge that the graze was a shallow one and likely wouldn't even need suturing, he smiled at his good fortune.

"Couple of close calls," Griff said. "Need me to check you out?"

Shaking his head, Cade said, "I'll be fine." He paused. "You still have those cards on you?"

"Cards?"

"The deck you were playing Hold Em with on the tarmac back at Peterson."

Griff retrieved the pack of playing cards from his ruck. "These?"

Nodding, Cade took the cards from him. Opening the pack, he noticed the cards bore the same gun-toting Grim Reaper as the Pale Riders patch riding on his shoulder.

"Where'd you get these?"

Griff replied, "Lola had them made up for me. Some printer dude in Springs supplies them to her."

"Can they be replaced?"

"Sure. Why?"

All business, Cade said, "I'm going to leave some of them behind. I want the PLA pukes who come looking for the general to know who to fear."

Dragging the prisoners along, Cade and Griff walked the parking lot. Dropping a card near each fallen PLA soldier, Cade called them out, saying, "Ace of spades. Queen of diamonds. Six of clubs. Suicide King ..." He went on like that until half the deck was gone and they were back to where they started.

Cross and Nat were waiting near the pen and watching the rangers loading the Ghost Chinook with the injured. A handful of those among the healthy prisoners who wanted to ride along to Colorado Springs were already aboard and strapped in.

Ten minutes after Jedi One-Two landed, it was filled to capacity and the turbines were beginning to spool up.

Cade and Griff instinctively ducked their heads as the heavy-lift helo launched. They were still standing, heads bowed and backs facing the LZ, when Jedi One-One slid in from the north and took One-Two's place on the parking lot.

Meeting Skip at the open starboard-side door, Cade said, "Good shooting, Tex."

Grabbing Fan by the arm, Griff said, "Where do you want him?"

"Port side, back to the cockpit. Put Baby Bird directly across from him."

Once the prisoners were strapped in with their legs bound at the ankles with zip-ties, Cade boarded the helo and sat on the seat beside Jinlong.

Cross and Griff clambered aboard. Taking the forward-facing seats beside Cade, they began removing their rucks and securing and stowing their rifles.

Boarding last, Nat snagged the rear-facing seat adjacent to the starboard-side minigun.

Showing Ari a thumbs up, Skip said, "All customers aboard. Preparing for launch," and started the cabin door motoring shut.

The red cabin lights flickered briefly as the turbines started to spool up.

Over the shipwide comms, Ari said, "Welcome aboard Night Stalker Airways. TF-160 wants you to enjoy your flight. As we prepare for launch, please return your seats to their upright positions and stow your seatback tray tables."

"The seats have one position," Griff complained. "Straight up and stiff as a board."

Cross and Nat fist-bumped Griff.

Feeling the ship go light on her gear, Cade said, "Take us south, please. To the riverfront park." He pointed to it on the map on Skip's lap.

Addressing Ari, Skip said, "It's just this side of the Sellwood bridge."

"There's like a dozen bridges across this river," shot Ari.

"Two miles south," Cade said. "It's impossible to miss." As the helo turned on axis and went nose down, he regarded the general. "Do you speak English?"

"Poorly," said Fan.

Cade growled, "I *asked* Baby Bird."

In fractured English, Jinlong said, "Very little."

"Why didn't you study abroad?" Cade asked. "Maybe learn the language before you come over here to fuck us."

Jinlong remained tightlipped.

Ari said, "Thirty seconds out."

Cade flipped his NVGs up. Regarding the general, he said, "When does the spring offensive commence? Give me a date. Troop strength. All the details. You do that and I'll find you something to cover that shriveled little worm between your legs."

The general said, "Fuck you," and spit in Cade's balaclava-covered face.

Having witnessed the ultimate sign of disrespect one soldier could show another, Griff, Cross, and Nat all voiced their displeasure.

"No he didn't," exclaimed Nat.

"Want me to break *his* nose?" asked Griff.

"Stupid move," said Cross, shaking his head.

Cade said nothing. He was busy removing his helmet.

"On station," Ari said. "Where do you want me?"

Cade said, "Hover over the parking lot. Southeast corner. About twenty … twenty-five feet above the deck."

Ari side-slipped the helo into position.

Removing the sweat- and spit-soiled balaclava, Cade fixed Fan with a hard stare. "Do you recognize me?"

Fan leaned forward as far as the safety harness would allow. After a few seconds spent studying Cade's face, he shook his head. "All you *round eyes* look the same to me."

Seething inside, Cade said, "Picture me tied to a chair in a Utah farmhouse." He tugged off one glove and held his hand up for Fan to see. "And with fingernails. I used to have *perfect* fingernails."

Seeing Fan's face go slack, Cade snugged his glove back on and turned to face the general. "The spring offensive? Spill your guts."

Nothing. The general stared straight ahead, unblinking, a firm set to his jaw.

Cade leaned forward and powered open the cabin door. Leveling a hard stare at Fan, he said, "If it's any consolation, *Sishén*, I didn't recognize your face when I first saw it on the 8x10 a friend gave me. Even when I saw it blown up on the monitor during the briefing back at Peterson, your piggy mug didn't register to me. The name *Li Fan* didn't ring a bell, either. However, as soon as one of your men called you '*Sishén*,' the wheels in my head started to turn. I'll never forget that name for as long as I live. Undeniable confirmation only happened when I heard you speak. Can't be very many Chinese torturers with a lisp who call themselves Reaper." He shook his head. "You're no *Reaper*, Fan. I'm still on the good side of the grass."

"It's all because I left you with my apprentice," Fan said. "I should have finished the job myself. I regret it, now."

Cade looked toward the ground. Though he wasn't wearing NVGs, he could still see ghostly shapes milling about in the parking lot. "Well, you didn't. And here we are. Two reapers face-to-face." He paused while he released the buckles on the man's safety harness. "But I'm not going to kill you, Fan. I'm just going to introduce you to what your people let loose on my country. Sishén, meet Jiangshi. Jiangshi, meet Sishén."

With Jinlong looking on in horror, Cade manhandled the torturer from his seat and shoved him into space. He didn't pause to savor the moment. Didn't give Fan time to beg or plead. Here one second, gone the next.

Cade leaned out and watched Fan fall the twenty feet to the ground. Saw him land atop a Z and bowl over a couple more before coming to rest on the asphalt, writhing in pain, face contorted in terror and staring straight up at the hovering helo.

Their raggedy clothes and greasy hair being whipped about by the rotor wash, the twenty or so Zs down below pig-piled on the fresh meat.

Staring into the general's eyes, in Mandarin, Cade said, "*Talk, or Baby Bird gets shoved from the nest.*"

The general swallowed hard, then began speaking rapid-fire Mandarin.

Cade silenced him with an upraised hand. Peering out the door, Cade regarded the feeding frenzy. On Fan's flailing arms were deep fissures pulsing blood. One creature was gnawing on his neck. Another plunged its gnarled fingers into the torturer's ample belly and ripped out a length of shiny intestine.

The man was on his way to meeting the mythical Pale Rider, that much was clear.

Having seen enough to know the man's fate was sealed one way or the other, Cade started the door closing.

Eyes narrowed against the rotor wash, Griff regarded Cade. "Adios, motherfucker. Shitbag reaped what he sowed. Where'd you learn that trick, Wyatt?"

"From an old Cowboy named Mike Desantos."

Ari came on over the comms. "That was savage, Wyatt. Know that it will not make it into my report. Where to now, boss?"

Cade said, "Home," and turned toward the general, eager to learn all of the man's secrets.

Chapter 81

Sunday, March 18, 2012

Colorado Springs, Colorado

"I hope it doesn't rain," Raven said to Max. "All those decorations they put up. Then there's the Pueblo survivors sitting on stage without umbrellas. It'll really *suck* if it does."

Sleeping on the floor nearby, Max didn't even stir when his name was uttered.

It was quarter to noon on Sunday and Raven was alone in the Founders Suite. She was standing on a chair she'd pushed against the window. Even then, she had to stand up straight in order to see over the head of Secret Service Agent Lyle Galt, who'd set up his overwatch position on the outside veranda.

We will have to secure your weapons ended up not being as bad as it had sounded the day before when Agents Woodson and Lowell first visited. Instead of removing everyone's weapons from the premises, cable and trigger locks were placed on all the rifles and pistols. The weapons were then stowed inside a pair of Pelican cases, which were then secured with padlocks. The agents had put the cases in a closet and, before leaving, had stressed that the door was not to be opened.

Next to the thirty-something agent behind the scoped sniper rifle was an Hispanic agent named Maria Diaz. The woman had pretty brown eyes, angular features, and a sinewy gymnast's body, no doubt a byproduct of surviving in the zombie apocalypse.

Diaz sat on a chair taken from the Founders Suite, elbows braced on the rail and one eye pressed to the eyepiece of a powerful spotting scope.

Thirteen floors below, Antlers Park was swathed in red, white, and blue. Banners and flags were draped on seemingly every flat surface. Of the thousand or so people in the park, Raven doubted if there were a dozen who weren't waving an American flag.

Surrounded by Jersey barriers and twelve-foot-tall hurricane fence, the park could only be accessed by the public on the two corners closest to the Antlers building. Each corner entry had a magnetometer of its own and was manned by several uniformed CSPD officers.

Nobody was sneaking a gun into this event.

The stage was dead ahead. Behind the stage was a tent where a reception was to follow. Parked beside the tent, with people in white aprons coming and going from their open rear doors, was a trio of black vans.

Railroad tracks ran behind the stage. They were paralleled by the western wall, a couple of blocks distant.

Wilson came in from the room opposite the Founders Suite. "Someone's going to be partying after this thing." He clapped his hands together. "And it ain't going to be us."

"I don't want to be anywhere near that park," Raven admitted. "If they would have caught Pirate and Snake and Pixie ... maybe I'd feel different about being seated a few feet from the President."

"Duncan and the others didn't seem too worried."

"How about you? Why didn't you go with Taryn and Sasha?"

Wilson said, "Sasha has Peter"—Raven made a face—"and Taryn gave me permission to listen to the ceremony on the AM radio I found down in Maintenance. I put batteries in and it works just fine. Signal seems pretty strong."

Raven said, "Admit it ... you're scared."

"OK, OK," he said, "Though I think you're blowing it out of proportion, I am a bit spooked."

"Since we can't go up to the roof, or even use our own damn *patio*"— hoping Galt and Diaz would hear her, she had said it with her mouth real close to the window, all the while drumming her fingers on the glass— "you might as well bring your radio in here." Turning to face Wilson, she added, "Please?"

"Sure," he said. "Just don't tell anyone why I stayed behind."

"No promises," Raven said. "Just hurry, it's almost noon." As Wilson neared the door, she called, "And bring binoculars."

Max rose and stretched. Seeing Raven, he strolled over and rubbed his head against her calf.

"Hey, boy. have a good nap?"

Max yawned, then sat down and stared up at her.

Fishing some venison jerky from a pocket, she shared it with the dog.

Wilson returned carrying the requested items, the music playing in the park already coming out of the radio's dual speakers.

Humming along with some country singer going on about how proud he was to be an American, Raven returned her attention to the park, where she saw the President's black SUV limousine pulling through the blockade. It gave off a *don't mess with me* vibe as it crept slowly, left to right, toward the stage.

Raven stuck a hand out. "Binoculars, please."

The music kept playing as the President's black limousine, nicknamed The Beast, stopped near the stage.

A trio of sunglass-wearing agents piled out. After poking around the stage, the agents returned and one of them opened the door for President Clay.

The President stepped from the highly modified Cadillac, waving and smiling at the cheering crowd. She wasn't wearing her trademark ball cap. Instead she wore her dark hair in a ponytail.

Instead of the usual outdoorsy garb—jeans, plaid shirt, hiking boots— President Clay wore a navy-blue pantsuit and sensible heels. Flanked by two Secret Service agents with submachine guns and dark glasses, she approached the stage.

The country ditty was starting to fade out.

"Before she speaks," Wilson said, "I have a question."

"What is it?"

"Where's your dad? And along those lines … where's my Tahoe?"

Raven said, "His message to me said he got in late last night. They were about to have a debriefing is why he didn't call. Apparently, the flight back was pretty eventful. I guess he was nursing a couple of minor wounds and couldn't sleep aboard the helicopter like he normally does. So, after the debrief he was going to stay there so he could get some sleep."

Throwing his hands in the air, Wilson said, "I might as well go out and find another rig."

"What's stopping you?"

He made a face. "I would, but this one still has the new-car-smell."

"Relax, Wilson. After today, my dad won't ever need to borrow it again."

The music on the radio was replaced by a recording of *Hail to the Chief*. It played for a couple of minutes and finished with a rousing conclusion.

Standing before a podium adorned with the Presidential Seal, Valerie Clay said, "My fellow Americans … please remove your hats, find a flag to face… not hard to do here—" laughter from the crowd—"and help me in singing our National Anthem."

Wilson mumbled something under his breath. Turning toward the window, he removed his boonie hat and placed it over his heart.

Raven put her hand over her heart. Just as the music was starting to filter through the radio speakers, she saw movement left of the stage. It was another black van. It had writing on the side. Writing she couldn't read from a couple hundred yards out.

The Secret Service agents manning the gate The Beast had come through were taking notice. Hands ducked into jackets as the protection detail went for their weapons.

"No, no, no," Raven said.

One of the detail approached a row of portable roadblock signs. He started a conversation with the black van's passenger.

Raven bellowed, "Give me the binoculars."

Shooting her an angry look, Wilson hissed, "The Anthem!"

Still standing on the chair, Raven forcibly removed the Steiners from around his neck. Putting them to her eyes, the van snapped into focus. She read the white lettering: *Loretta Jean's Pies*.

Panning the Steiners to the van's front end, she saw that Pirate was the one talking to the agent. Though it was clear to her the driver's arms were tattooed, thanks to the angle, she couldn't see his face.

"Stop them. Arrest them." Knowing the agents on the veranda couldn't hear her, she banged on the window, hoping to get them to listen to her. To do *something*.

Galt didn't flinch. Diaz, however, rose up from the spotting scope.

Wilson whispered, "That's the pie van, isn't it?"

Raven said nothing. She was looking Diaz in the eye and motioning for her to open the sliding door.

Diaz shook her head. Mouthing, "I can't," she returned her eye to the spotting scope.

Raven began, "Sasha and Taryn are down there—"

"—in the front section with the others," Wilson finished, his face whitening.

Max growled.

As the rendition of Francis Scott Key's song got to the *rockets' red glare* line, inexplicably, the agent allowed the van to drive forward.

Raven banged on the window, harder this time, as she watched the van park behind The Beast.

Nothing. Both agents were now fully ignoring her.

Just as Raven dragged the satellite phone from her pocket, Pirate and Snake stepped from the van.

Brewing beer my butt.

Thumbing the Iridium to life, she saw the agent walk away from the van.

She thought, *No, no, no. There's a bomb in the van.* Back to banging on the window, she screamed, "Shoot them. There's a bomb in that van. You have got to warn the President!"

Galt drew his eye from the scope, looked at her, then shook his head.

Max whimpered.

Binoculars in one hand and pressed to her face, Raven shook the sat-phone, saying, "Come on, damn it. Power the eff up."

By the time the agent had returned to his post behind the barricades, Pirate and Snake had looped all the way around the rear of the van. But instead of opening the back doors like Raven expected them to, they double-timed it toward the train tracks behind the park.

Hands shaking, Raven dialed Chief Riggleman's number from memory. As she waited for the connection to be made, she took her gaze from the phone and watched the terrorists through the Steiners.

The pair were now stopped by the western wall and appeared to be arguing about something. In Snake's hand was what looked to be a smartphone.

In a funereal voice, Raven said, "Snake has a detonator."

Wilson said, "If that van blows with us standing here, we're going to get a face full of broken glass."

Just as Raven said, "If that van blows, all of our friends are dead," a slew of things happened all at once.

Beyond the tracks, mouth moving a mile-a-minute, Snake shook the device in his hand and stabbed a finger at Pirate.

In response, Pirate took a step backward, drew a pistol from his waistband, and pointed it at the smaller man.

Clearly, they were having a falling out.

As that strange turn of events was registering with Raven, there came a knock on the door. Still balanced on the chair, Steiners pressed to her face and being attacked on multiple fronts by all kinds of stimuli, she ignored it.

A tick after the short flurry of knocks ceased, the doorknob rattled, and the door swung inward.

Reacting to the sound, Raven lowered the Steiners and jumped down from the chair.

Seeing Chief Riggleman in her CSPD uniform and filling up the doorway, Raven said, "I'm calling you. The pie van is down there right now."

Clutched in the chief's hand was a satellite phone. Though it was making no sounds, its screen was lit up with an incoming call.

"I know," said the chief. "What you just witnessed was totally expected by us. We provided the credentials that got the van and driver through the outer perimeter. The bomb in the van is inert. It was assembled with help from one of our people. The parts in it look real but are not."

Incredulous, Raven said, "You've known all along ... and didn't tell me? Hell, Agents Galt and Diaz knew and just let me go into complete meltdown mode." Jaw clenched, she banged the binoculars against her thigh.

Ending the incoming call without answering it, Riggleman said, "Couldn't be helped. We have been following this plot for some time now. Even though things have changed drastically because of Omega, Lady Justice is still blind. She *has* to remain blind. That's why we had to let it play out. Catch the cells in the act."

Puzzle pieces finally falling into place, Raven said, "*Cells?* Snake and Pixie are *the* cell … and Pirate is one of yours."

"His name is Rory. And, yes, he's FBI. He's also truly grateful you didn't shoot him in the gut the other night."

"I was so close to ending him," Raven said. "I thought he was a terrorist. I thought … maybe he could see me even though it was real dark and I was hiding in some bushes."

"He made you. He's *real* good at what he does," Riggleman said.

Interrupting, Wilson said, "But you said cells. Plural. How many more are there?"

Riggleman said, "Thanks to Raven and her dad figuring out the Klingon angle, we rolled up another cell that kept slipping our noose. There's still some threads we're following. We think they were ready to go when Omega was released. They were coordinated by various Chinese-run *institutes* on the West and East Coasts whose connections lead back to the mainland."

Raven said nothing. She figured it would take a talk with her dad to fully grasp what the chief was alleging.

Pointing to the radio broadcasting the President's speech, Riggleman said, "Keep listening, Raven, President Clay is going to mention the plot and thank those who helped expose it."

Wilson said, "Anonymously, right?"

Regarding Wilson, Riggleman said, "Of course." She paused and walked to the window.

Raven said, "I thought you were discounting me because of my age."

"I had to shine you on. And for that, I'm really sorry. You're bright and resourceful. Maybe one day you'll want to try out for CSPD?"

Wilson said, "Or the FBI."

Raven said, "If anything, it'll be Army Rangers. Then, maybe Delta."

Riggleman said, "Shooting for the moon," and handed Raven a small sack. Something inside it jingled as it hit Raven's upturned palm.

The chief went on: "Keys for the trigger locks. We had to do that so you would be less apt to rustle up a posse and go out on another late-night jaunt."

Raven nodded. "It did cross my mind."

Riggleman smiled at that. "I better go now," she said. "We've been asked to help the Bureau lock the crime scenes down so they can preserve all the evidence. There will be a trial."

"And hopefully a public execution," Wilson shot.

Riggleman said, "Let's not put the cart before the horse," and turned to go.

As Riggleman neared the door, Raven said, "Tell Rory I'm real sorry for pointing my gun at him."

"Will do," she said, then let herself out.

Raven tapped softly on the picture window. Drawing the attention of Galt and Diaz, she mouthed, "I'm sorry."

The pair on the veranda threw her mock salutes, then went back to the task at hand.

"Well," Wilson said, "since that's all settled, what do you say we go down and watch the rest of the ceremony from the good seats?"

Nodding, Raven said, "What do we tell the others?"

"The truth," Wilson said. "The whole truth and nothing but."

Epilogue

Wilson's lipstick-red Chevy Tahoe rounded the corner in front of the Antlers at exactly 3:00 p.m. Cleanup from the Pueblo Survivors ceremony was still ongoing, but the streets in the area were opened back up to civilian travel.

The rain clouds that had threatened the ceremony moved on to the west, giving way to blue sky dotted with high clouds.

Raven, Duncan, Taryn, and Wilson stood shoulder to shoulder on the curb, waiting. At Raven's feet, Max sat on his haunches, looking expectantly at the approaching SUV.

The Tahoe pulled smartly to the curb, the passenger window already motoring down. Hinging over, Cade met Wilson's gaze. "Want to drive?"

Hands on hips, Wilson simply shook his head.

Cade said, "Get in." Moving an overstuffed manila envelope off the passenger seat, he regarded Raven. "What's this *latest* clandestine operation you've cooked up?"

Stowing her SBR by her feet and closing the door, she said, "Patience is a virtue." Another one of Duncan's sayings.

Max jumped in back first and sat on the seat near the middle.

While Taryn took the seat behind Cade, on the other side of the Tahoe Duncan was forcing Wilson in ahead of him.

Wilson glared at Duncan. "Really? Bitch seat? In my own rig? Even Max here has a better view."

"Get in," growled Duncan. "I'm the one with the bad back."

Pulling from the curb, Cade said, "You've no one to blame but yourself, Old Man. Those helos didn't crash themselves."

"Controlled landings," grumbled Duncan.

Smiling at that, Cade said, "Where to, daughter of mine?"

440

Raven gave directions that took them past Penrose and deep into the Northern District. As they passed a burned-out convenience store, Cade directed her attention to the manila envelope. "Take a look inside."

From the backseat, Duncan said, "What did I get for Christmas, Santa?"

"If one of you can reach my ruck in the cargo area"—Cade met Duncan's gaze in the rearview mirror—"you'll find Old Man's present packed close to the top."

With his long wingspan, Wilson got ahold of a strap and dragged the backpack forward. "It's heavy," he said. "What's in here, rocks?"

"Yeah," Cade responded. "I got Old Man a box of them."

Raven had opened the envelope and dragged out a thick stack of pictures. Eagerly thumbing through them, she said, "Look, it's you and Mom on your wedding day." Her eyes suddenly glossed over from grief. She felt her throat constrict. "And one of me with Nana and Papa in Myrtle Beach. Oooh … this black and white one is of Grandpa and Grandma from a long time ago."

Taking his eyes off the road for a beat, Cade poked at a picture. "This is me, you and Mom … summer before last, I think."

"When we went to Bend?"

"Yes," Cade answered. "Got your baby pictures and some of you learning to walk, too."

In the backseat, Wilson had pulled a heavy object from the pack. It was wrapped in a stiff, new-smelling tee shirt. On the shirt was a helicopter silhouette and the words: STUMP TOWN AVIATION.

"Here's your rocks," Wilson joked. "Strangely, feels like they're in the shape of a gun."

Raven said, "Stop at this next intersection for a sec."

Craning over the seat, Cade said, "What do you think, Duncan?"

Duncan had unwrapped the *present*. It was a Colt .45 Model 1911. It felt familiar in his hand. Real familiar. Swiping at a stray tear, he said, "This is mine … isn't it?"

Cade said, "Affirmative."

"Was Charlie still there?" He paused. "I mean … Charlie's body."

"He was. Right where you left him." Cade explained how the three helos in the strike package had loitered overnight at the Troutdale Airport. "Ari and Haynes had some time on their hands, so they dug a deep grave inside the fence and buried your friend in it. Even had a short graveside service for him. Believe it or not, that was Ari's idea."

Duncan was crying now. "You thought of me while you were out there. I don't know what to say." He dabbed at his eyes with his sleeve.

Cade said, "No words are necessary. You'd do the same for me."

Wilson leaned over and wrapped Old Man in a bear hug.

Cade looked over at Raven. "Can I drive now?"

She pointed to the street sign.

Cade read it: "Boise Street." He looked at her. "Where'd you find that?"

"She made it herself," Duncan said. "With just a *little* help from Old Man. Hell, we almost died in the EZ so she could steal the signs to make it."

Taryn leaned between the seats. "But there's more. Right, Raven?"

Raven said, "Turn here."

The street was tree-lined and relatively clean, with only two abandoned cars parked on the entire block. Pointing to a Craftsman on her side of the street, Raven said, "That look familiar?"

Cade said, "It looks like home."

"It is," Raven said.

"How?"

"Cost me a bunch of ears. Lady named DeAngelo over at Reclamation helped me with the paperwork." She pointed at the homes flanking the Craftsman. "The bungalow is Duncan and Glenda's. The two-story next door is Daymon's place."

Interrupting, Cade asked, "Where is he?"

"On some kind of *vision quest*," answered Duncan. "Him and his new lady left the walls right after President Clay finished her thing."

Nodding, Cade said, "What about you kids? You all staying at the Antlers?"

Wilson shook his head. "No. That big white mansion down the street is ours."

Cade said, "Looks like the place on the U of O campus where they filmed Animal House."

"Exactly," said Duncan. "They want to behave as if they're in a frat, they had to be kept at arm's length. Far enough away so that we can't hear them, yet close enough to home we can pop in and check on them now and again."

Cade said, "Even the house number is the same as the old house."

"She worked hard to steal those, too," quipped Duncan.

Smiling, Raven said, "Pull forward and look in the driveway."

Cade took his foot off the brake and let the idling engine pull the Tahoe forward.

"Is that—?"

"Yep," she said, "it's Black Beauty. In the flesh."

Never in his wildest dreams did Cade think he'd ever see his F-650 again. "How?" he asked.

Duncan said, "Me and D paid Whipper a visit a couple of weeks ago. Believe it or not, the old coot was happy to help. He had a Chinook returning from a mission up Idaho way divert to the Eden compound. They put her in a sling and ferried her back to Peterson. He even took it upon himself to get her back into fighting shape."

Cade said, "Looks like he up-armored her, too. And is that new black paint that I see?"

"He did the Humvee treatment on her. The paint is that radar-beam-absorbing stuff they put on the new helos. He even added bulletproof glass, a Whipple supercharger, a third fuel tank, and beadlock wheels wrapped with run-flat off-road tires. She's a rig Mad Max would kill for."

Beaming, Raven said, "Did I do good?"

Tilt to his head, tone all business, Cade said, "Did you do anything I wouldn't do while I was gone?"

Raven said nothing.

Taking that as a "Yes," Cade said, "You did beyond good. I love you, Bird."

###

To be continued in a new *Surviving the Zombie Apocalypse* novel in 2020

Thanks for reading! Reviews help us indie scribblers. Please consider leaving yours at the place of purchase. Look for books in my bestselling series everywhere eBooks are sold. Please feel free to Friend Shawn Chesser on Facebook. To receive the latest information on upcoming releases, please join my no-spam mailing list at ShawnChesser.com.

Shawn's Facebook Author Page:
www.facebook.com/SurvivingTheZombieApocalypse/

Shawn on Twitter: http://twitter.com/@sdchess

ABOUT THE AUTHOR

Shawn Chesser, a practicing father, has been a zombie fanatic for decades. He likes his creatures shambling, trudging and moaning. As for fast, agile, screaming specimens ... not so much. He lives in Portland, Oregon, with his wife, two kids and their pooch, Holly. This is his sixteenth novel.